PRAISE FOR THE NOVELS OF
DEBBIE MACOMBER

Window on the Bay

"This heartwarming story sweetly balances friendship and mother-child bonding with romantic love." —*Kirkus Reviews*

"Where *Window on the Bay* really shines is in its portrayal of women who are done raising their children, but are far from done with life."
—*Booklist*

Cottage by the Sea

"Macomber's story of tragedy and triumph is emotionally engaging from the outset and ends with a satisfying conclusion. Readers will be most taken by the characters, particularly Annie, a heartwarming lead who bolsters the novel."
—*Publishers Weekly*

"Romantic, warm, and a breeze to read—one of Macomber's best." —*Kirkus Reviews*

"Macomber's patented recipe of idyllic small-town life with a touch of romance is sure to result in a summer best-seller." —*Booklist*

"A novel that warms like the summer sun."
—*People*

If Not for You

"Debbie Macomber has written another great novel letting the reader into the character's mind. All the doubts and insecurities two people in a new friendship can have when they find their feelings are changing, makes for a remarkable story for all to enjoy."   —Romance Junkies

"Wholesome and thoughtful, Macomber's latest is a heartwarming treat."   —*Library Journal*

"Debbie Macomber's heartfelt messages and authentic look at personal relationships definitely brought a smile to my lips throughout the majority of Beth and Sam's journey."
    —Harlequin Junkie

Sweet Tomorrows

"Macomber fans will leave the Rose Harbor Inn with warm memories of healing, hope, and enduring love."   —*Kirkus Reviews*

"Overflowing with the poignancy, sweetness, conflicts and romance for which Debbie Macomber is famous, *Sweet Tomorrows* captivates from beginning to end."   —Bookreporter.com

"Macomber manages to infuse her trademark humor in a more somber story that focuses on love, loss and faith. . . . This one will appeal to those looking for more mature heroines and a good, clean romance."   —RT Book Reviews

Blossom Street Brides

"*Blossom Street Brides* gives Macomber fans sympathetic characters who strive to make the right choices as they cope with issues that face many of today's women. Readers will thoroughly enjoy spending time on Blossom Street once again and watching as Lydia, Bethanne and Lauren struggle to solve their problems, deal with family crises, fall in love and reach their own happy endings."   —*BookPage*

"[An] enjoyable read that pulls you right in from page one."   —Fresh Fiction

"Fans will happily return to the warm, welcoming sanctuary of Macomber's Blossom Street, catching up with old friends from past Blossom Street books and meeting new ones being welcomed into the fold."

—*Kirkus Reviews*

"A master at writing stories that embrace both romance and friendship, [Debbie] Macomber can always be counted on for an enjoyable page-turner, and this Blossom Street installment is no exception."   —RT Book Reviews

"Rewarding . . . Macomber amply delivers her signature engrossing relationship tales, wrapping her readers in warmth as fuzzy and soft as a hand-knitted creation from everyone's favorite yarn shop."   —Bookreporter.com

ALSO BY DEBBIE MACOMBER

The Angels Series
A SEASON OF ANGELS
THE TROUBLE WITH ANGELS
TOUCHED BY ANGELS
ANGELS EVERYWHERE

Deliverance Company
SOMEDAY SOON
SOONER OR LATER
THE SOONER THE BETTER
(formerly MOON OVER WATER)

FAMILY AFFAIR

ONE NIGHT
MORNING COMES SOFTLY

The Miracle Series
MRS. MIRACLE
CALL ME MRS. MIRACLE
MR. MIRACLE

DEBBIE MACOMBER

Morning Comes Softly

AVONBOOKS

An Imprint of HarperCollinsPublishers

MORNING COMES SOFTLY. Copyright © 1993 by Debbie Macomber. All rights reserved. Printed in the United States of America. No part of this book may be used or reproduced in any manner whatsoever without written permission except in the case of brief quotations embodied in critical articles and reviews. For information, address HarperCollins Publishers, 195 Broadway, New York, NY 10007.

First Avon Books mass market printing: March 2007
First HarperCollins paperback printing: May 1993

Print Edition ISBN: 978-0-06-108063-0
Digital Edition ISBN: 978-0-06-176616-9

Cover design by Amy Halperin
Cover photograph © Sandra Cunningham/Trevillion Images
Author photograph by Dane Gregory Meyer

Avon, Avon & logo, and Avon Books & logo are registered trademarks of HarperCollins Publishers in the United States of America and other countries.

HarperCollins is a registered trademark of HarperCollins Publishers in the United States of America and other countries.

20 21 22 23 24   QGM   40 39 38 37 36 35 34 33 32 31

Acknowledgments

Most people will skip over this section of the book, unless of course, they expect to find their name, so please bear with me as I give a word of appreciation to those who deserve it.

Special thanks to my family, from my late parents, Ted and Connie Adler, to my husband, Wayne, and four children. Their love and encouragement have been a shield to me. To them every word I write is pure gold. I'm hoping their attitude rubs off on the rest of the country.

To Linda Lael Miller, my friend, for all the fun, crazy times we've shared through the years, from missed flights, hotel fires, and taxi drivers who've only been in America one day.

I need to thank Jayne Krentz, Katherine Stone, Anne Stuart, and Robyn Carr, who so winningly read my manuscript and offered quotes. I didn't bribe them the way I did Linda. A writer couldn't ask for better friends.

Last, but certainly not least, Carolyn Marino, my former editor. When Carolyn and I first started working together, another writer claimed Carolyn walks on water. It's true.

One

"It isn't a housekeeper you need, Mr. Thompson, it's a wife."

"A wife." The word went through Travis like a bullet, and he soared to his feet. He slammed his Stetson back on his head, shoving it down so far it shadowed the starkly etched planes of his jaw and cheekbones. He paled beneath the weathered, sun-beaten tan.

It had been two months since his brother and sister-in-law's funeral, and he'd barely stepped outside the ranch house since he'd been appointed the guardian of their three children. He might as well forget thirty-six years of ranch life and take up being a full-time mother. All he seemed to do was cook, wash clothes, and read bedtime stories.

The worst of it was that according to five-year-old Beth Ann and the two boys, Jim and Scotty, he wasn't doing any of those jobs worth a damn.

"Mommy wouldn't like you saying the 's' word," Beth Ann announced each and every time the four-letter word slipped from his mouth. The kid made it sound as though his sister-in-law would leap straight out of the grave to reprimand him. Hell, she probably would if it were possible.

"Mom used to say 'yogurt' instead," Beth Ann announced, her eyes a soft cornflower blue. Janice's eyes. Everything about the bundle-size youngster reminded Travis of his petite sister-in-law. The thick blond hair, the gentle laugh, and the narrowed, disapproving look. The look that spoke a hundred words without uttering a one of them. Janice had had a way about her that could cut straight through an argument and silence him as no one else had ever done. Travis stared at Beth Ann, and his heart clenched. Godalmighty, he missed Janice. Nearly as much as he did Lee.

"Your mother used to say 'yogurt'?" Travis had asked, confident he hadn't heard her correctly.

Jim nodded. "Mom said yogurt was a much better word than the 's' word."

"I think yogurt's a fine word," Beth Ann added.

"If one of us got into something we shouldn't," Scotty, who was eight, was quick to clarify, "Mom would say we were in deep yogurt."

That was supposed to have explained everything, Travis guessed.

His language, Travis learned soon enough, was only the tip of the iceberg. Within a week he discovered that washing little girls' clothes with boys' clothes damn near ruined the girl things. Hell, he didn't know any different. Okay, so Beth Ann wore a pink dress, one that had once been white, to church on Sunday. It could have been worse.

Church was another thing, Travis mused darkly. Generally he attended services when the mood struck him, which he freely admitted was only about once every other year, if then. Now it seemed he was expected to show up every week in time for Sunday school with three grade-school children neatly in tow. It was less trouble to wrestle a hundred head of cattle than to get those youngsters dressed and to church on time.

Raising God-fearing children was what Janice would have wanted, Clara Morgan had primly informed him on the first of her proven-to-be--weekly visits. Dear Lord save him from interfering old women.

God, however, had given up listening to Travis a good long time ago. No doubt it was because he swore with such unfailing regularity.

Everything had come to a head the day before. Heaven knew Travis was trying as hard as he could to do right by Lee and Janice's children. He'd damn near given up the management of his ranch to his hired hands. Instead he was dealing with do-good state social workers, old biddies from the local Grange, and three grieving children.

The final straw came when he'd arrived home with a truckload of groceries a few days earlier. The boys, Jim and Scotty, were helping him carry in the badly needed supplies.

"You didn't buy any more of those frozen diet dinners, did you?" Jim demanded, hauling a twenty-five-pound bag of flour toward the kitchen, helped by his younger brother.

"No. I told you boys before, that was a mistake."

"It tasted like . . ."

"Yogurt," Travis supplied testily.

Scotty nodded, and Beth Ann looked on approvingly.

Travis dealt with the fencing material he'd picked up in town and left the three children to finish with the groceries. That was his second mistake in what proved to be a long list.

When he entered the house, it was like walking into a San Francisco fog. A thin layer of flour circled the room like a raging dust storm. Beth Ann, looking small and defeated, held on to a broom and was swinging madly.

"What the hell happened in here?" Travis demanded.

"It's Scotty's fault," Jim shouted. "He dropped his end of the flour sack."

"It was heavy," Scotty said. "It caught on the nail."

The nail. No one needed to tell Travis which nail. The blunt end of one had been protruding from the floorboard for the last couple of days . . . all right, a week or more. He'd meant to pound it down; would have if it had been a real hazard, but like so many other things, he'd put it off.

"I tried to sweep up the flour," Beth Ann explained, coughing.

Travis waved his hand in front of his face and watched as a perfectly good bag of flour settled like a dusting of snow on every possible crevice of the kitchen. "Don't worry about it," he said, taking the broom out of her hand. He leaned it against the wall and surveyed the damage.

"If Scotty wasn't such a wimp, none of this would have happened," Jim said.

"I'm not a wimp," Scotty yelled, and leaped for his brother. Before Travis could stop them, the two were rolling on the floor, wrestling like bear cubs, stirring up the recently settled cloud. Travis broke the two of them up, ordered Jim out to the barn to do his chores, and did what he could to clean up the mess in the kitchen.

Dirty dishes lined the porcelain sink. Dinner dishes from the night before, breakfast dishes from the morning. The dishwasher was filled with clean dishes, or had been, but they were mixed with dirty ones, too. Pans, crusted with dried food, soaked on the stove, but he'd run out of burners. It seemed every piece of cookware he owned was strung out across the kitchen counter.

Added to the unappetizing scene was the scent of burned macaroni and cheese that lingered in the air like something that had died and had yet to be buried. It had been lunch, and he'd overcooked it in the microwave. The stuff smelled worse than the brownies he'd attempted the week before. He'd made one small mistake. The package had said to bake the brownies twenty minutes, and he'd set the microwave for that amount of time. It wasn't until he removed the rock-hard substance from the microwave that he realized his mistake. Twenty minutes had been the baking time for a regular oven. The brownies weren't the only thing ruined. He'd ended up tossing the pan, too.

A glass baking dish, however, was the least of his worries.

Jim returned from the barn a few minutes later, much too soon to have completed his chores. When Travis asked the twelve-year-old about them, he'd gotten defensive. Jim's bitterness ate like acid at Travis's pride. It took all the strength of will he possessed not to take that boy by the shoulders and give him a hard shake. He wanted to shout at Jim that he didn't like this arrangement either. They had to make the best of it. Work together. They were family.

But how do you say that to a grieving kid who just lost both parents? As with so many other things about parenting, Travis was at a loss.

He didn't know the answer to that any more than he knew what he was going to do about raising his brother's children. It was then that he'd decided he needed help. He'd driven into Miles City to find himself a housekeeper.

"I'm sorry, Mr. Thompson," the matronly woman from the employment agency continued, breaking into his heavy thoughts, her brown eyes sympathetic, "but there isn't anyone in our files who'd be willing to live on a cattle ranch in the middle of nowhere for those kinds of wages."

"I can't afford anything more." As it was, Travis was having a hard time making ends meet. Adding three extra mouths to feed and bodies to clothe hadn't helped matters any. Once the funeral bills had been paid, there was nothing left of Lee and Janice's estate, and the Social Security he collected didn't begin to cover the expenses.

He gave himself a moment to calm down. "What do you suggest I do?"

"What I said in the beginning. Find yourself a wife."

"A wife," Travis repeated, his face tightening with a frown.

He cringed, almost hearing Beth Ann chastise him.

"I'm sorry I can't be of more help to you," she continued, closing the file.

A sense of panic rose in Travis like floodwaters over the banks of a creek bed. "All right," he muttered, "I'll do it."

"Very good," she replied with a dignified nod of her head. "I believe it's the best solution to your problem. I imagine you have someone in mind?"

"No," Travis answered brusquely, honestly. "Do you know of anyone who'd marry me and take on a passel o' kids?"

Her laugh was polite and mildly shocked. "Oh, hardly, Mr. Thompson. Our agency did its best to locate a housekeeper for you, which is a stretch for us. We're certainly not in the matchmaking business."

Travis thanked her and left abruptly. His truck

was parked outside, with its dented fender and rusted tailgate, looking as beaten and old as he felt. A wife. Damnation, he didn't know anyone in Grandview who'd marry him, and even if he did, where the hell was he supposed to find the time to date?

Sitting in the pickup, his arms braced against the steering wheel, Travis did his level best to size up the situation. If something didn't change soon, he knew exactly what would happen. The state agency had already sent out a social worker to check on matters. Shirley Miller was helpful enough, or at least she tried to be. After her most recent visit, she'd suggested he hire a housekeeper. Although she hadn't issued any warnings, her message was rainwater clear. If things didn't work out for Jim, Scotty, and Beth Ann at the Triple T, then she'd have no other choice but to place them in foster homes. The unspoken threat hung over his head like a three-month-late mortgage payment.

Having to part with Lee and Janice's children was more unpalatable to Travis than the thought of marrying. The children were the only family he had left, and he wasn't about to let his brother and sister-in-law down.

A wife.

Travis just couldn't see himself as a husband. He'd never intended to marry. From everything he'd seen, women were nothing but troubles, always wanting things, never leaving well enough alone. From experience he knew they were constantly meddling in matters that were none of their damn business.

On the other hand, there were advantages to having a woman around. Travis certainly wouldn't be opposed to regular bouts of sex, for instance.

His infrequent trips into Billings usually netted him a night of pleasure with a waitress friend. Travis didn't flatter himself into thinking Carla's words of undying love were anything close to sincere. He was rugged and tough and some said a little dangerous. Carla claimed he was a real man, whatever the hell that meant.

If he was marrying a woman to keep him content in bed, he'd choose Carla, but it wasn't his carnal appetite he was looking to gratify. He needed a woman decent enough to be a mother to Lee and Janice's kids.

He sighed and rubbed his hand over his face, trying to think. One thing was certain, finding her wasn't going to be so easy.

On the long drive from Miles City back to Grandview, Travis stopped in at the Logger, the local watering hole. The kids weren't due to be out of school for another hour, and he needed a beer to help settle his mind.

He slipped onto a seat at the bar and set his Stetson on the polished mahogany top.

"Travis," Larry Martin greeted casually, claiming the stool next to him. "I haven't seen you around lately."

"Been busy." Travis tipped back the ice-cold beer and drank three huge gulps. Once his parched throat was relieved, he wiped the back of his hand over his mouth and turned his attention to his nearest neighbor. He liked Larry and counted him as near to a friend as he got. The two of them had a good deal in common. They spent more time on the back of a horse than they ever did in any bed. There was nothing soft in either of them. Neither of them would back away from a challenge, especially when their indignation had been fortified with a few beers. Sometimes it was each other they fought.

Neither one of them was much of a talker, either.

Larry lowered his gaze to the glass of beer between his hands. "How's it going?"

Travis shrugged. "Fine."

"I understand you've got your brother's three kids with you."

Travis replied with an abrupt nod.

"I was sorry to hear about Lee and Janice."

Travis's jaw tightened. He didn't like talking about the car accident that had claimed the lives of his brother and sister-in-law because it reminded him the person responsible for driving them off the road had yet to be found. If there was anything to be grateful about in this situation, it was the fact none of the children had been riding with them that night.

Travis took another long swallow of beer. He had problems enough without dwelling on the deaths of the two people he loved most in the world.

"Trouble?" Larry asked.

Travis nodded, thinking of the unspoken warning he'd gotten from the state social worker. "Looks like I'm going to have to find myself a wife."

Larry's gaze swung to him so fast it was a wonder he didn't put his neck out of joint. "A wife?"

"Trouble is, I don't know how I'm going to come up with one. There isn't a woman in town that would have me."

"What about Betty?"

The hairdresser lived in Pine Bluff, thirty miles south. She was pretty enough, as Travis recalled, but a little on the bony side. "She's divorced and has a kid or two of her own, doesn't she?" He already had three to worry about, and he didn't want to add to the problem.

"Tilly?"

Now there was a thought. Tilly worked as a waitress at the local cafe. A pretty thing, gentle as a kitten and all soft and tender.

"She's sweet on Doc's son," Travis muttered, and drank his beer. "Can you think of anyone else?" By this time he was growing downright worried. If *he* couldn't think of a woman he wanted to marry and if Larry couldn't come up with someone, then he didn't know what he was going to do.

It took a moment for Larry to shake his head. "I never thought I'd see the day you'd want a wife."

"I'm not all that happy about it," Travis admitted grimly. The beer bottle hovered close to his lips as he analyzed the situation, seeing the flaws in this plan as clear as cracked glass. "Hell if I know how it'll work out. I'm used to living my life as I damn well please. No woman's going to want to let me do that."

"You can say that again."

Travis didn't need to. He knew. Larry knew it, too.

"Women like to talk," Travis mumbled contemptuously, thinking of his times with Carla. "They don't say it's talking, though, did you ever notice that? They're much too sophisticated for something as simple as that. Oh, no, they say they're 'communicating.'"

"You're right," Larry concurred. "You make love, and what does a woman want to do? Sleep or eat like a normal person? Nope, she prefers to chat a while, and if you happen to drift off while she's cooing in your ear, it's a personal slight."

Travis finished his beer and pushed the empty bottle away. "Another thing. You allow a woman into your home and before you know it, they're fixing things. They can't leave well enough alone, wanting to paint here and put up frilly curtains there. As far as I'm concerned it's a waste of time and good money."

"You get married and that's exactly what'll happen."

Travis's frown grew darker and heavier as he waved for a second beer.

Stan, the bartender, bald and generally crabby,

strolled over to where the two men were sitting at the bar. "What are you two grumbling about now?"

"Travis here's got to find himself a wife."

"So?" Stan demanded. "What's so damn difficult about that? The world's full of women looking for an easy ride."

Any woman who married Travis thinking she was going to freeload off him would learn otherwise soon enough. Not that Travis planned on making her sweat blood out on the range the way he did. All he needed a woman for was rearing Lee's children.

"What kind of gal you looking for?"

Travis wasn't completely sure he understood. "Personally, I like long-legged women." A lot of men were turned on by big busts, but breast size didn't matter that much to him. As long as they filled his hands and mouth, then anything left over was pure fluff.

"Long legs," Stan echoed approvingly.

"Legs all the way up to her neck," Travis embellished. "I'm partial to a tight butt, too."

"That's not the only thing you're going to want that's tight," Larry said with a chuckle.

"You lookin' for a virgin, too?" Stan asked with an incredulous jerk of his head, as if he were holding back a rowdy laugh. "I didn't know there were any left here in Grandview."

Travis reached for his beer, but the heavy malt wasn't nearly as satisfying as the first one had been. "What I really need is a housekeeper. Problem is I can't find one, and even if I could, it's doubtful I could afford her."

"A wife ain't cheap," the bartender was quick to inform him. "I ought to know, I've been married three times, and each wife cost me more than the one before. What the hell do you think I'd be doing in a place like Grandview if I wasn't hiding out from those thieves?"

"What about one of those church ladies?" Larry offered as if struck by pure genius. "They're the marrying kind."

Travis had already given serious consideration to every woman he could think of in the entire Methodist congregation. Not that they'd have anything to do with the likes of him, mind you. As far as he knew, there wasn't an unmarried one in the lot of them, other than three widows well into their seventies and a couple of teenage girls in braces. If he were to approach either group, he'd likely get arrested. There wasn't a woman in town he could picture in his bed. And damn it all to hell, if he was going to have to marry, then he wanted it to be to someone he'd enjoy viewing naked.

"What do you suggest?"

"If you're serious about this, then advertise for one," Stan said.

Travis didn't find many things amusing, but he found Stan's suggestion downright comical. "You're joking."

"The hell I am. Men do it all the time."

"Where?"

Stan strolled out from behind the counter and across the room to a lopsided stand, where he picked up a local trade paper. He walked back and slapped it down on the bar. "There must be fifty ads or more right here, all from men looking for a wife or a quick lay. Sometimes even the women place the ads."

Travis exchanged an amused look with Larry. As far as he knew, the only thing the *Little Dime* advertised was used equipment, old furniture, and garage sales and the like. It covered a two-county area and was published bimonthly. The only time Travis read the *Little Dime* was when he ate at Martha's, the cafe where Tilly worked, and he couldn't remember ever seeing a personal column.

"If you don't want a woman from around here, then I suggest you put something in the Billings paper," Stan said, wiping down the scarred mahogany bar with a wet rag.

Travis peeled open the newspaper and spread it out, looking for the "Dateline" section. It took him a moment to locate the proper page. He read through each ad twice and discovered the majority of them were from men.

Larry was reading over his shoulder. "Here's one," he said, pointing to the three-line ad at the top of the page. "But what the hell does she mean by 'herpes okay'?"

Travis jerked the paper away. "Don't be stupid."

Larry chuckled. "Hey, buddy, who knows, she might have long legs and a tight butt."

Travis slapped some money down and headed out to his truck. The only way he would ever place one of those ads was if he got desperate. Frankly he wondered how much longer that would take.

The answer came in two weeks.

Travis had been working out on the range and returned to the house exhausted, hungry, and in no mood to deal with another social worker. He must have talked to three or more in the last couple of months. They were doing their best to help, but frankly, he felt a whole lot more harassed than he did encouraged. Each visit netted him another list of atrocities he'd committed. Another lecture on his inadequacies as a nurturing parent. Another voice suggesting he was a failure.

"Hello," Travis said as he strolled into the house. He stopped in the middle of his kitchen to find Shirley Miller sitting at the table, waiting for him.

"Hello, Mr. Thompson."

He set his hat on the peg just inside the kitchen, walked over to the refrigerator, and reached for a pitcher of iced tea he'd made that morning. Without pausing he drank directly from the pitcher, gulping down several cool swallows. He was annoyed to note Mrs. Miller entering a notation on her ever-present clipboard.

"I noticed there were several containers of food left uncovered in your refrigerator," she said. "I realize that sounds like a small thing to you, but it's terribly unhealthy."

"What the hell!" Travis couldn't believe it. They were actually going to make a fuss over a bowl of leftover stew. Canned stew to boot.

Beth Ann beamed at him proudly. "That's good, Uncle Travis. Hell's a much better word than the 's' word."

Frowning, the social worker quickly entered that tidbit on her clipboard as well. Travis had never been more frustrated in his life. This woman had been sent direct from the bowels of hell to harass him. She'd made his life a nightmare, dropping in unexpectedly for inspections, issuing unwanted advice. It didn't matter how hard he tried, he seemed to be doing something that was sure to place Lee and Janice's children in grave emotional and physical danger.

"Mr. Thompson, there have been complaints."

"From whom?"

Shirley Miller sat on the edge of a kitchen chair and sighed heavily. "I'm not at liberty to say, but the . . . person who contacted me did so out of genuine concern for these children."

"I'll bet."

"It's my understanding Beth Ann missed two days of school last week."

"She had a cold." His eyes refused to meet the little girl's for fear she'd call him a bold-faced liar. The kid had a way of announcing his faults to anyone who would listen. Generally she did so at the worst possible moment.

"You didn't contact the school to let them know Beth Ann wouldn't be in, nor did you write a note to explain her absence."

"Not writing a note has got to rank right up there with leaving a cover off a bowl of leftover stew."

The social worker sighed and then waited an inordinate amount of time before she continued. "Contrary to what you think, the state doesn't want to place these children in a foster home."

Leaning his six-foot-three physique against the doorjamb, Travis struck a relaxed pose. "Frankly, I'd like to see you try."

"I don't even want to. You're being difficult, Mr. Thompson, when all I want to do is help."

"Let's make sure we understand each other." He hardened his dark eyes until he was confident she got the message.

"I'm afraid we don't," the middle-aged woman said, and her voice dipped regretfully. "You're doing everything to the best of your ability, but frankly, it just isn't good enough. Look at this place. It's hardly a fit environment for these children."

Travis glanced around the kitchen, seeing it from Shirley Miller's point of view. The linoleum table had been around from the time he was a kid, the corners chipped and broken. The chairs were mismatched, the padding tattered. He couldn't remember the last time the walls were painted, but it couldn't have been that long ago. Ten years sounded about right. Okay, so the place could use a bit of renovation, he'd admit that much. If all she wanted was for him to paint a few walls and buy a couple of things, then no problem. Hell, he was willing to do about anything to get the state off his back.

In the deepest part of his being, Travis recognized the truth of what Mrs. Miller was saying, but it didn't alter the facts. Jim, Scotty, and Beth Ann were his to raise, and it would take a whole lot more than one social worker or, for that matter, the entire state of Montana to take them away from him.

"You can't feed growing children macaroni and cheese four nights a week."

How the hell she knew that, Travis could only speculate. It seemed the woman rode a broomstick, circled his place, and wrote down every move he made. He was convinced she knew he was lying about Beth Ann missing school because of a cold.

With the five-year-old enrolled in the afternoon kindergarten program, Travis had only a few hours late in the day to make up for the time he spent in the house babysitting her. Unfortunately, that didn't leave a whole lot of opportunity for cooking a three-course evening meal.

If the weather was decent, he took Beth Ann out on the range with him, but all too often he'd lose track of time and she'd miss her bus. Then he'd either have to chase down the transportation provided by the school district or drive her into town himself. It was easier to let her miss class. Frankly, he didn't believe kindergarten was important enough for him to ruin the few precious hours he had to race all over kingdom come. The kid could already read some words; it seemed a waste of effort to teach her the ABCs when she could recite them as well as he could.

"We didn't have macaroni and cheese every night," Beth Ann delighted in telling the social worker. "One night Uncle Travis fixed popcorn. We had strawberry ice cream for dessert."

Travis groaned inwardly but didn't say anything in his own defense. There wasn't much to say. He'd been tired and cranky, and when he asked Scotty what he wanted for dinner, Scotty had suggested his two favorites. Travis had complied willingly.

Beth Ann walked over to stand next to Travis, as if aligning herself with him. He appreciated the gesture but wondered how much weight that pulled with the social worker, if any.

"How long has it been since you combed Beth Ann's hair?" she asked.

Travis frowned. The kid wouldn't hold still long enough for him to braid it properly, the way her mother had. His hands were too large, and her hair kept slipping between his fingers. Besides, Beth Ann was tender-headed and cried when he tried to brush it for her. It tore at his stomach to hurt the child. He heard her sob most every night, and nothing he could say or do comforted her. Part of each evening he spent sitting by her side and gently patting her head because he didn't know the words to ease the ache of not having her mother.

"It's my understanding Clara Morgan is coming in once a week to help?"

"That's right." The retired schoolteacher might well be an old biddy, but she generally stayed long enough to cook dinner, and Travis appreciated it. The day of the funeral, several of the town folks had claimed they'd be out to lend him a hand. In his pain, he had lashed out that he didn't need any help, didn't want any. A few had come, but Travis had turned them away. Clara Morgan was the only one who'd ignored his protests and continued her visits.

The back door opened and the two boys strolled into the house, having finished their chores. As soon as they saw Travis with the social worker, Jim and Scotty walked silently into the kitchen.

"Hello, boys," the social worker greeted them warmly. She made a notation on her clipboard, and Travis strained to read it. He hadn't a clue what terrible crime he'd committed this time. Then he noted the small rip in Scotty's shirt, at the elbow. He could probably sew it himself, he'd been mending his own clothes for years, but as with so many other things, he simply hadn't gotten around to it.

"Hello," Scotty answered, glancing up at his uncle. His young face was filled with concern, and Travis grinned, attempting to reassure him.

Jim didn't respond to the greeting. He stood silently in the background, waiting, it seemed, for the bomb to explode, staring it in the face, refusing to flinch or back away.

"I'll give you more time, Mr. Thompson," Mrs. Miller said, standing. She paused and glanced around the room again, as if she were afraid she'd missed some infraction the first go-around.

"Thank you," he said, meaning it. He walked her to the door.

She hesitated a second time, and when she looked up at him, her eyes were filled with warning. With one look she told him she must put these children's best interests first, it was her obligation to do so. If that meant taking them away from him, she'd do it without batting an eye.

Travis literally felt sick to his stomach after she left. He was going to have to do something, and quick.

"What was she doing here?" Scotty asked, looking out the back door window as the social worker drove from sight, leaving a plume of dry Montana dust in her wake.

"Someone filed a complaint."

"I didn't have a cold," Beth Ann admonished him. "Mommy said we should always tell the truth."

"You're right." Travis lifted the youngster into his arms and hugged her. He might not be much good when it came to parenting, but he'd grown to love these children deeply.

"What are you going to do?" Beth Ann asked.

"I'm not going to live in any foster home," Jim said from behind him.

"You won't have to."

"We might not have any choice."

"Not true," Travis said, setting Beth Ann back down on the floor. He walked across the kitchen and took out a fresh piece of paper and a short lead pencil, then pulled out a chair and sat down at the table. One chair leg was shorter than the other and rocked under his weight.

"What are you doing?" Beth Ann scooted out the one next to him and crawled onto it, kneeling on the seat and leaning toward him.

"Writing an ad."

"For what?"

"A wife."

He expected someone to say something. Scotty for sure, who rarely kept his mouth shut. The kid could speak nonstop for hours, driving Travis to the point of insanity with his questions and idle chatter. Even Beth Ann was staring at him as if he'd lost his wits.

"We need someone around here to help out, and since no one wants to take on the job of house-keeper, I was thinking maybe some woman out there would be willing to be my wife."

Scotty jerked out a chair and climbed next to him. "You can write away and get one?"

"Sure." Hell, he didn't know what kind of woman would answer his ad, if any. He glanced up to discover three faces staring at him so trust-ingly that his insides knotted.

"All right," he said, licking the end of the pencil. "Let's make a list of what we want."

"She should be a good cook," Jim suggested.

The others were all quick to agree, and Travis entered that quality on the top line. After nearly three months of macaroni-and-cheese dinners, he was willing to marry the first woman who could bake a decent apple pie.

"And sew," Beth Ann added. The ruffle on her best dress had ripped, and Travis had tried to mend it by hand, damn near ruining it. He felt doubly guilty about that since it was the same dress he'd inadvertently dyed pink.

"She should like horses and cattle if she's going to live out here with us," Scotty added thoughtfully.

"Right." Travis quickly added those facts.

"Do you think Mary Poppins might come?"

"Who?" Travis repeated. This wasn't the time to revive fairy tales.

"Mary Poppins," Beth Ann said again. "She was in a movie Mommy took us to see once in Miles City a long time ago. Mary came to be a . . . a nanny to some kids just like us, only their mommy and daddy didn't die. She could fly with her umbrella and make a messy room all tidy." She paused and supported her chin in her palms as she leaned forward, closer to Travis and the list. "She sang real pretty, too."

"Beth Ann wants you to find a wife who can work magic," Jim explained quietly.

"A woman who does magic tricks and sings."

Travis added the two qualities to the growing list. To be blunt, Beth Ann's request wasn't that much out of line. He was looking for a woman who could perform miracles.

Now all he had to do was find her.

Two

"Did you see it?"

Mary Warner glanced up from her desk in the front of Petite, Louisiana's lone library. She took a second to adjust her reading glasses, scooting them from their perch at the end of her nose. Then and only then did she look up at Sally Givens, the high school junior who came in two afternoons a week. The teenager's pretty blue eyes were hidden behind ridiculously long bangs that swayed like a pendulum across her face when she walked.

"See what?" Mary quizzed softly.

"The ad. Karen found it when she was putting the Billings, Montana, newspaper back on the shelf." Giggling, she absently brushed the bangs away from her eyes. The sides of her head were shaved high above the ear as though a crazy man had gotten lose with a razor. Apparently the style was the latest rage, and both of Mary's young assistants had caved in to peer pressure.

Mary couldn't help wondering what they'd think ten years from now when they viewed pictures of themselves.

"Some rancher is advertising for a wife," Sally continued, her amusement high. "Can you believe it?"

"A rancher looking for a wife," Mary repeated, tucking around her ear a strand of pale brown hair that had strayed from her carefully coiled chignon. "Well, that's certainly original."

"Karen says she might answer him herself." Sally's words were followed by a bout of smothered laughter as Karen came toward the front desk.

"I said no such thing," she argued. Karen's hairstyle was almost identical to Sally's, only the second girl sported a long thin queue that reached halfway down her back.

"Right, Ted would never let you."

"You're jealous because he asked me to Homecoming instead of you," Karen shot back, and with a jaunty step returned to shelving books from the polished oak cart.

If Ted, whoever he was, had asked Karen instead of Sally, then Mary knew why. Karen wore her skirts several inches above her knees, several inches above discretion, to her way of thinking. Miniskirts had been popular in the sixties, as Mary recalled, but had apparently made a recent comeback. The girls wore leggings with the skirts now, clinging nylon pants with a lacy fringe at the ankles. The youth these days were certainly creative in their means of dress, Mary mused.

Both girls returned to their tasks, teasing one another about Homecoming. Impatiently Mary watched them go, wondering briefly if she'd ever been that frivolous. Or, for that matter, that young. One thing was for certain, she'd never had to worry about which young man would ask her to the Homecoming celebration. In four years of high school, she'd never once been invited.

A sting of regret, of sharp grief, caught her by surprise. It took her a second to remind herself what was important in life. While she was in high school it had been grades and the school newspaper. Mary had been the editor for both her junior and senior years, an honor that hadn't been bestowed on any other high school student before or since. Although Mary hadn't been asked to Homecoming or the junior-senior prom, she'd certainly never been as desperate for a date as Sally and Karen seemed to be. The two had been agitated for weeks, vying against one another for the elusive Ted's attention.

This rancher who advertised for a wife was clearly desperate. Daring and reckless, too, as far as Mary was concerned. There was no telling what kind of riffraff would respond.

The poor man was from Montana, no less. Personally Mary could think of no one who'd be willing to move to the harsh, unforgiving land of the untamed West. She equated Montana with thick dust, scrawny cattle, and frightfully cold winters.

A barren region. It was certainly no place where she would ever consider living. Not when her home was in the South. Her home and her life.

Petite was a small town, with fewer than five thousand inhabitants, situated between two bayous. It was encompassed by marshy waters, and a warm mist rose up in the mornings, giving the area about town a delicate air of mystery and romance. Mary loved Petite and the slow, easy pace of life. The hours seemed to meander just the way the quiet waters of the bayous stirred softly at dawn.

As a girl she'd often fished with her older brother. They'd leave early in the morning, and Clinton would take her in a pirogue, a small dugout, and they'd drift across the still water, their lines dangling just below the surface, teasing the catfish. Bearded in Spanish moss, the trees drooped heavy arms in welcome. Those had been the happiest moments of Mary's childhood, fishing with Clinton.

Clinton was gone four years now and she missed him still. No sister could have asked for a better brother. He'd been her protector, her knight in shining armor, her bright morning star. Her older brother possessed everything that was good in the Warners. Not only had he been strikingly handsome, he'd been clever and daring and fun. Their house had never been quiet when he'd visited.

Often, when the scent of magnolia blossoms filled the evening air, Mary and her mother would sit on the porch sipping homemade lemonade. Clinton would steal up behind them and set the swing in motion, then hoot with laughter at the way Mary and his mother would cry out with surprise.

Everyone in Terrebonne Parish had grieved at the tragic loss.

Montana. Mary sighed and shook her head sadly. The poor, dear man wasn't likely to attract many bridal prospects coming from that bleak part of the country. Due to her ignorance, she was sure, she viewed ranchers as a rough and coarse breed, hardworking, hard-living men. Certainly no Montana cattleman could hope to compete with a refined southern gentleman.

As Mary recalled, the West had little appreciation for good food, either. She likened Montana with Rocky Mountain oysters and thick, blood-filled steaks cooked over an open fire.

Louisiana's cuisine, on the other hand, was as rich and flavorful as its history. Early each morning Mary savored dark Creole coffee and often delicious hot crullers or doughnuts still warm from the stove. She'd read once that chuckwagons boiled coffee over an open fire and served it grounds and all. The mere thought caused her to cringe.

Louisiana had shrimp so plentiful that steaming bucketfuls were emptied directly onto the tabletop and shelled by eager hands. Louisiana was filled with soul and spirit, and try as she might Mary couldn't view Montana as anything but ruthless and desolate. It was little wonder the rancher had resorted to advertising for a wife.

Sally and Karen continued returning books to the shelf, and every now and again the sound of their giggles drifted to the front of the library. Once Mary thought she heard Karen telling Sally she should answer the ad herself just so she'd have a date for Homecoming.

For a moment or two Mary toyed with the idea of chastising the pair for being so insensitive, but she changed her mind. The two were only teasing. They'd never do anything so heartless.

Although Mary was fond of the girls, she found their amusement uncharitable. But they were young yet and didn't understand what it meant to be so hopeless and lonely that one was reduced to reaching out to strangers.

There'd been a time—years ago, of course— when she might have been tempted to be amused herself. Years ago. The thought echoed in her mind like a loud, unexpected clap of thunder. Agitated by her musings, she patted her hand down the front of her dark blue skirt. Years ago. Suddenly she felt dowdy and old. Although she was only thirty-two, she felt forty. More profoundly, she knew to the depths of her soul what it meant to be alone. Isolated. Removed. Her heart went out to the rancher because she understood all too well what had prompted his placing the ad.

These unwelcome feelings could be attributed, Mary realized, to her mother's death this past February.

She was alone, she reminded herself. Orphaned. Her father had died when she was sixteen, and Clinton, her dearly beloved older brother, had perished in a plane crash. Savannah Warner, her mother, had never recovered from the death of her son. Although she'd been in splendid health, Mary's delicate southern mother had carried her grief with her, dragging it from one day into the next until the weight of it had burdened her heart so terribly that it had eventually failed her. Mary had done battle with her own grief in the months following Clinton's death and then her mother's.

Sally and Karen left at closing time, waving and smiling to Mary as they bounced out the door. The pair reminded her of playful cocker spaniel puppies. Once they were gone, she set about closing the library for the evening.

She reached for her sweater and stood in the middle of the two-story structure, gazing proudly on row upon row of neatly shelved volumes. The polished mahogany stairway curved up to the second story, and a scent of lemon oil wafted lazily between the two floors.

There wasn't a sound, not even a hint of one. How empty the building seemed.

Empty.

Hollow.

She drew in a wobbly breath. That was exactly the way she felt inside. Knotting her hands into tight fists, she turned away. Rarely did she allow herself to be so open and honest about her life. Hearing about the rancher was responsible for this, and she experienced a flash of resentment toward him.

By all outward appearances she lived a busy, active life. There was her work at the library, which was fulfilling and challenging. In addition she sang in the church choir and was an accomplished seamstress. She had several friends, the best of whom was Georgeanne McKay.

Few would guess. None would recognize the emptiness of Mary's struggle. Today was worse than others. Worse than it had been in a good long while. It was as if the giant void inside her had yawned open to reveal itself and she was left to hurriedly stuff it back inside. She was reluctant to drag it out, examine it, weep over it. There was a certain comfort in denial. This fragile peace with her consciousness had to be maintained at all costs. Ignored and buried.

Standing as she was, alone in the library, the vast barrenness of her life seemed suddenly to echo against the walls, reverberating back not a song, as she longed to hear, but silence.

An empty, lonely silence. One so loud it was all she could do not to cover her ears to block out the lack of sound.

Hurriedly Mary collected her purse and the latest Jean Auel novel and headed toward the back door. Her delicate fingers rested against the light switch . . . when she hesitated.

A wife.

Mary paused as the word, so soft and gentle, fluttered through her mind, bringing with it the promise of what she'd always dreamed would someday be hers. Those dreams had faded over the years until they were little more than aspirations.

A wife.

The word exposed hidden feelings, forgotten hopes, and dug deep, rooting out the loneliness she battled so hard to hide from the world, and harder from herself.

Mary had forsaken the idea of ever marrying. Every eligible man in Petite, Louisiana, had long since stopped looking at her in that way.

She wasn't unattractive. She was small-boned and barely five feet two, as delicate as her mother had been before her. Some said she was lovely, but it wasn't the type of pretty that attracted attention. Her grandmother had told her from the time she was little what beautiful eyes she had. Blue, they were, as blue as a field of spring irises.

Mostly Mary was shy. Apparently men expected a woman to do the talking, and she could never seem to find much to say that would interest a man. From the time she was in grade school the boys had avoided her because she made top grades. Evidently girls weren't supposed to be intelligent. It did something to their fragile male egos, at least that was what Georgeanne McKay had once explained to her.

Being both quiet and clever had worked against Mary while she attended college, too. Later, after she'd been chosen to become Petite's librarian, she learned that she'd inadvertently shut herself off from opportunity.

When she hadn't married by age thirty, most everyone in the small bayou town had given up hope Mary would find herself a husband, including Mary herself.

With a determination she could barely understand, Mary turned and headed back into the main part of the library. She walked over to the section that displayed the newspapers and reached for the *Billings Gazette*. With trembling hands she turned page after page until she located the personals column. The ad was at the top and her eyes found it almost instantly.

**Need wife to help rear three orphaned children
ages 12, 8, and 5.
Must know how to cook, sew, and sing.
Appreciation of ranch life would be helpful.
Write for information:
Travis Thompson
Grandview, Montana 59306**

Children.

Sally and Karen hadn't said a word about there being children involved. Mary's heart softened at the thought of those three precious youngsters, then swelled with an excitement, an anticipation, she couldn't squelch. There was a family, a real family, in need. Little ones lacking a mother's tenderness, hungry for love and gentility.

Like most women, Mary had dreamed of someday rearing a family. But those dreams had been shelved, like the forgotten books in her library, among tightly packed queues of other romantic, whimsical fantasies.

Montana! Mary cringed, thinking of rodeos and vulgar cowmen. Surely the men who lived there possessed little or no appreciation for the finer things in life.

She shook her head firmly. What had gotten into her? She didn't know. For a second, a very brief moment, she'd actually considered writing the rancher herself. It was sheer craziness. If she ever was to marry, Mary had decided she would do so only for love. Never anything less. Every woman was entitled to a little romance in her life.

Romance. She nearly laughed out loud. What did she know of such things? Precious little. A few stolen kisses behind the gym when she was fifteen, a note someone left in her locker once back in her senior year of high school.

Her actual experience with men might be limited, but Mary was well read and not nearly as naive as those around her chose to believe.

"Travis Thompson." She tested the name on her tongue, liking the sound of it. It felt solid to her. The name of a man who was trustworthy and sincere. A man as despairing and as lonely as she was herself.

"He's probably looking for someone much younger," she argued with herself as she walked out the door, locking it securely behind her.

Once she was home, Mary stared into the living room. The polished oak floors shined back at her as untouched as they'd been when her mother had been alive. It was as if no one had ever stepped across the pristine wood. The drapes were made of a heavy chintz fabric and had hung precisely this way for the last thirty years. The furniture hadn't changed in two generations. A rose-colored velvet sofa with mahogany claw-shaped arms and legs had been a family heirloom, along with the matching chair. Her mother's tea cart rested against one wall, and the photographs of her somber-faced grandparents were there to greet her each evening.

The living room had been reserved for company, although neither Mary nor her mother had entertained in years. If the living room had an untouched feel to it, then so did every other room. How tidy everything around her was. How orderly and uncluttered. Just like her existence.

Pushing aside any additional pessimistic thoughts, she moved into the equally immaculate kitchen and prepared herself a sensible dinner of shrimp and rice. Everything about her, Mary realized, was ridiculously sensible.

Seldom, if ever, did she do anything rash. Answering a rancher's ad for a wife might well be the most absurd thing she'd ever contemplated in her life. For the second time she shoved the idea from her mind as though it were something ugly lying dead on the side of the road.

It was while Mary was dealing with her leftovers that she hesitated for no reason, standing in front of the refrigerator as though she expected a genie to jump out and grant her three wishes.

The weekend before, Mary had been to visit her friend Georgeanne and been amused by the crayon-colored papers proudly displayed on her friend's refrigerator door. Every inch of available space was covered, and the door was smudged with the grimy fingerprints from Georgeanne's two sons.

Mary's refrigerator door was so clean that her own reflection glared back at her accusingly. She stared at it for several moments, analyzing her small breasts. Men were said to appreciate a woman who was well endowed. It was little wonder she hadn't attracted much attention. Frowning, she turned away to wash up the few dishes she'd dirtied.

As she stood at the sink, Mary couldn't keep her mind from envisioning three children crowded around a kitchen table, chattering away like magpies, eager to share the activities of their day. Three children to love and to hold and to read to each night, the way her mother had read to her and Clinton.

Mary's thoughts only magnified her loneliness. With a determined effort, she reached for the novel she'd brought home from the library.

Fifteen pages into the book, she set it aside. Funny how she'd never realized what poor company a novel could be, what poorer company the nights had become.

Children. Three of them, and all so young.

Mary could feel her resolve shifting, and she closed her eyes against the onslaught of churning emotions. She didn't want to hope because hope brought with it the opportunity for pain, and there had already been so much pain in her life. She was an adult, old enough not to be seduced by the promise of being needed and loved. Promises were often empty, and there was enough emptiness in her life.

Nevertheless, fifteen minutes later, Mary weakened and reached for a pen and a sheet of scalloped-edged paper.

Dear Mr. Travis Thompson:

I am writing in response to your advertisement in the Billings Gazette. My name is Mary Warner. I'm thirty-two and have never been married. I'm currently employed as head librarian in Petite, Louisiana.

In regard to your ad, I meet the requirements you stated. I'm an excellent cook, my specialty being boneless chicken with oyster dressing and gingersnap gravy. My sweet fig pie recipe won a blue ribbon two years back, and I'd be more than pleased to share the recipe with your family, if you so desire. I also serve up a respectable etouffee and apple pie.

As for my ability to sew, I am an accomplished seamstress and have been making my own clothes from the age of sixteen. Over the years I've sewn several complicated patterns for friends and family, including my best friend's wedding dress, which entailed five hundred pearls to be stitched on by hand.

Now, in regard to my ability to sing. I have

been a first soprano for the Petite Regular Baptist Church for the past ten years and have given several solo performances. I've sung at weddings, funerals, birthday parties, and anniversaries. If you wish to review a tape of my singing voice, I will willingly supply you with one.

Other than the talents you requested, I'll add that I come from hardy southern stock with roots that can be traced back as far as the early 1600s. Some of my relatives include a Spanish conquistador, a soldier who fought in the bayous with Jackson, and an Acadian exile. There's no doubt in my mind that the blood of more than one pirate has mingled with the Warner line.

Having lived in Petite all my life, I'm afraid I know next to nothing about cattle and the like. Nor have I ever lived on a ranch. I do suffer from a few minor allergies, but to the best of my knowledge hay isn't one of them.

If you would be willing to consider me as a candidate for your wife, then you may write to me at the address listed on the top of the page.

Respectfully,
Mary S. Warner

Mary mailed the letter first thing the following morning, before she could entertain second thoughts. They came anyway, almost immediately after she'd dropped the letter in the mail slot, followed by an entire day in which she chastised herself for yielding to the fantasy.

She was too old. Too quiet. Her roots were in the South, her heritage, everything that was important to her. Travis Thompson and those three children wouldn't want her. He'd want a wife who was young and pretty. Not someone whose most appealing feature was blue eyes.

Only . . . only she could cook and sew and sing. And that was all Travis Thompson had claimed he wanted. He hadn't said a word about requiring a beauty queen and a fashion model.

The response came back so fast that it made her head spin. Within a week she was clenching an envelope postmarked Grandview, Montana.

Dear Miss Warner,

Thank you for your kind letter, which the children and I have read with interest. Since you've been so forthright about yourself, I figured it's only fair to share a bit of my own background. I'm a cattle rancher, age 36. Like you, I've never been married.

My brother Lee and I were born and raised in Grandview. Lee married Janice a few years out of high school, but the two of them were killed several months back in an auto accident. I was granted custody of Jim, Scotty, and Beth Ann. They're the only reason I need a wife.

If you're looking for romance, fancy words, and expensive gifts, then I'll tell you right now, I haven't got the money or the inclination for such things. My brother and his wife are gone, and I've got my hands full dealing with their youngsters. I don't have time to properly court a woman. I need a wife and these children need a mother.

My spread has over 15,000 acres, and I make a decent wage when the beef prices are fair, but I'm not a wealthy man, so if that's what you're thinking, then I suggest you withdraw your name from consideration.

I'm honest, although there are some who would question that. I work hard and play just as hard. I drink a little now and again, but I don't chew or smoke. I enjoy a game of poker with the men, but rarely play more than once or twice a month. I kinda hate to give that up. I swear a little, but Beth Ann's taken it upon herself to clean up my language. I'm not much of a talker and keep mostly to myself.

Each of the children have a question. Jim thanks you for the offer of the recipe for your sweet fig pie but wants to know if you can bake chocolate-chip cookies. He figures if you can cook up gingersnap gravy, you'll probably know how to cook just about anything.

Scotty says he doesn't care if you can sew wedding dresses. He's more anxious to find out if you can mend the tear in his favorite plaid shirt. He won't let me try since I ruined Beth Ann's church dress trying to fix the ruffle.

Beth Ann's biggest concern is if you can make up songs and would be willing to sing them to her when she goes to bed the way her mother used to do.

As you might have guessed, I sincerely lack any domestic talents. I can't carry a tune any better than I can cook.

If you decide after reading this that you're still interested, then please write again. A picture would be appreciated.

Sincerely,
Travis J. Thompson

Mary read Travis's letter straight through, twice. She read it so many times in the next few hours that the top edges of the pages started to curl. Of course she'd hoped to hear from him, but she hadn't allowed herself the luxury of believing he would actually respond to her letter. A thousand times she regretted the wording. She should have said this, deleted that. For days she'd been tormenting herself, regretting whatever weakness had possessed her to answer the Billings ad.

The instant she heard from Travis, all her doubt evaporated. She was thrilled.

She answered him that very night.

Dear Travis:

I lost a brother, too. Clinton died four years ago in a small plane crash. I know all about the pain of losing a loved one, of feeling guilty because they died and you didn't. Guilty because everything changes afterward. Everyone changes. You your-

self change, although you struggle against that very thing. At least I did, and the battle tired me so. Death leaves one feeling overwhelmingly powerless, doesn't it?

I learned that hope and despair feel so much alike that I couldn't tell the difference after a time. It was as if both paths crossed each other so often that one blended into the other. That's the best way I can think to describe the months following Clinton's death.

I apologize. I didn't mean to get started on that subject, but it struck me that the two of us, who are so outwardly different, share something so fundamentally important.

Yes, I'm still interested in becoming your wife, although I'm not sure I should be. You were prompt in telling me what I shouldn't expect. I hope you'll be as forthright in telling me what I can.

As for the children's questions, you may tell Jim that I can cook anything he desires. My expertise in the kitchen isn't limited to sweet fig pie. All he need do is let me know his favorites.

And Scotty, you don't need to fret, either. I know my way around a sewing machine just as well as I do a kitchen. If I can't mend his shirt, I'll sew him another just like it.

Beth Ann, sweetheart, I've been singing made-up songs for as long as I can remember. I'd be more than happy to sing them for you each night.

The picture I'm enclosing is from last year. It was taken beneath a blooming magnolia tree.

*I'm the one on the left. The woman standing
with me is my best friend, Georgeanne McKay.
I'll look forward to hearing from you again.*

*Warmest wishes,
Mary Warner*

Mary was on tenterhooks until she heard from
Travis again. She didn't have to wait long. Within
a few days there was another letter waiting for
her. Mary didn't wait until she was home to rip it
open and read what Travis had written. She tore
the letter open right inside the Petite Post Office.

Dear Mary,

*What can you expect? You're right, I was quick
to list what you couldn't, but I didn't bother to
tell you what I'm offering. Your question gave me
cause to evaluate exactly what I'm willing to give
to this marriage other than hard work and three
grieving children.*

*First and foremost is commitment. We're both
well aware this isn't a love match. I suspect that
matters to you far more than me, being that's the
way a woman thinks and feels. From what I know
of women, I suspect you'd prefer I sugarcoat this
agreement with a few romantic words, but I'd
rather we start out being honest with each other.*

*If you agree to marry me and move to Grand-
view, then I'll commit myself to you the same way
I have to Lee and Janice's children. This means*

I'll make myself responsible for your well-being. Your problems will be my problems. Your needs, my needs.

I promise to be faithful to you, to work toward making this ranch as prosperous as possible, so when the time comes we can enjoy the fruits of our labors together.

My home will be your home. Lee and Janice's children our children.

What I'm offering seems damn little when I look at it in black and white.

The kids and I talked, and of everyone who's written we like you the best. Instead of keeping us waiting for your letter, please phone with your response at the number listed below.

I look forward to hearing from you.

Affectionately,
Travis J. Thompson

Three

The afternoon Travis's letter arrived
was incredible. For no reason whatsoever, sitting
at the front desk, Mary burst into giggles. She
glanced around guiltily and then moved on to
some other section of the building only to laugh
again. People must have assumed she'd been
sniffing book glue.

"How are you this fine afternoon?" Mrs. Garrett
had asked her near closing time, no doubt expecting
Mary's customary reply of "Very well, thank you."

Only Mary hadn't given it to her. "I feel especially reckless today," she answered politely.

The retired nurse had stopped short and
frowned at her through narrowed eyes above
thick wire-rim glasses. "Did you say you were
feeling reckless?"

"As a matter of fact, I am." Mary punctuated
the comment with a warm smile.

"My dear, you should do something about this. I suggest you visit Dr. Hanley without delay."

Unable to hold on to her secret a second longer, Mary headed for Georgeanne McKay's house as soon as the library was closed.

"Mary, what a pleasant surprise," Georgeanne welcomed her warmly. Tall and as slender as a young poplar tree, Georgeanne had married a month after graduating from high school and gone on to live a fairy-tale existence. Two children and several years of marriage had done little to mar her classic features. Even after two difficult pregnancies, Mary's dearest friend had been able to maintain her svelte figure. Georgeanne had always been popular and outgoing, and Mary felt uplifted just being around her. Analyzing their friendship, Mary realized her friend was a pleasant contrast to her own dull existence.

"Have you got a moment to talk?" Mary knew it was the dinner hour, but she couldn't wait another second to share her news.

"Of course." Georgeanne led the way into the kitchen. The sink was piled high with dirty dishes, and the table crowded with plates and an empty milk carton. The salt shaker had spilled, and white granules had been scattered across the tabletop. "Benny took both boys down to buy them a new football. It seems the old one went flat. Here, sit down and let me get you something cold to drink."

Mary stood in front of the refrigerator and noted that the crayon-colored pictures were still there, along with a copy of the school lunch menu for the month. She reached out and brushed her fingers over the magnet holding the menu in place. Happiness crowded up inside her as she realized her life would soon be as cluttered and full as her friend's.

When she turned around, Georgeanne was standing with two tall glasses of iced tea. She studied Mary for a moment before asking, "Is everything all right?"

Mary smiled brightly. "It couldn't be better."

Georgeanne believed her, Mary could tell by the relaxed way her friend walked past the cluttered kitchen table and led the way to the front porch.

"I was just thinking the other day that we haven't seen near enough of each other lately. How about the two of us going shopping Saturday?" Georgeanne asked as she sat on the white wicker chair. Brown thrushes fluttered between the tree limbs while june bugs and katydids chirped a cheery song.

"Shopping . . . ah, sure." Mary's hand tightened around the strap of her purse as she sat down herself. The air was fragrant this evening, she noted, and realized with a pang how much she was going to miss her home. But Montana held something for her that Louisiana never would.

A husband, children, and love.

"Georgeanne," she said excitedly, "I have some wonderful news."

"I guessed as much. Your eyes are fairly twinkling."

"I need to know what you think of that pale pink material and the pattern I showed you last month. The one I planned to make with the lace overlay and the satin ribbon woven in at the yoke."

"I thought it was absolutely divine," George-anne answered thoughtfully. "Why? Are you thinking of sewing it up? I thought you said you were saving it for something special."

Mary's nod was eager. "The most important event of my life."

"Is the library holding another literary tea?"

Mary carefully opened her purse and withdrew Travis's letter as if she were bringing out the Hope diamond, as though she would never again in her life hold anything of more value. "I'm planning to wear it for my wedding."

The stunned silence stretched to embarrassing proportions. "You're getting married?"

"Don't look so shocked," Mary teased, knowing full well how much of a bombshell her news was. She, who hadn't been out on a date in over two years. She, who had given up the hope of meeting that someone special, of ever being loved or of loving a man.

"I . . . I hardly know what to say. I wasn't even aware you were dating."

"His name is Travis Thompson, and he lives in a little town a hundred or more miles outside of Miles City, Montana. I'm not entirely sure where the wedding will be held or even when, but I assume it'll be in Grandview since that's the closest city to Travis's ranch."

"Montana." Georgeanne's reaction was very much like Mary's had been when she'd first read the ad. It was as though Mary had announced she were marrying an alien from outer space.

Mary understood her friend's concern. She'd had her own share of misgivings in the beginning. She might as well explain everything at once, she thought with a muted sigh. "I really don't have much choice but to move to Montana, since that's where Travis's cattle ranch is."

"You're going to live on a cattle ranch?"

"Don't worry, I'm sure Travis has no intention of having me work the range." She'd meant it as a joke, but Georgeanne seemed to be taking her seriously.

"How . . . did you two meet?" her friend asked in a reed-thin voice.

"We haven't, at least not yet."

"You've never met the man." Georgeanne stood abruptly, then literally fell back onto the seat. Silence stretched between them, and the air filled with static electricity that arched between incredulity and disbelief.

"We will before the ceremony, of course," Mary assured her with a light laugh. "There's no need to look so worried. We're both going into this with our eyes open."

"If you've never met, then how . . . when did you find each other? It doesn't make . . ." The words quickly faded into nothingness.

"I answered Travis's ad for a wife," Mary explained, never considering telling her friend anything less than the truth, however painful. "He put one in the Billings, Montana, paper, and Sally Givens—you know Sally Givens, don't you?—found it."

Georgeanne's nod was decidedly weak.

Drawing in a calming breath, Mary forced herself to continue. "You see, Travis's brother and sister-in-law were killed recently, and Travis was granted custody of their three children. They're the reason he placed an ad in the paper."

There, it was out. The facts, stark and chilling. The truth that Mary was so despairing, so hopeless, that she'd resorted to answering an ad in the personals column. It hurt to admit it, but she was safe telling her friend, the person in Petite who knew her best.

"This rancher . . . advertised for a wife?"

"Yes, and I answered. We've been writing back and forth ever since, and he and the children chose me." She couldn't keep the pride from ringing in her voice. When Georgeanne continued to stare at her as though she were from Mars, Mary peeled the pages from the envelope and handed them to her friend as proof.

Perhaps Mary had been foolish to blurt it out this way, but she expected Georgeanne to share a small portion of her enthusiasm. Her lifelong friend was the single living soul she trusted enough to believe such a madcap scheme could be made to work. No one else would understand. Mary fully envisioned being called a fool, cautioned, and chastised by most everyone, but not by Georgeanne. Not her best friend.

"Children? The man was granted custody of the children?"

"Three."

"Dear God in heaven," Georgeanne whispered in words that weren't meant to be a prayer. Then again, maybe they were.

"Georgeanne, please," Mary said, reaching for the other woman's hand and gripping it tightly between her own. "Be happy for me. A man, a good, honest man, wants me for his wife."

"B-but you haven't even met him."

"But I know him. We've been writing." Mary shuffled through the pages of the letter.

"Not for long, otherwise you would have mentioned him before now. How could you even consider anything this crazy? It just isn't like you." The words burst like caps out of a toy gun, quickly fired, loud and demanding.

"I'm going to marry him," Mary said with quiet dignity.

"Have you told anyone else? Don't you think you should at least discuss it with someone? Mary, please, you've got to think this through very carefully. Naturally you're feeling confused. Your mother died this year, and I know Clinton's death was terribly upsetting to you. Surely this idea of yours . . . of marrying this man sight unseen is somehow linked to losing Savannah and Clinton. You're feeling disoriented and bewildered by the blow. You aren't yourself."

"I know exactly what I'm doing."

"You can't," Georgeanne argued, "otherwise you wouldn't have agreed to this . . . this strange proposal."

"I haven't actually agreed. At least not yet."

Georgeanne closed her eyes briefly. "Thank God," she whispered. "You can't leave Petite, Mary, you just can't. What would I do without you?"

"You'll be just fine. You always have."

"But this just isn't like you."

Her friend had given Mary pause, had dented the confidence she'd been nearly drunk with earlier. Hearing herself explain out loud what she was doing made it suddenly seem preposterous. Absurd and foolish. Still, she longed to marry Travis Thompson more than she'd ever wanted anything in her life.

"Travis asked me to contact him by phone once I'd reached my decision."

"I take it you haven't phoned him."

"Not yet," Mary confirmed. She was trying to think clearly, weigh her decision with a logical mind, and examine the pros and cons without emotion. There was no need to coat the fairy-tale picture of marriage she'd built in her mind; she knew what she wanted, and she also knew what she was getting.

It was either a mistake to have come to Georgeanne or the best thing she could have done. Mary didn't know which.

She reached for her iced tea and took a sip. As

she did, she recalled her friend's cluttered refrigerator door. Her heart ached, throbbing with a need so strong it was all she could do not to burst into tears.

Through all the years that their friendship spanned, Mary realized sadly that Georgeanne McKay hadn't really known her. Georgeanne, whose life was so littered and happy, couldn't possibly understand what it meant to live in the sterile, tidy world of loneliness. Her friend, who'd been loved and desired by one man from the time she was in high school, had no conception of what it meant to be a thirty-two-year-old virgin. Her friend's reaction had been one of selfish need. Georgeanne could never appreciate what Travis's offer meant to someone like Mary.

Within her hand Mary held the only opportunity she might ever have to find happiness with a man. There were children involved, young, grieving children who needed her. For the first time in years she had hope, and it was a damn sight better than filling the emptiness with faded dreams.

Okay, Mary was willing to admit marrying a stranger did sound like the action of someone desperate and hopeless. So? Those were the very feelings she'd been stuffing deep inside her all these years. She was sick of pretending otherwise. Sick of denying the lack and all that went with it.

Georgeanne must have sensed Mary's attitude because she released a labored sigh. "I don't mean to sound so skeptical. For all I know your cowboy may be . . . wonderful. I assume you've had him checked out? I mean, he could be a mental patient or have a criminal record or any number of things that you should know about."

"I don't need to do that," Mary responded defiantly. Now her friend seemed to be questioning her ability to judge character.

Georgeanne looked all the more concerned. "Please tell me this is all some silly joke. You really aren't seriously thinking of going through with this, are you?"

"Yes, I most likely will marry Travis." Georgeanne had given her something to think about, Mary admitted. As for taking the time to have Travis checked out, as Georgeanne put it, she didn't feel it was necessary. If the state of Montana considered him fit enough to raise three children, there couldn't be that much wrong with him.

Georgeanne meant well, but for the first time Mary recognized a side of her friend's personality she'd never viewed before. As for marrying Travis, Mary's mind was set.

"How could you even consider marrying a man you've never met?" Georgeanne reached for her iced tea, jerking it so hard that it sloshed over the sides. She took a sip, then set it back down on the glass-top table with a thud.

"He and the children need me. It's enough. I don't expect you to understand what it means to be needed," she returned sadly.

"This isn't you, Mary, it just isn't you. You've always been so levelheaded. My instincts tell me it's all wrong, you can't honestly mean to move half-way across the country to marry this cowpoke."

"Why can't I?"

"Well because . . . because if you want a husband, this isn't the way to go about getting one. Did you ever stop to think the only reason he wants a wife is because of those children?"

"Of course. They're the reason I'm marrying him."

Mary's answer seemed to confound her friend even more.

"I . . . thought you were happy. You've always seemed to be . . . this just isn't something you would normally do."

"Oh, but, Georgeanne," she disputed, amazed that her friend didn't know her at all, "it is me. I don't think I've ever been more excited in my life. I feel so rich inside, as if I've won the lottery."

"Have you thought about his motives? Have you honestly considered why he's willing to marry someone he's never met? He's using you."

Mary smiled softly, dismissing her friend's fears. Georgeanne had used her, too, as a sounding board, to help her with the children when they were younger, to sew her clothes. "Don't be so hard on Travis. I'm using him, too. We're both doing this because of the children. They need me, and it feels so wonderfully good to be needed."

"I need you, too," Georgeanne argued, her voice growing urgent. "We've been friends nearly our whole lives. I'm trying, Mary, honestly trying to understand, but I just don't. You're willing to toss away everything you've ever worked for because some cowboy needs a wife, and because some children you've never met need mothering? You're risking so much, and for what? What do you expect in return?"

In some ways Mary appreciated her best friend's concern, but it wasn't going to make the least bit of difference. Her course had been set from the instant she'd heard Sally and Karen talking about Travis's ad. In that moment some unnamed emotion had scooted down the length of her spine, and she hadn't been the same since. She sincerely doubted that she ever would be again. The ad had been the pivotal point of her life. It had forced her to take an honest look at her existence. She couldn't bear to go on another day the way she had been. Pretending to be happy. Imagining so much that was never there and never would be unless she took action. Travis was giving her the opportunity, and she was so overcome with gratitude that it was all she could do to refrain from dancing down Petite's oak-lined streets.

"It doesn't matter what I say, does it?" Georgeanne whispered. "You've already made your decision."

The brown eyes staring at Mary so intensely persuaded her that she really should have led into this discussion with a little more tact. But after so many years of friendship, she hadn't thought it would be necessary.

"I feel as though I've lived my entire life in a

glass bowl," Mary said in one last effort to explain. "Georgeanne, look at me. I'm thirty-two years old, don't you think it's time I lived a little?"

"But marrying a stranger is like learning how to fly by leaping off the Brooklyn Bridge."

"Perhaps," Mary agreed, but she never had been afraid of heights, and for the first time in more years than she wanted to count, she was ready to soar.

"Promise me one thing," Georgeanne pleaded, gripping Mary's hands with her own. "Give it a week. Think through every detail of this before contacting him. A week shouldn't be so long to wait. Will you do it? For me? Please?"

Mary sighed, then nodded reluctantly.

"You know what I was thinking?" Scotty said, his elbows propped on the kitchen table, his freckled face buried between his small hands. He paused, his expression dour.

"What's that?" Travis was busy scrubbing out the bottom of a cast-iron stew pot. He'd gotten distracted and left it on the stove several hours too long. Hell, he didn't know something could get this badly burned. The meat was scorched, the vegetables had cooked so long they were an unrecognizable mass, and it looked like he'd damn near destroyed the best pot he owned.

"I was thinking," Scotty continued, frowning, "that Mary's decided she doesn't want to marry us."

Travis muttered a cuss word under his breath. The truth of the matter was he'd been having those same thoughts himself. By his calculations, Mary had received his letter a full seven days earlier. Seven days. She should have been able to make up her mind in that amount of time. He'd laid his cards on the table, been as honest and straightforward as he knew how to be, and ruined everything in the process.

He'd give her a few more days, then sort through the other letters he'd received and answer one of those. Hell, finding a woman willing to marry him was proving to be as difficult as locating a housekeeper.

"Did I just hear you say a bad word?" Beth Ann asked, stalking in from the living room, arms akimbo. Travis swore the kid had better hearing than some bats.

"I might have muttered something just now."

"Something bad?"

"He's worried," Scotty explained patiently. "A man should be able to let off a little steam when he's got something heavy on his mind."

For being eight, the kid was all right. Travis saw more of Lee in Scotty than the other two kids. At times it was almost painful watching the lad, and at others . . . at other times Travis's heart felt a bit lighter seeing bits and pieces of his brother's wit and charm sparkling from the boy's eyes.

Jim physically resembled Lee the most, but his personality was more like Travis's. He didn't say much but stood back and soaked in what was going on around him. Of the three, Jim was the cynic, the pessimist. Travis tried to be patient with the boy, but frankly he was getting sick of dealing with his sour, critical moods. If Jim behaved this way at twelve, then Travis hated to think what he'd be like at fifteen.

"We might as well accept the fact she's not coming," Jim announced. "Why should she?"

"I liked her the best," Beth Ann said sadly, scooting out the chair and sitting down next to her brothers. The five-year-old's shoulders slumped forward as if her head weighed too much. Travis had managed to comb her hair into pigtails, and although they were lopsided he was downright proud of his efforts.

Scotty leaned across the table and whispered in a voice Travis wasn't supposed to have heard but did. "We've got to do something quick before Uncle Travis poisons us with his cooking."

"I heard that," Travis muttered. "No one ever died because something was a little overcooked."

"A *little*," Jim complained loudly. "It's going to take you a week to scrub the burnt stuff off the bottom of that pot."

"If you're going to complain, I'll let you do the scrubbing."

"How long will it be before Mrs. Morgan comes to visit us again?" Beth Ann asked wistfully.

"Six days," Scotty answered, as though they were sure to be the longest six days known to mankind.

The old lady continued to drive out and visit every week. In the beginning, fool that he'd been, Travis had resented the intrusion. Several women from town had wanted to smother him with advice and drown him in their charity. He hadn't wanted any part of it. He'd been gruff and unfriendly when they'd driven out to the Triple T carting food and cleaning supplies, too damn proud to accept their help. Four months had altered his opinion. Anyone who made the trip to the ranch hauling anything edible was given a welcome fit for royalty.

No one came, however, with the exception of Clara Morgan. The retired schoolteacher stopped by weekly with dinner fixings, stayed long enough to talk to each of the children, and then promptly left. Travis half suspected she was the one who'd contacted the Children's Protective Services with a long list of complaints. He hadn't figured out if the old woman was friend or foe, but since she served up the only decent meal they could plan on for the week, Travis didn't ask.

The phone rang, and all three kids turned bright eyes toward Travis. He should never have said anything about asking Mary to phone. He regretted that now. His own disappointment was keen enough without having to deal with theirs.

"You going to answer that?" Scotty demanded after the second ring.

"Give me a minute, will you?" he returned brusquely, reaching for a dish towel. He never thought he'd see the day he was suffering from dishpan hands.

"She might not wait a minute," Scotty argued.

"It isn't her, anyway," Jim said with a sneer. "She isn't goin' to call."

Travis pointed his index finger at the older boy.

"I told you before to quit being so damn negative," he reprimanded as he reached for the telephone receiver. Jim's rotten attitude nagged at Travis. "Triple T," he barked into the mouthpiece, frowning. He needed to do something about Jim, only problem was, he didn't know what.

"Hello . . . Travis?"

The voice that came at him was soft and feminine, with a warm southern drawl. Travis's hand tightened around the receiver as his heart tripped. "Mary?" He flashed a triumphant look toward the kitchen table as though he'd known it was her all along.

"Yes, it's me. You asked me to phone."

"Have you decided?" Travis hated the eagerness he heard in his own voice. He should sound cool and collected, as if her response didn't matter to him one way or the other. There were plenty of other letters to sort through. Even a few worth considering. None that matched hers, but she didn't know that.

"You didn't send a picture." Her words were mildly accusing.

"Did you ask for one?" He tried not to let his impatience show, but he was having a damn hard time of it.

He could almost hear her smile, which was nonsensical. "Listen, if you want something, you're going to have to learn to ask for it. I'm not a mind reader."

"Are you tall?"

"Six three. I'm a little on the scrawny side."

"That's because he has to eat his own cooking," Scotty shouted, and the three gathered around the table all laughed. The tension had broken, and for that, at least, Travis could be grateful.

He silenced them with a look. He didn't want Mary to think he was marrying her just because she was a good cook, although that was part of it. Heaven knew he'd lain awake nights thinking about the meals she'd make. If she could win a blue ribbon for a fig pie, then it didn't take much of an imagination to figure out what she could do with apples or peaches.

"If you want a picture, I'll mail you one," he said a bit more gruffly than he intended. He could have told her some women thought he was handsome, but he didn't want to sound conceited. It was generally accepted that he was good-looking.

"Mailing me a photo won't be necessary."

It was all Travis could do not to demand why the hell she'd asked for one in the first place, then. Furthermore, he wished she'd answer his question. The way he figured it, if he said nothing, she'd eventually get around to telling him what he wanted to know.

A painful silence fell between them. It was all Travis could do not to blurt out the question once more.

"The reason I phoned," Mary said after several torturous moments, "was to let you know that I've given thoughtful consideration to your proposal and have decided to marry you. That is, if you still want me?"

Want her! He hadn't met the woman, and everything within him longed to bring her into his arms and tell her how grateful he was. The weight of ten years was lifted from his shoulders in that moment.

"Great," he said, struggling to disguise his enthusiasm and not succeeding. He gave the kids a thumbs-up sign and grinned when the three clasped arms around one another's waists and danced around the table.

"I'd like to speak to each of the children, but before I do I thought we should agree on a date so I can make the travel arrangements."

"Fine. I'll call the airlines and have a ticket waiting for you at the desk. Is Saturday convenient?"

"This Saturday?"

When else did she think he meant? "Yes. The children and I are eager to meet you."

"I'm sorry, but I couldn't possibly be ready so soon."

A man could get used to a voice that soft, Travis mused. It was like listening to a flow of liquid honey.

"There are several matters I must see to before leaving Petite," she added. "I've decided to put the furniture in storage and rent the house. There's so much to sort through. Why, it could take weeks."

"Weeks!"

"I was thinking two months would be adequate."

"Two months?" His hold tightened on the telephone to a punishing force. "We can't possibly wait that long." Not with the state social worker breathing down his neck. Not with him ruining every pot and pan in the house. If that wasn't enough incentive, he had a ranch to run. He needed a wife, and he needed her now.

"All right," Mary said genially enough. "One month. That will be pushing it, but I'll need at least thirty days to conclude my affairs in town."

"No way." His tone was sharp enough to stop the children cold. Three pairs of anxious eyes turned to him. "One week," he said firmly. "That's all the time I've got. Either take it or leave it." He sounded far more confident than he was feeling.

"Uncle Travis," Scotty reminded him, waving his hands wildly, "she can cook real good."

"Well?" Travis pressed, ignoring the boy.

"She sings made-up songs," Beth Ann added in a soft, pleading voice.

"If that's the case," Mary said with an abrupt sigh, "then a week will just have to do."

She wasn't pleased, Travis could tell that much, but it couldn't be helped.

Mary hesitated, and then her voice dipped slightly. "I'm looking forward to meeting you all."

"I'm anxious to meet you, too." Travis was convinced she didn't have a clue exactly how much.

Four

Mousy. It was the only word Travis could think to describe Mary Warner when she stepped off the plane. His heart sank and took a moment to rally itself. Long legs, that was all he'd asked for, and what did he get? Minnie Mouse.

All right, he was willing to admit, he was being unfair. She'd sent him the photo, and he'd known she wasn't an Amazon. He just hadn't expected her to be quite so . . . so diminutive.

Travis didn't know when he'd seen anyone who looked more like a librarian than Mary did. She couldn't have weighed more than a hundred pounds, and as best he could calculate she was a full foot shorter than he was. The top of her head barely reached his shoulders. If her plain features and size weren't discouraging enough, she looked as if a stiff wind would topple her, and God knew there were plenty of those in Grandview. Travis doubted that Mary Warner had much if any stamina. She didn't look strong enough to shift the gears on his truck, let alone cook and clean for an entire household. As for living on a ranch, she'd be as out of place as a palm tree in Alaska.

She was wearing a pale lavender dress, and the soft color enhanced her features, which were—he hated to say it—ordinary. She seemed a tad pale, until he realized she wasn't wearing makeup. Not even a little blush or lip gloss. Her glasses were the huge horn-rimmed variety that took up nearly all of her face. Her classic navy blue coat was left unbuttoned, and she wore sensible black shoes. A book was tucked in her arm, and he glanced down to note it was one on child rearing. Apparently she didn't know any more about the subject than he did. They were certainly going to be great parents, he told himself sarcastically. Funny he hadn't thought of that before.

In any other circumstances Travis was convinced he would have passed her by without even giving her a second glance. Damn, but she was small.

The entire scrutiny took all of two seconds before he gave himself a mental shake, removed the Stetson from his head, and stepped forward.

"Mary Warner?"

"Yes." She looked up at him with clear blue eyes.

She had lovely eyes. She wasn't his type, not in the least, but he appreciated beautiful eyes when he saw them.

She stood absolutely still as they stared at each

other. For the longest moment she said nothing, as if she too had been expecting something much more than he'd ever deliver. He straightened, uncomfortable under her scrutiny, wishing he'd taken the time to shower and shave before he left the ranch.

"I'm Travis Thompson."

"I thought you must be." Her voice was deeply southern, and her smile was shy, sweet. Gentle. A Mary Poppins sort of smile. Beth Ann, at least, was going to get her wish. As for him, there was no hope.

Travis felt as though he'd been duped. The photo she'd sent had been vague and nondescript. The shot was much clearer of Mary's friend than of herself. He'd studied her image for a good long while, sensing a rare beauty beneath those pale eyes and gentle features. He should have looked closer. Any beauty he'd detected from the photo had been in his imagination.

Apparently everything she'd written about what a good cook she was had blinded him to the truth, because he experienced little, if any, of those feelings now. He'd needed someone for the children so badly that he'd made Mary into something she would never be. He should have known better, but by the time he'd read her letters and received her picture, he'd gotten fanciful.

The number of women who'd responded to the ad had shocked Travis. He received fifteen replies that first week and more later, but by then he'd heard from Mary. Of all the women, she was the only one he considered suitable to help him raise his brother's children. He'd like to see the state social worker find fault with a librarian!

Some of the others who'd written had tempted him plenty. Pretty ones, desperate ones, sexy-as-hell ones, but Travis had repeatedly gone back to Mary's simple, straightforward letter.

He'd known long before he sent her the airfare that Mary Warner wasn't a candidate for Miss America. He just hadn't been prepared for a shy little mouse.

"I thought the children would be here," she said, glancing around for them.

"They're back at the ranch waiting." He didn't own a vehicle large enough for everyone to fit into and hadn't gotten around to buying one. He probably wouldn't until he'd sold off the rest of his herd.

"I was hoping to meet them." Once again she offered him a gentle smile, then quickly lowered her eyes to the floor.

Mary Warner wasn't the type of woman he'd ever dated, but he found himself growing to like that sweet smile of hers. And those eyes.

"You'll meet the children soon enough." Pressing his hand against her elbow, Travis led the way to the luggage carousel. He wondered what the hell they'd find to say to each other during the two hours it would take to drive into Grandview.

He was so much larger than Mary had envisioned. Six three had never seemed so formidable. His

size was downright threatening. He wasn't smiling, and his look, so dark and intense, intimidated
her. His hair was brown and untamed and needed
to be cut. She noted that he set his hat back on his
head a second after he'd introduced himself, as if
he felt uncomfortable without it. She found that
somewhat endearing.

His eyebrows were bushy and bleached nearly
blond from too many hours in the sun. She didn't
know what to make of his eyes. They were an
odd shade of brown—uncommon, really, a cross
between brown and green—and when he smiled,
which was rare, she noted, their color resembled
Kentucky whiskey. His look was unreadable,
as if he'd had a good deal of practice hiding his
feelings.

His face was nearly bronzed, weathered and
beaten. He'd written that he was thirty-six, but he
looked older. He might have been handsome if it
weren't for the chiseled hardness of his jaw. The
contours were angled and abrupt.

There was nothing soft in this man, nothing
delicate or subdued, she noted. He made no apol-
ogies for who or what he was, nor did he make
any attempt to hide it.

If she were to have walked past him on the
street, her first thought would have been that he'd
stepped off the pages of a Louis L'Amour novel.
A cowboy from a hundred years past, wearing
faded denims, a blanket-lined jean jacket, scuffed
boots, and a black hat. Mary strongly suspected
he'd leaped from the back of a horse and hur-

ried into Miles City to meet her plane. He hadn't dressed for the occasion, but she wasn't offended by that. He was a rancher, and from what he'd written, the hours he could spend working his spread were precious few since the arrival of the children.

One thing did concern her, however. Travis Thompson was more man than she'd ever seen in her life. Having him touch her, even lightly at the elbow, unnerved her.

Once they were outside, the wind cut through her like a hunting knife. Shivering, she buttoned her coat as fast as her fingers would cooperate and hunched her shoulders against the cold. Travis had warned her winter was setting in. It had gone without saying that the mild weather in Petite would be nothing like the bitter cold of Montana. Mary had thought she was prepared, but she wasn't, not for anything like this, and it was barely October.

Travis set her two large suitcases in the back of a dilapidated pickup. The rest of her things were being shipped. She didn't take time to examine the truck carefully, other than to note that it didn't look like it would last more than a few hundred miles.

After helping her inside, Travis joined her. He started the engine, which roared to life with surprising energy as though to prove her wrong. She ran her hand along the tattered cushion in unspoken apology for having judged the truck harshly, and perhaps the man, too.

The ride into Grandview took nearly two hours. Neither of them spoke much, although they both made a single attempt at polite conversation. Travis inquired about her trip and she asked about the children, and after that there seemed nothing more to say.

The landscape as they rode along was as Mary had envisioned from the beginning. Stark and barren. They drove for miles on end, traveling up one rock-strewn hill and down another in what seemed to be an endless stretch of monotony broken by tumbleweeds that scooted across the road, carried by the howling wind. Mary had hoped to find grass rippling in the wind as the sun caressed the land. Only there was no grass and there was no sun.

"It's Mrs. Morgan's day at the ranch," Travis explained as they pulled off the highway and down a long, narrow roadway bordered on both sides by fenced land as rocky and barren as everything else around them. Curious, Mary wondered how anything sustained life in such desolation.

"Clara Morgan visits once a week," Travis went on to explain. "She does what she can to help with the children."

Mary nodded, not sure how to comment or even if one was needed.

"I had the boys clean up their room. You can sleep there until the waiting period is over." His hands tightened about the steering wheel as though suggesting she might be having second thoughts. Mary couldn't help wondering if maybe he was the one who would rather not go through with the ceremony.

"Is sleeping in the boys' room all right with you?" he asked gruffly.

"That'll be fine."

Just when Mary was beginning to wonder how much longer it would be, Travis slowed and turned into a gravel-packed driveway. The road was hardly one at all. It was steep and rocky and filled with ruts large enough to swallow half the truck. The ride was so jarring that she clung to the cushion in an effort to keep from being tossed about.

Travis slowed as they reached the house and immense yard. Mary wasn't sure what she'd expected. What she saw caused her heart to sink several notches. In her mind she'd conjured up a ranch that was something out of reruns from the old television series *The Virginian*, with a large, immaculate house set on a hill above pristine pastures and well-maintained outbuildings. What she found could best be described as a hodge-podge of dead and dying vehicles and neglected buildings.

The house was there all right, but it was small and dingy looking. The wood had been exposed for so many years that whatever paint had been there had long since faded. The outbuildings, of which there were several, looked in even worse condition. A few were leaning slightly to one side as if all it would take was a brisk wind for them to collapse altogether. She counted four rusting cars and doubted that a single one of them was drivable.

"It's not much," Travis said, apparently reading her thoughts. He studied her as if waiting for her to announce the whole thing was off and that she refused to marry him. If that was the case, Travis Thompson was going to be disappointed. Mary hadn't agreed to this marriage expecting to be met by servants and the promise of room service. Her imagination had run away with her, that was all, but she could accept reality.

"It's a very nice place, Travis."

He cast her a surprised look, as though he wasn't sure he should believe her. She smiled at him briefly and looked away, a little embarrassed.

The back door opened and three children crowded on the porch when Travis helped her out of the truck. Mary paused, and her tender heart warmed at the sight of them. They were exactly as Travis had described them in their two brief conversations following her phone call. Stair steps. All three were ogling her, their expressions blank except for their eyes, which were incredibly round and wide. If she didn't know better, Mary would have thought the three were posing for a poster of farm children back during the Great Depression of the 1930s.

"Don't be bothering Mary with a bunch of questions," Travis warned as he guided her into the kitchen. After viewing the outside of the house, Mary thought she was braced for what she would discover inside. A surprise awaited her as she scanned the large room. The appliances, although they weren't anything to brag about, were surprisingly modern. There was even a microwave oven. The walls were a cheery shade of yellow, but then Travis had mentioned having painted recently.

Wordlessly the children followed her from the porch, gathering around her, looking as though they expected her to say or do something.

"Hello," she said softly, smiling down at them. If she was disappointed in Travis and the ranch, then these precious children more than made up for it. They'd spoken briefly on the phone, and each time Mary had come to know them a little better.

The youngest smiled back shyly. "Can you do magic tricks?"

"No. Was I supposed to?"

"Yes, just like Mary Poppins."

"That's stupid," Scotty said. He was nearly as tall as his brother, with two front teeth growing awkwardly into place. A dash of cinnamon-colored freckles garnished his nose.

"More important," Jim argued, stepping forward, "when can you start cooking?"

"As soon as you like."

"It's a good thing, because Uncle Travis's dinners are about to kill us all."

"For Pete's sake, give her room to breathe," Travis demanded, coming through the door hauling both of her suitcases. "They'll talk your head off once you get to know them."

"We weren't pestering her."

Travis closed the door with his boot and paused halfway across the kitchen floor. "Introduce yourselves proper like while I put her suitcases away." He disappeared down a long narrow hallway.

"I'm Jim."

Mary walked over to him and smiled. "I'm very pleased to meet you." She held out her hand for the youth to shake, which he did.

"You're not very pretty."

Mary didn't take offense, but the words stung nevertheless. "I know, but I can cook, and from what you said earlier that was all you wanted."

"I think she's pretty," a boyish voice announced from behind her. "Well, sort of."

Mary turned around to face Scotty.

The youngster stuck out his hand. Mary shook it, then framed his face between her hands and smiled at him. "Thank you for saying I'm pretty."

The eight-year-old blushed profusely. "Well, you are."

"Sort of," she reminded him.

"I'm Beth Ann, and Uncle Travis ruined my best dress, and I need someone to make me another one."

"I'll see what I can do with it first thing after dinner."

"Where's Mrs. Morgan?" Travis asked on his way back from the bedroom.

"She had to leave early, but she left you a note."

Travis nodded, walked over to the bulletin board, and removed the tack from a folded piece of paper. All three of the children were watching him, waiting for his response. Because they did, Mary did, too. She noted that his jaw tightened as he crumpled the note and tossed it in the garbage.

"Is something wrong?' Mary asked.

"Nothing," Travis answered, and reassured her with a smile, but it was weak at best and didn't begin to reach his eyes.

"Mrs. Morgan sent her congratulations and said something about the ladies group at the Grange holding a reception for us after the wedding."

Scotty whispered for Mary's benefit, "She said she was looking forward to meeting you."

"I don't have much to do with the folks in town," Travis said darkly. "If you don't object, I'd rather skip the reception." His intense eyes studied hers.

"Whatever you prefer."

"I think a party would be nice," Scotty said.

"Scotty," Travis barked, "shouldn't you be doing your homework?"

"I'm hungry."

"Me too," Beth Ann announced. "Mrs. Morgan got so busy cleaning up for Mary that she forgot about dinner."

"She brought everything with her the way she always does," Scotty explained. "It just needs to be heated up."

"I'll do that," Travis said to the children, "while you show Mary her room."

The three hesitated. "Remember what happened the last time?" Beth Ann whispered to Travis as though it were a secret she didn't want Mary to hear.

"I can warm something without ruining it," Travis thundered, stalking across the kitchen.

The children turned to cast pleading looks toward Mary. She hadn't anticipated traveling for several hours and then being expected to manage dinner. But she'd do it without thinking twice, without question, because there were three sets of eyes staring at her expectantly.

In all her life no one had ever needed Mary the way these four did. The warm sensation it created within her was like slipping into a tub of hot water on a winter day. It felt good all the way to the marrow of her bones.

"You three show Mary to her room and then give her a tour of the house," Travis instructed, opening the refrigerator and taking out several items.

"I'll do that," Mary offered.

"No, you won't," he returned gruffly. "Not after the day you've had. Contrary to what the children may say, I'm capable of warming up dinner."

"You're sure?"

"Positive."

Still Mary hesitated, until Beth Ann slipped her small hand into Mary's. "I want you to see my room first, okay?"

Mary nodded and allowed the children to drag her down a narrow hallway. It was apparent they'd all made an effort to tidy up for her, but little could disguise the disorganization that greeted her in each and every room.

The boys' bedroom was the worst. A thin blanket covered the window, tacked to the frame with large nails. The curtain had been torn, Beth Ann explained, when Scotty had used it as a grapevine to swing from his bed to the floor. In the process he'd ripped the rods out of the wall.

Each and every room was wallpapered, Mary noted, but the paper was badly yellowed with age, lending a dingy, dark feeling to the house.

The master bedroom gave her pause. The curtains were closed, and dark shadows bounced against the hardwood floor. The closet was narrow, and Mary wondered how she and Travis would possibly find room to store their clothes in one so compact. The bed had been hastily made, and Travis's boots and socks were strewn in one corner as if he'd carelessly tidied it that very morning.

The living room was the largest room of the house, and she hesitated when she noted that Travis had arranged the long sofa so that it blocked off the front door. Surely he'd made a mistake, or else no one had come to call in a good long while. A massive stone fireplace took up one entire wall, bordered on each side by bookshelves. She smiled as she scanned the titles, pleased he appreciated good fiction as much as she did. Everything wasn't so bleak after all, she reasoned. They had more than a love for these children in common.

* * *

"I saw Travis Thompson in town the other day," Hester Johnson said, loudly enough for everyone in the group to hear. They were gathered at the Grange for their weekly game of pinochle.

"He's doing a good job with those children," Clara Morgan said, setting her cards on the table while she reached for her glasses. She hated having to wear them, to admit she was getting too old to play cards without them.

Everyone at two tables was staring at her when she'd finished, casting her doubting glances. She'd been thinking a good deal about Travis in the last day or so. Her weekly trip to his ranch had netted her a juicy piece of information that she'd been sitting on all morning.

"I'd say he's doing the best he can, which is a far sight short of what those youngsters need," Hester countered sharply. She sorted the cards in her hand and then glanced upward. "The man needs help, but the fool's too damn proud to admit it."

"You're just upset because he turned down the pear preserves you offered him."

One fine day Clara intended on having a nice long talk with Travis Thompson. He'd mocked Hester's good intentions and was paying the price. What folks said about hell having no fury like a woman scorned was true.

Hester muttered something Clara couldn't hear, but she knew Travis was a sore subject with the president of their ladies group. Hester had gone out of her way to visit Travis and the children shortly after the funeral, and he'd practically chased her off the Triple T. Travis had tried that with Clara as well, but it hadn't worked. She'd taught that boy English when he was in junior high, and she'd surrender her pension before she'd allow him to boss her about.

Briefly Clara wondered if Travis even remembered that he'd been in her class. Junior high had not been a good time in Travis's life. Now wasn't a good time, either.

Travis had been a troublesome youth, Clara recalled. His reputation as a rabble-rouser and a troublemaker had preceded him from grade school. She never knew what happened to his mother, whether she'd abandoned her family or died. Whichever it was, Travis's father had taken to drowning his sorrows in a bottle of whiskey. She admired Travis for the way he'd looked after his younger brother, Lee. She only wished he'd taken as good care of himself. My oh my, but that boy could fight. He didn't back down, even when he knew he was going to lose, and lose badly. Clara had lost count of the times he'd been suspended for fighting.

By the time he was in high school, Travis had been brought before the courts for any number of minor offenses. Criminal trespassing for one, spray-painting the back of the library for another, repeatedly letting the air out of the sheriff's tires. No one had much good to say about the boy, not that his deeds were unforgivable. It was his attitude, the belligerence, hostility, and disrespect, that people remembered.

A girlfriend might have helped, but Travis never dated much, as she recalled. Plenty of girls would have welcomed his attention, despite what their parents would have said, but Travis never showed much interest.

Like everyone else in town, Clara had heaved a sigh of relief when Travis enlisted in the marines. It would do him good. Make a man of him. In retrospect she had to admit she wasn't all that certain military life had changed him. He kept mostly to himself these days, and few, if any, of the good people of Grandview had forgotten his past.

Clara had never defended Travis, how could she? She'd lost her patience with him countless times herself. What had endeared him to her was the way he'd loved and cared for his younger brother. When she'd learned of Lee's death, her heart had immediately gone out to him.

"You've gotten quiet all of a sudden, Clara," Hester said, pulling her from her thoughts.

Clara hesitated, deliberating how much she should say to her friends about what she'd learned from the children. It was unfortunate that several in the group hadn't forgiven Travis for the way he'd rejected their generosity. Their hearts had been in the right place, and Clara knew most of them had been shocked at how ungracious he'd been.

She had the advantage of knowing Travis a little better than the rest. He was acting like an injured bear. The pain of losing Lee had him snapping at everyone and everything around him. It was as though he had to hover over and protect what was left of his family, and he didn't want anyone interfering.

"It seems Travis is marrying," she announced, waiting for her news to settle over the group. The reaction didn't take long.

"What did you say, Clara?" Hester asked loudly.

"Travis Thompson's getting married."

"Travis . . . marrying?" Martha Johnson demanded. "Who?"

"Certainly no one I know in Custer County would marry the likes of him," Hester muttered. When everyone paused at the uncharitableness of the comment, she added in her defense, "The man told me to stick my pear preserves where the sun don't shine."

"Hush, let Clara speak."

Now that she had their full attention, Clara regretted having said anything. Her peers would have found out soon enough without any help from her. "Apparently she's from Louisiana. Travis drove into Miles City to pick her up at the airport."

"Louisiana?" Hester repeated slowly, as though Clara had declared Travis's wife-to-be had arrived from the farthest reaches of civilization.

"I left a note suggesting our group would hold a reception for them after the ceremony."

Her words were followed by a stunned silence, then, "You did what?"

"Clara, after the way he treated us following the funeral, how could you?"

"I for one will have nothing to do with any reception," Hester declared righteously, her mouth pinched.

The venom in those words jarred Clara. She rose awkwardly out of the chair and straightened to her full height. A militant light came into her eyes, and she struggled to keep her voice even. "That man is willing to lay down his life for those children. It seems to me that we, as his neighbors, would be generous enough to do everything we can to help him."

The others looked ashamed of themselves. "Clara's got a point."

"Perhaps," Hester Johnson agreed reluctantly. "The man certainly needs someone. I've heard rumors of how poorly those dear children are faring."

"They're doing just fine, considering what they've been through," Clara countered.

Hester didn't look convinced, but it was apparent she didn't want to argue. "How'd he meet this . . . woman from Louisiana?"

"I have no idea."

"Surely he mentioned her?"

Everyone seemed to be waiting for Clara to respond. "I can't recall that he has."

Scotty had been the one to announce that his uncle was off to the airport in Miles City to pick up his bride-to-be. The news had been as much of a shock to Clara as it was to the ladies at the Grange.

"A wedding reception would be a good way

for us all to meet Travis's bride," Clara reminded them.

The women shared a significant look, then each one nodded in turn, their decision made. With the exception of Hester Johnson, who apparently hadn't changed her mind. Slowly she shook her head from side to side, silently declaring she would have nothing to do with the project. Clara smiled to herself, sincerely doubting that Travis would do anything to convince her friend he wasn't a sin-riddled troublemaker. It was unfortunate that he'd turned down those pear preserves.

Travis couldn't sleep, not for the life of him. Darkness closed around him as he lay in the middle of the double bed, his hands supporting his head as he stared up at the ceiling. He didn't know what to do. Mary wasn't anything like what he'd imagined or what he'd hoped.

For one thing, she was so dainty and delicate. For another, he couldn't ever imagine himself falling in love with her. Not the way a man should love his woman. His imagination had always been healthy, but for the life of him he couldn't picture that fragile body of Mary's stripped bare and stretched out on this bed next to his. He'd touch her, and in his mind's eye he could see her pull away from him, frightened half out of her wits.

Sweet heaven, he wouldn't blame her. The two of them were as different as anything he could imagine. His size alone must terrify her.

Sex was only a small part of marriage, Travis

reasoned, but damn it all, it was too important to gloss over lightly. He couldn't live with himself if he ever hurt Mary. When the time was right, he wanted to initiate her to the pleasures their bodies could bring each other without her shying away from him.

If only she wasn't so dainty. He'd watched her when she'd returned to the kitchen after the kids had given her a tour of the house. He'd studied her closely then, half expecting her to complain about the mess. She hadn't. Instead she'd removed her coat and insisted upon helping with the meal. He'd frowned as he realized how unbelievably small she was beneath that pretty wool coat.

For both their sakes, he should explain that he didn't feel this marriage would work out between them. By all that was right he should send her packing. She could catch the first flight out. . . .

Before he could accept the idea of sending Mary away, another thought filled his mind. He recalled how, after dinner, Beth Ann had crawled onto Mary's lap with a book of fairy tales in her hand. Mary must have been exhausted. Not only had she spent several hours traveling across the country, but she'd ridden two more in his truck. They'd arrived at the ranch in time for her to help him get dinner on the table, and then she'd topped off the day by reading Beth Ann bedtime stories. The fact his niece had gone to sleep without sobbing for the first time in months hadn't escaped his notice, either.

This frumpy librarian was a natural with the

children, and when he'd commented on it, she'd blushed and claimed story time at the library in Petite had been her favorite duty.

Travis had to admit she read a story better than anyone he'd ever heard. Beth Ann had been mesmerized by the tale of Sleeping Beauty. Soon Jim and Scotty had crawled up on the sofa to join their sister. It took one hell of a lot to hold the attention of those three, but Mary had managed without hardly seeming to try.

For the first time since Lee's children had come to live with him, they hadn't made a fuss about going to bed.

Travis rolled onto his side, and the bed creaked. He expelled his breath and bunched the thick goosedown pillow under his head.

Shit, he didn't know what to do. If he went ahead and married her, then he might as well accept the fact it would take a good long while before anything physical could develop between them. If ever. That thought was downright discouraging.

Of course, he could go on doing what he had been for the last several years, satisfying his carnal needs with Carla whenever he was traveling. But the thought left a bitter taste in his mouth. Furthermore, he'd already promised Mary he intended to keep his vows, and that included being faithful to her. He didn't know where he'd learned the importance of vows, certainly not from his mother, and not likely from his father, but he felt marriage should be taken seriously.

Travis must have tossed and turned for another

hour before he heard a noise coming from the direction of the kitchen. He held himself still and listened again. The sound was so faint he had to strain to hear it.

Throwing back the covers, he came off the bed and reached for his jeans. As he suspected, Mary was sitting at the table, silhouetted by the moonlight, staring into the dark.

"Mary?"

She twisted around and looked up at him. "I'm sorry. I didn't mean to wake you."

"You didn't."

A soft, powerful silence followed before she spoke. "I know. I heard you."

"I kept you awake?"

"No. I couldn't sleep myself."

Travis pulled out the chair across from her. "What are you thinking?"

She hesitated so long, he wondered if she'd heard him. "That you're probably looking for the kindest way possible to send me back to Petite." Her voice was calm and even, but Travis would have sworn that quality had been hard won. She looked so vulnerable, sitting there in the moonlight, holding herself stiff. Watching her was oddly painful for him. He had been having exactly those thoughts, but not for the reasons she assumed.

"What I don't understand is why you chose me. We don't have a thing in common other than books, and—"

"You had a brother that died." He hadn't realized it was the reason until exactly that moment. Yes, she'd written about her expertise in the kitchen, but it was what she'd told him about Clinton that had seared his heart. She understood the ache that consumed his soul.

"Yes." Her eyes were incredibly round in the dark, round and guileless.

"You know what it's like to lose someone you love."

She nodded.

"I liked your picture, too," he told her honestly.

"I'm not beautiful. . . . I wrote on the back of the photo that it was flattering. . . . I don't feel I misrepresented myself. In fact—"

"Mary," he said, interrupting her. He couldn't bear to listen to her defend herself when the problem was with him. She was a cultured, gentle soul and deserved much more in life than he'd ever be able to give her.

"What?" she asked softly.

"Despite everything, are you willing to go through with the wedding?"

She hesitated. Travis had thought, or at least he'd hoped, she would answer him positively, without even needing to think over her response. "Before you answer, you should know something."

"Yes?"

He needed her, and feared he'd lose the children if she declined, but he couldn't be anything less than honest. "I don't mean to be cruel, but you should know up front that I may never love you."

"I . . . wasn't expecting that you would."

She sounded so matter-of-fact, so unconcerned by what had been plaguing him most of the night. All the doubts he'd entertained came back to haunt him. Mary Warner was a refined, delicate woman, and he was a hard-ass, redneck rancher. What chance was there of her ever finding happiness with the likes of him? Damn little, he decided. Yes, he'd been thinking of sending her away, but it wasn't because he didn't want to marry her.

He half rose from his chair, convinced her silence was all the answer he needed. "If we do marry, there's something else you should know. There'll be no divorce. I refuse to put the children through that, so if you're entertaining second thoughts, then—"

"I wouldn't leave the children," she interrupted with a choked whisper. "Yes, I want to go through with the wedding. I have from the first, otherwise I would never have come. But . . . are you sure, completely sure, you want to marry me?"

Travis was so relieved, he sank back onto the hard chair without giving her question a second thought. "Yes, I'm sure. Damn sure."

Five

Travis impatiently paced the living room, glancing at his watch every few minutes. What in tarnation was taking so damn long? He hated this whole wedding business but considered it a necessary evil. If it had been up to him, they would have quietly visited the justice of the peace and been done with it. He should have known better than to give Mary a free hand. Before he knew it, she'd contacted Pastor Kennedy at the Methodist church, bought each of the kids a new outfit, ordered flowers, and damn near ruined what he was hoping would be a perfectly normal day.

Wearing a suit was torture enough. His tie felt like a noose stretched around his neck, and he eased the starched collar from his throat in order to swallow more comfortably. The last time he'd donned this suit had been for Lee and Janice's funeral, and the memories stirred awake the growing anger and frustration he experienced over their accident.

"Mary?" he called restlessly, pacing to the far end of the living room. The room was tidy; Mary's impact on his home and his life had been immediate. Within a matter of days she had the place looking better than he could ever remember. "We're going to be late."

"I'll only be a minute more." Her soft southern drawl meandered from the hallway without a trace of urgency.

Jim and Scotty joined him, sagging onto the sofa cushions. They didn't look any more eager to be wearing a suit than Travis. It was best they learned early that there were certain things in life a man had to accept in order to placate women. Occasionally donning church clothes was one of those things.

"Just how long is this wedding going to take?" Jim wanted to know.

"Too long," Travis muttered under his breath. As soon as the ceremony was over, he fully intended on having a talk with Mary. Apparently she didn't appreciate all that a rancher's life entailed. He was willing to give in to her wishes over this wedding business, simply because he wanted their marriage to get started on the proverbial right foot. But he couldn't be taking time off in the middle of the day for such frivolity again any time soon.

Weddings were important to women, Travis

was willing to grant Mary that much, but there was a limit to his endurance.

The length of his stride increased. He paused and looked at his watch once more and sighed expressively.

The ceremony itself wasn't anything more than a formality. As far as Travis was concerned, it was an obligation he'd prefer to avoid but couldn't.

"Do women always take this long to pretty themselves up?" Scotty asked, loosening the knot of his tie by jerking it back and forth several times.

Travis shrugged. Hell if he knew, he'd never lived with one before now. If today was any indication, he could well spend the rest of his life in a constant state of agitation.

"Maybe it's because Mary needs so much help getting pretty," Jim offered smugly.

Travis turned on the boy and glared, fighting back a fiery rage. The tension between him and Lee's elder son grew thicker every day. Travis didn't know what the hell he was going to do about it, if anything. The kid was grieving, they all were, and this animosity toward him was the way Jim had chosen to release his pain. Notwithstanding, he refused to allow Jim to talk about Mary in a derogatory manner.

"I won't have you say that about Mary. Understand?"

"Well, she's not much to look at, is she?"

Travis felt his nerves stand on edge the way they did before he entered a fight. By heaven, he wasn't going to let a twelve-year-old punk kid get his goat.

"She's about to become my wife and as such is due your respect," he said calmly. "Is that understood?"

Resentment flashed into the boy's eyes.

"We should just be grateful she agreed to marry me," Travis said stiffly, doing his best to avoid yet another confrontation.

"Right," Jim continued, snickering. "Beggars can't be choosers."

"Listen here, you smart ass," Travis exploded, taking hold of the twelve-year-old by the elbow and jerking him to his feet.

"Travis." Mary's soft drawl reached through the fog of his anger, reminding him he was playing directly into Jim's hands. "I'm ready to leave now."

Indignantly Jim pulled his arm free of Travis's grasp and straightened the sleeves of his suit jacket with an air of superiority.

Exhaling sharply, Travis composed himself before turning to face his bride. He wasn't expecting miracles. Mary was as sweet and gentle as a lamb, but it was going to take a whole lot more than a pretty dress and her hair done up all fancy to transform her into a beauty.

"Mary . . ." Scotty was the first one to speak, and he did so with a youthful enthusiasm. "You're pretty."

"She's downright beautiful," Travis added, struggling to sound convincing.

Mary blushed becomingly and lowered her long lashes. Beautiful was a stretch, but it made Travis feel good to know that he'd pleased her. Her dress was a delicate shade of pink, with lace and other girly stuff. She held on to a small bouquet of flowers, as did Beth Ann, who was standing demurely at her side.

Mary did look nice, and it was clear she'd gone to a good deal of effort. Every woman deserved to be told she was lovely on her wedding day, Travis reasoned, even if it was an exaggeration. He'd made it clear from the first that he wasn't one for a bunch of romantic words, but for her sake he tried.

Mostly he was grateful for Mary's willingness to marry him and help him raise Lee's children. At the moment he didn't feel especially lucky to be saddled with a soon-to-be wife and three children; nevertheless this was his fate, and he was determined to do his damnedest by those he loved.

"Can we leave now?" Jim's surly voice intervened.

"Yes, of course," Mary answered, her gaze seeking out Travis's. She smiled shyly and steered the two younger children out the door.

Mary couldn't think of much to say on the twenty-minute ride into town. Beth Ann was wedged in the cab of the pickup between her and Travis while the boys rode in the back. At the best of times Travis wasn't much of a talker, and after darting a look in his direction, she decided they really didn't have a whole lot to say, either.

Doubts had crowded her heart from the moment she'd arrived in Montana, but the din of her questions had quieted with Travis's compliment. He was trying so hard to make this day special for her. His effort touched her heart far stronger than anything he might have said or done.

Within an hour she was about to pledge her life to this man she barely knew and these children who so badly needed her love. She hoped . . .

Hope.

It seemed like such a fragile thing to base her future upon. So intangible and frail. In many ways Mary felt as though she were looking to achieve the impossible. Travis had bluntly warned her that he wasn't likely ever to love her. Although his words had cut at her pride, she recognized what it had cost him to admit as much. He was an honest man, hardworking, gruff in some ways, gentle in others. All things considered, she could have done a lot worse.

Travis drove the truck into the church asphalt parking lot and cut the engine. For a moment no one moved or spoke. Mary studied the small white church with the tall, spindly steeple and silently approved. This was exactly the sort of picturesque church she would wish for her wedding. It wouldn't be filled with organ music, orange blossoms, and a parade of friends who'd shower her with rice, but then she'd never expected to marry anyway.

Travis turned to Mary. "You're sure you wouldn't prefer a justice of the peace?"

Mary smiled at his less-than-subtle attempt to persuade her to forgo a church wedding. "I'm sure."

Grumbling, Travis opened the cab door and climbed out of the pickup. "I don't hold much with religion," he announced unnecessarily when he came around and helped her out of the truck. "Never have and never will."

"He makes sure we go to Sunday school, though," Scotty complained, jumping down from the truck bed. He landed solidly on both feet. Jim leaped directly behind him.

"Churching you three is what your mother would have wanted," Travis muttered. "Women are like that," he added as though it were a character fault.

Travis stood, arms akimbo, feet braced slightly apart, as he stared at the Methodist church. From his stance, one would think he was facing a gunslinger in the streets. Or something he dreaded.

Mary was much too practical to fill her head with romantic dreams. For that matter, so was Travis. This wedding was a major ingredient to melding their lives together, and she refused to be shortchanged. Especially since she'd been cheated in so many other areas. That they would be married by clergy had been her one and only stipulation, and Travis had agreed. He hadn't liked it, but he'd agreed.

"Come on," Travis said, stiffening his shoulders. "We might as well be done with this." His smile was apologetic as he reached for Mary's hand, lacing their fingers. Other than helping her in and out of the truck, it was the first time she could remember him touching her.

Pastor Brian Kennedy looked up from his desk when they walked into his office. He unfolded his lanky frame from the chair and nodded toward Travis and the boys.

"You must be Mary," he said, stepping around his cluttered desk.

"I am," she returned, holding out her hand, which he gripped and shook politely. "I'm honored to meet you."

"You too. Hello, Travis, it's so good to see you again," he greeted.

"I understand you talked to Mary yesterday about marrying us."

"Yes, I did." The reverend spoke slowly, rubbing his palms together. "Generally I don't perform the ceremony without several counseling sessions first. This arrangement is highly unusual."

"We don't have time for any counseling."

"Our circumstances are a bit out of the ordinary," Mary assured him with a warm, confident smile. "We know what we're doing."

"Are you going to marry us or not?" Travis demanded with a complete lack of patience. "If not, Judge Green will, so I suggest you make up your mind."

Reverend Kennedy looked decidedly uncomfortable. "Perhaps if I could speak to each of you alone for a few moments."

"For what purpose?" Mary asked softly.

"He wants to talk you out of marrying me," Travis flared.

The reverend wiped his brow and shifted his weight from one foot to the next. "I assure you that's not the case. It's just that this is all rather unusual, and—"

"Then shall we get on with it?' Travis asked impatiently.

"Of course. I never intended . . . Why, I think it's wonderful that . . ." He let the rest fade, then nodded eagerly, looking like a convict who'd been granted a stay of execution.

Tilly was busy delivering three plates of Martha's chicken-fried steak with mashed potatoes and country gravy when Travis, a sweet-looking woman, and Lee and Janice's three youngsters entered the cafe. They sat in the large circular booth in the corner in her section.

When she had a free moment, Tilly filled five water glasses and tucked the plastic-coated menus under her arm. Every movement she made was appraised by Doc Anderson. She'd been as nervous as a worm in hot ashes from the moment Logan's father had walked into the cafe a half hour earlier.

One minute she was convinced Doc knew about her and Logan, and the next she would have staked a month's wages that he didn't have a clue. Logan loved his father, but from the little he'd said, she knew the two men didn't get along well. When Tilly had first met Logan he'd told her he'd moved to Grandview to be closer to his father, yet it seemed the two were barely on speaking terms. One thing was sure, Doc would never approve of her dating his son.

"Howdy, Travis, kids," Tilly said with her brightest smile as she set the glasses on the table.

"Uncle Travis just got married," Beth Ann announced without forewarning, leaning against the tabletop. Her hair was curled in pretty blond ringlets, and she wore a lacy white dress, new from the looks of it.

"Congratulations, you two," Tilly said to the happy couple. She hadn't seen Travis's bride around town, but she'd heard a rumor he'd found himself a woman. His new wife was a bit on the plain side, but outward beauty didn't hold much weight with Tilly. She'd seen just how shallow it could be in her own life. Frankly she was surprised Travis didn't put more stock in good looks. Most men did. Since she was so freely tossing stones, Tilly had to admit women were often guilty of the same thing.

"Tilly, this is Mary," Travis said.

"Hello, Mary."

"Hello."

Her voice was soft, with a soothing smoky molasses drawl. Tilly didn't know where Travis had met up with Mary, but then the cowboy had always been full of surprises. The way he'd taken his brother's children under his wing had given most folks in town pause. Nearly everyone viewed Travis Thompson as a hotheaded troublemaker. Personally, Tilly never had understood why. He worked his ranch as hard as the next man, and if he chose to let off a little steam now and again, that didn't make him any different from several other more "respectable" ranchers she could name. That he'd gone and found himself a wife, someone who was clearly a lady, was sure to set tongues around town wagging.

The gossip mongers would forever find fault with Travis, but the problems he'd had raising his brother's youngsters were sure to be eased now. Tilly wished them all a truckload of happiness. God knew it had been in short supply the last few months.

"Can we order dessert first?" the middle boy asked, looking to his uncle.

"Why not?" Travis answered, setting aside his menu. "It isn't every day a man gets married."

It seemed to Tilly that his voice was a tad loud, as though it were important for everyone in town to know he'd found himself a wife. Which was likely the reason he'd stopped in at Martha's. Most folks frequented the cafe for coffee and idle chatter. News spread faster than a brushfire once it hit Martha's. Not only did the grandmotherly owner serve the best food in town, but the cafe was like a watering hole for the latest gossip.

Working at Martha's had complicated Tilly's

own sense of what was happening between her and Logan. She was convinced anyone watching her with Logan knew of their affair, but she wasn't sure if it had become common knowledge.

Doc didn't often drop in, which led her to believe he'd heard something. A rumor, perhaps an innocent comment. Tilly was left to guess, but whatever the reason for his visit, she was convinced he was there to scrutinize her, to determine if she was worth his only son's affections.

It didn't take much of an imagination for Tilly to know what Doc was thinking. She was a two-bit waitress who'd circled the block more times than the ice-cream man. She wasn't good enough for Logan, but she knew that already. It was the reason she'd insisted they keep their meetings clandestine despite Logan's protests. Even now, as she walked back into the kitchen for five slices of warm apple pie for Travis and his family, Tilly could feel Doc's gaze following her.

She didn't know how to explain to someone as dignified and respected as the local doctor that a waitress was crazy in love with his lawyer son. What she felt for Logan, what they shared, made every other relationship she'd ever been in seem dirty and cheap. She'd never felt like this with any other man. Only Logan.

Maybe Logan had mentioned her to his father. Surely he would have said something if he had. The least he could have done was warn her. But the last time she remembered Logan saying anything about his father had been several weeks earlier, after he and Doc had had a falling-out over . . . Logan hadn't said, now that she thought about it.

Her stomach clenched in painful spasms. They'd fought over her. Dear God, she should have realized it sooner. It all added up now. Of course, that was it. That was the reason Doc had come. He was here to size her up.

"Excuse me?"

Tilly turned to face the man who'd occupied her thoughts from the moment he'd walked in the door. Her heart filled her throat. Somehow she was able to speak normally. "Is there anything more I can get you, Doc?"

"Yes. My check. I've been waiting five minutes for you to bring it."

"I'm sorry . . . I got busy." Her hands fumbled inside the small apron pocket, fishing for the slip. "I hope you'll come again soon."

The older man scowled and reached for his wallet. He seemed in a hurry to leave. "I'm sure I'll be back." He stood, reached for the tab, and headed for the cash register.

She'd tried so hard to impress him, to be the best waitress he'd ever seen, prove to him she was worthy of Logan's love.

But she'd failed. Dear God, why did it always have to be like this?

Travis, Mary, and the kids all ordered the chicken-fried steak special and left the cafe a half hour later. Tilly, who'd worked a split shift, was home by six. Her feet hurt, but that didn't keep the nervous energy at bay. By eight she'd run three loads through the washing machine, mopped the kitchen floor, and cleaned out her bedroom closet.

Logan knocked at her front door shortly after eight-thirty, then let himself in. She'd given him his own key. There wasn't any reason for him to risk being seen standing under her porch light, Tilly reasoned.

"You told him, didn't you?" she demanded, holding a load of freshly laundered dried towels against her middle.

Stunned, Logan paused. "Told who? What?"

Tilly jerked a strand of hair around her ear, hating the way her hand trembled. "Your father . . . about us. He stopped into the cafe this afternoon."

"Dad?" Logan's features tightened. "Did he say anything to you?"

"He didn't have to. He knows, and you told him."

Logan's shoulders sagged. "Baby, I swear I didn't say a word, but not because I don't want to. I've thought of it a half a dozen times. Why should I care what Dad thinks? I'm long past seeking his approval."

"I don't want him to know about us."

Logan raised both hands in abject frustration. "Why not?"

"Logan, we've gone over this a hundred times. I don't see the need to rehash it all now."

"I'm not ashamed of you."

"I'm a waitress. Your father isn't ever going to accept me." She set the towels aside.

"Why should you care what Dad thinks, anyway?"

The last thing Tilly wanted to do was fight. She'd had a rough day, and she needed Logan, needed his touch, his tenderness, his love.

"Tell me what happened," he said, shrugging out of his jacket and tossing it on the recliner.

Without giving him warning, Tilly rushed to him, wrapping her arms around his waist. She'd spent the afternoon under a microscope and was left feeling small and inadequate. What she needed now was Logan's special brand of comfort, and she wasn't going to be cheated out of it by rehashing an old argument. Not tonight.

"Kiss me," she whispered. "Don't ask any more questions, just kiss me. I need you." She brought her hungry mouth up to his. Logan sighed as their tongues mated. Soon their panting breaths echoed each other.

Logan broke off with a groan. "I want to talk about this."

Tilly sighed softly and shook her head. "He doesn't like me. I could tell."

"Who cares if he does? Not me. I'm crazy about you, Tilly. It doesn't feel right for the two of us to sneak around like this. It never has. I don't care what people think, and you shouldn't, either."

"Logan, please, can't you see I need you?"

"I think we should talk first."

She rotated her hips against him and sighed

with satisfaction at the hard evidence of his need. "Why don't we do that later?" she suggested softly. "There seem to be more pressing matters to attend to first."

Travis had made it known from the time Mary stepped off the plane in Miles City that their marriage would be a real one. If she'd held on to some doubt about her place in his life, he'd dispelled it the first night.

Now that they were man and wife, she was to share his bed. The fact they'd soon be sleeping together had had a vague, unreal quality about it, until they'd walked into the house following their wedding.

When they'd arrived back on the ranch, Travis had hurried into the house, immediately changed clothes, and gone out to finish up the day's chores. Mary had been left standing in the kitchen, feeling like an unwanted guest.

The dinner in town had been a nice touch, and the children had enjoyed the outing. Mary had seen Travis's motive almost immediately. He wanted the word out that he'd married, and this was the best way to do it. Whoever was filing complaints against him could stop now. He had taken the necessary measure to correct the problem. Marrying Mary.

Okay, she reasoned as she tucked Beth Ann into bed, he hadn't followed tradition and swept her into his arms when they arrived home. She hadn't expected to be romanced and wasn't disappointed. Little about this marriage would ever be traditional. Except that she was expected to sleep in his bed.

Mary's heart was pounding as she turned off the light to the five-year-old's room and stepped into the dimly lit hallway. She should probably tell Travis she was a virgin. The thought mortified her. Could she speak of such a thing, even to her husband?

She could hear Travis rumbling around in the kitchen. His back was to her as she entered the room. He was bent in half in front of the refrigerator.

"Are you hungry?" she asked.

"Yeah. I don't suppose there's any of that meat loaf left over from last night, is there?"

"Jim ate it earlier."

She thought she heard him swear under his breath. "It figures," he said as he straightened and closed the door.

"I've rearranged our things in your . . . our bedroom." She could feel the heat invade her cheeks. She wasn't sure what to expect from him.

He nodded and bit down on a cold, crisp apple. The sound echoed like a sonic boom in the room. How quiet the house had become. Both boys were in their room, tired from the day's activities. Beth Ann had been asleep from the moment her head touched the pillow.

"I've got some paperwork that needs to be done," Travis commented flatly, turning away from her.

Mary blinked back her surprise. On their wedding night? Travis had forewarned her that he wasn't much of a romantic, but she'd expected something more than this careless disregard for her feelings.

"I . . . I'll take a bath, then."

"Good idea."

"Good idea," she muttered. He said it as though she'd gone six weeks without bathing. Her irritation with him lay just below the surface as it was. If they were going to make a go of this marriage, some changes needed to be made, and soon.

Her thoughts were as turbulent as the flowing bathwater. Without thinking she added perfumed salts. Roses scented the air.

Before Mary had left Petite, Georgeanne had given her a lovely silk nightgown. The gift had gone a long way toward mending the rift between them. Georgeanne had wept openly at the airport before Mary boarded her flight. Already Mary missed her friend's wise counsel. Without a doubt Georgeanne would know what to do in this awkward situation with Travis. She'd be able to advise her on how to act this first night they were together.

When she finished with her bath, Mary brushed her hair and tied the satin ribbons of the robin's-egg-blue robe. Travis was having trouble hiding his uneasiness the same way she was, Mary decided. He wasn't an unreasonable man. What they needed to do was sit down and talk this out.

It was with a sense of relief that she padded out

of the bathroom in her fuzzy slippers, another gift from Georgeanne, into the small den where Travis was working.

Only he wasn't there.

Nor was he in the living room, or the kitchen. An inspection of the house and barn showed he wasn't there, either. It wasn't until she was coming in from the barn that she noticed the truck was missing.

Travis had abandoned her on their wedding night.

Six

Mary was so outraged that she could hardly think. Marching into the bedroom, she slammed the door with an uncharacteristic display of temper. Apparently he was so averse to sleeping with her that he'd opted to run and hide.

That was just dandy with her. She wasn't all that keen on sharing his bed, either. But to leave her, with no explanation . . .

The gall of the man!

By all that was right, she should pack her bags and leave. Let him return to an empty house. It was what he deserved.

But leaving Travis would mean abandoning Jim, Scotty, and Beth Ann, and she couldn't bear to do that. The children had been through so much emotional trauma already, she couldn't, wouldn't, subject them to more.

With few options left her, she moved across the room and turned back the bedsheets. She'd been up since five and was exhausted. If Travis opted to booze it up with his buddies on their wedding night, so be it, but she'd be damned before she'd lie in bed like a subservient wife and wait for him.

The lovely silk gown Georgeanne had given her mortified her now. She shed it quickly, reaching instead for her sensible flannel pajamas. She stuffed the gown in the bottom drawer, feeling embarrassed and foolish for ever having donned it. It had been sheer folly to believe a mere nightgown would transform her into a desirable woman.

If there was anything to be grateful for, it was that Travis hadn't stayed to view her clumsy attempt.

In her present state of mind, even as exhausted as she was, Mary knew it would be impossible for her to sleep. So she tackled the master bedroom with a gusto of unleashed energy.

The room was all wrong. She stood in the middle, hands on her hips, and mentally rearranged the furniture. The bed was close to the hallway door, which made no sense. She much preferred to sleep beneath a window. In the hottest part of summer she'd be able to feel the cool, cleansing breeze wash over her.

It took some doing, but she was able to push the double bed up against the wall. When she was finished, she surveyed her efforts and was pleased. She made a few other minor changes, including shuffling the contents of their dresser drawers and organizing the dresser top.

By the time she was satisfied with her labors, it was nearly midnight. Mary refused to wait up for Travis, refused to allow him to believe his actions had disturbed her one iota.

If anyone was to blame in this situation, it was she. She'd behaved like a romantic fool, taken leave of her senses while strolling lazily through fantasy land.

She'd assumed that because she was married, the heavy burden of loneliness she'd carried since her brother's and mother's deaths would automatically diminish. But she was wrong.

Loneliness was insidious. It knew no border or boundary, was without mercy, and couldn't be bribed. That was what Mary had attempted to do, bargain with the deep well of pain within her by marrying a man who by his own word would never love her.

Mary turned off the light, climbed into bed, and lay on her back, staring at the shadows that flickered about the ceiling.

Travis had traveled this same stretch of road a hundred or more times in the last several months, sat in this same spot, and mentally reviewed what had happened the night Lee and Janice had died.

He was missing something; he had to be, otherwise he would be able to accept the accident and get on with his life. But he couldn't, not until everything was straight in his mind.

There would be no serenity for him until the answers clicked into place, until he was convinced he understood the events that had led to the tragedy. With nowhere else to go, he returned again and again to the accident scene. For the hundredth time he analyzed the events of that night, searched every avenue of explanation, a clue that would fill in the blanks. But there was nothing.

That was the way it had started this evening. Only it wasn't the accident that plagued his mind now. It was Mary and the children. Never before had he felt the weight of his responsibilities more.

Not only had he taken on the care and well-being of Lee's family, but now he had a wife to deal with. He knew nothing of being a husband. Absolutely nothing. Mary was a stranger to him. He was grateful for her willingness to marry him, but he didn't love her. She harbored no feelings for him, either. Yet they were bound together by vows he was determined to live up to no matter what price was required of him. He had little else to offer her.

Until they stood before Pastor Kennedy, Travis had looked upon this marriage as a business transaction. It wasn't until they were home and the children were down for the night that the enormity of what they'd done hit him. He was expected to be a husband now. Even the word felt clumsy in his mind.

A husband. A role he felt completely unsuited to fill. He was expected to be tender and kind, considerate and understanding. He was a rancher, not some bleeping Romeo. He'd seen the look in Mary's eyes and known what she expected.

Travis rarely tasted fear. Death held no terror for him. The only one who would have grieved at his demise was his brother. So he'd lived a foot-loose lifestyle and enjoyed the reputation of being something of a hellion. Those days were gone forever. He was a husband. He didn't know what the hell he was going to do.

He sat in the truck for nearly an hour, staring into the cloudless night. The moon was a crescent shape in the sky, and the stars sparkled in abundant array.

He felt crippled with doubts and expectations. Mary was gentle and warm and exactly what the children needed. But what about his needs? What about his wants? He'd married an old maid. Everything about Mary reeked of it. From the tidy way she wore her mousy brown hair to her sensible black shoes. He'd done his damnedest to make this day special for her, and then when it really mattered, when it was just the two of them, he'd panicked and failed her. Failed himself. Travis was a lot of things, but he'd never thought of himself as a coward until now.

He exhaled sharply, climbed from the cab of his battered truck, walked the path down the side of the steep, root-tangled hill, and sat on a bolder that jutted out from the side of the incline. He didn't want to think about Mary. Instead of berating his inadequacies as a husband, he should be counting his blessings.

Mary was wonderful with the children. Beth Ann and Scotty had taken to her immediately, and now even Jim was coming around. She'd brought stability and order to all their lives. Collectively, the four of them had heaved a sigh of relief at her arrival. She cooked, she cleaned, she organized. When it came to domestic chores she was perfect. Two days following her arrival, Beth Ann had slept through the entire night for the first time since she'd moved in. Nor had she wet the bed.

Mary was exactly what the children needed. He'd chosen well in that department, and as for all his inadequacies, Mary had known what she was getting into. He'd known, too.

Long legs, that was all he'd asked for, and what did he get? Minnie Mouse.

He didn't know what she was expecting of him for their wedding night. Hell, he hadn't known what to expect himself.

He had to return to the ranch and to Mary because there wasn't any place else for him to go. Heaven help him. His disappearing act hadn't built any bridges, of that much he was sure.

He leaped off the boulder and climbed the steep hill to where the truck was parked. Might as well face the music now and be done with it, he decided.

When he pulled into the yard several minutes later, Travis was relieved to find the house dark and silent. If his luck held, he could slip in undetected. Apparently Mary was asleep. Good. He was exhausted himself and in no mood to talk.

It took a moment once he was inside the house for his eyes to adjust to the lack of light. He took off his jacket, set his hat on the post, and slipped out of his boots. The less noise he made, the better.

The bedroom door was closed, and taking care to be as quiet as possible, he turned the knob. The room was pitch black. All the better. Gingerly he stepped inside and closed the door.

The only sound he heard was Mary's soft, rhythmic breathing. As silently as possible he stripped off his shirt and pants and tiptoed to his side of the bed.

The sound of a loud bang and immediate cursing was what woke Mary. Startled, she bolted upright in bed and reached for the lamp switch on the nightstand.

Travis was sitting on the floor in his underclothes.

"Damn it all to hell, woman, you moved the bed! What were you trying to do, kill me?"

Mary blinked, unsure of what had happened. Then she remembered, and a slow, angry resentment festered within her. "If you hadn't come sneaking in like a thief, you would've seen that yourself."

"A thief!" he exploded, righting himself awkwardly. She was satisfied to note that he was rubbing his bruised posterior with both hands. He made for an interesting sight standing there in his briefs and T-shirt, wearing socks. If she hadn't been so furious with him, she might have laughed.

Travis continued to glare at her. "What kind of woman rearranges furniture in the middle of the night?"

"What kind of man disappears without a word?" she fired back.

"Ah," he said, wagging his finger at her. "So that's it. You were looking to punish me?"

"Don't be ridiculous," she snapped. "It was a simple matter of turning on the light, which you opted not to do."

"I was being considerate."

"Considerate," she echoed as if the word were a source of amusement. "Right. In that case, so was I."

He muttered something she couldn't hear, but from the snatches she did catch, it was better she not know what he'd said. Travis marched across the room, limping slightly, and sat on the edge of the mattress. Mary lay back down and turned onto her right side so that her back was to him. Anger boiled within her, and she took out her frustration on the pillow, punching it several times as if to stuff the down farther into its case.

"I don't want you moving anything again without talking to me first," he demanded.

Mary had never thought herself sarcastic, but it seemed her husband brought out the very worst in her. She laughed.

"I mean it."

She laughed again, louder this time.

Travis peeled back the covers with enough force to lift them away from her shoulders. Mary sat up and reached for the blanket, jerking it back. Travis yanked it toward him, and for one wild moment the two were immersed in a furious tug-of-war.

"Do you mind!" she said, pulling with all her might.

He released his grip, the blanket went slack, and Mary nearly toppled onto the floor. She took a moment to compose herself, then calmly reached for the light switch. The bedroom was bathed in a blanket of darkness, but the tension between them crackled like static electricity.

Crowded as close to the edge of the mattress as possible, Mary shut her eyes, determined to ignore Travis. She'd die before she'd give him the satisfaction of knowing how much he'd hurt her.

"Damn fool woman," Travis grumbled, flipping himself onto his left side.

Mary didn't need to roll over to know he was positioned on the very edge of the mattress, the same way she was. The space between them was like a mine field, ready to explode with the least provocation.

"Damn fool man," she said after a moment of silence.

"Woman," he stated louder.

Mary ignored him, but her chest burned with righteous indignation. Her temper was frayed, to say nothing of her nerves, and she was still so angry she didn't know if she could bear to be in the same room with him and not explode.

Mary wasn't aware any silence could be this loud. It was so uncomfortable that she knew she'd never sleep. Before another minute passed she'd turned from her side onto her back, then rolled onto her stomach before returning to her side once more.

"Damn it, can't you hold still?"

"I'm trying to sleep."

"So am I, but you're making it damned impossible."

"I was sound asleep before you came crashing into the room," she felt obliged to remind him.

While they were arguing they'd both apparently let loose of their holds on the bed. The mattress sagged badly in the middle, and before Mary was aware of it, they were facing each other, their upper bodies pressed together.

All of a sudden her throat went dry. Even in the dark, she felt Travis's gaze burn into hers. They were so close she could feel his heart beat, so close she could smell the scent of the spicy rum aftershave he'd put on that morning before the wedding ceremony. So close his breath fanned her face.

"I know why you left," she whispered through her pain, "but it wasn't necessary to mock me."

"Mary—"

"I know I'm no raving beauty, but—"

"Mary, stop." He cupped her shoulders. "That wasn't it, I swear it wasn't."

"Then why?"

A sigh rumbled through his chest. "I . . . I wish I knew. Suffice it to say—"

"You don't need to tell me." Her voice lost its urgency and echoed her pain. "You don't want me . . . that way."

"That's not it at all. I was afraid if we went to bed together that my . . . needs would frighten you. I'm making a mess of this." He rubbed a hand down his face.

"I'm not a prude."

"But you're a virgin, and—"

"How do you know?" she flared, embarrassed and furious to be having so intimate a conversation. She resented him implying that he'd left her because he knew how inexperienced she was, how inept.

"Mary, you have to understand, a man has ways of—"

"Oh!" Furious once more, she backed away from him.

"I'm not saying that's bad, you being a virgin," he said quickly, in an effort to make amends, "it's just that, well, damn it all to hell, it makes it more difficult, you not knowing about men and all."

"You make me sound like a child. Do you honestly believe I'm so naive I don't know what happens between a man and a woman?"

"I said nothing of the sort. Quit twisting everything I say into an insult. I'm doing my damnedest to do right by you."

Some of the steam escaped her fury. She, too, was working toward that end. "I'm doing my damnedest," she whispered, "to do right by you, too."

Travis relaxed, and so did Mary. "Then we're both working toward the same end."

He was on his back now, and so was she. They stared at the ceiling as if there were something for them to read, something that would tell them how to make matters right. Her fingers gripped hold of the sheet, poising it beneath her chin.

Travis rolled his head toward her. "I was thinking," he began.

"Yes," Mary said eagerly, turning her head to face him.

"Maybe we should start easy like, getting to know one another first, get comfortable with each other."

"All right." Some of the terrible tension eased from her. She'd feared he was going to suggest they both go to sleep. But Mary knew, and apparently so did Travis, that neither of them was going to rest until this matter was settled.

"Could I hold you?"

"I suppose that would be all right." She scooted closer and rolled onto her side. Travis stretched out his arm, cupping it around her shoulders. She nestled her head against his chest and could hear his heart pound. They were both stiff and silent, but it didn't stop her from realizing how warm and vital he was.

"This is nice," Travis whispered. "You're no bigger than a minute, but you're soft and you smell nice."

"Thank you. You smell nice, too."

"I do?"

Mary struggled not to laugh. Travis made it sound as if she'd insulted him.

After a while he moved his arm from her shoulders to her back, lightly stroking the length of her spine. "Would you like to kiss?"

Mary's pulse quickened. "That would be a natural progression, don't you think?"

His hand beneath her chin lifted her mouth to his. Mary closed her eyes, unsure what to expect. Travis pressed his moist lips to hers in a gentle, unhurried exploration. As he had earlier with his hand against her back, his lips now began to stroke hers.

The sensation was unfamiliar and a bit strange, but pleasurable. She allowed it to continue, even participated, although she was unsure what she should do, if anything.

Travis's kiss continued lightly at first, then playfully, as if enticing a response from her. Of their own accord, her lips parted for him, and his tongue moved forward, outlining her mouth, coaxing and enticing her own.

This was good, much better than she'd ever been led to believe even in the books she'd read. Her heart was pounding hard and fast. Shyly at first, her fingertips rested against the hard angles of his jaw.

"Mary . . ." His breathing was heavy as he broke the contact. She was so disappointed that her eyes flew open. She'd done something wrong, offended him, botched her one chance of showing him she was woman enough to satisfy him.

"I did something wrong?"

"No. You were doing everything just right."

"Then why did we stop?"

"Because." He left it at that and pressed his forehead to hers. Threading his fingers through her hair, he sighed deeply. The room went silent and still, but it was unlike the dark, throbbing silence they'd experienced earlier.

"Good night, Travis," she whispered.

" 'Night, Mary, and don't worry, you did everything just right."

Logan held Tilly close and breathed in the fresh scent of her. He didn't want to leave, although it was nearly three A.M. and he should have slipped away hours ago.

He found contentment with Tilly. A peace he desperately needed came over him whenever he was with her, even though he was aware that Tilly was holding back a large part of herself.

When he was first attracted to her, he wanted to date her, wanted to get to know her. He was emotionally raw after his divorce, and it had taken him a good long while to decide he was ready to date again.

He liked Tilly, her quick wit, the friendly way she smiled when he came into the cafe. She was a breath of fresh air in a life that had been spent in a musty basement. She was sunshine after a week of rain.

Tilly was attracted to him, too, at least he assumed she was until he asked her to a movie. Damn but it had taken him a week to gather up the courage for the simple request. His heart had been pounding like a schoolboy's by the time he'd casually issued the invitation. Her quick refusal had set his ego back on its tail.

It took a week for him to put the rejection behind him and try again. This time, when she refused him, he was ready. He laughed and told her he wasn't going to give up. He wanted to take her to a movie, and by heaven he meant it.

Tilly's eyes had studied him, as if she were looking for something more. There was an edge to her; sometimes it shocked him how sharp and cutting it could be. She used it on him then, laughing sarcastically at his determination.

A few days later Logan was back with another invitation to the movie. She smiled regretfully and suggested he give it up and date someone more his type.

That was when Logan changed tactics. He found out where she lived and then one evening dropped by unannounced, claiming if she wouldn't go to the movies with him, then he'd bring the movies to her. He handed her a video and walked into her dingy apartment.

In retrospect, as he analyzed that evening now, Logan realized he'd made several costly mistakes.

They'd made love that first night. He hadn't intended to sleep with Tilly, not nearly so soon. He'd wanted to date her, court her, but as soon as he kissed her, she was all over him. He blamed himself for being so weak; it'd been months since he'd last made love, and Tilly was so damned tempting, so damned enticing. Before he realized matters had gone so far, she was naked beneath him, tears spilling from her eyes.

He apologized, held her close, tried to explain that it had been a long time for him. Tilly said nothing. She barely even looked at him, giving him the impression she'd given him what he expected.

Their relationship had gotten off on the wrong foot that night and had been headed down that same crooked path ever since.

Logan loved her so damn much it frightened him, yet he'd never said the words, mainly because Tilly didn't want to hear them. She gave him her body, but she held her heart and soul in reserve. More times than he could count, she'd frustrated him. Not physically, never physically, but emotionally. While her body fulfilled his, she held him at arm's length.

He never had gotten her to agree to date him. Every time he suggested they go out, she found an excuse. He felt as if he were butting his head against a brick wall. If he wanted to be with her, it was on her terms, not his.

He breathed in the warm, musky scent of her and kissed the crown of her head, wondering if he'd ever crack those defenses she'd erected.

Tilly stirred and lifted her head from the pillow of his chest. "What time is it?"

"Late. I was thinking I'd spend the night."

His words were met with a soft, undecided silence. "I'd rather you didn't."

"Why not?"

"Someone might recognize your car."

"I couldn't care less."

"I care."

The more she protested, the stronger his determination became to override her objection, to make some headway, however slight, into their twisted relationship. "I don't want to leave you, not tonight."

She rubbed her hand over his bare chest, and her fingers toyed with the short, dark hairs there. Although she appeared outwardly calm, he knew her well. Her sweet mind was racing at Indy 500 speed.

"If you stay, I think we should talk."

This was welcome news. "All right, we'll talk. It's time, don't you think?"

"There's a few things I want to know about you."

"All right, fire away."

"You'll answer anything I ask?"

His smile widened. "Within reason."

"We'll start off easy, then. What's your middle name?"

He hesitated. "Don't laugh, it's Alvin."

"Logan Alvin?"

"It was my grandfather's name."

"I think it's very nice. Dignified like."

He stroked her hair, loving the silky feel of it against his fingers. "You would. Next question."

"How come you're so incredibly sexy? It's unfair, you know. I moved to Grandview determined I wasn't going to have anything to do with men again. Every time I fall in love, I end up getting hurt. Then along strolls this incredibly handsome lawyer who won't take no for an answer."

"I guess you're just lucky."

She laughed, but he noticed she didn't echo his sentiment about being lucky to have him.

"I remember when you first came into Martha's," she continued.

"I remember it, too." They'd chatted and she'd put him at ease immediately. It was that first night he started watching her, thinking this was the kind of woman he wanted to know better.

"I have another question."

"Fire away." This was rather enjoyable, lying here with her, warm and content in his arms.

"Where do you go every Tuesday night?"

Logan tensed. Suddenly the conversation was no longer fun. Probably he should have told her about his Tuesdays long before now. It wasn't something he was proud of, and then again he was. "I drive into Moser to get sane."

"You're seeing a psychiatrist?"

"No, I'm attending a meeting."

"What kind of meeting?"

Logan released a breath while he collected his thoughts. He might as well explain and be done with it. If he knew of a way to decorate the truth, now would be the time for it. But he'd gotten too honest for such games. The honesty had attached itself to his sobriety.

"I'm an alcoholic, Tilly. I'm surprised you hadn't guessed before now."

"An alcoholic?" She repeated it as if she thought he were playing some kind of sorry joke. "But I've only seen you drunk once, and that was months and months ago."

"I know. I've only had one slip in the last five years."

She went still, and in that moment Logan knew he'd made a mistake.

"I didn't know."

"Do you want me to leave?" he asked, knowing he sounded defensive. "I'm repugnant to you now, is that it?"

"No, of course not, it's just that I'm surprised."

"Why? It happens in the best of families. Just ask my father." He started to break free of her hold, but she stopped him.

"Don't leave."

"I think I should," he said.

"Why? You wanted to stay a few minutes ago."

"I'm flawed, Tilly, I have a disease, but this one isn't going to disappear with a refillable prescription. I'm one drink away from ruining my life."

"Do you think I'm perfect?" she asked in a small voice. "Everyone has at least one skeleton in their closet. I'm no different."

Logan relaxed. "So you've got a deep dark secret yourself?"

"Yes," she admitted reluctantly. "I've got my secrets the same as you."

"Are you going to tell me about them?"

She was silent for a long moment. "No."

"I told you mine."

"Well, maybe I've got more than one."

"It doesn't matter to me, Tilly. There isn't anything you could have done that would change what's between us."

She gave a short, embittered laugh. "Sure."

"I mean it."

"So do I. I don't want to talk about it, all right?"

Logan didn't have much choice. Already he could feel her withdrawing from him. "Of course. You don't ever have to tell me if you don't want."

"Besides," she said, forcing a strained lightness into her voice, "I thought I was the one asking the questions here."

Seven

The first rays of dawn banked the horizon as Travis sat on the edge of the mattress, smiling to himself. It was a rare morning when he woke up grinning, a rare morning indeed. He certainly hadn't expected to be in a good mood, especially after the way he and Mary had argued when he'd first arrived home. Imagine . . . He'd thought she was meek and mousy, when in reality she was a spitfire. He'd felt as if he'd wrestled with a cougar when she'd finished with him.

Quietly he slipped out of the bedroom. He was tired and aching inside and out, but he didn't have all day to laze around. There was work to be done.

Pausing in the doorway, he looked back at Mary, sleeping so soundly in his bed. The morning shadows fell across her face, and her baby fine hair fanned out across the pillow. Once again he wished he knew more about women.

As was his habit, Travis put on a pot of coffee, waited for the first cup to drip through, took a couple of tentative sips, and then headed toward the barn.

The morning was chilly. The sheen of a frost glinted in the early morning light as he made his way across the dusty yard and into the barn. The horses greeted him with loud snorts of welcome. Mad Max, the temperamental gelding, impatiently pawed with his hoof against the stall door, seeking Travis's attention.

Travis reached for the pitchfork and speared a bale of alfalfa. He fed the horses, gave them fresh water and grain. It was while he was walking back toward the house that he caught sight of something silky and white and a small footprint. Stooping down, he realized it was a feather, all fluffy and shiny. The footprint didn't belong to any of the kids. Where the hell had it come from?

In a heartbeat he knew. Mary.

It made sense to him that she'd come into the barn looking for him. His heart quickened. She was a city girl, born and raised. She knew nothing of a rancher's life. There were a hundred unseen dangers lurking around each corner for her to stumble upon. It would be just like her to decide to make friends with Mad Max.

Travis could easily envision her walking into the paddock and coaxing the gelding with a sugar cube, unaware she was in any danger. With him working on the range, the horses and Mary were an accident waiting to happen.

With that thought in mind, he hurried back to the house.

Mary was up and dressed. She wore her hair down, tied loosely at her nape, and the style offered her a softer, gentler look. It was almost possible to forget she was a prim librarian. He might have pushed aside his concerns if he hadn't noticed the clothes she was wearing. She had on pretty slacks and a bulky knit sweater the color of winter wheat. Travis sincerely doubted that she owned a decent pair of jeans, which strengthened his conviction that she was a babe in the woods. He couldn't be out on the range, tending his herd day after day, while worrying about what was happening to her at the house.

"Good morning," she said, offering him a shy smile, but he noticed that her gaze skirted past his. She hadn't forgotten about their encounter any more than he had. She walked over to the refrigerator and removed a slab of bacon. "The children are awake and dressing. Breakfast will be ready in a few minutes."

"Were you in the barn last night?" he asked starkly.

Mary set the bacon on the counter and turned to face him. "Briefly. Why?"

"It's dangerous."

"How's that?" she asked, stopping to rub her hands down her apron, studying him.

"Listen, I don't mean to be bossy or gruff or say things that are going to upset you, but the barn is no place for a city girl."

"But, Travis—"

"For now," he interrupted, knowing she was going to put up a fuss, "just until you're familiar with the way a ranch is run."

"That's the silliest thing I've ever heard."

"I expect it is. All I ask is that you humor me."

She pinched her lips closed and set a pitcher of orange juice on the table. She wasn't pleased with him, but that wasn't something he could fret over now. He had a full day ahead of him. He couldn't be out working the range and worrying about her getting herself into trouble with animals and tools she knew nothing about.

Travis downed a glass of orange juice and three slices of bacon. "I don't want to fight over this. Go ahead and be mad at me if you want, but I'm saying this for your own protection."

"Do you intend to be this high-handed in other matters as well?"

He reached for his hat and set it on his head, taking his time adjusting it. "I expect I will."

"Then this is something we're going to need to discuss."

Travis eyed the door, wanting to escape a confrontation. Mary didn't seem to understand that there were men waiting and cattle to be fed. "Do you mind if we don't discuss it now?" he asked, walking toward the door.

"As a matter of fact, I do mind."

"Mary," he said with an ill-concealed attempt at patience, "I've got a ranch to run."

"This is important, too." Her hands were braced

against her hips, her stance combative. It didn't take much to envision her in a library, reprimanding a card holder for overdue books.

"We'll talk later," Travis promised as he headed out the door toward his truck.

Mary was too furious to think, let alone argue. She turned around and headed for the stove, only to find the children standing in the middle of the kitchen studying her.

"Are you and Uncle Travis having a fight?" Scotty asked.

"No, sweetheart, everything's fine."

"He was yelling at you," Beth Ann whispered.

"I don't think he meant to," Mary said as calmly as her pounding heart would allow. Last night, after Travis had come home, after they'd stopped yelling at each other and started really *talking* . . . and especially after they'd kissed, Mary had thought maybe they might begin to behave like . . . well, like man and wife. She had put so much stock in their forming a solid relationship. A friendship rooted in their mutual desire to become a family. But overnight, it seemed, Travis had become domineering and unreasonable. Instead of building bridges, they were detonating the little bit of common ground they shared.

"Can we bake cookies?" Beth Ann asked, breaking into Mary's thoughts. "Chocolate-chip ones, the kind my mommy used to make."

Mary's eyes rested on the five-year-old, and her heart constricted for the little girl holding on to memories of her mother. It wasn't for Travis that Mary had forsaken her home and friends and moved beyond the reach of civilization as she knew it.

It hadn't even been love or the opportunity of building a life with Travis that had prompted her away from Louisiana. No, she'd accepted Travis's marriage proposal for herself, to banish the lonely emptiness of her soul.

"With walnuts," Scotty added enthusiastically. "Mom used to let me and Jim lick the beaters."

"That's kid stuff," Jim muttered.

Mary studied the oldest of Travis's nephews. To the best of her memory she couldn't even remember seeing the boy smile. Her heart ached for the boy who felt he was too big to cry, yet was too young to carry the overwhelming weight of his grief alone.

"Let's eat breakfast first," Mary suggested. "When we're finished with chores we'll bake cookies."

Beth Ann smiled happily, her pretty blue eyes sparkling with pleasure.

"If Jim doesn't want a beater, can I have it?" Scotty asked as Mary set the skillet on the burner and peeled off thick bacon slices.

Jim looked to Mary, trapped between maintaining his superiority and letting go of a favorite treat. The decision seemed to be a weighty one.

"I'm probably going to need Jim's help," Mary said. "I might not have all the right ingredients in the dough. If Jim tasted it, he'd probably know if anything was missing. I'd appreciate you helping me out in this."

Jim's solemn dark eyes studied her. "Okay, but only this one time. If you bake cookies again, you're going to have to ask Scotty to do your tasting for you."

Mary nodded gravely. "I appreciate the help."

As the morning progressed there were several other things Mary decided that she'd appreciate. Peace and quiet, for example. She wasn't accustomed to all the noise three young children generated.

A piercing yell jerked her away from the sink, followed by Scotty, who raced toward her, gripping hold of her sweater and hiding behind her.

"Give it to me," Jim demanded, rounding the corner, his face red and furious.

"Children, please, don't argue," Mary said evenly.

"It's mine!" Scotty shouted. If he didn't let loose of her sweater soon, it would be stretched all the way to her knees.

"Give it back," Jim said menacingly, edging his way toward Mary.

"I will not tolerate fighting," she said in her most authoritative voice. Intent on each other, both boys ignored her. She turned one way and then another, wanting to reason with them before she realized they were playing a game of ring-around-a-rosy using her as tag center.

"I said I wouldn't tolerate any fighting," she said again, more forcefully.

"You have to tell them they can't watch television if they fight," Beth Ann suggested from the doorway.

Mary wasn't accustomed to accepting advice from a five-year-old, but she was growing desperate. "Stop this right now!" she shouted. They ignored her, and she reached for Scotty, but he was as slippery as new shoes. Jim was worse, escaping her frantic grasp with no problem.

"Stop this minute!" she shouted again. She might as well have been speaking to shelves of books for all the attention they paid her.

Jim caught his brother by the arm, tossed him down on the floor, and threw himself on top. Scotty's head hit with a decided clunk, and Mary gasped, thinking he might be seriously injured. Arms and legs were kicked in every direction, making it impossible to separate them.

She bent over the boys, trying desperately to pry them loose from each other and having as much success with that as she'd had quelling their argument.

The sharp, discordant explosion of noise behind her sounded like a plane taking off a runway. Mary straightened and whirled around.

Beth Ann was standing on a chair, slamming a wooden spoon against a black skillet. The racket was so loud, Mary placed her hands over her ears.

Both boys struggled into a sitting position and glared at their sister.

"Look what you've done to Mary," Beth Ann cried, and waved the spoon at them dictatorially.

"No television for a week, otherwise Mary will have to tell Uncle Travis."

Jim leaped upright and straightened his shirt.

Scotty followed and reluctantly handed his brother a card.

A baseball card, Mary realized as she slumped onto a chair. They'd been ready to pulverize each other over a stupid baseball card. She swallowed tightly and brushed the hair out of her face, using both hands. It wasn't until then that she realized how badly she was shaking.

"Are you all right?" Beth Ann asked.

Mary forced herself to smile and nodded.

"Don't worry, boys do that sometimes, you just have to be firm with them."

"I see," she whispered, waiting until the trembling had passed before she stood. What in heaven's name did she think she was doing, taking on the rearing of these three youngsters? Beth Ann knew more about being a mother than she did. Dear, sweet heaven, what had she gotten herself into?

The sound of a car door slamming in the yard announced Travis's arrival home later that afternoon.

"We're baking cookies," Beth Ann announced excitedly as he walked in from the porch.

Travis grinned and removed his hat, placing it on the peg just inside the house. "I wonder what a man has to do to get the first cookie out of the oven."

"Mary already promised me the first cookie," Scotty said, "because I helped the most." He eyed her, anxious, it seemed, for her not to mention the fight. Mary wouldn't, but not for the reasons he assumed.

"Yes, but I'm the man of the house, so I should get the first cookie."

"I worked the hardest."

"Are you going to argue with your uncle Travis?" he challenged.

Scotty grinned from ear to ear and nodded.

Travis reached for the boy, grabbing him around the waist and scooping him into the air. Scotty squealed with delight as his uncle whirled him around, all the while yelling he wasn't giving up his cookie no matter what.

Mary found herself smiling as well, pleased that the terrible tension from the morning had passed.

The oven timer buzzed, and using pot holders, she brought out the cookie sheet before inserting the fresh one Beth Ann and Scotty had dotted with dough.

The sound of a second car pulling into the yard diverted everyone's attention from the cookies.

"Someone's here," Jim announced, peeling back the curtain and looking out the window.

"It's Larry Martin," Travis said after glancing out the back door window. He stepped outside to greet the other man.

"Howdy, Larry," Mary heard Travis say. "What can I do for you?" Busy scraping the warm cookies off the sheet, she didn't look up until she finished. Then she automatically acknowledged Travis's friend with a smile. Being hospitable had been an important part of her upbringing. The Warner family had been well known for their southern hospitality.

The second man had a friendly, open face. He was about the same height and weight as Travis, and his gaze flickered toward her with undisguised curiosity.

His ready smile warmed her. "I stopped in at Martha's this afternoon," Larry explained. "Tilly told me you'd gotten yourself a wife. Stopping by to introduce myself seemed the neighborly thing." Although he was talking to Travis, his gaze continued to rest on Mary.

"This is Mary," Travis said.

Mary couldn't be sure, but she thought she heard a note of reproach in his voice and wondered at its cause. Larry was just being sociable. Apparently their dinner at Martha's following the wedding ceremony had served its purpose. Word of their marriage was out. Travis Thompson had found himself a wife.

"The cookies are warm from the oven," Mary said. "Would you like one, Larry?"

Larry slapped his hat down on the peg next to Travis's and nodded appreciatively. "I don't mind if I do. It's been a good long while since I've feasted on homemade cookies. From the looks of it, they're chocolate-chip, my favorite."

"Travis?" She couldn't help being flattered by

Larry's apparent approval of her, but Travis was the man she'd married.

He accepted the cookie and dispensed napkins to the three children.

"So you went and got yourself hitched," Larry said companionably, making himself at home at the kitchen table next to Travis. "When did all this happen?" he asked as Mary delivered two cups of coffee to the men.

"Yesterday," Travis answered.

"We got out of school for it," Scotty said.

Larry grinned at the boy. "So what does it feel like to be a newlywed?"

Mary was curious herself as to Travis's response. He shrugged. "The same, I guess."

Larry's gaze returned to Mary, and she felt the blush infuse her cheeks with color. It seemed both men were studying her, and, uncomfortable, she returned her attention to the cookies.

"I can't say when I've enjoyed anything more," Larry said, reaching for a second cookie.

The two men spoke easily for several minutes, then stood and wandered outside. It was an hour or so later when they strolled back into the house. By then Mary was busy with preparations for the evening meal.

"Would you like to stay for dinner?" she asked when she noticed Larry eyeing the fresh green salad she was making. "We're having veal scaloppine."

"If you're sure it's no problem."

"None whatsoever. There's plenty, and we'd be

happy to have you." He was their first guest, and Mary was pleased he'd taken the time to stop by and introduce himself.

"I'd be honored to join you," Larry told her, sounding almost gleeful.

Mary knew she'd made a mistake when she looked at Travis. He was frowning and seemed withdrawn throughout the meal, which turned out to be something of an uncomfortable ordeal. Mary was eternally grateful for the children, who helped carry the dinnertime conversation, plying Larry with a variety of questions.

It didn't help matters any to have Travis sitting at the head of the table brooding while Larry gushed with compliments over her cooking.

When Travis's friend left for the evening, Mary was relieved. She cleared the dishes from the table while Jim and Scotty took turns taking their baths. Beth Ann, who occasionally still needed a nap, grew cranky and restless. She knelt down on the floor and placed her head on the chair seat.

"I want my mommy."

"I know, sweetheart," Mary whispered, lifting the little girl into her arms.

Beth Ann pressed her head against Mary's shoulder. "I'm glad you married Uncle Travis."

"I'm glad I did, too." And she meant it, despite her morning, her disagreement with Travis, and the struggle with the children. She had a good deal to learn when it came to managing a family, but she'd seen progress from both sides. They were opening up to her, and they had helped abate her own loneliness.

When the boys finished in the bathroom, Mary bathed Beth Ann, tucked her into bed, and read to her from her favorite book. When she finished she sang to her. By the time she'd finished the first verse, Beth Ann was sound asleep.

Travis was in and out of the house. By the time Mary finished with Beth Ann, the boys were in the living room watching television.

She was at the sink, finishing up the last of the dishes, when the back door opened and Travis stepped inside the kitchen.

"I want to talk to you," she said, turning around to face him. She reached for a hand towel and briskly dried her hands as she prepared to do battle.

"I want to talk to you, too," he returned stormily. "First off, we need to set something straight. You're my wife, and I don't appreciate you flirting with my friends."

"Flirting with your friends!" Mary was so aghast, it took her a moment to speak. "Perhaps speaking now isn't such a good idea after all," she said, waving her hand in a dismissive gesture.

"Why not?"

"Because I'm about to forget I'm a lady and say something I'll regret later."

"Like what?"

"You wouldn't want to know."

"I'll tell you what *I* know, then. I don't like my wife of two days behaving like a siren in front of my best friend. If you find that so objectionable, then we'd better clear the air right now."

They stood half a kitchen apart physically, half a universe emotionally. Mary couldn't believe what she was hearing. Travis was more than unreasonable, he was insulting.

"Teasing Larry . . . a siren . . . me? You've got to be joking!"

Two giant strides and Travis ate up the distance between them. "I've never been more serious in my life. Larry was gawking at you, and you ate it up."

"I ate it up . . . gawking?" She was too furious even to speak coherently. Mentally she counted to ten before attempting to make sense of his accusations. "I've never known a more domineering, pigheaded, unreasonable man in my life. How in heaven's name are we ever going to stay married when we can't even talk civilly to one another?" She was fighting her outrage for all she was worth and losing the battle.

"It didn't help to have you all agog over Larry."

"Agog? I did nothing more than invite him to dinner."

"Because you're attracted to him."

Mary stared at Travis, strongly suspecting he'd spent too many hours in the sun. Either that or he'd gone daft. His face was hard and immobile. She might have deemed this a sick joke if his eyes hadn't been so intense.

"It doesn't help matters any that he feels the same way about you."

Mary went still. Travis honestly believed his friend was captivated by her. She, who knew next to nothing about men. What enthralled Larry had been her cooking. Mary guessed he hadn't eaten a home-cooked meal in months. It wasn't her wit or her stimulating conversation as much as the veal and the homemade cookies.

"The charm was oozing out of you." Each word was hard and precise, as if it wrenched Travis just to utter them. "My goodness, it was like falling into a jar of honey just watching you cozy up to Larry."

"You make me sound like a hussy," she whispered, on the verge of tears. This relationship wasn't going to work, she realized with unbearable sadness. Married two days and already she tasted the bitterness of defeat. It was impossible to reason with Travis; he'd already tried and judged her, found her guilty, and nothing she could say or do would alter what had happened. Knowing that, she turned and walked out of the kitchen.

Travis heard the bedroom door close, and his heart sank to the pit of his stomach. The problem wasn't with Mary, but with him. He was jealous, pure and simple. It had started when Larry had complimented the cookies and she'd blushed with pleasure. *He* should have been saying all those things to her, not Larry. *He* should have been the one telling her the veal was as tender as he'd ever tasted and that his grandmother had never made biscuits this light and fluffy. It should have been *him* saying how lucky he was to have married a woman like Mary. Instead it had been his friend.

The morning had gotten started wrong when they'd had that tiff about Mary going into the barn. Travis berated himself for the thousandth time for not being more subtle. If only he'd sat down with her, confessed his concerns. Mary would probably have agreed willingly, understood his worries.

Unfortunately he had never been a man for words. His lack hadn't been important until the children and Mary had come into his life. Not only was he expected to know all the things a husband did, things like romance and compliments. Now it seemed he was obliged to explain himself as well.

Travis had managed the ranch for too many years on his own to have his decisions questioned. When he wanted something done, he assigned the task to one of the hands.

Apparently Mary didn't take kindly to orders. It looked as though he was going to have to change his ways. The knowledge produced a series of unsettling questions. Now if only he could come up with the answers.

Travis poured himself a cup of coffee and sat at the kitchen table to mull over the problems he and Mary were experiencing. He was at fault, but admitting it was harder than he realized. If he felt more comfortable, he'd go to her now. But she was upset and angry, and frankly, he feared he'd unwittingly say or do something more to infuriate her. It was better to wait, let matters settle down, and then approach her.

Carrying his coffee with him, Travis moved into the living room, where Jim sat watching television. The youth barely acknowledged him.

"Did Scotty go to bed already?"

"No."

"Then where is he?"

Jim shrugged, his attention focused on the police show. Travis didn't think anything more of it until fifteen minutes had passed and Scotty still hadn't appeared. Travis knew the eight-year-old was as keen on this particular show as his older brother.

Stretching his legs, he wandered down the hall to the boys' bedroom. The room was neat and tidy, a stark contrast to the way they'd kept it before Mary's arrival.

Beth Ann was sound asleep.

Travis checked the barn and around the outside of the house, calling Scotty's name. Mary must have heard his increasingly frustrated shouts because she joined him a few minutes later.

"What happened to Scotty?" she asked, wrapping a light jacket around her to ward off a chilly evening wind.

"He isn't in the house."

"What about the barn?"

"I already looked."

"Is he hiding?"

"Hell if I know," Travis snapped, and immediately felt guilty. "Jim doesn't seem to know where he went, either."

"Do you think he might have run away?" she asked timidly.

Travis hadn't considered that. "Why would he do anything like that?"

"I don't know. Why do any of us do the things we do?"

It was the same question Travis had been asking himself all night. "Where would he go?"

"I don't know." Her voice was laced with alarm.

Travis was beginning to experience a healthy dose of anxiety himself. It was growing darker and colder by the minute.

"Did you find him?" Jim asked. He stood on the back porch, the tips of his fingers tucked in the back pockets of his acid-washed jeans.

"Jim," Mary said earnestly, "we can't find Scotty anywhere. Is there any possibility he might have run away?"

The wind was picking up, and Travis moved closer to Mary, wanting to shield her from the strong gusts. He longed to put his arm around her and tell her he was sorry, but the words stuck in his throat.

"He might have," Jim said thoughtfully after a minute.

"Where would he have gone?"

"Home," the youth suggested sadly, his eyes downcast.

"Home?" Travis repeated, and his heart ached with the lone word. This was Scotty's home now. Lee's place had been sold in probate a couple of months earlier. The older couple who bought the ranch had made several changes. Travis had avoided driving in that direction, not wanting to dredge up unhappy memories.

"Come on," Mary said, jogging toward the truck. "We've got to find him."

Travis experienced the same sense of urgency. The thought of Scotty wandering alone in the dark down a country road filled him with alarm.

Mary rolled down the side window of the pickup. "Jim, we'll be back as soon as we find Scotty. Watch Beth Ann, all right?"

Travis watched in his side mirror as the boy nodded. Jim, generally sullen and hostile, seemed eager.

"He might have cut across the field and got onto the road down by Patterson's," the boy shouted. "We used to do that sometimes."

"Damn fool kid," Travis muttered as he sped out of the yard. A plume of dust exploded behind him. He was going to wallop Scotty when they found him, teach him a lesson or two. But first he was going to hug him and find out what had troubled him so deeply that he'd decided to leave.

They'd gone about a mile when Travis saw him. Mary caught sight of him at almost the same moment.

"There," she cried, pointing to the small figure walking along the road's narrow shoulder. He was wearing a jean jacket, which was inadequate against the cold and the wind. His young shoulders were hunched against the bluster. The sun had set, and the only available light came from the truck's headlights.

Scotty turned, and when he saw it was them, he took off running. Travis let him wear himself out, then pulled onto the side of the road a few feet in front of him.

Mary was out of the cab even before he cut the ignition.

"Scotty," she pleaded, "where were you going?"

The eight-year-old sniffled. "Away."

"But why?"

Scotty rubbed the back of his hand under his nose. "Because."

"That doesn't answer the question." Travis knew he sounded gruff, and Mary sent him a scathing look that silenced him. She was right, he'd only make matters worse. It was best to let her do the talking. He was glad she'd come with him. He might be more familiar with the roads and the territory, but she was more familiar with the heart.

"I don't want to live with you and Uncle Travis anymore."

"But, Scotty, I'd miss you so much," Mary said softly. "You're my best helper. I need you."

Travis heard the tears in her voice and noticed the traces of moisture that ran unrestrained down her ashen cheeks.

"I need you, too," Travis ventured. "Just as much as Mary."

"You were yelling again," Scotty accused. "My mom and dad never yelled like that. They loved each other. I don't like it when you fight."

"I don't like it, either," Mary told him. "It makes me feel sick inside."

"Me too."

Travis exhaled sharply. "It's my fault, Scotty. I'm ill-tempered and unreasonable. I don't know much about kids and even less about being a husband. So if I've flubbed up, all I can ask is that you give me a little slack."

Scotty stood stock still and studied them both. "I've seen movies. . . ."

"Yes," Mary encouraged.

"When two people argue they sometimes kiss and make up. Will you and Uncle Travis do that?"

Eight

"Here?" Travis asked, looking at Scotty. "You want me to kiss Mary here?"

Mary bristled. The man made it sound as if he were being asked to do something repugnant.

Scotty nodded. "Like Mom and Dad used to."

"Mary?" Travis eyed her speculatively. "Would you mind?"

"Dad never asked Mom, he just kissed her," Scotty instructed, sitting between them, looking from one to the other. "Sometimes Mom fussed a little, but then she got real quiet and put her arms around Dad's neck."

"You're right," Travis said, grinning, and reached for Mary. But with Scotty trapped in the middle it was difficult getting close.

"I'm moving," Scotty said as he crawled over Mary's lap.

The moment the boy was out of the way, Travis

had his arms around Mary. He bent his head and kissed her. It was a sweet, gentle kiss, more of a meeting of the lips than anything passionate.

Mary blinked when it ended.

Travis's gaze swung to Scotty, and he arched his brows.

"Not good enough," Scotty said, crossing his arms and shaking his head. "I want to see a real kiss so that I know you aren't going to fight anymore."

"Kissing isn't going to insure—" Mary wasn't allowed to finish. Travis caught her in his arms and pulled her forward, his hot, moist mouth covering hers.

The action surprised Mary, and she gasped. He took immediate advantage of her opened mouth, and his tongue probed inside. Mary's eyes flew open at the unexpectedness of the assault. Holding herself perfectly still, she closed her eyes. As the kiss intensified, a slow, strange heat began to warm the pit of her stomach, and she sighed and slowly raised her arms to Travis's neck.

Travis's tongue continued to stroke hers, lightly at first, then playfully, enticing a timid response from her. He appeared to gain pleasure from her attempts and encouraged and rewarded her with more of the same.

Pressed against him the way she was, her nipples began to tingle and ache in a way that embarrassed her.

"That's the way." Scotty beamed from beside her. "That was real good."

"Yes, it was," Travis said, looking down at Mary. The smile she offered him was timid, but she tried to tell him she'd enjoyed it, too.

When they returned to the house, Mary wanted to talk to Travis, but it was difficult with Jim and Scotty around. She decided to wait until they could be alone, and that wasn't until much later.

Sharing her feelings with Travis proved difficult because Mary wasn't sure what she should say. Her thoughts were heavy as she prepared for bed that night.

She pulled back the sheets and climbed inside the bed, which creaked as it accepted her weight. Travis, fresh from the shower, followed; reaching for the switch, he turned off the light. The room was bathed in dark stillness. They both lay on their backs, staring at the ceiling, each waiting expectantly, it seemed, for the other to speak.

"Travis, I—"

"Mary, listen—"

They spoke simultaneously, and then the words got tangled as each insisted the other go first.

"All right," Mary conceded, although she'd rather he be the first one to speak his mind. "There are several things you should know. First off, I'm afraid my lack of experience in the mothering department is causing problems. Jim and Scotty got involved in a scuffle this morning, and I was utterly useless. Beth Ann broke them up." It hurt to admit her failure. "I don't appear to be doing all that much better in the wife department, either."

He was silent for a moment. "It isn't you, Mary, it's me. I behaved like a jealous fool this evening. Larry was saying all the things I should have, telling you what a good cook you are and how nice the house looked. I felt like a heel and took everything out on you."

"I feel like such a failure."

"You?" he said with a sarcastic laugh. "Scotty's the one giving me instructions on how to be a decent husband."

Travis stretched out his arm and brought Mary to his side. She accepted his comfort because she needed it so badly. He was warm and safe, and she sighed when he kissed the crown of her head.

"I like kissing you," he admitted.

"I like it when you kiss me, too." She smiled because he made it sound as if he were surprised by how good it was between them.

After a while Mary yawned, exhausted from the day's activities. When she rolled onto her side, Travis moved with her, cuddling her spoon fashion, his hand tucked around her stomach. His touch soothed her, and she was drifting off to sleep when he whispered something.

"Hmm?" she asked groggily.

"I was just saying that I'm going to do my damnedest to be a better husband."

Mary smiled to herself. "I'm going to try harder, too."

"Uncle Travis is going to church with us," Beth Ann whispered as Mary hurriedly stirred a bowl of pancake batter the following morning. "He's got his suit on and everything."

"Morning," Travis grumbled as he stepped into the kitchen and poured himself a cup of coffee.

Mary felt Scotty's gaze resting on the two of them. "Dad always kissed Mom in the morning."

"Is that a fact?" Travis asked with a devilish smile.

"Yup, every morning. First thing. I used to hide my eyes 'cause it got mushy sometimes."

Mary cursed herself for blushing. Apparently Scotty had appointed himself keeper of the marriage. The boy seemed determined that she and Travis behave like other married couples.

Travis removed the spatula from Mary's unresisting fingers and set it aside. Slowly her gaze followed the course of his hands. Placing his index finger under her chin, he raised her mouth to his and kissed her soundly. Mary's knees went weak and her hand crept up his chest and closed around his suit lapels.

"That's real good," Scotty praised.

When Travis finally lifted his mouth from hers, he smiled at her. "It *was* good," he whispered.

Mary trembled and nodded.

"I think my brother may have stumbled onto something," he said, kissed her lightly on the cheek, and headed toward the table.

Mary hummed softly to herself as she reached for the spatula and resumed her task. Beth Ann was right. Travis was wearing the dark suit he'd worn for the wedding, with the starched white shirt and string tie. He'd shaved, too, and wetted down his hair. He caught her look and grinned once more. Mary couldn't keep from blushing, but she managed to smile back at him, too.

"I thought it would be a good idea if I attended services with you and the kids," he announced.

"That's very thoughtful of you, Travis," she said, delivering a second plate of pancakes to the table. Apparently he'd meant what he'd said the night before and was doing his best to be a good husband and father.

"You're going to church?" Jim asked Travis, a forkful of pancake halfway to his mouth.

"I thought I would. Do you have a problem with that?"

"You've never gone with us before," Jim continued. "Why now?"

"Because I want to," Travis muttered, spearing a hot pancake with his fork and delivering it to his plate. He lathered it with butter and poured warm syrup over the top.

He was determined to do his best, and so was she. Over the course of their meal, she caught him watching her, as though he were seeing her for the first time, really seeing her, only now he was less weary. He seemed ready to deal with the reality of who and what she was, the same way she'd had to do with him.

They were married, for better or worse, and sooner or later they'd consummate their union. Her inexperience intimidated him, she realized. He'd wait, Mary reasoned, for some sign from her, some signal that would tell him she was ready for the physical side of their relationship.

If that was the case, what exactly was she supposed to do? She'd never attempted to lure a man until now and felt grossly inadequate. She tried to remember what it had been like in high school with her friends. Georgeanne had been crazy over Benny from the time she was a sophomore. The pair seemed to gravitate toward each other and had married a few weeks after graduation. Her other friends had known intuitively how to attract a man. A pretty dress, a smile, and a charming, submissive disposition had been all that seemed necessary. At the time, Mary had thought it rather foolish and certainly beneath her dignity. Furthermore, she was certain she'd never care for a man who could be so easily manipulated.

Now she wished she'd paid more attention.

Their arrival at the church caused something of a stir. The five of them walked down the center aisle in single file. Mary had never felt more of a spectacle. Word of their rushed marriage had spread through town by now, Mary suspected, and she was the subject of blatant curiosity. She found it discomfiting to be the center of attention, but stares were less disturbing with Travis and the children at her side.

Travis chose a pew in the middle of the church, and they filed into it. Mary went in first, followed by the three children and then Travis. She caught him looking her way once and smiled. He grinned back, and she relaxed.

Within minutes of their appearance, the old church filled with the melodious sounds of the pipe organ, and the assembly rose to its feet. Mary helped Scotty and Beth Ann with their hymnals and joined in with the congregational singing. She noted that neither Jim nor Travis sang. Both looked as if they'd swallowed something distasteful and were wondering if they should spit it out. Mary found their attitude amusing, and her smiling eyes found Travis. Soon a grin was quivering at the edges of his mouth. Mary was gratified to notice him reach for the red hymnal himself, although she was certain he wasn't partial to singing, especially music from the nineteenth century. Nevertheless he made a pretense of doing so in order to please her.

Pastor Kennedy looked out over his congregation, and when his gaze landed on Mary and Travis, he smiled approvingly. The service went amazingly well. The children were a bit restless, but that was to be expected.

As soon as the last notes of the closing hymn dimmed, Travis vaulted to his feet. He leaned across the children to whisper to Mary, "I'll meet you and the kids outside," then edged his way through the crowd. Mary lost sight of him as he made his way out the door, sidestepping Pastor Kennedy.

Several people stopped to introduce themselves, including Clara Morgan, who invited Mary to a reception in her honor at the Grange. Mary was detained ten or more minutes. When she walked down the church steps, she caught sight of Travis in the parking lot.

"Who's Travis talking to?" she asked Jim.

Jim's gaze followed hers. "The sheriff."

Mary frowned, wandering what Travis had found so important to mention to the sheriff.

"He's probably asking about my mom and dad's accident," Jim explained. "Uncle Travis promised me he was going to find who was responsible."

"I thought it was an accident."

"They were driven off the road," Jim said bitterly. Mary's heart ached at the pain she heard in the youth's voice. She placed her hand on his shoulder, but Jim shrugged it off, not wanting her comfort.

"Uncle Travis convinced the sheriff it was vehicle . . ."

"Vehicular homicide," Mary supplied.

Jim nodded. "My dad was a good driver. He'd never have hit that tree if he hadn't been forced into it. Travis found a second pair of tire tracks at the scene and then farther down the highway, too. Whoever was driving the other car was all over the road that night."

"Oh, Jim," Mary said softly. "I'm so sorry."

"Why?" he demanded sulkily. "They weren't your parents."

"I lost my family, too. It doesn't matter if you're twelve or thirty when it happens, it still hurts."

He nodded, and his look was apologetic when

he added, "Travis has been pressuring the sheriff about the accident. He was the one who insisted they make plaster molds of the tire tracks."

Mary was momentarily distracted, but she heard raised angry voices coming from the parking lot. She cringed inwardly as she heard Travis swear. It seemed the entire congregation was milling on the front lawn outside the church. They too stopped and stared.

Travis said something more that Mary couldn't hear, then turned away and stalked to the truck. Only then did he remember Mary and the children, and he looked around anxiously, eager to leave.

Mary quickly steered the three children toward the truck. Travis climbed inside the cab, his face a grim line of restrained fury. He didn't say a word as he peeled out of the parking lot.

Beth Ann, who was sandwiched between them, held on tightly to Mary, her round eyes revealing her apprehension. Mary wrapped her arm around the little girl and brought her close to her side.

"Travis . . ." Mary attempted conversation when they left the outskirts of town, her voice soft and nonjudgmental. "What happened?"

"Nothing," he barked. His face remained stony, giving away nothing.

He'd tell her later, she suspected, when there weren't three pairs of ears listening in on the conversation. Now wasn't the time to pressure him; she'd wait until he'd worked out his frustration.

The ride back to the ranch took an uncomfortable twenty minutes. Once they'd pulled into the yard and parked, Travis leaped from the truck and headed for the house like a storm trooper, leaving Mary to deal with the children.

She'd barely gotten the kids inside when Travis wordlessly marched past her again on his way out the door. Mary was amazed that anyone could change clothes so quickly. He ignored both her and the children. Vexed, she instructed the kids to get ready for lunch and followed her husband outside.

"Travis," she called after him, racing down the porch steps.

He stopped and his gaze flickered to her, but for only a heartbeat.

"What happened?" she asked again.

"Nothing."

"Then why are you so angry?"

"It's none of your business."

Mary made a valiant effort to swallow the pain his words inflicted. His face was hard, his jaw set and immobile. Even his dark eyes seemed colorless.

"I see," she whispered, feeling disheartened and dejected. She'd been wrong to confront him so soon, especially when he wasn't ready to talk about the incident. Turning, she headed for the house. Each step felt weighted. Just when she'd dared to hope they were making progress, something unexpected happened and she was promptly reminded she had no place in his life other than with the children.

"Mary." His voice was filled with regret.

She hesitated and then turned back. Travis stood several feet away from her, his face tight, his eyes raw with pain.

"I was talking to the sheriff. After my brother's accident, I insisted he make a plaster mold of both sets of tire tracks from the scene." He stopped long enough to rub a hand over his face as though to wipe the events of the terrible night from his mind. "The lab report came back weeks ago, and there were no distinguishing marks in the tires. I thought there might be something more to go on, but I was wrong." The last word was uttered with despair and hopelessness. "I swore I was going to bring whoever killed Lee and Janice to justice, but I keep running into dead ends."

Mary didn't know the words to say that would ease his mind. Platitudes were useless. She'd heard them herself. She yearned to offer Travis something substantial, something more.

"Can I help?" she whispered.

He shook his head. "I need to get away, vent some steam. Will you be all right with the kids?"

"Of course."

They stood looking at each other, and it was as though the first bridge of understanding had been forged between them.

"Thank you." His words were little more than a rough sigh.

Travis turned away from her, heading for the barn. Mary was halfway to the house when she saw a rider approaching on horseback. Whoever it was seemed to be in an all-fired hurry. He pulled in the reins and came to a grinding halt.

"The wolf got another calf," the man shouted.

Travis cursed and raced for the barn. A few minutes later he led out a handsome gelding. Mary took a moment to admire the horseflesh and watched as Travis deftly climbed into the saddle. When she noticed the rifle and saddlebags, her heart pounded with alarm.

Then, almost in afterthought, Travis pulled back on the reins and looked to Mary.

"I don't know when I'll be back. A wolf's been terrorizing the herd. I've already lost three calves."

"Be careful," she called after him.

He nodded. "Don't worry, I was born careful." Then with a smile, he galloped out of the yard.

Storm clouds banked like armed paratroopers on the horizon, ready for the signal to attack. Mary stood with her arms wrapped around her middle, gazing out the small window in the back door. She watched the thick gray clouds rolling in, darkening the sky and threatening her serenity.

"Can I have another piece of pie?" Scotty asked from behind her.

"You've already had one slice. That's enough for now." She half expected an argument and was mildly surprised when she didn't get one.

Scotty pulled a chair over to where she was standing and stood on the seat, looking out the window with her. "What are you watching for?"

"I'm not sure. I was just wondering when Travis was going to be home." It would be dark within the hour, and a storm was sure to hit soon. She could feel the heaviness in the air. The sky was filled with warning, and Travis was riding around heaven knew where, seeking out a wolf, which she knew he shouldn't be doing. She didn't know much about ranch life, but she did know the U.S. Fish and Wildlife Service didn't take kindly to ranchers hunting down an endangered species.

"It's cold outside, isn't it?"

Mary nodded.

"Are you worried?"

"No." It was a small lie. She couldn't help but be concerned. Knowing her anxiety would alarm the children, she moved away from the window and finished the dinner preparations, determined to appear undisturbed by Travis's long absence.

They ate in silence. The storm arrived just after they'd finished washing the dishes. Sheets of rain pelted against the window, and the wind howled like a wounded animal.

Mary's nerves were stretched taut, but she did her utmost to disguise her fears from the children. Surely Travis should have been back before now. It was dark and cold.

At Beth Ann's insistence, Mary read another chapter from *The Secret Garden*. Beth Ann and Scotty listened attentively, but Jim seemed restless. He roamed from one room to another, claimed he had homework, but if that was the case, it took him only a few minutes to complete the assignment.

Beth Ann went to bed at eight. Scotty and Jim followed at eight-thirty.

"Aw, Mary," Scotty whined when she insisted he go to bed.

"Travis will tell you all about the wolf in the morning."

Scotty looked as if he wanted to continue the argument, but she silenced him with a single look. She was mildly surprised by how effective the tactic was on the eight-year-old.

For a short while Mary treasured the solitude. It was times like this that she missed Petite and her own small home, her friends, and the library.

By nine, however, she was pacing, wringing her hands, worrying about Travis. She'd expected him home long before now. Her stomach was in knots. She would have felt better if there were someone she could phone, but there was no one, so she talked to herself, whispering reassurances that soon rang flat and unconvincing.

The winds raged outside, howling and whistling around the house. The lights flickered and she froze, not knowing what to do. Collecting her wits, she started searching the drawers so she'd be prepared in case they lost power.

"Travis keeps candles in the kitchen." Jim spoke softly from behind her. "In the drawer next to the telephone."

Mary thanked him with a smile, so grateful he was awake that it was all she could do not to hold him and weep. "You couldn't sleep?" she asked, hoping she sounded cool and composed. Knowing she didn't.

He shrugged and walked past her. He set matches, candles, and a flashlight on the table. He looked out into the night and then back to Mary. "He's okay, don't worry."

"How can you be so sure?"

"Travis knows how to take care of himself."

Restless, she circled the kitchen table. "Do you want some hot chocolate?"

Jim shook his head. "No thanks."

"I . . . I appreciate what you told me this morning about your parents' accident," she said, rubbing her palms together.

He didn't say anything for a moment, then, "I better get back to bed."

Mary nodded. "I'll see you in the morning."

"You going to be all right?"

"Me?" She laughed. "Of course."

"You're not afraid of the dark, are you?"

"Not at all." That was only semitrue. She wasn't so concerned about losing power, not when her husband of three days was riding the range in the middle of a rainstorm in the dead of the coldest, darkest night she'd ever seen.

"Good night," she said as brightly as her fears would allow.

" 'Night, Mary."

Jim hadn't been in bed more than fifteen minutes when the lights flickered once more. A second later the house went pitch black. Mary fumbled in the darkness until she found the flashlight Jim had set out for her.

Not knowing what else to do, she made her way into the living room, sat on Travis's recliner, and wrapped a hand-sewn quilt that had been her grandmother's around her legs. Every five minutes or less, she turned the light on her watch.

The slightest sound coming from the yard was enough to propel her from the chair and send her stumbling through the dark. She waved the light through the glass, but the yard was empty.

Her heart sank and she bit into her bottom lip. Please God, she prayed, bring him safely home soon.

Cold rain ran in rivulets down his back. Travis was soaked to the skin as he led Mad Max into the barn. The electricity was out and he flipped the switch generator, wondering why Mary hadn't done so earlier. He fed Mad Max an extra portion of grain and made sure he had plenty of fresh, clean water before racing through the rain toward the house.

Mary was standing in the middle of the kitchen, and when she saw him she vaulted into his arms.

"Travis," she sobbed, hugging him with surprising strength, "thank God you're home. I was so worried. I thought . . . I didn't know what to think."

He felt her warmth all the way through his heavy jacket. He gathered her in his arms, lifting her from the floor and holding her against him as he breathed in her warm, womanly scent.

It was unclear who started kissing whom, not that it mattered to Travis. Mary couldn't be any more pleased to see him than he was to be with her. He'd spent one of the most miserable evenings of his life. He was wet, cold, and hungry.

"I should be furious with you." She sobbed, bracketing his jaw with her hands.

Travis wove his free hand into her hair, pressing her softness against him. The kiss was brutal, and he sent his tongue deep inside her mouth, ending it only when it became necessary for them to breathe.

"I thought—"

"I know, I'm fine, don't worry," he interrupted, his mouth fiercely moving back to hers, unable to get enough of her. Until now they'd been flirting with the physical side of their relationship. A few kisses now and again had been the extent of their experimentation. Travis was finished playing games. He realized that if they didn't stop soon, he was liable to do something stupid and frighten her.

He tore his mouth from hers, twisted his head away from her, and inhaled deeply. "A man could get accustomed to being welcomed home this way."

Mary laughed softly. "I was afraid." She seemed embarrassed, then recovered quickly. "I imagine you're starved."

He was, but food wasn't the only thing on his

mind. Damn, he felt like he was sixteen all over again.

"I'll get your dinner," she said, her cheeks a bright shade of pink as she turned away from him.

"Let me take a shower first." He was close to having hypothermia as it was, and it had dulled his wits. Surprisingly, though, it seemed to have heightened his senses. No woman had ever felt as good in his arms. No woman had looked more becoming. Travis didn't dwell on his thoughts. He was too cold and miserable.

Standing under the stinging spray from the shower, he let the warm jets revive him. Two of his men, plus Rob Bradley, another rancher, had tracked the wolf most of the day. The tracker sent by the U.S. Fish and Wildlife Service hadn't had any luck, and Travis strongly suspected the animal had rabies, which lent their search urgency. They'd followed the wolf farther than Travis would have normally traveled under these conditions. When the storm arrived, pummeling them in the downpour, they'd decided to call it quits and return home. The night, complicated by the storm, made for dangerous riding. Several times Travis thought about Mary and the children. He wished there were some way to contact them. When he was the coldest, he remembered her standing in the kitchen that morning, all flustered and uncertain when Scotty had announced Travis should kiss her. He recalled the way her gaze had drifted toward him during the church service and how she'd smiled so sweetly at him. She'd been almost pretty.

Mary at the house with the kids had dominated his thoughts, along with their discussion from the night before and the promises they'd made to each other. Rob had offered to let him spend the night at his spread, but Travis had declined, eager to get back to the ranch.

When he saw the house was dark he'd assumed she'd gone to bed and was swamped with disappointment. Nothing could have surprised or pleased him more than to have her rush into his arms the instant he walked in the door. He hadn't been joking when he'd told her a man could grow accustomed to being missed this badly. He wasn't used to being fussed over, but having Mary care felt good.

Once he'd finished with his shower, Travis dressed and headed for the kitchen, following his nose. The last time he'd had anything to eat had been that morning at breakfast, and he was famished.

Mary brought him a plate piled high with mashed potatoes, thick slices of roast beef, both swimming in gravy, along with corn, warm biscuits, and a thick slice of pecan pie. He dug into the meal as though he hadn't eaten in a week, which was very much how he felt.

Her biscuits were even better than they'd been the night before, and he swore he'd never tasted better pie. Travis maintained Mary would put Martha out of business if she ever chose to open her own restaurant.

"This was excellent," he said when he finished.

He pushed back the chair and pressed his hands to his stomach, sighing his full appreciation. Larry Martin wasn't the only one who could dish out compliments, especially ones as well earned as this.

Mary flushed with pleasure, less shy than usual. He guessed it was because she was in her element in the kitchen. Somehow she appeared softer, more feminine, than he could remember. He found himself studying her as she carried his plate to the sink and poured him a fresh cup of coffee. He stood close to her, leaning his hip against the counter while she rinsed off his dirty dishes.

Soft blue light danced in her eyes as she chatted with him, telling him about the children and how much better their day had gone than on Saturday. It was a good thing she didn't ask him to repeat what she'd said because Travis paid far more attention to her than to the words she spoke. One soft brown curl had escaped the tie at her nape and flirted with him, until he reached out and tucked it around her ear.

Mary froze and Travis stepped back, surprised that he would feel comfortable enough to touch her. "I'm sorry, I didn't mean to frighten you."

"You didn't," she assured him softly.

He continued to watch her, wondering what had changed. He'd viewed her as a mousy frump when she'd stepped out of the jetway from Louisiana, and now he found her captivating. Her sweater had seemed bland and bulky earlier, and even that was different. He noticed the way it outlined her breasts, the way the fabric moved over her nipples as she worked.

Her sweater wasn't the only thing that made an impact on him. He was looking at her like a woman instead of his housekeeper. By heaven, he was looking at her like a wife. The realization struck him mute for a moment. He actually found Mary lovely. Not because she was beautiful, but because she cared for him, worried about him, was there waiting for him.

Travis didn't want their time together to end, but he wasn't sure how they should continue. He didn't want to rush her into the physical aspect of their relationship, but he discovered to his chagrin that he was looking forward to it.

"I'd like to hold you," he found himself saying. He didn't need Scotty to encourage him this time.

Shyly she moved away from the sink and toward him. He edged toward her and brought her into his arms as if this were where she belonged. His cheek was pressed to hers, and he closed his eyes. Neither spoke. He held her until her warmth, her scent, cinnamon and something else, some flower, he guessed, became too much for him to resist. Turning his head ever so slightly, afraid of destroying the mood, he nuzzled her ear with his nose, then her neck. She sighed softly as though she found as much comfort in their embrace as he did.

He wanted to make love to her. There wasn't any use lying to himself about it, but the time wasn't right, although he would have liked it to be. Using restraint, he kissed her cheek, her ear, and her hair before finding her mouth. He experienced that deep, almost painful sense of waiting and wanting. She trembled, and he knew she too was deeply affected by their kisses.

"Can I touch you?" he asked her next.

"If you want."

Travis held his breath and carefully eased his hand under her sweater. She bit into her lower lip when he pressed his hand to the silky-smooth skin of her abdomen, but she didn't impede his progress. Gradually, moving slowly, he traced his fingers upward until he reached and covered her breast.

Her fullness filled his palm, and when he rotated his thumb over her nipple it rose hard and proud to greet him, to welcome his touch.

"Mary." He groaned her name and pressed his forehead to hers. "You feel so damn good in my arms."

"I'm plain and small and—"

"No," he said brusquely, and slid his hand from beneath her sweater. "I won't have you saying that about yourself." He lifted his head from hers and pressed his palm against her cheek, directing her gaze toward his.

Their eyes met and locked hungrily, and he lowered his mouth to hers, kissing her deeply. Bracing his feet slightly apart, he rotated his hands up and down her back to press her softness intimately against him.

He wanted her physically so much that his body throbbed with the need. For a wild moment it demanded all his strength to resist her.

"Thank you for the wonderful dinner," he said, releasing her when he felt confident he could do so.

"Would you want to go to bed now?" she asked, looking up at him shyly.

Nine

"Bed," Travis repeated.

"You must be exhausted," Mary explained, unable to understand why he found it such an odd question. She finished her tasks in the kitchen and walked toward the hallway, pausing in the doorway and looking back at him.

Travis stood with his arms dangling lifelessly at his sides, seeming to be at a complete loss for words. "I might stay up a while."

She blinked, surprised and disappointed. She'd enjoyed their kisses and even having him touch her breasts, but he looked now as if he were in pain. "I assumed you'd be exhausted."

"I am." He paused and studied her, his dark eyes intense. "Do you *want* me to come to bed now?" he asked her.

Mary hesitated, not knowing what to say.

"You don't seem to understand what happened

just now," he said. He stopped abruptly, his gaze skirting past hers. "You . . . turned me on."

"Touching me did that?" Pride lifted her spirits. Her less than voluptuous body had stirred a man. The high she experienced was incredible. "I didn't know I could do that," she whispered.

"Do you or don't you want me to come to bed with you?" Travis asked once more with less than sterling patience.

Mary hesitated. "What exactly are you asking me, Travis?"

He walked toward her and lifted his hand as though to touch her face. Apparently he changed his mind because he lowered it to his side. "If I come to bed with you now," he explained, "we might end up making love."

She didn't know how to answer.

"It's soon, but I'd like to work toward that end. I'd like to touch you and have you touch me, so we can get accustomed to one another. That's what going to bed with you means. Now do you want me to join you or don't you? The choice is yours." His words were gruff and stiff, as if the decision didn't affect him in any way.

"I . . . liked it when you touched me before. Come to bed, Travis, and we'll work out the details there."

By tacit agreement they didn't turn on the lights, preferring to undress in the dark. Travis was under the sheets first, and when Mary slipped onto the mattress, he scooted close, wrapped his arm around her, and held her against him.

It comforted her to realize he was as nervous as she was.

"I want to kiss you again," he told her in a husky whisper, "but if I do anything to frighten you, let me know, all right?"

She nodded.

Travis threaded his fingers through her hair and dragged her lips to his. She parted her mouth to him, eager to accept his tongue and experience again the powerful surge of pleasure. Warm sensations glided effortlessly though her blood, and she sighed, wanting more and not knowing how to ask for it.

Travis stroked her breasts, leaving her wanting and needy. His hand moved lower, under the elastic waistband to her flat stomach. For several moments he caressed her abdomen in soft, circular movements.

Not knowing what to expect next, Mary tensed. Travis paid no heed to her hesitation but continued his movements.

"No more," she said.

"Okay," Travis whispered, rolling away from her. He was on his back, his breathing labored. "Did I hurt you?" he asked after a moment.

Mary took time composing her reply. "No, but it felt strange, and I . . . I don't know—different. I'm not explaining myself very well, am I?"

"I think I understand. The problem is that you've got romance confused with sex."

"I do?"

"You think sex is all moonlight and roses, but

you're wrong. It's urgent and sweaty, and from what I understand it isn't any picnic for a woman the first time. If you're looking to wrap it up in a fancy satin bow, it'll never happen."

Mary's cheeks burned, they were so bright. "Are you angry with me?"

"No."

"But you're so far on your side of the bed. I like it when you hold me."

"That's the problem. I like it too much. You tempt me, Mary, and I don't want to do anything that's going to frighten you."

"I tempt you," she repeated softly on the last dregs of a yawn. "Oh, Travis, that's the most lovely thing you've ever said to me."

"We overslept?" Groggily Mary sat up and rubbed the sleep from her eyes. She looked warm and pink, and acting on impulse, Travis gathered her in his arms and kissed her. Her ready, eager response sent his blood racing. Mary's fingers tunneled in his hair, holding him against her, and she sighed heavily when he reluctantly eased away from her.

"I have to go."

"I know," she whispered. "The kids will be late for school."

Still, he couldn't force himself to leave her. "I enjoyed holding and kissing you last night."

She lowered her gaze and blushed. "I enjoyed it, too."

Travis kissed her again, and she wound her arms around his neck and opened her mouth to his.

A knock sounded at their door and they were interrupted by Scotty, who walked into the room. Travis was conscious that he was only half-dressed and kissing Mary.

"That's real good, Uncle Travis," the boy said with a wide grin. "Real good."

"Hurry and get dressed," Mary instructed. "We forgot to set the alarm."

"Okay." Scotty closed the door and scampered away.

"I have to go," Travis said with heavy reluctance. He would have liked nothing better than to send the children off to school and spend the day with his wife. Unfortunately he couldn't.

"Have a good day," she said as he pulled away from her.

"You too."

Travis reached for his socks and boots. He couldn't help but have one hell of a day, especially when he was looking so forward to the coming night.

Mary's morning was hectic. The boys were out the door just seconds before the school bus arrived. The kitchen was in complete disarray. Scotty had spilled a box of cold cereal, and some had fallen onto the floor. Wanting to help, Beth Ann had scattered the corn crispies in every direction so

Mary heard crunching noises each time someone took a step. Within minutes a sawdust of sticky cereal blanketed the spotless linoleum.

Jim tore apart the living room looking for his homework assignment, tossing cushions and pillows into the air like a bulldozer attacking the furniture.

The minute they were out the door, Mary collapsed on the kitchen chair. Her head was spinning. She hadn't even taken time for a cup of coffee.

Beth Ann climbed on the chair across from Mary, cupped her chin in her palms, and sighed expressively. "Those boys need to get their act together."

Mary laughed. The boys weren't to blame. If Travis hadn't forgotten to set the alarm . . . Her mind drifted back to the events of the night before, and she felt warm and content.

Once she'd downed a cup of coffee, tidied the kitchen, and got the washing machine going, Mary felt as though she'd put in an eight-hour day.

At ten Clara Morgan stopped in for a visit. She was dressed in her thick wool coat and a pillbox hat and carried a black purse and small wicker basket lined with a red-and-white-checkered napkin.

"I hope you don't mind my arriving unannounced like this," the older woman said primly, setting a basket of homemade jams on the table. "But it seemed best that we make the arrangements for the wedding shower as soon as possible. The ladies at the Grange are anxious to meet you. But first, you must tell me how you ever convinced Travis Thompson to attend church services with you."

Mary smiled to herself as she poured the other woman a cup of coffee and carried it to the table. "It wasn't the least bit of a problem," she said. "He volunteered."

"I swear, you're exactly what that boy needs." Clara added a teaspoon of sugar into her coffee and stirred it briskly.

Beth Ann came into the kitchen and smiled. "Hi, guess what? You don't need to bring us dinners anymore. Mary cooks better than Uncle Travis."

"I'm pleased to hear that." A smile quivered at the edges of the older woman's mouth, and her gaze met Mary's briefly.

Mary studied the woman. With her gray hair tucked neatly into a bun at the base of her neck, her modest dress, and sensible shoes, it was like seeing a picture of herself thirty years in the future. Without Travis. Without the children.

"Travis is a former student of mine," Clara went on to say. "He was a real hellion as a boy, but I saw through him then, the same way I do now. He insulted the others, you know."

"Uncle Travis was rude to some of the church ladies," Beth Ann explained in a loud whisper.

Clara sipped her coffee. "He was rude to me, too, but I wouldn't put up with any nonsense from him and he knew it."

Now it was Mary's turn to smile. She liked

Clara, perhaps because she saw so much of herself in the older woman. Travis appreciated Clara, too, but he wasn't comfortable showing it.

"I won't keep you from your duties," Clara said. Her cup made a clinking sound as she set it back in the saucer. "I know how busy you must be. Would next Tuesday be agreeable with you? One of the ladies from the Grange will be contacting you soon. We want to officially welcome you to Grandview." She frowned as though displeased about something. "You're going to be very good for Travis. I can see that already. At least that boy had a decent head on his shoulders when it came to choosing a mate. I was worried when the children first told me he had written away for a wife."

"Our marriage was a bit unusual." Which was an understatement.

"Scotty offered to show me your letters, but I felt that would be an invasion of privacy." She reached for her white cotton gloves. "Beth Ann assured me you could sing, Scotty was more concerned about your cooking, and Jim"—she hesitated—"Jim, well, he didn't say anything one way or another."

That sounded like her oldest, Mary mused. *Her oldest* . . . Jim wasn't her son, yet she felt as though the bonds were as thick as blood. She was fiercely attached to each of the children, but more so to Jim. Mainly because he was hurting so terribly.

"I'd like it if we could be friends," Mary said as

Clara stood and reached for her purse, which she tucked protectively under her arm.

Clara looked both pleased and surprised. "I'd like that very much."

The words began to blur in front of her eyes, and Tilly squeezed the bridge of her nose. This was the first time in her life that she even remembered coming purposely into a library, let alone checking out any books. She'd never been much of a reader, even when she was young. Boys had always been more important than her studies. It had hurt her, too. A man had gotten in the way of her graduating from high school. He'd been an error in judgment in what proved to be a long line of errors as far as men were concerned. Tilly didn't dare hope Logan would be any different. For now she interested him, but she could think of no logical reason for their affair to last more than a month or two. Yet her heart refused to believe Logan was like all the rest.

Just walking into the library proved once more how unlearned she was. It took her ten minutes or more to realize the fiction books were categorized by alphabet. The nonfiction ones were more difficult to understand. One thing was certain, she wasn't going to ask the librarian and make an even bigger fool of herself.

Logan was the reason she was visiting the library. He'd made several comments in passing about certain classic works of literature. Tilly knew next to nothing about tragic heros, mythology, and the like. He'd mentioned how much he enjoyed books. The last novel Tilly could remember reading all the way through had been written by Sidney Sheldon. One of the girls at work had raved about it, and Tilly read it. Her friend was right, the plot was great, but it had taken her a month to finish the book.

Logan read a lot, and sometimes he told her the plots. If she was ever going to make something of herself, she would need a little culture. So she struggled with a collection of short stories published in the *New Yorker* between 1927 and the mid-1970s. Half the time she didn't even know what she was reading, but this was supposed to be good literature.

"Hello. You're Tilly, aren't you?"

Tilly looked up from the book to see Mary Thompson, Travis's bride. "Oh, hi," she said, welcoming the intrusion. Mary picked up one of the volumes Tilly was researching and studied the spine. She arched her brows, apparently impressed. "So you enjoy opera."

"Not really. I might, but I don't know very much about it. Sit down," she said, gesturing to the chair across from her. Her brain was swimming with all the things she was learning. She never realized a person could overdose on knowledge.

"Actually I was just leaving," Mary said, smiling.

Tilly reached for the pile of books and gathered them in her arms. "So was I. Do you have time for a cup of coffee?" Being new in town, Mary probably hadn't made many friends. Tilly remembered what it was like for her that first month when she'd barely known anyone. At least she'd found a job at Martha's, which had helped, but Mary spent the majority of her time holed up on a ranch twenty miles outside of town.

"I'd love a cup of coffee."

Together they traipsed across the street to Martha's.

"You'd think I'd be sick of this place," Tilly said as she slid into the booth closest to the kitchen. "But Martha serves the best coffee in town." She raised two fingers to Sally, who worked the day shift, and her co-worker promptly delivered two mugs.

"So, how's married life treating you?"

Mary's gaze lowered to her coffee. "Very well."

"Have you met many folks about town yet?"

"A few. Tilly, listen, I was wondering if you wouldn't mind answering a few questions for me. I know this is unusual, but I'd like to talk to someone other than Travis and the children about this."

Frankly Tilly was curious and a bit flattered that Mary would seek her out. "Fire away. I'll tell you what I know."

"It has to do with Travis's brother and his wife. What do you know about the accident?"

Tilly released a labored breath. "Now that was really sad. It happened nearly five months ago now. It was early morning, and from what I understand they'd gone into town to dance. The Logger has a live band come in once a month. Lee and Janice really enjoyed dancing. From what I heard they left the tavern sometime after midnight."

"Had Lee been drinking?"

"Maybe a beer or two earlier in the evening, but I heard he was stone sober when he left. Janice, too."

"Does anyone know what happened?"

"No. There's been plenty of speculation, of course. The first word we heard was that Lee had taken the corner too fast and lost control of the car. That made sense to everyone but Travis. He was the one who insisted Lee was too good a driver to let that happen. I heard Travis was at the accident scene for hours, trying to come up with some answers. He was the one who insisted Sheriff Tucker classify the accident as vehicular homicide. When the facts were made public, there wasn't any doubt Lee was driven off the road."

"But who would do such a thing?"

"A drunk. As best they can picture it, Lee was coming around the corner and met another vehicle that'd crossed the center line. From the tire marks, it looks as if they both tried to swerve out of the way. Lee's car went over the ledge. The markings on the car showed they had some contact. It probably dented his fender. There couldn't have been much damage to the other car since the driver took off. Whoever it was apparently didn't even bother to stop."

Tilly paused. She remembered the accident clearly because Logan had come to her apartment early the next morning staggering drunk. He'd wanted to make love and she'd refused, and they'd had their first and only fight. She'd never known him to drink before or since.

The muscles in her stomach tightened. Dear, sweet Jesus, could Logan be the one responsible? The mere suggestion set her heart into a panic. Logan could never do anything like that, she reasoned, trying to calm herself. She couldn't love him as much as she did and believe he'd drive away from an accident scene.

"The children came to live with Travis right away, then?"

It took a moment for the question to filter past Tilly's confusion. The accident happened the night Logan had gotten drunk, she was sure of it. Why hadn't she made the connection before? She should have realized, should have put two and two together.

"Travis drove over and got them himself," she murmured. "Apparently someone from the sheriffs department had already been there, so the kids knew what had happened. Those poor kids, imagine losing both their mother and their father at the same time."

Mary nodded.

"A lot of folks in town didn't think Travis was the right person to be raising those youngsters. From what I heard, Travis was something of a hellion when he was growing up and hasn't been able to shake the image. You have to admire the way he stepped in and took full responsibility. He didn't need to do that. He feels as strongly about his brother's children as he does about finding whoever's responsible for the accident."

"It hasn't been easy on him, either."

"I bet it hasn't." Tilly was quickly tallying the changes in Logan since the night of the accident. She'd known something was troubling him and had been for weeks. He never spoke to her about it. He'd admitted to being a recovering alcoholic. Oh, God, it could have been Logan.

Tilly felt she was going to vomit. She broke out in a cold sweat and couldn't seem to get enough air in her lungs.

"Tilly?" Mary's soft voice was filled with concern.

"I'm . . . not feeling very well all of a sudden." Her body ached, but not nearly as much as her heart. For once, just one lousy once, couldn't she fall for a decent man? Was that too much to ask? She'd thought he was respectable, decent, gentle.

She should have known, should have figured it out much sooner. If Logan was so wonderful, what was he doing hanging around someone like her?

Tilly felt numb inside. Dead. Dead to the man she wanted so desperately to love. But mostly her dreams had died.

"Tilly, are you all right? You're looking terribly pale."

"I'm fine," she whispered, and it was probably the biggest lie she'd ever told.

Mary hurriedly unloaded the groceries from the back of the pickup and got dinner started. She'd stayed in town far longer than she intended. Although Tilly had gotten ill, Mary had enjoyed their time together. She wanted to learn what she could about Lee and Janice without asking Travis or the children. Mrs. Morgan would have been a good choice, but she didn't want Beth Ann overhearing the details of her parents' accident.

Mary liked Tilly. The waitress was a little rough around the edges, but her heart was as big as her ready smile.

Mary was busy peeling potatoes when the school bus arrived. Jim, Scotty, and Beth Ann raced toward the house like bear cubs. Hearing the sound of their laughter, Mary stood in the doorway smiling as the three tore down the driveway, their feet stomping the ground in their hurry to reach home.

Since Jim was the oldest, he reached the porch first. Panting, he paused and pressed his hands against his knees while he caught his breath.

Scotty wasn't all that far behind Jim, and Beth Ann followed, looking disgusted with her two older brothers. She swung her backpack from her shoulder as though to suggest that if she hadn't been carrying the extra weight, she might have won the footrace.

"Are there any more cookies left?" Scotty asked between gasps.

"Lots. You can have two each. Put away your school things and do your chores."

The three piled into the house, and Mary returned to the pile of potatoes. Jim grabbed his cookies and headed for the barn, but Scotty and Beth Ann chose to eat theirs at the table.

"I drew a picture in school today," Beth Ann said. "Wanna see it?"

"I'd love to," Mary said, wiping her hands dry. She followed Beth Ann to her bedroom. The kindergartner sat on the edge of her bed and carefully unzipped her backpack. After sorting through several folded papers, she found what she was looking for. She was grinning proudly when she handed it to Mary.

"Why, Beth Ann, this is very good." Mary wasn't entirely sure what the five-year-old had drawn. Five stick figures marked the page with a row of colored flowers.

"It's our family," Beth Ann explained. "Look, there's Uncle Travis." She pointed to the tallest stick figure. Mary studied the sketch and realized what looked like a doughnut was actually a cowboy hat. "That's you," Beth Ann explained, pointing to the second figure in a skirt. "And Jim and Scotty and me."

A family. Mary's chest tightened with emotion. She'd never been one who cried easily. She hated to cry, hated the way the moisture felt on her face, the way her nose got all red and started to run.

"It's beautiful," she whispered, savoring this feeling of belonging, of being a part of Beth Ann's world. "Let's put it on the refrigerator, okay?"

"Okay."

Mary continued to sniffle as she finished peeling the potatoes. It was such a small thing, yet it meant so much to her. Until she'd come to Montana her heart had felt dry and barren, parched with loneliness. She lived each day, survived each disappointment, holding on to the belief that someday, somehow, she'd find where she belonged.

That day had arrived.

The back door opened, and thinking it was Jim, Mary turned around to ask him if he'd set the table.

But it wasn't Jim.

"Mary," Travis whispered softly, clearly shaken. "What's wrong? What's happened?"

around every one before. Until she'd seen the picture she imagined every year getting progressively colder and drearier until she gave up hope ...

Ten

The last thing Travis expected when he walked into the house was to find Mary in tears.

"Mary, what's wrong?"

"It's nothing." She continued to weep.

"Did one of the kids upset you? Was it Jim?" The twelve-year-old was growing more and more sullen and uncommunicative. If he'd upset Mary somehow—

"Not Jim," Mary assured him.

"Then, tell me. Can you tell me what happened?"

She nodded. "Beth Ann drew me a picture."

Travis went still. Beth Ann had offended Mary with a drawing?

"Look," Mary said, motioning to the refrigerator. "Isn't it beautiful?"

Travis stared at the creased picture, wondering

if Mary saw something he didn't. As far as he was concerned, the kid didn't reveal the least amount of artistic ability. Five stick figures and a bunch of odd-shaped flowers wasn't worthy of such emotion. He studied Mary, thinking he might have missed something.

Mary smiled softly and brushed the tears from her face. "You don't see it, do you?"

Travis squinted and scratched the side of his head. "Nope."

Mary laughed and resumed preparations for dinner.

Still puzzled, Travis moved into the bathroom to wash his face and hands. Scotty came in and sat on the edge of the tub, watching him.

"Howdy, kiddo. How was school?"

"All right, I guess. Jim got in trouble, though."

Travis tensed. This was exactly what he'd been afraid of. "What kind of trouble?"

"I don't know. He wouldn't tell me, but he was in the principal's office. You're supposed to sign a note."

Travis slapped the washcloth against the side of the sink. "Where is he now?"

"Doing his chores."

Travis should have guessed something was wrong when he arrived home and found Jim working in the barn. The boy generally had to be reminded two and three times before he did what he was told. Travis couldn't look at Jim and not feel the aggression in the youth that raged just beneath the surface. Mostly the hostility had been aimed at him. This confrontation had been stewing for weeks. The kid had an attitude, and by God, he was going to be set straight once and for all.

Travis marched out of the bathroom and through the kitchen, not pausing, not even when Mary whirled around and asked him what was wrong.

Jim was cleaning stalls when Travis came upon him. He certainly didn't seem to be working with any degree of energy. Every movement was sluggish, as if he resented each lift of the pitchfork.

"Tell me what happened at school today."

Jim's shoulders tensed, and he stabbed the fork into a fresh bale of hay. "I suppose Scotty couldn't wait to let you know I got in trouble."

"Never mind your brother, I'm asking about you."

"I got in a fight, all right?" Defiance flashed in his eyes.

"No, it isn't all right. Let me see the note."

Jim stood with his feet braced apart, and Travis realized the boy meant to defy him. They glared at each other for several moments, their eyes drilling one another. Jim's were filled with open hostility, as if he welcomed the chance for them to fight. What the boy needed, Travis thought, was to be taken down a peg or two, and by heaven, he was the man to do it.

The stand-off lasted only a matter of seconds before Jim sighed and reached inside his hip pocket. He removed a folded slip of paper and handed it to Travis, who peeled it open. He read Mr. Moon's letter and cursed under his breath.

"You started the fight and wouldn't stop even when two teachers were pulling you off the other boy."

"Billy asked for a fight. I gave it to him. If you want to get all mad about that, fine. I don't care."

"You've been asking for trouble yourself," Travis snapped. "Billy's a year younger than you. If you're going to start a fight, at least be man enough to pick on someone your own size."

"He started it," Jim shouted, his fists clenched at his sides.

"And you were glad, because you've been looking for a reason to fight someone for a good long while. You think I don't know that?" Travis shouted. "You've been in a rotten mood for months. You think I don't know you don't want to live with me? You think I'm so stupid I haven't figured that out?" He paused, not wanting his anger to get the better of him, not wanting to say something he'd regret later. "Listen, hotshot, we're stuck with each other, and we better damn well make an effort to get along. Otherwise we're both going to be miserable."

"Go to hell."

Travis grabbed hold of Jim's arm. "I won't have you talking to me or anyone else like that, you hear me? You aren't so big that I can't wallop your behind."

Jim snorted and jerked his arm free. "I'd like to see you try."

"I'd welcome the pleasure."

They glared at one another, each apparently waiting for the other to move first. Travis's threat had been empty. He had no intention of turning Jim over his knee. At twelve Jim was too old to be spanked. Travis wasn't sure what to do with him. Something. Ground him, he guessed. Give him extra chores.

"You were always in trouble in school!" Jim shouted.

"I learned the error of my ways and was man enough to admit when I was wrong," Travis told him.

"What makes you so sure I was in the wrong?" Jim challenged. "You didn't even bother to ask my side of the story. You automatically assumed that because Billy Watkins is a year younger that I should let him get away with pushing me around. You can beat me if you want. Mr. Moon can expel me from school, too. I hate school. I hate living with you."

"Well, that's tough, because you don't have any damn choice."

Jim's face was beet red, and his shoulders were heaving with restrained anger. For a moment Travis thought the boy was going to break into tears. He could see him struggling to hold back the emotion.

Travis would have given everything he owned to know what to say to Jim. He understood better than his nephew realized what it was like to hate home and school. To feel he didn't belong either place, to have people look for the opportunity to think bad of him. His home had been lost to him when his mother deserted the family. That was when his father had given up on life and taken to drinking more than he should. Like Jim, Travis had lashed out at those around him. He'd learned life's lessons the hard way and hoped Jim could avoid repeating the mistakes he'd made.

"If you're going to get in trouble at school, then you'd best learn you'll pay the consequences at home as well."

"What are you going to do?"

"Double your chores. When you finish here you can oil the saddles and the rest of the tack." That would keep Jim busy for a couple of hours if not more.

"But—"

Travis silenced him with a look. "You want to make trouble, fine, then I assume you can take what you dish out. There'll be no dinner for you until you're finished. Understand?"

Jim glared at him, belligerence simmering in his eyes. Travis didn't give the boy the opportunity to antagonize him further. "Let me know when you're done and I'll check your work. When you're finished, you'll write Billy Watkins a letter of apology." With that he stormed out of the barn and headed for the house, taking the porch steps two at a time.

Mary was setting the table and looked up when he came into the kitchen. She paused, holding the dinner plates against her stomach expectantly, as if waiting for some explanation.

"Jim brought home a note from the principal," Travis said. He walked over to the stove to see what she was cooking for dinner. He was pleased to note it was hamburger gravy, one of his favorites. Mary certainly knew her way around a kitchen.

"You talked to Jim?" she asked stiffly.

Travis nodded.

"What did he have to say?"

"Jim started a fight."

"Why?"

"It doesn't matter why. Jim knows better."

"Maybe so, but there could have been extenuating circumstances."

"There weren't." Travis felt the weight of her censure, and he didn't like it. "I gave him some extra chores. When he's finished with those he'll be writing the other boy a letter of apology." He was rather proud of the fact that he'd kept his cool. It hadn't been easy with Jim's bad attitude, but he hadn't allowed him the upper hand.

"You might have discussed this matter with me first." Mary straightened to her full height, squared her shoulders, and glared at him. It was like squaring off with Jim all over again, but this time Travis didn't doubt for a moment she was going to take the upper hand.

Dinner was strained. Jim's empty chair left a huge gap at the table, and in Mary's heart. She was irritated with Travis for not discussing the incident with her before confronting Jim. They should have

approached the boy together, asked for an explanation, and then decided what course they would
take to right the matter. Instead Travis had reacted
in anger. Depriving a twelve-year-old of his dinner
until he'd finished his chores was inhumane. Jim
was a growing boy. He needed his strength.

Scotty, who normally chatted through the dinner hour, remained strangely quiet. He barely
touched his meal, and that wasn't like him, either.
Even Beth Ann's appetite wasn't up to par. What
Mary found more surprising was the sight of the
five-year-old sucking her thumb.

Jim came into the house and stood just inside
the door halfway through the meal. "I'm finished
now."

"All right," Travis said. His chair made a grat-
ing sound as he pushed away from the table and
stood. "I'll check and see what kind of job you
did, and then you can sit down for dinner."

"I made you a plate," Mary told him softly. She
remembered the night she'd been near frantic
with worry over Travis in the storm and how Jim
had reassured her. He'd gathered the flashlight,
candles, and matches for her. A knot developed in
her throat, and her own appetite fled.

"Jim can have my piece of cake if he wants,"
Scotty offered.

"Mine too," Beth Ann echoed.

Wordlessly Travis followed Jim out of the
kitchen.

"Can I be excused?" Scotty asked, his eyes
downcast.

Mary looked over his half-finished plate and nodded. She was finished herself. She carried her plate to the sink.

"Me too," Beth Ann said.

"You both can have applesauce cake later," Mary said. "There's plenty for everyone."

Tears brightened Scotty's eyes. "I shouldn't have told Uncle Travis," he whispered, not wanting his sister to hear.

Mary placed her arms around his shoulders and squeezed lightly. "Travis would have learned sooner or later anyway."

"Jim will think I'm a squealer. I wouldn't have said anything, but he wouldn't let me play with his Matchbox cars. He keeps them hidden from me, and it made me mad."

"We all do things we regret," Mary assured him. "What's important is learning from our mistakes."

"I'm never going to tell on Jim again. Never. It makes my stomach hurt." He sobbed once and buried his face in Mary's abdomen, crying softly.

"Jim will forgive you, sweetheart. You're brothers."

Mary couldn't help remembering how close she was to her own brother and how dreadfully she missed him even now. Travis had been close to Lee, too. In time the squabble between Jim and Scotty would right itself.

Jim returned to the kitchen a minute later, and

Mary brought him the plate she had warming in the oven. His eyes refused to meet hers or Scotty's.

"Scotty, clear the table for me when Jim's finished," she said. "I'm going outside to talk to Travis. I might be a while, so keep an eye on your sister."

Mary grabbed her sweater and hurried down the back porch steps. It was dark by now, and the yard was illuminated by the lights from the kitchen and the ones in the barn. By the time she met up with Travis, who was halfway across the yard, she was furious.

She refused ever again to let him discipline Jim when he was angry. Furthermore, she should have had some say in the matter. If she was going to be a mother to these children, she had a right to a say in their upbringing.

"We need to talk," she said angrily.

"About what?" He looked taken aback.

"Jim."

Travis frowned. "What about him?"

When she was this agitated, Mary had problems properly expressing her feelings. What disturbed her most was Travis's attitude. It was the "me Tarzan, you Jane" thing all over again.

She knew the best way to communicate her discontent was to speak to him on his level.

She dragged the heel of her sneaker through the dirt, creating a deep groove in the compact soil.

"What's that?" Travis demanded.

"The line, and you've crossed it."

Travis's frown deepened. "What the hell are you talking about?"

"You've crossed the line with Jim and with me. I won't have you disciplining him again without conferring with me first." She steadied her hands against her hips and glared at him. "If we're going to raise these children, we need to stand together as a united front. A house divided against itself is doomed."

Travis rubbed his hand along the back of his neck. "You're really upset about this, aren't you?"

"You're damn right I'm upset."

"Then we need to talk about it."

"Exactly." Mary was somewhat surprised by his attitude. She'd fully expected a major argument to evolve from this. "But I don't want to do it in front of the children. Especially not Jim."

"Fine, we'll talk in the barn."

Mary gathered the sweater more completely around her and followed him.

Several bales of hay and feed were stacked in an empty stall. Travis went in there and gestured for her to sit down. He sat across from her and leaned forward, pressing his forearms against his thighs. "Go ahead, what is it you want to say?"

"First off, I don't appreciate your disciplining Jim without discussing it with me first. Furthermore, withholding dinner from a growing boy is barbaric. I won't stand for it."

"I see," he said thoughtfully.

She felt adamant. "I mean it."

Travis wiped his hand down his face. "Dinner was a pretty miserable affair, wasn't it?" he muttered almost to himself.

"A disaster. I can't ever remember seeing Beth Ann suck her thumb."

Travis glanced her way. "She does every now and again when she's overly tired or upset. She fell into the habit for a time following the funeral, but stopped because the kids on the school bus were teasing her."

"Scotty's upset, too, because he tattled. Apparently Jim wasn't willing to let him play with his cars. Telling you about Jim's run-in with Mr. Moon was how he chose to retaliate. He's miserable."

"They'll work it out."

"I'm sure they will."

"You're right," Travis said after a moment. "I should have conferred with you, and we could have talked to Jim together. It's just that I'm accustomed to taking matters into my own hands. I'll do better next time."

Mary watched the play of emotions cross his face. She guessed the admission that he was in the wrong had cost him dearly.

"Are you still angry?" he asked.

Appeased, she shook her head and smiled softly.

"Good." He transferred himself to her bale of hay. "Wanna kiss and make up?" He wiggled his eyebrows suggestively.

"Here?"

He slipped his arm around her waist and

dragged her closer to him. Mary couldn't dredge up a smidgen of resistance. There wasn't any available when he kissed her, either.

She tried to imagine what her life would have been like without Travis and the children. She'd been with them only a short while and couldn't help feeling they'd always been the most important part of her life.

Travis brushed a wisp of hair from her face and looked down at her. He kissed her again, urging her mouth open even wider. His tongue sought hers, involving her in a lazy erotic play. When he raised his head she noted that his eyes were dark with passion.

"Mary, I thought about you all day, about us, wondering if we could make this marriage real."

"I did, too," she admitted softly. "I was so afraid of what it would be like, but I'm not anymore."

"You're not." His kissed her until they were both breathless, then pulled his mouth away and pressed his forehead to hers. "You're in trouble now."

She heard the humor in his voice and responded with a smile. "How's that?"

He stood and closed the bottom half of the stall door. "I mean to have my way with you, woman."

"Here?" She feigned deep shock.

"Right here and right now." His large hands were busy with the buttons of her blouse. It surprised her how agile his fingers could be.

"What about the children?" Her voice was little more than a husky murmur. She did nothing to impede him, nothing to deter him from his mission.

"They won't bother us."

"How can you be so sure?"

"I'm sure." He peeled the blouse from her shoulders and deftly removed her bra. "Oh, Mary," he said with a deep sigh of satisfaction. "You're so damn beautiful." As he spoke he swathed her nipples with his tongue. His tongue curled around the delicate bud, drawing it deep into his mouth. He sucked gently, and again Mary felt the effect of it all the way through her.

"Am I shocking you?" he asked.

"No . . . no, this feels as good as the kissing."

He heightened the pressure, sucking at her greedily, roughly, then gently again.

Mary threaded her fingers though his hair and let the warm passion melt over her. Travis was making sounds, too, the kinds of sounds Mary had never dreamed she'd hear from a man, the type a husband made when he needed his wife.

Travis paused and looked at her, his face tight with desire, the planes of his face chiseled and hard.

Mary urged his mouth to hers and instinctively raised her hips to meet his. "I need you, too, Travis."

He seemed to have stopped breathing. "Does this mean what I think it means?"

She lowered her lashes and nodded.

Travis traded positions with her, so that she lay sprawled atop him. He touched his forehead to hers and closed his eyes. "Not in a barn, Mary, not your first time."

His thoughtfulness touched her as few things ever had.

"Tonight?" he asked. "After the children are in bed?"

Mary nodded. She was a mature woman, not some teenager with stars in her eyes. Where once there was loneliness now there was joy. It had seeped silently into her soul.

"Travis . . . the children. We need to get back to the house."

"I know." His words were filled with regret.

Mary leveled herself away from him and buttoned her blouse. Travis's hand reached for hers, and his eyes burned into hers. "You make me feel strong." He kissed her fingertips. "And alive."

Mary understood. Grief had overwhelmed her following Clinton's death. It had taken nearly a year for her to notice the world kept right on going when she'd been trapped in her pain. A year had passed before she'd realized the roses continued to bloom and the sun continued to shine. It had taken a full twelve months before she felt alive again.

Mary and Travis went into the house together. Jim was washing the dinner dishes without having been asked. Scotty was sitting at the table doing his homework, and Beth Ann was sitting on the kitchen floor playing with her Barbie dolls.

"Mary?" Beth Ann asked, her eyes round with concern. "Did you fall down?"

"No, sweetheart, I'm fine."

"But there's straw in your hair."

Eleven

"Tilly, damn it, I know you're in there. For the love of heaven open up and talk to me."

Tilly stood on the other side of the door, her hands pressed to her trembling lips. Her head and her heart were involved in a fierce battle. She desperately loved Logan, and at the same time she hated him and wanted to punish him for the agony he was putting her through.

By all that was right she should have gone directly to the sheriff and reported what she suspected. Each minute she kept the information to herself, it weighed her down more.

"Tilly." The pounding grew louder.

The knot in her throat increased until it was nearly impossible to breathe. She felt as though someone had stuck a fist down her esophagus.

Silently she cursed Logan. He'd made a believer

out of her. No one had ever been more cruel. Not even Davey when he'd stolen her ATM card and emptied her checking account, then left town. Not Phil when he'd slapped her around and left her with two black eyes, bruised ribs, and a broken heart.

Logan had made her feel good about herself. He'd brought out the best in her, helped her heal. They'd helped each other. Or so she'd believed; now she understood what her real role had been. She'd soothed away his guilt.

Tilly had always been a slow learner. Life's lessons had never come easy. Everything, it seemed, had to be learned the hard way. Phil had taught her that if she continued to love someone who was hurting her physically and mentally, eventually she would stop loving herself.

Davey had been a multiple lesson awardee. Lesson number one: Try to save a drowning man and you risk going down with him. Tilly had made the plunge three times. If Davey hadn't left town first she might never have survived their affair. Lesson number two had come when she realized there was a limit to how much pain and confusion any man was worth.

Now Logan was the teacher and Tilly was convinced his lessons would be the most pain-filled by far. From him she learned she'd lost the ability to judge character.

She'd been so sure this time. Logan hadn't dragged her down, he'd built her up. Because of Logan she wanted to better herself. For the first time in years she was becoming involved in her community. For the first time in years she was truly happy. What a farce happiness was, Tilly realized, closing her eyes to a fresh stab of pain.

"Tilly, damn it," he shouted, "are you going to make me break down the front door?"

It wasn't an idle threat. Exhaling her frustration, she unbolted the lock and threw open the door. She stood defiantly on the other side of the threshold, dredging up each bit of backbone she could muster.

"What the hell's the matter with you?" Logan asked angrily. "You've been avoiding me for two days now. If we've got a problem the least you can do is talk to me about it."

Tilly knew he was right, but knowing that didn't change things. She could think of no way of asking him if he was the driver responsible for the deaths of Lee and Janice Thompson. She'd gone over the details in her mind until she couldn't bear to analyze them any longer. No matter how she tallied the facts they led to the same inevitable conclusion.

"Don't you have anything to say?" he demanded when she didn't speak.

Staying away from Logan had been damn difficult. The first day she'd called in sick to Martha's. She hadn't answered her phone either. The second day, when he showed up at Martha's, she had Sally wait on him while she slipped out the back door.

Now he stood before her and she saw him with

fresh eyes. He was a distinguished-looking man, handsome as sin, gentle and good. And he loved her. He honestly loved her.

"Baby, tell me what's wrong," he pleaded.

Tilly shook her head wildly from side to side.

"Damn it, Tilly, what the hell happened?"

He was angry with her, but she read the confusion and pain in his eyes.

"I did something?"

Unable to look at him any longer, Tilly lowered her gaze. She couldn't make herself say it.

"Tilly," Logan exhaled sharply. "For the love of God tell me what's wrong! Don't you know I love you? This is killing me. Baby, if we've got a problem, let's face it together."

She didn't know who moved first, but before another moment passed she was in Logan's arms, holding on to him and sobbing uncontrollably. He felt so strong and warm, and so damn comforting. She longed to lose herself in him, and blot out everything else.

Driven by her fears, her mouth found his and their kisses took on a frantic wildness. Tilly knew Logan was as confused as she was, but he withheld nothing from her. His arms were locked around her waist and he lifted her so her feet dangled above the floor. Holding her against him, he carried her into the house, their mouths locked together. Kissing became far more important than breathing.

A scary kind of sexual excitement filled her. Logan, who'd always seemed to be in tune with her needs, moved directly into the bedroom. They barely had time to get their clothes off. Tilly undressed first and clawed at Logan, demanding that he hurry. Rushing was essential otherwise she'd be forced to look at what she was doing.

Their lovemaking was as fierce as their kissing had been. When they finished, they were both left exhausted. Logan gathered her in his arms and kissed her temple.

"Can you tell me what's wrong?"

Tears welled in her eyes and she turned onto her side so he couldn't see her face.

She felt exposed and weak, more emotionally insecure than she'd ever been with anyone else. More than her heart was involved this time. Logan had wrapped tentacles of hope around her soul.

"It's my father, isn't it?" Logan whispered, tucking his arm around her waist and cuddling her spoon fashion.

"No."

"Don't lie to me, Tilly. He said something to you, didn't he?"

"No," she said again, stronger this time. "He has nothing to do with this."

"I don't believe you." Taking her by her shoulders, he twisted her onto her back so he could look into her eyes. Tilly knew they were red and swollen from crying. She hated to have him see her like this but there was no help for it.

"I can't stand the thought of anyone hurting you," he whispered and kissed her gently. "You're the best thing that ever happened to me. If you say my father doesn't have anything to do with this, then I don't have any choice but to believe you." As passionate as his kisses had been earlier, now they were filled with a warm tenderness. "I need you so damn much," he whispered. "I swear the last few days have been hell without you."

"I need you too," she told him, looping her arms around his neck and holding him against her.

"Listen to me," Logan said, lifting his head and cupping the side of her face with his hand. "I'm through sneaking around. Who do you think we're fooling? Anyone with a lick of sense knows how I feel about you. In case you hadn't noticed, our romance is old news. No more of this, Tilly. We're dating the same as any other couple. I'm proud to have you at my side. Personally I don't give a damn what my father thinks. I'm through living my life to please him."

"Oh, Logan, you don't understand."

"No arguments," he said and kissed her soundly. "We're attending the Harvest Moon Festival together and that's the end of it."

"I can't," she said, her mind racing frantically for an excuse.

"Yes, you can. I won't take no for an answer, Tilly. We're through sneaking around behind closed doors."

"But . . ." A couple of days earlier she was going to turn what information she had about Logan over to the sheriff's office, and now she was considering attending the Harvest Moon Festival with him.

"No buts," he said, kissing the end of her nose. "We're going."

Tilly pressed her hands to his face and stared into his beautiful eyes. "You'd never hurt anyone, would you, Logan, and leave them behind? You wouldn't do that, would you?"

A sadness crept into his face and he smiled weakly. "No, Tilly, I'd never do that."

She had to be wrong, Tilly reasoned frantically and her heart lightened. He'd said he had to accept her word that his father hadn't confronted her, now it was her turn to trust him. Logan wouldn't lie to her. Not about this. Not about something so important.

It wasn't him, her mind shouted. It couldn't be.

Mary was lying still, dressed in the silk gown Georgeanne had given her. She waited for Travis to join her, feeling like a goose dressed up for Christmas dinner.

She tensed when he came into the room and turned off the light. "Are the children sleeping?" she asked.

"Yep." He sounded nervous.

Shadows flickered against the wall as he undressed. She caught the scent of his cologne and smiled, knowing he'd put it on for her. The mattress dipped with his weight as he climbed in beside her.

For a moment neither spoke nor moved. Mary's heart was racing in her ears like a revved-up car engine. Travis was tense too; his body seemed to be pulsing with anxiety. Mary knew she'd feel more relaxed if he'd kiss her again the way he had in the barn. When he was holding and touching her everything felt right and good.

Travis rolled onto his side and, supporting himself on his elbow, he looked down at her in the moonlight and grinned sheepishly. Mary saw the lingering light of need in his eyes and her heart constricted with love. Never would she have deemed it possible to have fallen in love with Travis so quickly. But love him she did, until her heart felt as though it would burst with the emotion. Smiling, she slid her hands up his shoulders, gently tracing the shape of him, reveling in the sleek, smooth feel of his skin. She linked her hands at his nape and tentatively lifted her mouth to his.

The kiss was slow and deep. Mary felt its impact all the way to her toes. Travis had taught her much in the art of kissing and she welcomed his tongue and teased him with her own. His chest expanded with a sharp intake of breath and he wrapped his arms around her waist and rolled onto his back, taking her with him so she was poised above him.

The kissing continued, but it was no longer a leisurely exploration, but one of hunger and urgency. He braced his hands at the back of her thighs and gathered the silk fabric of her gown until it collected at her waist.

The small pleasure this afforded her was something of a surprise. He'd touched her like this before, on her stomach, and she'd felt threatened and a little afraid. Not now. He was introducing her to the world of sensual enjoyment and the limits seemed to constantly expand.

He broke off the kissing and exhaled slowly as if he needed to do something to compose himself, to slow down their momentum. He brushed the hair from her face and gazed into her eyes. "Are you afraid?"

"A little," she admitted shyly. "I know all the technicalities of what we're going to do, but . . . you're so big."

Travis grinned, looking inordinately pleased by her words. "We'll go slow and you can stop me if I hurt you."

"I'm not going to want to stop."

He smiled again and lifted his head to give her a moist kiss. "Me either, but I will. I don't want to hurt you." Taking hold of her sleek gown, he stripped it from her so that she was completely bared to him. Mary felt her breasts tighten as they were exposed to the cool air. Pleasure mingled with heat darted through her as he touched her breasts with his hands, gently lifting one in his palm.

"Perfect," he murmured, "just perfect."

With one easy, deft movement, he rolled so she was beneath him. "I want to touch you. All right?"

Mary closed her eyes and nodded.

His callused palm lovingly traveled downward, over her ribs to her stomach until his fingers tangled with the silky triangle of curls.

"Mary," Travis whispered urgently, "look at me."

She found him studying her with an intense, loving expression and whatever fears she was experiencing fled immediately. Instead she was proud that this man should want her so desperately, that he cared so much about making this first time pleasurable for her even if it meant taking away from his own enjoyment.

"I could shoot Georgeanne," Mary whispered into the silence.

"Georgeanne?"

"My best friend. At least I thought she was. She never told me lovemaking was this good, I'd always thought . . . I don't know, that it was all hot and sweaty."

"It is," Travis said, and she heard the smile in his voice.

"Maybe, but it's a whole lot more."

Travis kissed the crown of her head. Within minutes he was asleep. Content, Mary smiled and sighing, she contemplated what a miracle it was to be nestled in her husband's loving arms.

Twelve

Mary's sewing machine had recently arrived and she'd set it up on the kitchen table. In front of her was a pile of mending. Travis was the worst offender. No fewer than fifteen of his shirts were badly in need of repair. Jim ran a close second.

The phone rang and she gazed absently in its direction, resenting the intrusion into her morning. She removed the pins from her mouth and reached for the receiver, tucking it against her shoulder.

"Hello."

"Mrs. Thompson, this is Mr. Moon from the school."

Mary's heart fell like dead weight to her knees. Jim was in trouble again, she knew it even before the grade school principal could say the words.

"I'm afraid there's been an accident on the

playground," Mr. Moon continued. "Beth Ann fell from the swing and her right arm seems to be causing her a good deal of pain. I'm afraid it could be broken."

"Oh, no."

"We have her arm packed in ice for now. How long will it take you to come for her?"

"I'll be there as soon as possible. Thank you for calling." Numbness set in as Mary hung up. Her head was whirling so badly that for a moment she remained immobile.

Beth Ann was in pain with a possible broken arm. Her baby. Mary grabbed her coat and purse and was all the way into the yard before she realized Travis had the truck. There were three other vehicles scattered about the place, all in a state of disrepair. An old Chevy that didn't have an engine was rusting alongside the barn. Plus two other vehicles, one without tires, another without doors. Travis had said something about fixing one of the cars up for her, but unless she specifically told him she needed the truck for errands and the like, he generally took it himself.

Mary scrambled toward the house, but paused at the foot of the porch steps before whirling around and racing toward the barn.

It was high time she became acquainted with Mad Max.

Travis was mending fences. The wolf had gotten another calf and he'd spent the better part of the morning battling his frustration. No rancher could continue to sustain these kinds of losses. Something had to be done. And soon. The beast had attacked cattle on two neighboring ranches as well, but their hands were tied behind their backs. The U.S. Fish and Wildlife Service still had a tracker hunting down the wolf, but apparently the animal had outwitted him as he had just about everyone else.

In a manner of speaking, Travis was mending fences with Mary as well. They'd come a long way in a few short days. What had started out as a problem over the way he'd handled Jim had been settled most satisfactorily. He smiled to himself, lifting the last post from the truck bed.

She was right about the way he'd handled the situation with Jim. When he thought about it, he could see her side of the matter. He'd been wrong to withhold the boy's dinner, wrong, too, not to have discussed how to deal with the problem with Mary. It was an understandable mistake, since he wasn't in the habit of discussing his decisions. Nor was he accustomed to having a wife, but he was learning.

"You're looking mighty chipper," Jake Roth, his hired hand, said as he lifted the last fence post from the truck bed. "I can't ever remember you whistling much before."

Travis stopped. He didn't realize he'd been whistling.

"It seems to me married life agrees with you."

Travis shrugged. "It has its moments."

Jack laughed. "So I've heard. Personally I

wouldn't want a woman messing up my life. Too damned demanding. They're always wanting something."

Travis's thoughts had run along those same lines when he'd first considered looking for a wife. He'd dreaded what marriage would do to him. A woman would be an intrusion, and by heaven he'd been right.

He couldn't very well claim that Mary hadn't been an imposition. Hell, she'd turned him inside out, upside down, and every which way. What he hadn't understood was the balance she'd brought into his life. There was no getting around the fact she was a woman. One hell of a woman.

She'd tackled the house the way an offensive fullback goes after the quarterback in football. Why she'd scrubbed down every room until even the windowsills shined. Only a day or so ago she'd gone into town and brought back paint chips and sample materials. As best he figured she'd have the entire house redecorated by Christmas.

What she brought into his life was something Travis hadn't figured. Stability. The weight of his responsibilities had shifted. His burden had lightened substantially. There were drawbacks. She had a tendency to move furniture around in the middle of the night, but he could live with her small idiosyncrasies. She also cooked, cleaned, and organized. She offered the children something Travis felt at a loss to provide. A mother's tenderness. The most incredible part of the arrangement was that he hadn't been left without rewards himself.

To think he'd found this extraordinary wife through a want ad. It flabbergasted him. What astonished him even more was how he'd been disappointed when he first saw her. Long legs. That was all he'd wanted. That seemed laughable to him now. He wanted Mary, his Mary, and he didn't give a double damn what her legs looked like.

"Someone's coming," Jake announced, looking toward the west. He was leaning against the shovel handle, his feet crossed. "A rider."

Travis glanced in the same direction and hesitated. If he didn't know better he'd say it was Mad Max. The figure was riding hell-bent for leather too.

It took another second or two to realize the rider was the woman who'd so recently occupied his thoughts. Travis tossed aside the shovel and started racing toward her. He wasn't a man who tasted panic often, but he did so now. The woman was crazy to come racing across the range like this. From the looks of it, she was about to break her tomfool neck.

Mad Max came to an abrupt halt.

"Are you trying to kill yourself?" Travis shouted furiously.

Mary ignored him and practically leaped off the horse. "It's Beth Ann," she whispered, unable to get her breath. "She's fallen in the school yard . . . possible broken arm. No way . . . to get into town."

"Jake," Travis said urgently, turning to his hand. "Take care of the horse."

"Right away," Jake promised.

Travis was halfway to the truck before he realized Mary hadn't moved. Apparently her legs had lost the ability to move, so with his arm around her waist, he lifted her, carried her to his vehicle, and helped her inside. Before another minute passed they were on their way.

Travis noted that Mary's breathing was deep and labored as he shot across the range land. Although he did his best to avoid the ruts, it was impossible. His petite wife was tossed about the cab of the truck like a Ping-Pong ball.

"Hold on," he shouted irritably.

"I am," she snapped back.

Travis was relieved to hear the sass was back in her voice.

"Mr. Moon said she was in pain."

"Did you call Doc Anderson?"

"No, I didn't think."

"Don't worry. He's been treating the kids for years. He'll take Beth Ann right in."

"Just hurry," Mary shouted.

He tried slowing down.

"Hurry," she cried again.

"But you're—"

"Don't worry about me."

"If you weighed a little more it'd help," he complained.

The highway was in sight and Travis heaved a sigh of relief. He cast a worried glance at Mary and saw that she was holding on for all she was worth. Not that it did a damn bit of good.

They both sighed with relief when Travis

reached the highway. With any luck they'd be at the school within minutes.

Each one of those minutes seemed to take a month of Travis's life. Although he tried to appear calm for Mary's sake, he was anything but. Years ago, he'd forgotten how many now, he'd broken his own arm. The memory of the pain remained with him even now and the thought of Beth Ann enduring that kind of agony sent chills down his spine.

He pulled into the school yard and parked in the bus zone. Mary was out of the truck before he'd cut the ignition. She waited for him at the double doors and they entered the building together.

The receptionist took them directly to the nurse's office. Beth Ann was huddled in a chair against the corner, her face red and streaked with tears. She was holding her arm protectively against her side, clinging to a dripping ice bag.

She looked up when Mary and Travis entered the room and shuddered with soft, vibrating sobs. "I fell."

"It's all right, sweetheart," Travis said, gently picking her up with both arms. "You're going to be all right now."

"It hurts real bad."

"I know."

"Mary, open the door for me," Travis instructed. He turned around to find his wife signing some papers. She finished and hurriedly did as he requested, racing ahead to the front doors of the school and then to the truck. She leaped inside and Travis gently placed Beth Ann in her arms. He might have been mistaken but it seemed to him that the five-year-old sighed as she nestled into Mary's comforting arms. Funny, that was the way he felt when Mary held him too.

Travis drove far more sensibly to Doc Anderson's office.

Doc saw her immediately. Mary went with Beth Ann into the X-ray room while Travis paced the outer office. A row of patients followed his movements and after a moment, he explained. "Beth Ann broke her arm."

He heard the five-year-old scream and stopped abruptly. Not another second passed before he slammed through the door, nearly knocking Doc Anderson's nurse down as he came tearing into the inner office.

"What happened?"

Mary met him in the hallway, her features ashen. "Doc had to move her arm for the X ray."

"Is she all right?"

Mary nodded, but not before Travis noticed the tears in her eyes.

Mary and Travis stayed with Beth Ann while Doc developed the film. Beth Ann sat on Mary's lap, her head resting on Mary's shoulder.

Doc came into the room a few minutes later, carrying the film with him. "Well, young lady," the white-haired doctor said, holding the black sheet up to the light. "It looks like we're going to have to cast up that arm. Look here." He used the end of his pencil to outline Beth Ann's small bones and reveal the crack.

Travis squinted, but he didn't see anything.

"Where did I break it?" Beth Ann asked softly.

Doc brought the picture down to the five-year-old's level. "Here. See?"

Travis did then, but if Doc hadn't pointed it out he would have missed the infinitesimally small line. "It's not a bad break," Doc said, apparently for their peace of mind. "Painful, but within six weeks, it'll be healed, good as new."

"I have to wear the cast that long?"

"I'm afraid so, but you can have all your friends sign it. What color do you want? I can have Frieda make us up a pretty pink one."

"I like blue better," Beth Ann whispered, sniffling. She used her good hand to wipe her nose.

They moved into the casting room where Frieda, the nurse Travis had nearly mowed down, was busy soaking plaster strips. Mary continued to hold Beth Ann in her lap.

"It would be better if she sat up on the table," Doc said in passing as he brought out a roll of thick cotton.

"No," Beth Ann sobbed, clinging to Mary with her good arm. "I want Mary."

Doc hesitated. "Fine, Pumpkin, we want to make you as comfortable as possible."

Travis was grateful the older man was so understanding. But then he'd been dealing with injured children for a long time. Travis watched the process with a good deal of interest. Doc's able hands efficiently wrapped Beth Ann's forearm in the plaster strips. He chatted amicably, but was unable to draw Beth Ann into conversation. She continued to cling to Mary, who whispered soothingly to the youngster.

By the time they stopped off at the pharmacy for a prescription and drove back to the house, Travis felt as if he'd put in a twenty-hour day. After taking the pain medication, Beth Ann went down for a nap.

"Is she asleep?" Travis asked when Mary reappeared.

She nodded, walked to his side, and slipped her arms around his waist. For several moments they did nothing but hold each other. Travis drank in her warmth, grateful once more for Mary's presence in his life. He didn't know how he would have survived this day without her. If she hadn't been at the house to answer the call, Beth Ann would have been forced to sit in the nurse's office until he'd come back to the house. Heaven only knew how long that would have been.

Pressing her hands against the side of his face, Mary directed his mouth down to hers. His body flared awake at her touch.

When they broke apart, Travis was breathless and weak. "What was that for?"

"To thank you."

"For what?

"I haven't got that figured out yet. I . . . I just wanted to kiss you."

Amazed, Travis stared at her, not knowing what to say. "I've got to get back to Jake."

She nodded. "I've got plenty to do myself." Without another word, she sat back down at the table, in front of the sewing machine, and reached for one of his shirts.

Mary rolled onto her back and sighed. Although she was exhausted, both mentally and physically, she couldn't sleep. Travis seemed to be having the same problem.

"You awake?" he whispered into the dark.

"Bright-eyed and bushy-tailed."

He chuckled softly. "It's been one hell of a day, hasn't it?"

"I could do without another like this for a good long while."

"Me too," he agreed. He hesitated and reached for her hand, bringing it to his lips. "Beth Ann's broken arm was bad enough, but I swear you frightened me ten times worse."

"Me?"

"Riding Mad Max like a wild man across the open range like that. You might have been killed."

"I was perfectly safe."

"Who taught you to ride like that? You certainly aren't a novice to the saddle."

"I've been riding from the time I was a girl. A good many southern women do, you know." It was difficult keeping the smile out of her voice.

Travis was silent for a moment. "You might have said something."

"You might have asked."

"Is there anything else I should know about you that I don't? Do you fly planes and jet ski too?"

She laughed at his bemusement. "No."

"How'd you know where to find me?"

"That was easy. I overheard you talking to Jake this morning. I wasn't exactly sure where you were, but I know which way east is. All I had to do was keep the fence line in view. I knew that sooner or later I'd find you."

Travis muttered something under his breath. It sounded almost like a compliment, as if he were impressed with her deductive powers.

"I made a call after dinner."

Mary had noticed him on the phone earlier, but hadn't thought much about it. "To whom?"

"Slim Jenkins. He sells used cars. I can't afford a new one just now, but I can't have you trapped at the house either. Besides, we need a vehicle everyone can ride in safely."

Rolling onto her stomach, Mary looked down into her husband's handsome face. She hadn't thought of him as handsome when they first met, but she did now. She loved every sun-kissed crease and line, especially the ones that fanned out from his eyes.

"I've made arrangements for us to go in and talk to Slim tomorrow afternoon. Is that all right with you?"

"It's perfect."

He reached up and wove his fingers into her hair and brought her mouth down to his. Their kiss was leisurely and deep. His lips were soft beneath hers. When they finished, Travis released a long, uneven sigh.

Mary smiled to herself. "What was that all about?"

His hands cupped her breasts. "I can't get over how randy you make me feel."

"Randy?"

He chuckled and rubbed his thumbs across her nipples which puckered responsively. "It means, my innocent wife, that you turn me on."

"I do?"

"Yes," Travis answered with more than a trace of amusement. "You do."

She curled her arms around his neck and pressed her lips to the pounding pulse at its base.

Travis's hands caught her hips and shifted her closer to him. Her gown had slipped up over her thighs. When the bare skin of her hip met his, he hesitated. "Mary, you don't have anything on underneath this gown, do you?"

"Nope," she said with the same inflection she'd heard him use countless times. "I thought it'd save time."

His long legs tangled with hers as he brought her mouth down to his. They kissed again with renewed vigor. Travis's hand was at her breast and Mary sighed with the immediate spark of pleasure that he was capable of igniting with the slightest touch.

The knock at their door went unnoticed at first. Certainly Travis didn't hear it. Mary jerked her mouth from him.

"Who is it?"

"Beth Ann," came the muted reply. "I couldn't sleep. My arm hurts."

"Come in, sweetheart," Mary said, righting her nightgown.

The door opened and Beth Ann stepped into the darkness. "Sometimes when I was sick Mommy and Daddy let me sleep with them."

Mary looked to Travis who was frowning fiercely. Disregarding his warning, she scooted over until there was a wide space between her and her husband, then patted the bed.

"Come on, sweetheart, you can sleep with us for tonight."

Beth Ann hurried forward, crawling onto the mattress at the foot of the bed.

"But only tonight," Travis warned.

"Okay," the five-year-old agreed with a sigh as she settled in between them.

Thirteen

"*I want to go on the hammer,*" Scotty said excitedly from the backseat of the minivan as they rode into town for the Harvest Moon Festival. The three children were too excited to sit still and bounced around the backseat like popcorn kernels in hot oil.

Amused, Mary glanced toward Travis. "We'll see."

"You'd probably throw up again," Jim muttered just loudly enough to rile his younger brother. Mary strongly suspected Jim felt obligated to tease Scotty now and again just to keep in practice.

"I won't either," Scotty cried. "I like scary rides."

"You're a sissy and you know it."

"Enough," Travis snapped.

"Scotty's afraid of the hammer," Jim jeered in a singsong voice.

"Am not."

"Ask him what happened last year."

"It wasn't my fault I got sick," Scotty shouted in outrage, half flinging himself over the backseat.

"Enough," Travis said more forcefully this time.

Mary sighed when the tentative peace was restored. She eased the strap loose across her front and shifted position so she could look to the children without being strangled by the seat belt. They'd purchased the car a few days earlier, and she wondered how they'd managed without it this long.

"I don't want to go on any rides," Beth Ann announced in a thin, sad voice.

"They probably won't let you because of your cast anyway," Scotty informed her, appointing himself the authority on such matters.

"Why don't we just wait and see." Mary suspected Scotty was right. But surely there'd be something special for Beth Ann. The kindergartner was doing as well as could be expected, dealing with a cast that stretched from her fingertips to her elbow. Mary knew it was upsetting that Beth Ann's right arm was the one broken. Nevertheless, the little girl was making a gallant effort to write and dress herself. Having the Harvest Moon Festival to look forward to had helped ease her frustration. Letting Beth Ann attend the wedding shower held in Mary's honor had helped.

The local newspaper had been filled with details of the annual festival for two weeks running.

The Grange ladies were responsible for baking the cakes for the cake walk. Mary had baked one herself and delivered it earlier that afternoon. While she was there, she'd signed up as a volunteer for Fish, one of the games that involved the younger children. From seven to eight on Friday night, she was responsible for tucking a prize on the end of a fishing pole.

All day the children had been excited about the community festivities. They'd chatted like magpies from the moment they'd stormed into the house after school. The three hurriedly finished their chores, anxious to be on their way, unwilling to miss a single minute of fun.

"Let's eat first," Mary suggested when Travis parked the minivan. The football field at the high school had been transformed into a huge parking lot since the smaller school lot was being used for the carnival rides.

Huge spotlights were set up at the far end of the field and crisscrossed the evening sky. The school gymnasium housed the games and other activities, including sit-down space for eating.

"I'm hungry," Scotty admitted enthusiastically.

"When aren't you?" Jim demanded, and Beth Ann laughed as if her oldest brother had told a hilarious joke.

"Enough," Travis interrupted for the tenth time as they piled out of the car.

"Can I have cotton candy and a candy apple and popcorn?" Beth Ann asked, tucking her good hand into Mary's, tugging her along.

"Not for dinner."

Beth Ann sighed with mock disappointment.

"You go on ahead," Travis instructed, walking several steps in the opposite direction. "I'll only be a few minutes."

Mary hesitated, surprised. Then she nodded, doing her best to suppress her disappointment. Like the children, she'd been looking forward to this family outing. Mary had hoped they'd present a united front, Travis, her, and the children, for the inspection of the good people of Grandview. Perhaps then the inquisitive looks, the unasked questions, and the curious stares would cease, and their marriage would be accepted. To have Travis wandering off by himself, leaving her with the children, was sure to cause speculation.

"Where's Uncle Travis going?" Scotty asked, walking backward in order to watch his uncle.

"I . . . I'm not sure." Mary glanced over her shoulder and noticed her husband, his hands stuffed in his pockets, moving slowly down the line of parked cars. Every now and again he paused to study a vehicle before moving on reluctantly.

"Can we have hamburgers?" Beth Ann asked, tugging at Mary's hand to gain her attention.

Mary turned back to the children and nodded absently. Her wistful gaze returned momentarily to Travis. She'd put a lot of stock in this outing.

"Mary?"

"Hamburgers? Of course, hamburgers would be great."

"With lots of curly fries."

"With curly fries," she agreed, amused. No doubt their menu would extend itself as they passed the various booths.

"Lemonade, too."

"That won't be any problem," she continued.

"Corn on a stick and big pretzels with lots of salt?"

"Ice-cream bars?"

"Later," she promised, laughing, "if you're still hungry."

"I will be," Scotty assured her, then turned a bright shade of pink as Jim and Beth Ann glared at him.

They waited in line a good fifteen minutes for their hamburgers. It seemed everyone else in town had gotten the urge for a hamburger at the same time. Mary guessed it had something to do with the appeal of the huge barbecue that was set up just outside the doors of the large school gymnasium. The aroma of fried onions and beef with barbecue sauce scented the evening air.

The Harvest Moon Festival reminded Mary of the crayfish celebration in her own town. Folks from miles around flooded and overfilled the streets of Petite. At the memory, she experienced an unexpected rush of homesickness. She corresponded regularly with Georgeanne, but she'd been so busy in her new life with Travis and the children that she hadn't had time to miss Louisiana. Georgeanne's letters had been filled with welcome gossip. It seemed that Mary's best friend was waiting patiently for her to announce she'd made a mistake and would soon return home. It was what Georgeanne expected.

Purposely Mary turned her thoughts from her best friend. As the line approached the grill, she glanced over her shoulder, hoping to find Travis.

He still hadn't joined them by the time they'd reached the front of the line. Mary ordered for the children, deciding she'd eat later with Travis.

The children followed her, each carrying thick paper plates, to the beige folding chairs set up along rows of paper-covered tables. Mary helped Beth Ann with the ketchup and mustard, all the while keeping her eye on the door, waiting anxiously for Travis. Scotty wanted chocolate milk instead of lemonade, so Mary saw to that.

"Where's Uncle Travis?" Beth Ann asked, looking around when Mary returned. Using her left hand, she awkwardly dipped a curly fry in the glob of ketchup, then carried it to her mouth. "I want him to ask about the rides."

Mary was also anxious to learn exactly where her husband was. The last thing she expected when they arrived was to have Travis abandon her with the kids. She was reminded of what had happened to her on their wedding night, when he'd up and disappeared and left her stewing.

"I'll be right back," Mary murmured, thoroughly impatient by the time Travis had been gone nearly twenty minutes.

"Where are you going?"

"To find Travis."

"You'll be back, won't you?"

Mary smiled down at Scotty and Beth Ann, who were both looking up at her anxiously. Jim didn't seem concerned one way or the other, at least not outwardly.

"I'll be back so soon you won't even know I'm gone," Mary promised. The gym was filling up, and the sound of laughter and good cheer echoed off the walls. The country-western radio station from Miles City was broadcasting live, and the songs rang out over the school's loudspeaker system. Everyone around her was filled with the spirit of celebration, but Mary felt immune to the gaiety.

Edging her way outside the crowded gym proved to be something of a task. She paused and scanned the sea of faces, looking for Travis. It could be that they'd simply missed each other, and that he was searching for her and the children, not knowing where they'd gone.

As hard as she tried, she couldn't keep a slow, burning resentment from brewing. They'd come to the festival as a family. In years past, Mary was convinced, Travis had probably gone off with his cronies, drinking and carousing. If he assumed he could continue with his bachelor ways, he had another thing coming.

She searched the carnival area. Brightly colored lights flashed, and the cheers and screams echoed through the excitement of those participating on the wide selection of daring rides. Several attempts were made to entice her to try her hand at small tests of skill. Mary ignored them. Popping balloons with a dart and tossing pennies into fishbowls were low on her priority list at the moment.

Discouraged, she hurried past the rides and games to the farthest end of the festivities. She scrambled between a row of trailers at the far end of the football field.

"Hello there, pretty lady." A lanky man with dull brown eyes smiled at her approach. He was sitting on the steps leading into a trailer, studying her as she approached.

"Hello," Mary said with little enthusiasm. She didn't want to appear unfriendly, but there were three children waiting for her. And a husband to locate.

"You're looking mighty pretty this fine evening."

"Thank you." She hurried onto the field, which was quickly filling with cars. Already nearly every space was occupied. It was by pure chance that she happened to catch sight of Travis. He was in the parking lot, walking between the lengthy rows of vehicles, almost exactly where she'd left him.

"Travis," she shouted, and raised her hand, wanting to attract his attention. She purposely stepped away from the trailer area.

Apparently Travis didn't hear her.

She called out to Travis again. This time her voice must have carried with the wind, because he turned around abruptly, his face illuminated in the light from the two huge spotlights.

He started walking in her direction, and Mary raced toward him, meeting him halfway.

"I'll have you know, Travis Thompson, I don't appreciate this," she flared.

"Appreciate what?"

"Your . . . abandoning me and the children."

Travis frowned. "I didn't abandon you."

"What exactly were you doing, then?" she demanded.

"I was busy," Travis answered. His frown darkened, as though he resented her questions.

He could be downright angry for all Mary cared. The children were waiting and no doubt restless by this time. They didn't have time to dawdle or argue.

"I was looking at the cars."

"Why?"

"I wanted to see if any had recently been in an accident," Travis explained, his voice dropped several degrees toward ice. "Sheriff Tucker may have forgotten about Lee and Janice, but I haven't."

"Travis," Mary whispered, sick at heart, "for your own sanity you've got to lay what happened to rest." Nothing would bring back his brother and sister-in-law. It had been several months, and if Sheriff Tucker had found no leads in all that time, it wasn't likely Travis would, either.

"No, I won't forget," he said between clenched teeth, gripping her shoulders and pivoting her around so they stood face to face. "I'm not ever going to forget it. Not until I've found whoever was responsible. I promised the children, but more important, I promised myself. Whoever drove Lee off the road is going to pay for what he did."

"Travis, please . . ."

"Please what?" he said, his eyes as hard as steel. "Forgive whoever's responsible and get on with my life?"

"Yes," she pleaded, gazing up at him. His eyes were dark and so fierce that he would have terrified her if she hadn't known him better.

"You can forget that right now, because I won't give up. Not this year or the next. I'll keep looking if it takes the next twenty years. Not you or anyone else will persuade me otherwise. Understand?" This last bit was shouted, the words dark with emotion and spoken from a man who'd stared into the fires of hell.

Mary blinked at the barely restrained violence she saw and felt in Travis. His fingers dug into her shoulders, but she was certain he was unaware he was hurting her.

"I . . . I have to get back to the children," she said, stunned by his vehemence, unsure of how to respond.

Travis closed his eyes momentarily, breathed in deeply, and then exhaled. "This shouldn't take much longer." He pushed back the pain from his eyes and stared down at her, his cold anger dissipated.

Mary looked toward the gym, fearing she'd left the children far too long. "I . . . need to get back." She turned to leave, but Travis caught her fingers, halting her.

For a long moment he said nothing. "I didn't mean to yell at you."

"I know."

He mumbled something under his breath and then hauled her into his arms, as if he were in desperate need of her softness. His arms banded her waist, and for a moment he did nothing but hold her against him.

"Mary," he whispered huskily as his mouth swept down on hers. His tongue sought hers as he pressed their bodies together intimately, flattening her breasts against the hard wall of his chest. "I'm sorry," he whispered, nuzzling her neck. "You were looking to have fun this evening, weren't you?"

"It's all right. I understand."

"Come on," he said, tucking her hand in the crook of his elbow. "Let's go find the children and enjoy ourselves."

Tilly couldn't remember a date she'd anticipated more eagerly. Logan was scheduled to pick her up at the house shortly before five. She'd spent nearly the entire day getting ready for their first official outing together.

Having been cheated out of her high school prom, she'd spent as much time and energy on this evening with Logan as she would have had she been seventeen all over again.

The morning began with a hair appointment, followed by a shopping spree that netted her a pair of classy designer jeans with white leather stars that decorated the two hip pockets and a row of leather fringe that stretched from hip to cuff. A bright red western-style shirt with the sleeves rolled up past her elbows and a scarf were the perfect accents.

Logan came for her promptly at five. When she opened the door he paused and gazed at her, and in true classic form his mouth fell open.

"Tilly, my goodness, you're beautiful. Why, you look good enough to eat."

Tilly had long assumed she'd lost the ability to blush, but she did so now. The pleasure of his words soaked straight to her heart.

"Do I dare kiss you?"

It was as if he were seeing her for the first time and was afraid to touch her. Tilly couldn't have been more pleased by his response.

"We can kiss as long as you don't mess my hair."

The kiss was long and sweet and shockingly thorough.

"Oh, Tilly, you taste so damn good," he murmured, reluctantly pulling his mouth away from hers.

"We don't have to go," she offered, afraid and unsure all at once.

"We're going!" With his hands on her shoulders, he kept her at a safe arm's distance. "There'll be plenty of time for making love later."

With a heavy heart, Tilly glanced over her shoulder toward the bedroom. "We could be a few minutes late. Nothing says we need to be there right at five-thirty."

Logan's hungry gaze followed hers. "You're not going to distract me this time." Having made the decree, he relaxed somewhat. "And when we do make love, it'll be at my house, and you're spending the night with me. All night. When I wake up in the morning I want you with me, Tilly. Understand?"

Tilly went stock still. They'd been lovers for several months and she'd never been inside Logan's house. Not once.

"No arguments, understand? It's high time you saw my place."

Tilly thought her heart would burst wide open; such happiness was too much to hold to oneself.

"Tilly," Logan said with a groan. "Don't do that."

"What?"

"Smile at me like that."

Tilly blinked. "Like what?"

Logan ground a hungry kiss over her lips. "Like you just did. That sweet, womanly smile."

Tilly was thrilled. "I have a sweet, womanly smile?"

"Yes, baby, you do. It drives me crazy."

"Like this?" She tried it again and was gratified by a low moan from Logan. He grabbed her arm and literally pulled her out of the house.

"Shouldn't I bring a pair of pajamas?" she whispered, although there wasn't anyone close to overhear.

Logan laughed outright. "Whatever for? You certainly won't be needing a stitch of clothing as far as I'm concerned."

Tilly laughed and accepted Logan's hand as he helped her inside the car. She nestled on the passenger seat and reached for the seat belt, stretching it across her front and snapping it into place. The leather scent reminded her the car was new. He'd purchased it shortly after his arrival in Grandview. Tilly remembered being impressed with the leather interior. To the best of her knowledge it was the first time she'd ever ridden in a brandnew car. Her own vehicles had been sorry excuses for cars, abused and discarded by their previous owners. In many ways Tilly was like those secondhand cars. Try as she might, she couldn't understand why a Mercedes would fall in love with a Ford, but she wasn't going to let the questions plague her, not tonight.

The carnival was crowded and fun. Tilly wasn't sure what she expected. For the first hour she waited for someone to comment about the two of them together, but it never happened, and she soon relaxed.

Logan insisted they go on a variety of wild and daring rides. Tilly had never found much excitement in being whirled about in every direction, but Logan insisted. And because she was so happy, she couldn't make herself refuse him. Countless times Logan had assured her it would be fun.

Tilly suffered her first doubts while they were suspended thirty feet above the ground, hanging upside down. Her carefully styled hair fell over her eyes and mouth. "For this I spent two hours at the beauty parlor?" she muttered.

Logan chuckled. "I promise to make it worth your while later," he whispered, and kissed her neck.

Tilly stared down at the ground far below them and was surprised by how high they were. From this distance it was doubtful anyone recognized them, and that lent her courage. Her hand unhurriedly wandered up the inside of Logan's thigh.

"Tilly," Logan whispered, his hand stopping her, "behave yourself."

"I am. My oh my," she whispered, smiling at how tightly his free hand was gripping the bar.

"What are you trying to do to me?"

"Make you pay for dragging me onto this stupid ride."

"No more," he pleaded. "I promise. We're heading for my place the minute we're out of here."

"But I'm hungry," she said, pouting prettily.

"I'll feed you later. Lobster, hell, anything you want, just move your hand before you drive me out of my mind."

Tilly thrilled at the awesome power she held over Logan. It had never been like this with the others. Both Phil and Davey had held her firmly in their grasp until she'd lost all respect for herself. To be the one in control of the relationship was a powerful aphrodisiac.

By the time they were back on the ground, Tilly was as eager to leave as Logan. She changed her mind, however, as they raced past the booth selling cotton candy.

"Logan," she said breathlessly. She was forced into taking two steps to his. "I'd like some cotton candy."

Logan pretended to be exasperated, but the smile that wobbled at the edges of his mouth gave him away. "First you drive me wild with need, then you frustrate me within an inch of my life. Cotton candy?"

Tilly nodded.

"All right," he said, bringing out his wallet. "I might as well get a candy apple while I'm at it." He laid a couple of bills on the counter and kissed her neck. "Heaven knows I'm going to need my strength later."

"Hello, Tilly."

The friendly southern drawl caught Tilly off guard, and she turned around to find Mary Thompson standing behind her. "Mary," she said, genuinely pleased to see her newfound friend. "Hello."

"I thought that was you," Mary said. "You look wonderful. I wish I could get my hair to go like that."

"Listen, honey, two hours in a beautician's chair and a can of hairspray and they can do anything."

Mary laughed, and Logan cleared his throat, seeking an introduction.

"Mary, the man with candy apple smeared all over his face is Logan Anderson," she said, slipping her arm around his waist and easing him forward. "Logan, Mary Thompson, Travis's wife."

"I'm pleased to meet you," Logan said. "Are you enjoying the carnival?"

"I just finished an hour behind the raging waters of Gold Pan Creek," Mary said, looking mildly flustered. "In other words I was the fish in Fish."

"Oh, the kids' game."

Mary nodded. "Travis was going to meet me here at eight, but I can see he's behind schedule. Beth Ann's probably roped him into taking her on the merry-go-round. They wouldn't allow her on any of the other rides because her arm's in a cast."

"That's right," Logan said absently, "Dad mentioned Beth Ann to me recently. She broke her arm in the school yard last week, didn't she?"

Mary nodded. "And frightened Travis and me out of five years of our lives. She'll heal nicely, but I don't know if Travis or I'll recover anytime soon."

The sound of raised, angry voices captured Mary's attention, especially when one voice was so familiar. Tilly turned to discover Travis having a heated argument with Sheriff Tucker.

"What's happening?" Tilly asked.

"I don't know," Mary said, biting her lower lip. Her soft blue eyes revealed her worry. She loved him, Tilly noted, and was pleased.

Travis poked his finger in the sheriff's chest.

"If you'll excuse me," Mary said urgently.

"Of course."

"It was very nice to have met you, Mr. Anderson. Your father was wonderful with Beth Ann."

"Thank you."

By tacit agreement, Logan and Tilly edged toward Travis and Mary. By the time they reached the outskirts of the milling crowd, Tilly realized Sheriff Tucker was having as difficult a time holding his temper as Travis. His ears were bright red, and his jaw was tight and clenched.

"Listen here, Travis, you push this much further and I'm going to haul your butt to jail."

Tilly studied Travis. The cold look in his eyes seemed capable of freezing out the sun. His jaw resembled granite, and when he spoke, his words sounded like bits of chewed-off concrete. His hands were knotted into fists as if he would swing with the least provocation.

"Travis . . ." Mary was trying to gain his attention, but to no avail. "What is it? Tell me what's happened."

"Sheriff Tucker is closing the investigation into my parents' death," Jim Thompson announced. "He said he hasn't got a single lead. He's going to list the accident as unsolved and stuff it in a drawer somewhere."

"I don't have any choice," the sheriff said. "Even if we could afford to keep the case open, we don't have any clues. If you're looking for someone with Firestone radial tires, then I'd be dragging half the folks of Custer County in to be questioned. I can't do that."

With a grunt of disgust, Travis lowered his arms, pivoted sharply, and stalked toward the parking lot. Mary and the three children hurried along after him, having trouble keeping up with his lengthy strides. Mary's arms protected Beth Ann and the middle boy. The older youth held his back ramrod straight. The pain and outrage pulsated from him as clearly as it did from Travis.

Sheriff Tucker glanced about him, eyeing the crowd of curious onlookers that had formed to watch the scene.

"There isn't anything more I can do," the lawman stressed to no one in particular. His frustration seemed as keen as Travis's. Several folks were mumbling, and it seemed most sympathized with Travis. "Break it up, folks," he said, shooing them away. "There's nothing here to see."

Logan pitched his half-eaten apple into the waste bin. "Let's get out of here," he told Tilly, reaching for her hand.

"Do . . . you still want to go to your place?" Tilly whispered.

Logan glanced toward the retreating figure of Travis, Mary, and the children, and a shudder went through him. Slowly he shook his head. "Not now."

Fourteen

Travis couldn't sleep. Over and over again his mind replayed the horror of the night Lee and Janice had died. Every time he closed his eyes, the vision of his brother trying frantically to avoid a head-on collision seared into his brain. The tires screeching against the dry payment, Lee's cry for his wife to protect herself, screamed through his mind. He felt Lee's panic and terror as the car propelled off the road and swerved toward the tree. Unspeakable pain tore through him to think how Lee must have realized there was no avoiding the inevitable.

By four A.M. Travis acknowledged sleep was useless. The anger crawled like a serpent, winding its way around his soul. The frustration ate at the lining of his stomach like acid.

Had his brother screamed? Had Janice? Had their deaths been instantaneous, or had they suffered agonizing pain? Oh, God, please, please, Travis begged mutely. He didn't want to know.

But he had to know. To feel. The hate needed to be fed in order to thrive.

Sheriff Tucker had done his duty. The entire investigation had been wrapped interminably in red tape, bogged down in a sea of inefficiency and cold disregard. Two lives had been snuffed out that night, and no one seemed to care.

"I won't let it happen," he shouted, his fury propelling him upright. He rubbed his face with his hand, and the sound of his raspy breathing filled the silence of the night.

"Travis?" Mary's soft voice came to him in the fog of his agony.

"Go back to sleep," he said, and plowed his fingers through the unruly thatch of his hair.

"What's wrong?"

"Nothing," he said less vehemently. He hadn't meant for his restlessness to wake her.

She sat up, and her hand unerringly located his cheek in the still darkness. Her skin felt smooth and warm against his. It was all Travis could do not to drag her into his arms and breathe in her softness. She was his only link to reason; if he continued to dwell on Lee and Janice, he felt that he would surely go mad.

"Do you want to talk about it?" Mary asked with gentle concern.

Travis removed her hand; the temptation to accept her comfort was too great. "No. This doesn't concern you."

"It's about Lee and Janice, isn't it?" she asked in a whisper. "And what Sheriff Tucker said."

"I told you," he said forcefully, "this doesn't concern you." He tossed aside the covers, leaped from the bed, and reached for his jeans. He yearned to immerse his pain in Mary's gentleness. Her love would heal him, her love would make him whole again. He was in desperate need of her softness, of her comfort. With everything in him, he longed to bury himself in her warm body, seek the emotional sanctuary she offered.

Instead he was forced to plunge headfirst into the pulsing bitterness that surrounded him. He dared not release it lest he forget his promise to Lee, to the children, and to himself. He'd find whoever was responsible, whatever the price.

He stood by the kitchen counter in the darkness while the coffee brewed. Mary wandered into the room, dressed in her housecoat. He watched as her shadow migrated against the opposite wall, and it seemed that she was moving in slow motion. She stood directly behind him, looped her arms around his waist, and pressed her head to his back.

"It's all right, you know," she assured him in a delicate whisper.

"What is?" he growled. "That Lee and Janice are dead? Is that what's all right? Well, it isn't with me. Ask Jim if he's willing to forget it. Ask Scotty and Beth Ann." He released himself from her hold. Her touch was too potent to ignore. He had to push her away, although it hurt him more than she'd ever know.

He needed her then, her body, but it wouldn't be love, it'd be sex. Brutal and demanding. Mary deserved better than that, far better. He refused to vent his frustration on her, refused to force the brunt of his pain on her fragile body.

"Go back to bed."

"Please, I want to help."

"Just do as I ask," he snapped. "Don't fight me, just for once."

She stepped away from him as though she'd been burned. Even in the darkness he could see the tears glistening in her eyes as she spun away and returned to their bedroom.

Travis exhaled and toyed with the idea of following her and apologizing. Loving Mary was too damn easy, and he needed to remember, not forget. He couldn't afford to go soft now, not when his sinister mood had to be fed. He couldn't allow himself the luxury of burying his mission. Everyone else had given up finding Lee's killer, but he wouldn't. He'd die first. The sooner Mary accepted the inevitability of that, the better.

Travis remained in the kitchen for several hours. He sat at the table, his hands cupping a hot coffee mug. The heat in his palms radiated up his arms.

Jim was the first one awake, and Travis barked out the oldest boy's chores without so much as looking at the youth. Jim didn't utter a word before dressing and heading for the barn. The slamming door was the only indication Jim gave of his feelings.

As soon as the back door closed, Scotty strolled into the kitchen in his flannel pajamas. It looked almost as if the boy were sleepwalking. He yawned loudly and sank down in front of the cupboard. Apparently Scotty was unaware of Travis because he reached for a box of cold cereal. He opened the lid and inserted his hand. From the looks of it, there wasn't much left because his elbow disappeared inside the cardboard box and when he withdrew his hand, his fingers were coated in crumbs, which he took delight in licking.

"Get dressed," Travis snapped unreasonably.

Scotty started and turned around. "I'm hungry," he said.

"Get dressed and then you can eat."

"But—"

"Don't argue with your uncle," Mary's gentle voice intervened. "By the time you're back I'll have toast ready for you."

"With strawberry jam?"

"With strawberry jam," Mary promised.

The muffled sound of her slippers moved behind Travis. "There's no need to snap at the children," she said evenly, without censure.

"I'll do as I damn well please."

Her sigh suggested a wealth of impatience. "You're behaving like an angry bull, Travis Thompson. I suggest you go about your day before we do or say something we'll both regret."

Travis knew she was right. He didn't like admitting it, and wouldn't, except he didn't have the energy or the desire to tangle with Mary. He was angry and irrational, and he knew it, but he had no intention of altering his mood.

"I'll be chopping wood."

"Good," she said approvingly. "Maybe you can vent some of that frustration with an ax. I'll keep the children out of your way."

He nodded, carried his coffee with him, and slammed out of the house. He passed Jim in the yard. The boy glared at him with undisguised malice, which was fine with Travis.

Mary's shoulders sagged with relief when Travis vacated the kitchen. He was in one bear of a mood. She realized he was dealing with the frustration of his talk with Sheriff Tucker. With the local police working on the matter, Travis had been content to sit back and let them do whatever they could to find Lee and Janice's killer. The law had access to equipment and information unavailable to a cattle rancher.

Now that the investigation was closed, Travis would want to take it up on his own. He'd never accept Sheriff Tucker's decree. Nor would he give up. He meant to find the driver responsible for his brother's death, and heaven help whoever stood in his way.

"Is Uncle Travis gone?" Scotty asked, sticking his head around the hallway corner. "He nearly bit off my head."

"He got up on the wrong side of the bed, is all," Mary explained. She doubted that Travis had slept. She'd wakened several times during the night, and each time he'd been awake. He'd tried to let her think he was asleep, but she'd known otherwise.

The back door opened and Jim walked slowly into the house.

"I think Jim got up on the wrong bed, too," Scotty whispered.

"The wrong what?" Jim demanded.

"Is anyone interested in pancakes?" Mary asked, hoping to divert an argument. Like Travis, Jim had taken the sheriff's news hard.

"Me," Scotty piped up enthusiastically.

Jim shrugged.

"I like pancakes," Beth Ann said, pulling out the chair and climbing onto the seat, "but I like them best the way Mommy used to make them."

"Yeah," Scotty agreed, his eyes growing wide. "I'd forgotten. Mom used to cook them in weird shapes, then she made up funny names for them and told us how brave we were for gobbling up monsters."

"It was stupid," Jim muttered.

"It wasn't," Scotty cried, refusing to allow his older brother to destroy the happy memory. "It was fun."

"That's because you're a kid."

"Jim," Mary said in her finest disciplinary tone, leveling the full force of her gaze on him. "Drop it."

"I've forgotten lots of things about Mommy," Beth Ann said sadly, and laid her head on the table. "Sometimes I forget what she looked like."

"Her picture's in the living room," Mary reminded her gently.

"She didn't look like that . . . exactly," Scotty explained. "Her hair was shorter, and her eyes . . ."

"Mom wore glasses," Jim added.

"I don't want to forget Mommy," Beth Ann whined. "I want to remember Daddy, too." It sounded as though she were close to tears.

"Dad's easy to remember," Scotty said, brightening. "Uncle Travis and Dad look alike."

"Travis isn't our father." Jim's words bordered on desperation. "He'll never be our father. Never."

"What can I do to help you remember?" Mary wanted to know, unwilling to let the precious memories the children had of their parents fade.

"I want to go see them," Scotty suggested, and his voice wobbled with emotion.

"You can't, stupid, they're dead."

"Jim," Mary pleaded. "Don't be so cruel. Scotty knows that, and so does Beth Ann. Your brother's asking to go to the cemetery and visit their graves, aren't you, Scotty?"

The eight-year-old nodded and kept his gaze lowered. Mary noticed the tears that brimmed in his eyes and the boy's effort to hide them from his sarcastic older brother. When Jim wasn't looking, Scotty rubbed the back of his hand under his nose.

"As soon as we've finished with breakfast, we'll drive out to the cemetery."

"I'm not going."

Mary's gaze sought out the twelve-year-old. How cold his eyes were, not unlike Travis's had been that morning. His young jaw was clenched, and he seemed to be waiting for Mary's comment, possibly her insistence.

"I'm not going to force you," she assured him.

"It wouldn't do you any good, even if you tried. My parents aren't there, anyway. What good is looking at a lump in the ground going to do? It isn't going to help Beth Ann remember Mom and Dad any better. All it'll do is make us miss them more. If Scotty wants to be so dumb, fine, but I won't." With that he slammed out the door.

A strained painful silence followed his departure.

"Why's Jim so mad?" Beth Ann wanted to know, cocking her head to one side as if that would help her understand.

"Because he misses your mom and dad so much," Mary offered, feeling Jim's pain as strongly as if it were her own. How vulnerable he was, standing on the threshold of his teen years, trapped and miserable. Too old to suck his thumb like Beth Ann or cry like Scotty, but too young to carry such a heavy load of anguish all on his own. Her heart went out to him, but she didn't know how to reach him.

"I . . . I don't think I want pancakes." Scotty's words brought an added ache to her heart.

"I don't, either," Beth Anne echoed, and Mary noted the five-year-old was back to sucking her thumb.

She poured herself a cup of coffee while the two youngest children ate their cereal. She wasn't sure she was doing the right thing by taking them to the graveyard. Instead of soothing their loss, it might rip open half-healed wounds, destroy the trust she'd worked so hard to construct since her arrival. As much as she loved the children, she'd never be their biological mother. She was a sorry replacement, and visiting the gravesite might well remind them of that.

"I'm ready," Beth Ann announced shortly after she'd finished breakfast. She came out of the bedroom, hauling her backpack, which seemed to be stuffed with a wide assortment of items.

"What are you taking?" Mary asked.

"The things I want to show Mom and Dad," Beth Ann announced proudly. She held up a molded clay pumpkin that she'd made in school for Halloween. A quick inspection revealed several paintings, including the one of the five stick figures that had touched Mary's heart so profoundly.

Scotty hesitated, as though reconsidering the wisdom of such a visit.

"You don't have to go," Mary felt obliged to tell him.

"I know, but I am," he said bravely.

Mary reached for her own coat. The sky was overcast, and a thick frost had settled over the ranch like a shiny white quilt. Mary strongly suspected it would snow soon.

She debated whether to tell Travis her destination, then decided against it. He was working with a vengeance in the yard, splitting a pile of wood. He'd removed his jacket and was swinging the ax with an energy that defied description. He wouldn't be able to maintain the killing pace for long.

For a moment she watched, fascinated to see his muscles ripple with each swing of the ax. He seemed to be unaware she was there, confirming her suspicions.

Beth Ann and Scotty climbed onto the backseat. Mary had just started the ignition when Jim came racing out of the house. His blue jacket was in his hands as if the decision had recently been made. He didn't look at Mary as he scrambled across the yard, threw open the passenger door of the car, and climbed inside.

"I didn't think you were coming," Scotty said, sounding inordinately pleased his brother had chosen to join them.

"I'm not staying alone with Uncle Travis. Not when he's being a major jerk."

Jim didn't look at Mary, as though he were afraid she'd say something that would embarrass him. Mary's heart constricted. She knew Travis's mood was a convenient excuse and loved Jim for being man enough to follow his heart. She yearned to tell the boy how proud she was of him, but she couldn't. Not then, but sometime later, perhaps a few months down the road, she'd be able to speak freely.

Grandview's cemetery was located on the outskirts of town, in what looked to have once been a churchyard. Apparently the church had been torn down sometime in the past, but Mary could see where it had once reigned over the area.

The cemetery was edged by a three-foot-high rock fence. Sunlight splashed and glistened on the frost-covered lawn. Large tombstones, some as high as seven feet, haphazardly speckled the rolling landscape.

"Mom and Dad are over here," Jim said, determinedly leading the way. His footprints left deep grooves in the frozen grass. "Here." He stopped, pointing toward the ground.

Mary looked down at the two plain marble markers. She read the simple words engraved in the stone. Their names, the date of their births, and their deaths. That was all that was listed. There wasn't a Bible verse, as there had been with her brother and parents. No epitaphs or words of shared wisdom. It seemed like so little for two lives that had had such a strong impact on Mary's own.

The tears came as a surprise to Mary. They seemed to leap into her eyes even before she was aware the emotion was there. They came hard and fast, as if they'd been held at bay far too long.

Mary wished it were possible for her to speak to the children's mother. She would have loved to tell Janice what a beautiful job she'd done. This woman who'd given birth to these three seemed very real to Mary. From the little she'd learned about Janice Thompson, Mary knew she would gladly have counted her as a friend.

"Hi, Mom and Dad." Scotty spoke first. His hands were folded as though he were in church and about to pray. "I miss you a whole lot. Do you miss me?"

"Of course they don't," Jim said with a snicker.

Mary reached for Jim's shoulder and squeezed, effectively silencing him.

"I made a goal in soccer on the playground, even though I was playing with the fourth-graders," Scotty continued, and then cast his older brother a dirty look. "Jim got in trouble because he was fighting, and Uncle Travis got real mad at him, and then Mary got mad at Uncle Travis. You know about Mary, don't you?"

"Uncle Travis married her," Beth Ann explained. "We were real glad because he was having a bad time with us. I don't think he knew what to do with kids."

"He couldn't cook, either," Scotty interjected. "And he was extra rude to Mrs. Johnson, and the social workers didn't like him very much. Everything's much better now that Mary's here."

"I broke my arm," Beth Ann told them, and held out her right arm, encased in the plaster cast, as though waiting for them to comment. "It hurt worse than anything. I tried real hard not to cry, but it hurt too bad. Doc Anderson hurt me more. I don't like him anymore."

Mary moved behind Beth Ann and cupped the small shoulders with her hands.

"Do you get to talk to God?" Scotty asked.

Jim snickered again, but Scotty ignored him.

"Jim's mad almost all the time. The next time you talk to God ask him if He can help Jim not be so mad."

Beth Ann stuck her hand in her bag and brought out a blue ribbon she'd been awarded for knowing all the sounds of the letters of the alphabet. She squatted down and placed it on the marble headstone.

"I want Mommy and Daddy to have it," she explained, looking up at Mary.

Mary nodded her approval, knowing deep within her heart how very proud and pleased Lee and Janice would be. "Do you want to say anything?" she asked Jim after a silent moment.

The youth shook his head. "No."

She was sure that he did, but he wasn't comfortable doing it when his brother, sister, and Mary were there listening. "I'll take Scotty and Beth Ann to the car," Mary whispered, sensitive to his unspoken needs. "You can meet us there in a few minutes."

Mary steered the two younger children toward the station wagon. "What's Jim doing?" Beth Ann quizzed, looking over her shoulder toward her older brother. "We aren't going to leave him, are we?"

"No," Mary assured her, "we won't leave him."

"You shouldn't have tattled on Jim," Beth Ann said, glaring at her older brother. "He's not mean all the time. Just sometimes."

Scotty climbed onto the backseat and reached for the seat belt. Snapping it into place, he released a deep sigh. "I feel better," he announced as though recovering from a lengthy illness.

"Me too," Beth Ann echoed. "Can we come again?"

Mary nodded. Inexplicably she felt much better, too.

Jim joined them a few minutes later, and Mary noticed his eyes were red. She yearned to comfort him but knew he wouldn't welcome her touch. Given the opportunity, he would shun her the same way Travis had earlier that morning.

When they returned to the ranch, Mary was surprised to find Travis still chopping wood. Heaven only knew how he'd been able to maintain such a killing pace. Just watching him made her want to cry out that he stop.

"Go inside," she instructed the children.

She waited until they were in the house before she called to him. "Travis, for the love of heaven, stop."

He pretended not to hear her.

"Travis, please." She tried again, more desperate this time. It was killing her to see his mindless struggle with emotional and physical pain.

"Mary." Standing on the porch, Jim called for her. "There's someone on the phone for you."

"For me?" Mildly surprised, she pointed to herself. There were only a handful of people she knew in town. She ran up the steps and into the house.

"This is Mary Thompson," she said into the receiver.

"Hi, it's Tilly."

"Is everything all right?" It sounded as though the waitress had been crying. She certainly didn't seem to be her chipper self.

"I'm fine. I guess I caught a cold last night at the carnival. It's nothing. I . . . was wondering if we could have lunch together one day next week. There's something I'd like to talk to you about . . . that is, if you have the time."

"I'd like that very much," Mary said, touched by the invitation. "Would Wednesday be all right?" She had several library books to return and was hoping to do some shopping. Spending the afternoon with Tilly held a good deal of appeal.

"Great, I'll see you on Wednesday, then."

"You get over that cold, okay?"

"Sure," Tilly said almost flippantly. "I'll be fine by then."

"Good."

When Mary replaced the receiver she turned to find Jim standing at the back window, studying Travis. When he found her watching him, he released the curtain and turned away.

"I'm going to my room."

"That's fine."

"I know it's fine," he snapped, and raced down the hallway as though he couldn't get away from her fast enough.

Mary walked over to where Jim had been standing. Travis's arm swung the ax with punishing force against a fat section of log. The force of the blow was so strong that two thick slices fell away.

He paused, leaned against the ax handle, reached for another section of wood, and placed it on top of the block. He staggered but caught himself.

Mary decided to try once more. She had to, otherwise she feared he'd grow careless and hurt himself.

The sun hid behind a thick gray cloud as Mary stepped outside the house. Standing on the top step, she gazed into the angry sky. Fat drops of rain fell onto the dry, moisture-hungry ground. Small round puddles formed in the dirt.

"Travis," she shouted, "you've got to stop."

Again it was as though he hadn't heard her. His actions had slowed now as physical exhaustion set in. It was almost more than he could do to lift the ax. He seemed to stagger under the weight of it. His body rocked right, he caught himself, then he rocked left, only to brace himself before falling once more.

Mary hurried down the steps. "Travis, please."

He ignored her, lifting the ax high above his head and letting it slam down against the wood.

Wobbling, he fell to his knees. Mary rushed to him and removed the ax from his unresisting hands. Kneeling beside him in the soft dirt, she wrapped her arms around his middle and held on to him.

His breath came in strangled gasps as if he couldn't get enough oxygen to fill his lungs. It was a miracle he hadn't collapsed earlier. Her heart felt wide open and vulnerable, heating with her love for him, with her desire to help him deal with his pain. He made it so difficult, rejecting her at every turn. No longer. She couldn't allow this torment to continue. Somehow she had to find a way to reach him.

Suddenly she couldn't bear it. Tears flowed from her eyes.

"Travis, dear God." Her hand trembled as she reached up and cupped his face. Her touch seemed to ripple through him, and with it came a sob imbedded deep within his chest. It worked its way upward and escaped on a low, howling moan of such grief that Mary buried her face in his neck, sobbing.

The rain pounded the earth, first in greedy drops that teased the soil, then in a wild torrent. Within moments Mary's hair was plastered to her face. The cold water ran unrestrained down the small of her back. She hardly noticed.

Travis's shoulders shook, and the low moans eased into sobs that rocked his torso with such force, it was as if he were being lifted physically from the ground.

"Why Lee?" he shouted with such vengeance and fury that Mary gasped. "Why not me?" he demanded.

His arms reached for Mary, and he hauled her against him with enough force that the air was knocked from her lungs. Burying his face against her shoulder, he wept as she'd never heard a man weep before. His sobs tore at her soul. Over and over she stroked the back of his head and between her own tears whispered reassurances.

The sound of the downpour obliterated her words, she realized, but it didn't matter.

Grief seemed to claw at him. She circled his neck with her arms, holding his head against her, weeping with him. His tears fell without restraint now, without thought, mingling with hers.

Travis raised his mouth to hers, and the kisses were wild. His lips feasted on hers, his passion a greed he couldn't seem to satisfy. Their tongues warred and caressed and danced with each other. The rough fierceness of his touch frightened her, yet she trusted him completely. In her heart she knew Travis would never knowingly hurt her.

When he tore his mouth from hers, his breathing was labored and erratic. He clung to her, his arms protecting her from the cold and the rain.

"He had everything to live for," Travis whispered. "A home, Janice, the children. He loved them so much . . . they were his life."

"I know."

"God in heaven, why would anyone want to kill him?"

Mary had no answers, no solutions. All that was left were questions.

Fifteen

Travis needed Mary again. No more than a few hours had passed since they'd last made love, yet his body ached with renewed desire. He was a beast, a sexual glutton. His wife was a lady; he couldn't wake her and ask that they make love again. Not until a respectable time had passed.

If he did wake her, she would know how weak he was when it came to loving and needing her. She'd realize how badly he craved her touch.

This crippling desire was something he didn't understand himself. Mary had awakened his vulnerability and made him feel again. Hell if he knew what to do about it. He didn't like being vulnerable. If he was going to concentrate on emotions, then they should be anger and vengeance, not her goodness, not her sweetness.

When he was buried deep inside Mary he felt

powerful and alive. Her softness wrapped silken cords around his heart. The softness of her touch, the softness of her life, lured him like nothing he'd ever experienced.

He'd never needed her more than he did right then. This craving went much deeper than the physical. He craved her softness as an absolution, to obliterate his hate, if only for a moment, because the price of maintaining it was so damn costly.

Stuffing a groan, he rolled onto his side, away from her, hoping that would help. He closed his eyes and forced his mind to other matters. The renegade wolf had struck again. Rob Bradley had phoned with the news. It couldn't continue. If the U.S. Fish and Wildlife Service couldn't capture the beast, then the local cattlemen had no choice but to take matters into their own hands. That, however, could be an expensive proposition, especially if they were caught.

The mattress shifted as Mary rolled, tucking her warm body against him. Her breasts flattened against his back. Her nipples puckered and seared his flesh. Travis stifled a groan.

"Mary," he whispered, and faced her. His hand cupped her breast, lifting it in his palm.

"Hmm?"

"I'm having a bit of a problem sleeping." If ever he'd made an understatement, this was it.

"Hmm? Do you want me to get you something?" she asked sleepily.

"Not exactly, but you might be able to help."

"Okay."

Okay! She didn't even know what she was agreeing to and yet she was willing. From the time she'd flown to Montana to be with him and the children, Travis had recognized that he'd found a rare and good woman. He hadn't fully appreciated how much until this moment.

His mouth claimed hers in a moist, gentle kiss, and his hand eased past the elastic waistband of her pajamas. He flattened his palm against the smooth, heated skin of her abdomen, not daring to go farther just yet until she understood his unspoken request.

"You want to make love . . . again?" She sounded both surprised and pleased.

Travis would have preferred not to voice his wants, especially since he was self-conscious about it. His teeth captured her earlobe, and he sucked on it while inching his fingers lower until he encountered the downy curls that nestled her femininity.

Mary kissed him, her hunger growing as he eased between her legs. Travis felt humble with the strength of his desire. Grateful for this woman who so willingly gave of herself.

They sighed their pleasure in unison. Travis gathered her in his arms, almost afraid to breathe, so intense was his gratification.

He held Mary for a long time afterward, his breathing hard. She pressed her mouth to his throat.

"Can you sleep now, cowboy?"

He chuckled, warmed by her love. "Like a log."

"Me too."

Travis didn't know who drifted off first, but when he woke, he couldn't remember a time he'd slept better.

Mary felt wonderful. Clara Morgan had called to invite her to attend the monthly meeting of the Grange ladies. The older woman's invitation came on the heels of Tilly's offer to join her for lunch.

Mary felt she was making friends. She longed to become an accepted member of the community. She continued attending church, but most of the meetings were in the evenings, and there always seemed to be so much to do after dinner. Perhaps later, when she was more familiar with the roads and unpredictable driving conditions of late autumn and winter, she'd join the choir.

Monday and Tuesday were her busy days. She did the wash and the deeper cleaning and baked fresh cinnamon rolls, which generally disappeared by Wednesday afternoon.

While the rolls baked, Mary wrote Georgeanne a long, chatty letter, telling her about the Harvest Moon Festival plus a detailed synopsis of the children's activities. As she reread her letter, Mary realized how much she sounded like a proud mother, bragging about her children. It was the way she felt. She was happy, happier than she'd anticipated.

She sat chewing on the end of her pen as she mulled over the changes in her life since she'd married Travis.

He was a card-carrying chauvinist, but that wasn't unexpected. She'd known that before she married him; indeed, she'd often gained a good deal of amusement from his attitude. There were times, however, when he drove her to distraction with his high-handed notions.

Mary frowned and held on to the pen, rubbing it between her palms. Her husband never had been the talkative sort, but he seemed even less so lately. She knew his brother's death continued to weigh heavily on his mind. He hadn't said anything to her, but she knew he'd contacted a couple of private investigators, although he hadn't shared with her what he'd learned, if anything.

Any communication between her and Travis recently had taken place in bed. There had to be a physical limit to how much a man could perform sexually. If Mary hadn't known better, she would've suspected he'd been looking to set some sort of world's record.

For the last three nights they'd made love when they went to bed, and later he'd wake her again, wanting her, often with a desperation that rocked her. He appeared apologetic about his need, embarrassed, and even a bit shy. Mary didn't understand it, and she felt equally certain Travis didn't, either.

If she were more experienced about men, if she'd been in other relationships, she might have been more insightful. She guessed that in some way his sexual prowess was connected to his anger over what had happened in the investigation involving his brother and sister-in-law. She wasn't sure how the two were linked, but she felt strongly that they were.

Twice now, when she woke in the morning, she learned he'd already been up, eaten, and left the house. His disappearing act maddened her. She felt emotionally bruised and abandoned. If she hadn't believed he was at a loss to explain his strange behavior himself, she would have taken offense.

Each night she meant to talk to him about his early morning habits. It would be nice if they talked before he left the house. But when she slipped into bed, Travis was there waiting, eager, needing her. Her irritation evaporated under the wonder of his kisses and the golden feel of his hands over her. Afterward, content in his arms, she felt drowsy with love and disinclined to bring up any unpleasantness.

Soon, she promised herself, she'd talk to him soon. Having reached an agreement with herself, she returned to her letter to Georgeanne.

"Tilly," Sally called as she slipped past, carrying three orders of fried chicken with mashed potatoes and Martha's special gravy. "Martha wants to talk to you when you've got a free minute."

"She does?" Tilly tucked the pencil behind her ear. "Did she say what it was about?"

"No. Don't look so worried, kid, she needs you more than you need her."

Tilly sincerely doubted that. She fretted until the dinner crowd had thinned out, then headed toward the kitchen. Martha was busy giving orders to the relief chef. The older woman was one of the best cooks Tilly had ever seen, but she never ate her own food, or so it seemed. She couldn't remain this thin and sample her own cooking. She wore her gray hair short and in her white uniform resembled a nurse more than she did a cook. "Sally said you wanted to see me."

"Let's talk in the back room," Martha suggested. "Grab yourself a cup of coffee."

"I didn't do anything wrong, did I?" Tilly was tense and worried. She couldn't help it. She wasn't making money hand over fist, but she liked the job and the town and was hoping to stick around for a while. A long while, especially if Logan was going to be an important part of her life.

Martha led her into a small storage area. She'd set up a desk and did her paperwork there among rows of huge cans of fruit and vegetables. A bulletin board posted on the door listed shift times.

"Sit down," Martha said, motioning toward a dilapidated chair that looked like a Goodwill reject.

Tilly took the chair. "Are you going to fire me?" She'd rather know that flat out. No need prettying it up with a bunch of fancy words when it all boiled down to the same thing. She wasn't needed any longer.

"Don't worry, kid, you've got a job here for as long as you want."

Tilly relaxed so much that she nearly sagged off her seat.

"Something's been troubling you lately, though, hasn't it?"

Tilly's relief was short-lived. "What makes you ask?"

Martha chuckled. "I got eyes. You've been tense and unhappy. Is it Doc's boy? Has he been doing you wrong?"

Tilly hid a smile at the old-fashioned term. It wasn't her Logan had hurt. Each day the same nightmare greeted her when she woke. She could barely look at Travis or those three precious children without wanting to weep.

For days she'd tried to convince herself that she'd misread Logan the night of the Harvest Moon Festival, but no amount of self-talk could persuade her she was wrong. After listening to Travis and Sheriff Tucker's argument, Logan had changed. It was like he'd been hit with a flu bug. He'd gone pale and had started to shake. When she asked, he'd claimed he wasn't feeling well. Which was true enough.

He'd brought her to his house as promised, but they hadn't made love. Instead Tilly had lain in his arms all night while he'd clung to her. She swore neither one of them got a wink of sleep.

"Tilly?" Martha asked again, pulling her from her musings. "Has that lawyer man been using you?"

"No," she said, surprised by how strained and unnatural her voice sounded.

"You love him?"

Tilly lowered her gaze and nodded.

"You sleeping with him?"

"That's none of your business."

The older woman chuckled. "You're right, acourse. Besides, it's written all over you. Naturally you're sleeping with him. What red-blooded girl wouldn't fall in love with that handsome cuss? Just be careful, you hear? Them lawyers can be slick with words, and I don't want you hurt. Understand?"

"I'll be careful," Tilly promised.

"Now cheer up. You're much too pretty to be so unhappy. Smile, child."

Tilly did, then laughed and hugged the cook who was more of a friend than she'd ever realized.

Mary was helping Scotty with his homework when she heard the back door close. Travis had seemed even more pensive than usual over dinner, adding only a comment or two to the mealtime conversation. Scotty and Beth Ann had filled the silence with their happy chatter. Scotty had gotten a good grade on his math paper and bragged about it for several minutes. Beth Ann was excited, too. She'd been chosen to play the part of a rabbit in a dramatization that afternoon. She'd loved it and had decided to become a Hollywood actress. Even Jim seemed more agreeable than usual. At least he hadn't purposely started an argument. It had been a red-letter day, or would have been if it hadn't been for Travis.

"Where'd Travis go?" Mary asked.

Jim was sitting at the table with his homework. "I don't know. He didn't say," he answered without looking up.

"He probably went out to the barn," she suggested, more to herself than the boy.

"If that's the case, he took the truck."

Mary was stunned. Travis had left without a word to anyone? Without even letting her know where he was headed? It was as if whatever he did was his business. As if she were nothing more than his housekeeper, certainly no one he need concern himself with. No matter what he said or did, she'd be there to care for the children, cook his meals, see to the house, and satisfy his sexual needs. The setup was ideal. For him!

Her head buzzing, Mary sank onto the chair next to Jim. She crossed her arms and tapped her foot, the rhythm fast-paced and frenzied.

"Mary," Jim cried, slamming his pencil against the tabletop. "Stop, would you?"

"Stop what?"

"Your foot. It's knocking against the table."

"Oh," she said, surprised, and stood up. "I'm sorry." She crossed the room, brushed the hair from her face, and reached for her coat.

"Where are you going?"

Mary jerked her arms into the satin-lined sleeves. "Outside." She wasn't entirely sure what she intended to do, but it was necessary to do something. Anything was better than sitting in the house stewing. For days she'd avoided confronting Travis in front of the children so as not to upset them again. That had been a mistake.

The wind was cold and cutting, whipping around her like a blue northerner. Stuffing her hands deep inside her lined pockets, she hunched her shoulders against the wintry blast and headed toward the barn.

Jim was right. Travis's truck was gone, and everything was surprisingly quiet in the barn. She traipsed from one end to the other, thinking, hoping she'd gain some clue, some indication of what had been so important for Travis to leave without a word.

Naturally there was nothing; she didn't really believe there would have been. He'd done it on purpose—a slight to let her know how unimportant she was in his life. She bit her lower lip. Damn, but it hurt, it really hurt.

As she left the barn she saw Beth Ann's anxious face watching her from the kitchen window. Mary waved, then raced across the yard and into the house.

Scotty met her at the door. "Jim said you were running away."

"Jim," Mary said sternly, "you know that isn't true." She squatted down and hugged both Beth Ann and Scotty. They wrapped their arms around her neck and squeezed tight. "I'd never leave you, not ever," she whispered.

"Maybe you wouldn't," Jim said coldly, slapping his textbook closed. He stood with enough energy for the chair to topple backward. "But Travis would."

"That's not true."

"He doesn't keep his promises. Not a single one, not ever." With that Jim raced down the hallway to his room. Mary flinched at the sound of the slamming door. She debated whether she should follow him, have this out now, then decided against it. Jim's problem evolved from his relationship with Travis and the promise to find whoever had been responsible for Lee and Janice's death. Her heart softened at the pain she read in the twelve-year-old. Confronting him now, without Travis there, could prove to be another mistake in a growing list.

"Someone's here," Scotty said, pushing aside the window curtain and peering out intently.

"Who is it?" Beth Ann crowded next to her brother.

"Children, please," Mary said, steering them away from the window. "It's not polite to stare at visitors."

"I didn't see who it was. I don't think you should open the door." Scotty rushed ahead to the back door and spread his arms, blocking Mary's way.

"Scotty, you're being ridiculous."

Her curiosity aroused, Mary glanced out the window and recognized Logan Anderson, the man who'd been with Tilly at the Harvest Moon Festival. They'd talked only briefly, but Mary had liked him. It was plain Tilly did, too. Her friend had glowed with happiness.

"You don't need to worry, Scotty, it's Mr. Anderson," Mary said, opening the door to Logan.

Scotty eyed the man suspiciously until he recognized him. "We saw you at the carnival, didn't we?"

"That's right." Logan smiled down at the eight--year-old. His gaze lingered momentarily on the boy before shifting to Beth Ann. Mary wasn't an expert at reading people, but she sensed a deep pain in Logan as he studied the children.

"Would you like a cup of coffee?"

"No thanks," Logan answered, pulling his attention away from Scotty and Beth. "I've come to talk to Travis."

"I'm sorry, he isn't here. I'll be happy to give him a message if you'd like."

"No, no," Logan said quickly—too quickly, it seemed to Mary. Funny, but he looked almost relieved that Travis wasn't available. She wasn't sure what to make of it.

"I'll tell him you stopped by."

"That would be great, thanks, Mary." He patted the top of Beth Ann's blond head and shook hands with Scotty, then looked to Mary. "It was good to see you again."

"You too." She opened the door for him and watched for several minutes until he'd climbed inside his car. It wasn't until after he'd left that Mary realized how quick his steps had been as he'd walked away.

How very strange.

The Cattlemen's Association meeting had dragged on far longer than usual. Several of the ranchers were up in arms with the wolf problem. Travis addressed the issue himself, suggesting the cattlemen trap the wolf themselves, and a number of the others agreed with him.

The U.S. Fish and Wildlife Service had sent a representative to reassure the cattlemen that everything possible was being done. It would be only a matter of time before the wolf was located and moved to another area, he promised.

"A matter of time" didn't sit any better with Travis's neighbors than it did with him. The time for talking was past. They'd given the federal boys the opportunity to handle matters their own way. It hadn't worked. Not even a helicopter had been able to flush out the cagey beast.

Like the others, Travis had already lost several calves. His patience had long since worn thin. If the wolf moved onto his land again, he was going after it himself.

The meeting broke up some time later, and Travis drove to the Logger with several of his friends. The cattlemen convened in groups, eager to share their dissatisfaction with what had taken place at the meeting.

Larry Martin sat on one side of Travis at the bar. Rob Bradley was on the other side. The three ordered beer.

"I'm telling you right now," Larry said, red-faced and angry, "I'm not going to worry about protecting any wolf. If this keeps up much longer, my cattle are going to be an endangered species."

"Amen." Rob raised his bottle in salute.

"I can't afford any more of these losses."

"You?" Travis muttered, as disgruntled as his friends. "No one can."

Stan, the Logger bartender, walked over to the three men, drying a shot glass with the frayed edge of the white apron tied about his waist.

"What are you three grumbling about now?"

"We got troubles," Larry explained.

Stan laughed. "That's what I understand. I heard you boys got yourself a wolf who hankers after veal."

"You'd think he'd be so fat by now, he wouldn't be able to run," Bill muttered, and downed another swallow of his beer. When he finished he slammed the glass against the counter. "I'll take another."

Stan eyed the others. "What about you two?"

"Sure," Larry agreed.

"Travis?" Stan held up a third bottle.

"No thanks."

Stan looked surprised, then chuckled. "Ah, I forgot. Word has it you found yourself a wife."

"You heard right," Travis returned without emotion. "Her name's Mary."

"Cooks like a dream," Larry said, placing his fingertips against his lips and making a loud smacking sound.

"Yeah, but what's she like in bed?"

It seemed all three men were studying him. The question angered him, but if he showed his feelings, they'd take delight in riling him more, so he shrugged. He didn't mind bragging about his conquests, but his wife was another matter.

Stan rested his arms against the bar and leaned toward Travis. His eyes twinkled with curiosity. "She got long legs?"

"Nope," Larry answered for him. "I swear she only stands this high." He put his hand out level with his hip.

His friend's assessment disturbed Travis. Sure, Mary was small, but she made up for that in a hundred different ways. "She may be tiny, but then I've found there are advantages to petite women," Travis supplied.

"Oh?" He had their full attention now.

"Like what?"

Travis regretted having fallen prey to their questions. Every time he opened his mouth he dug himself in deeper. "When I put that ad in the paper," he said, "I thought I was getting the short end of this deal."

"You mean you didn't?"

Travis grinned sheepishly and pushed his empty beer bottle toward the bartender. "Just think, when I get home tonight, I've got a warm, willing body waiting for me." That should shut up his friends.

"You're putting us on."

Travis shook his head. "Have I ever lied to you before?"

Larry slowly shook his head. "Never."

"I'm not now."

Rob turned to Larry. "You believe him?"

"I don't know. Travis ain't usually one to lie."

"Yeah, but he's never had a wife before, either. A woman can do strange things to a man."

Both were studying Travis closely.

"My guess is he's telling us the truth."

"Yeah," Rob said with a sigh, "you could be right."

Larry just stared at him, the bottle raised halfway to his mouth.

Travis slapped some change on the counter. "I'll be seeing you boys later."

"Later," Stan muttered, and raised his hand in farewell.

Travis stepped outside and into his truck, pleased with himself. Talking about his private life with Mary was something he was uncomfortable with, but he couldn't have his friends thinking she'd twisted him around her little finger, even if it was partially true.

As for that part about her in bed waiting for him, he hoped it was true. Talking about their sex life had made him eager, but there wasn't a time lately that he hadn't been. This intense need for the physical side of their union continued to plague him. He felt like a kid with a hormone problem.

Now more than ever he felt it was time he asserted his independence from Mary. That was the reason he'd left for the Cattlemen's Association meeting without telling her. Keeping her guessing would be good for their marriage.

He was traveling well past the speed limit now in his eagerness to get home. A hot river of desire pulsed through him as his mind filled with images of Mary in his bed, eager for his arrival home. Within minutes they'd be making love and she'd fill the aching emptiness that closed in on him at night.

The house was dark when he pulled into the yard. He glanced at his watch, surprised to realize it was nearly midnight. Not wanting to disturb the kids, he moved through the kitchen without turning on the lights. Just beyond the kitchen, he removed his boots and slipped silently down the hallway.

He opened the bedroom door and saw Mary, under the window, silhouetted in the moonlight in his bed. In seconds his clothes came off, tossed in several directions. He'd just peeled off his underwear when Mary bolted upright and reached for the lamp. The room flooded with harsh light.

"Travis?"

"It's me," he said, squinting against the light. He held his shorts in front of him, hoping to hide the evidence of his desire.

Mary tossed aside the sheets and leaped out of bed as if he'd announced he'd placed a snake in the sheets. Her hands were digging into her hips and she glared at him like a woman scorned. "Just where the hell have you been?"

"Ah . . ." He turned away from her and slipped back into his shorts. Things didn't look as promising as he'd hoped they'd be.

"Answer me!" she flared with enough righteous indignation to sink a battleship.

Travis could see he was going to be on the losing end of any argument they had tonight. "Why don't we discuss it in the morning, darlin'?"

"We'll discuss it right now."

"Mary, please . . ."

"Is there anything you have to say for yourself?"

"Yes," he muttered, sinking onto the edge of the mattress. "At least you didn't move the bed this time."

Sixteen

Mary couldn't recall a time she'd been more outraged. Her hands and legs trembled with the power of it, like a race car engine revved before the start of the Indy 500. If Travis made one more wisecrack about her moving the furniture, she was going to punch him. How dare he come toddling to bed, hot for a tumble, when he didn't have the common decency to tell her where he'd spent the last six hours!

"Is that beer I smell?" she flared, disgusted all the more. So he'd been carousing with his friends in some tavern, probably looking for a willing woman.

"Mary, for Pete's sake, one beer. You make it sound like a federal case. Okay, I had a beer with the guys, shoot me if you want."

"So you went off for a night with the boys. Two can play this game, fella." She fell back into bed with enough force to cause the mattress to buckle. Positioning herself on her side away from him, she jerked the blankets so hard that they pulled free from the foot of the bed.

"What is that supposed to mean?" Travis demanded. She ignored him, reached for the lamp, and turned off the switch. The room went dark. And still.

"Mary?" Travis coaxed softly in the quiet.

"I'm free to disappear any time I damn well please. Have girls night out. Tilly and I can drive into the city, view a couple of male strippers. No need to mention it to you until after the fact."

"Oh, no, you won't."

"Want to try and stop me?" She'd enjoy the challenge.

The mattress heaved again as Travis shifted his weight onto the bed. He tugged at the blankets with such force that they both were left with their feet bare. "Don't try it, Mary. I won't have you making a fool of me."

"That comment, Travis Thompson, isn't worth a response."

Mary didn't know how long it took her to fall asleep, but the next thing she knew the phone was ringing. Travis mumbled something obscene under his breath and literally stumbled out of bed. Being so close to the edge of the mattress, he nearly fell onto the floor. He caught himself in time, then staggered forward a couple of steps before righting himself. He swore loudly when he stubbed his toe and did an interesting jig on his way out the door.

Mary didn't hear the telephone conversation, which was just as well since she was exhausted. Her eyes burned and she wondered if she'd gotten more than a few minutes' sleep all night.

The next thing she knew Travis was back in their bedroom, dressing in the dark. She waited for him to say something, anything, then realized he had no intention of doing so. Apparently he preferred that matters between them remain as they were, strained and pressure-filled.

Mary waited a few minutes, wondering what she should do, if anything. She could hear the cupboards opening and closing several times, then she heard the back door close. He was doing it again. Sneaking away like a cat burglar, without telling her where he was headed or when he planned to return. She waited five minutes or more, then couldn't stand it any longer.

Reaching for her housecoat and stuffing her feet into fuzzy slippers, Mary followed her errant husband. Moonlight splashed across the yard as she moved onto the porch steps. Frantically she searched the area for signs of Travis, thinking she might be too late, but his pickup was parked where it generally was. The lights in the barn told her he was probably saddling Mad Max.

She returned to the house long enough to grab her coat and was halfway through the yard when Travis appeared, leading the gelding out of the barn. Mad Max didn't look any more pleased to have his sleep disrupted than Mary did.

A pair of saddlebags were flung over Travis's shoulder, and she noticed he was dressed for winter. Apparently he didn't notice Mary.

"Where exactly are you going?" she demanded.

Travis ignored her.

Mary's heart went still. The anger and fury vanished under the weight of her pain. The wind was cold and cutting, but she barely felt them. "Travis," she pleaded, "don't do this."

"Do what?" He lifted the stirrups to adjust the rear cinch while Mad Max nervously shifted his hind legs. It was impossible to see Travis's face, but there was no mistaking his grim tone.

"Leave again."

Travis placed the saddlebags onto the gelding's back. "I don't have any choice."

Mary brushed the hair from her face and held it back with her hands pressed against her temples.

"Mary, this is men's business. It doesn't concern you. I'm sorry you're taking such offense. I explained it to you when we first married, so you don't have any right getting all upset about it now."

"Explained what?"

"Men's work and women's work. This is men's work. The line's there, Mary, it always has been and always will be."

"In case you haven't noticed, that line disappeared a long time ago. The rain washed it away. The children's footsteps wiped it out." The wind and cold stung her face, but she ignored them. She was too proud to plead with him again. "I'd hoped I'd proved to you that lines weren't necessary between us."

"Mary, I can't waste time talking about this now. There'll be plenty of that later. I have to go." He hoisted himself into the saddle. The leather creaked, and Mad Max shuffled backward a few steps as Travis adjusted his weight. He hesitated, then said in obvious concession, "I don't know where I'll be. I'd tell you if I knew."

She looked away. "So you want to maintain those lines of yours?"

"Mary, for the love of heaven—"

"Do you?"

He sighed with exasperation. "Yes," he shouted, pulling back on the bridle as Mad Max danced about.

"Okay," she said, stiffening her shoulders. She stepped back several steps, then smiled up at him ever so sweetly. "I have a few lines of my own, Travis, and one of them runs down the middle of our bed."

Travis reared back on the gelding. "Tarnation, woman, I've got wolf problems, I don't need trouble with you, too."

"As far as I'm concerned, cowboy, you asked for this. I won't cross your precious line again. I won't ask for a single explanation. If you want to stay out half the night, drink beer, and carouse with your bachelor friends, that's your prerogative." She forced herself to sound serene and composed. "Just don't try and cross my line, either. Deal?"

She smiled smugly at Travis's one-word response and returned to the house, climbing the steps with a dignity reserved for royalty. It wasn't until she was inside that she started shaking again. Her hand reached for the back of the chair in order to steady herself. With her free hand covering her mouth, she willed herself not to cry.

The jingle of spurs and heavy footsteps behind her told her Travis had followed her into the house. He caught her by the shoulders and turned her around.

"Damn fool woman," he muttered, dragging her against him. "I wouldn't last another night without you." His mouth swooped down and plundered her lips. The kiss was hard, hot, and compelling, and so wonderfully savage that he took her breath away. Involuntarily her lips parted, and he thrust his tongue forward. As his arms closed around her waist, her own hands slid convulsively around his neck, clinging to him.

"No more lines?" Mary asked when she could.

"None. You play dirty, Mary Thompson."

She smiled, nestling her head against his chest. "I play fair."

"I was at a cattlemen's meeting last night."

Mary melted more securely into his arms. She'd tried not to think where he'd been, tried not to let her mind wander. The insecurities she'd suffered most of her life had taunted her like banshees.

She wasn't pretty enough, she was too small. Her fears had been rampant.

"Larry, Rob, and I went out for a beer afterward, if you're wondering about that. This morning, Larry phoned. The wolf got another steer." His jaw caressed the crown of her head.

"What are you going to do?"

"We don't know yet."

"The fines . . . you could go to prison."

"We know." He tucked his glove-covered hand beneath her chin and raised her mouth to his for a lengthy farewell kiss. "I can't say when we'll be back."

"I'll be waiting for you," she told him, bringing his mouth back to hers.

Reluctantly Travis broke away. "I'm counting on that." With that he turned and walked out of the house.

Mary's morning was a busy, happy one. Once the boys were off to school, she'd taken Beth Ann into town with her to do some shopping. They'd purchased fabric for curtains in the five-year-old's room, paint, and several rolls of brightly colored wallpaper. They'd chosen light, airy tones of pale green, daffodil yellow, and creamy white, a stark contrast to the heavy blue walls and curtains that currently decorated the little girl's room.

Mary was hoping to start work in the bedroom that weekend. For part of it she'd need Travis's help. He didn't know that yet, but she'd find ways of making him willing.

Each time she thought of their confrontation that morning, she found herself smiling. There just might be hope for that chauvinist cowboy yet.

"Hi, I hope I'm not late," Mary greeted Tilly as she slipped into the booth across from her friend. "I needed to drop Beth Ann off at the school." She'd been looking forward to this luncheon engagement all week.

"No, you're right on time," Tilly said, offering her a feeble, slightly off-center smile.

Mary checked her watch again, thinking she might have irritated Tilly by her tardiness. But she was two minutes early.

"It was a great idea for us to meet for lunch," she continued, wondering at Tilly's mood. She reached for the menu and studied the list of entries. She made her selection quickly. When she glanced up, she noticed how ashen Tilly's features were, although she'd done a good job of disguising it with cosmetics. Her cheeks were pale except for two rosy smudges, and her eyes seemed sunken and empty. She looked as if she'd recently recovered from a lengthy illness.

"Are you feeling all right?" Mary asked, chastising herself for not noticing right away.

"I'm fine."

Although Tilly's smile was big and warm, Mary knew she was anything but fine. Tilly continued to study the menu, which disturbed Mary even further. Knowing it as well as she did, Tilly certainly seemed to be taking a long time deciding.

"I heard the chicken-fried steak is good here, ever tasted it?" Mary teased.

Either Tilly didn't hear her, or she missed the joke.

Sally approached the table, pad and pen in hand. "You two ready to order?"

"I'll have the chef's salad," Mary said, handing her the plastic-coated menu, "no olives, with diet dressing on the side. Don't bring me the roll, either."

Sally wrote down Mary's order. "It isn't any wonder that she has such a slim figure, is it, Tilly? No olives, no bread, and diet dressing." She giggled, thinking herself amusing.

Tilly didn't find that funny, either, although Mary was far more willing to approve of Tilly's lack of humor this time.

"You ready to order, Tilly?"

"I'll have the same thing."

Sally wrote it on the pad. "You want me to give her olives to you?"

"Olives?" Tilly repeated blankly.

"Never mind," Sally muttered, turning away.

Mary watched as Tilly's hand circled her water glass. Something was very wrong. "Tilly," she said gently, "what is it?"

The other woman opened her purse and reached for a tissue, dabbing it at the bridge of her nose. "I . . . need to talk to you."

"Is it bad?"

Tilly nodded. "It doesn't get much worse than this."

"You're in love with Travis and are carrying his child?"

Tilly laughed. "No . . . that's crazy." She wiped the tears from her face and giggled. "Everyone knows Travis's in love with you. He's got the look."

"He does?"

Tilly nodded. "Most of the women in town used to view Travis Thompson as one rugged cowboy. Women really go for that macho image, you know? But lately, any woman interested in Travis can tell that he's taken. He doesn't even bother to look much anymore."

"Much?"

"Listen, Mary, a man's always going to look. He wouldn't be a man if he didn't. But Travis's gaze doesn't linger. He appreciates a pretty woman, but that's all he does. He values what he's got waiting at home for him, and it shows."

Mary felt all warm inside hearing that. Maybe it was the lack of sleep, or the tension from their fight, or a hundred other reasons she couldn't name, but hot, salty tears brimmed in her eyes.

"Look what you're doing to me," she said, her voice wobbling with emotion. She pressed her index fingers under her eyes. "If we aren't careful, we'll drive away Martha's customers."

"Damn, but I like you, Mary," Tilly said softly.

"I'm happy that Travis married you. You deserve a man who loves you, and he deserves you."

"You know about love yourself, don't you?" Mary whispered. She reached for the paper napkin. This crying was getting out of hand. She'd never been given to fits of tears, and having cried twice in one day was definitely out of character for her.

"I'm crazy about Logan Anderson," Tilly admitted, reaching for the chrome napkin container herself. "I love him more than I thought it was possible to love a man."

"Does he feel the same way about you?"

"I . . . don't know. I want to believe it so badly that I don't trust my own judgment anymore. The problem is I'm not nearly good enough for him."

"Don't you dare say that."

"It's true. He's an attorney, esteemed in the community, a doctor's son. I dated college boys a few times. They seemed to think *waitress* was another word for hooker."

"Logan's not like that."

"I know. He's so good to me. That's why it makes everything so much more difficult. You see, I have the habit of falling in love with the wrong guy. I thought it was different with Logan, but now I'm beginning to wonder."

Sally returned with their order and a bowl of olives for Tilly. Tilly swatted her friend across the rump.

"Logan drove over to talk to Travis last night," Mary said, making conversation.

Tilly's head jerked up. "Logan went to see Travis?"

Mary nodded.

"Did he . . . talk to Travis?"

Mary shook her head. "Travis was at the Cattlemen's Association meeting."

"Oh." The word was emitted on an elongated sigh.

"Travis didn't get home until late, and I forgot to mention it this morning, but I'll make sure he gives Logan a call tonight."

"That's a real good idea," Tilly said, brightening visibly.

"There was something you wanted to tell me?" Mary pressed.

"Tell you?" she echoed blankly. "Oh, that . . ."

"It doesn't get much worse than this," she reminded her friend.

"Oh, that." Tilly appeared hesitant, almost embarrassed, undoubtedly uneasy. "It was nothing."

"Nothing. Tilly, I don't believe that. You've been a wreck over this meeting, and I want to know why."

Tilly wadded the paper napkin into a tight ball and lowered her head. "Forgive me, Mary, I was . . . involving myself in something that was none of my business. Sometimes it's best just to leave matters to take care of themselves, and I'm beginning to think this is one of those times."

"You can't do this to me."

Tilly stretched her hand across the Formica tabletop and reached for Mary's hand. "I know it's a lot to ask of you, but would you mind waiting a while longer? I'm convinced everything will come out in time, and it's much better if you learn it from someone else."

"Learn what? Tilly, be reasonable."

"I don't blame you for being upset. I know I would be, but as your friend, I'm asking you to wait."

Mary could see arguing wasn't going to convince Tilly to tell her what she'd found so important only a few moments before. She reached for another napkin and dabbed the tears from her face. "I don't know what's the matter with me lately," she admitted hoarsely. "I almost never cry."

Mary felt Tilly's steady gaze, watched as a slow smile began to appear. "Is there any possibility you might be pregnant?"

Seventeen

Logan was waiting for Tilly inside her apartment when she arrived home. He stood in the doorway leading to her kitchen, a dish towel tucked in at his waist. His grin was warm and wide when she opened the door.

"Logan, what are you doing here?" Tilly hadn't expected to see him, nor did she want to. She'd made her decision and had hoped to have some time and perspective before she told Logan. He was making that impossible now.

He saluted her with a wineglass and sipped from the edge.

"You're . . . drinking." The words barely escaped the tightness gripping her throat. Damn, but his timing was perfect.

"It's Cherry Coke, so don't look so worried."

"It's late."

"I hope you're hungry, because I fixed you my specialty."

The last thing on Tilly's mind was food. Her appetite had vanished the night of the Harvest Moon Festival. Her weight loss was becoming noticeable. Even Sally had commented on it.

"Baby," Logan said, discarding his makeshift apron and setting aside his drink. He moved toward her, his dark eyes revealing his dismay. "What's wrong?" He guided her to the overstuffed chair and brought her onto his lap. "Tell me, Tilly, please, I can't bear to see you so unhappy."

Tilly gently pushed against him, but he refused to release her. She knew where this was leading, and she wanted no part of it.

"Is it something I've done?"

Tilly didn't answer. How could she? When Logan had told her he was in love with her, it had seemed like a miracle. An attorney in love with a waitress. He'd touched a cord in her that she'd assumed was long dead. Phil and Davey had assassinated that deep inner part of her soul that made her free to love. Over the years she'd been in other relationships. She did it for the good times and for the sex, but no man had really loved her. They'd used her, and on rare occasions she'd used them, but in no other relationship had she received such unselfish tenderness.

"Kiss me," she pleaded, her hands clenching his shirt and her voice barely audible. When he made love to her, she was able to blot out her suspicions. Then and only then did the pain fade.

"Tilly, something's troubling you. You've got to tell me what's making you so unhappy."

"Make love to me," she begged. Her hands directed his mouth to hers, and she kissed him as though she were starved, as if he could wipe out all her pain with his mouth.

"Tilly," Logan moaned, dragging his lips from hers. "Not until we've talked. We can't continue like this."

"Okay," she said, her eyes avoiding his. Her fingers were nimble as she unbuttoned her blouse and released the snaps of her bra. Her breasts sprang free of their confines.

Logan said nothing.

"Tilly, dear heaven." He squeezed his eyes closed.

In the back of her mind, Tilly realized what she was doing, why she found this crude scene so necessary. It was only when they were making love that she felt in control. The pattern was a familiar one, the scene identical to those played out with Phil and Davey.

A three-time loser, that's what she was. She hadn't learned anything. For a while she'd believed it was different with Logan. He'd taught her to feel again. She'd lowered her guard, trusted him. For a while it had been ecstasy, but no more. All that was there now was pain. It felt almost comfortable because she'd become accustomed to dealing with it in so many other relationships.

"Oh, baby," Logan moaned, replete. "The things you do to me."

Tilly didn't dare look at Logan, knowing how weak she was, fearing her untrustworthy heart would easily veto the dictates of experience.

"It's been fun," she said, hating and applauding her directness. She sounded cold and hard, but for her sanity's sake it was necessary. "I gave you what you came for. It's time you left."

Logan's stunned gaze connected with hers. He sat as though he'd been struck dumb. "Came for?" he repeated.

"Yeah," she said, reaching for her purse. She kept a pack of cigarettes handy for times such as these. Although she hadn't smoked regularly in years, every now and again she still needed a nicotine fix.

Her hands shook when she struck the match, but she didn't think Logan noticed. Sitting across from him, she crossed her long legs and aimed a puff of smoke toward the ceiling.

"It's over," she announced coolly.

"What's over?" he demanded. He straightened his clothes and sank back onto the chair. He looked disoriented, as if he weren't sure he was hearing her correctly.

"Us." The cigarette tasted like crap, and she stabbed it out on a plate. "I know, Logan. I'm not stupid, although I have to admit it took me far longer than it should have to figure it out."

It amazed her how well he was able to maintain a look of innocence. "Know what?"

"That you were the driver who killed Lee and Janice Thompson."

He paled so quickly, she feared he might pass out.

"You don't need to worry. I'm not going to tell anyone," she assured him, knowing that would be his first concern. "I invited Mary to lunch. I wanted to find out what Travis was doing to find the driver and how much information he had. If he was close to figuring out it was you, I was going to go to him, plead with him on your behalf. But before I could say anything Mary told me you'd gone out to see Travis yourself." She gave him adequate time to explain the reason for his visit, and when he didn't she continued. "You chickened out, didn't you? I can't say that I blame you. No one wants to spend time in prison."

"Tilly, listen to me—"

"If you're thinking what I suspect you are, you can forget that as well."

"Forget what?"

"Me being your alibi. I'm not lying for you, Logan."

"I'd never—"

"Sure you would," she said coldly.

He didn't say anything for a couple of tension-strained moments. "What did you say to Mary?"

"You're worried about that, are you. Well, you needn't be. I realized I was a fool to involve myself in something that was none of my business. I do that, you know, try to fix things for everyone else, instead of taking care of myself. You'd think I'd know better."

"Please, hear me out."

"Excuses? No thanks, I've heard them all. This time, for once in my life, I'm going to play it smart. I'm bailing out before I end up planning my weekends around prison visitation hours. It would have been far better for you if you'd turned yourself in the night it happened. I'd think you'd know that, being an attorney and all." She kept her voice cool and as unemotional as possible. "It's been fun, Logan, don't get me wrong, but it's over."

"Tilly . . ." Logan gestured weakly with his hands, vaulted to his feet, and paced the area in front of her.

"Your one slip in sobriety happened the same night as the accident," she reminded him.

"I know, I know," he said quickly, rubbing the back of his neck.

"You've been restless and unhappy for months."

He closed his eyes and nodded.

"Did you think I hadn't noticed?"

He paused and lowered his gaze. "I've needed you so badly."

"Yeah, it generally works that way. Phil and Davey needed me, too."

"I never knew you could be this cold." He lifted his eyes to hers, studying her. "We didn't make love just now."

"Not really. That was sex. It was my way of saying good-bye, of proving to myself you aren't any different from the others. If I'm cold, it's because I have to be. I can't afford to care about you anymore, because ultimately it'll hurt too much." She looked away, not wanting him to notice the tears that were filling her eyes. "It always seems to boil down to that."

"To what?"

"Love hurting me."

"Not this time, baby, I swear to you—"

"I'm sorry, Logan, I really am, but for once I'm playing this smart and bailing out while I still have my sanity," she said quickly, cutting him off. "There isn't anything you can say that will change my mind."

"Nothing?" He stared at her, his eyes dark and intent. "Not even the truth?"

"The truth? I already know the truth."

"No, you don't." He knelt in front of her and reached for her hand. "Tilly, I swear to you by everything I hold dear, I didn't do it."

Eighteen

*Mary fretted all night. The slight-*est sound, a rustle of wind whispering against the window, the hoot of an owl as it flew across the face of the full moon, sent her scurrying to look out the window, watching, waiting, for Travis.

Sleep was impossible. Each time she attempted to put her concerns aside, her mind filled with visions of her husband and his friends riding across the range. Her imagination ran wild with countless episodes that would place them in harm's way. Her concern was compounded by the thought of the penalties federal and state governments imposed on anyone who purposely killed a wolf. With fewer than seventeen hundred wolves left in all of Montana, the U.S. Fish and Wildlife Service took the welfare of their charges seriously. No one knew this better than Travis and the other ranchers, yet they'd chosen to disregard the warnings and take matters into their own hands.

Mary was sitting in the dark kitchen, stewing in her worries, when Jim wandered out. He paused when he saw her. "Travis didn't come home?"

Mary shook her head. "I'm worried, Jim. Anything might have happened."

"He'll be all right."

She nearly choked on her panic. It was times like these that she was convinced she'd never make a good rancher's wife. Other women sent their husbands off seemingly without a qualm, trusting completely in their mate's abilities to overcome any obstacle. Mary didn't doubt Travis's skill. It was the wolf that worried her. The wily beast had outmaneuvered federal and state officials, the best trapper in three states, and every rancher within a hundred miles. Mary didn't know what Travis and his friends hoped to accomplish, but it didn't seem promising, whatever it was.

"You'd better get Scotty up for school," Mary said to Jim, leaving the table. She walked over to the kitchen counter and then forgot what she was there for.

The boy hesitated. "Are you going to be all right?"

Tears came to her eyes, and she reached for him and hugged him close. Jim was at a point in his life when he felt he'd outgrown any display of affection from family, but Mary didn't care. She wanted to thank him, and because she was so close to breaking into sobs, she couldn't do it with words.

"You want me to call someone?" he asked, gently patting her back. "Mrs. Morgan would be glad to come and sit with you. She was real good to us, and she likes you."

"No-o, I'll be fine." Mary released him. Jim looked grateful to have escaped her embrace. "Thanks for the hug," she whispered.

"That's all right. Women need a man every now and again." He sounded so grown-up, so like Travis, that it was all Mary could do not to gather him in her arms a second time.

A couple of moments later Scotty rushed into the kitchen, dressed in his flannel pajamas. He'd apparently gone to bed with his hair wet because it swept upward like a skateboard ramp against the side of his head. "Where's Travis?"

"He didn't come home, but there's no need to worry."

Scotty didn't say anything for several moments. "That's what happened with Mom and Dad," he whispered brokenly. "They didn't come home and they didn't come home. The babysitter got upset and called her mother and then . . . then the sheriff came and . . ."

"Travis is fine, sweetheart, don't worry."

"But he didn't come home." Scotty's young voice shook forcefully. "Not all night."

Beth Ann's whiny voice came from her bedroom. "She wet the bed," Scotty whispered. "She always whines when she wets the bed."

Scotty's prediction proved to be accurate. It amazed Mary how easily the children had absorbed her tension. All evening she'd tried to hide her concern, but with little success. She'd expected Travis back by dinnertime, and when he hadn't shown, she'd tried to make light of it. Apparently her acting skills were a bit rusty.

Travis had been gone over twenty-four hours. Although Mary hadn't seen what he'd packed, she knew his saddlebags would hold only so much. He was probably hungry, cold, and near desperate by now.

The phone rang while she stood lifelessly stirring the pan of oatmeal. The children glanced at her, eyes revealing their fears. She reached for the receiver and prayed with everything in her that it was some word regarding her husband.

"Mary, it's Travis."

"Travis," she cried, and it seemed the four of them collectively sighed their relief. "Where are you?"

"Jail, listen—"

"Jail?" Mary cried. "For the love of heaven, what are you doing there?"

"I don't have time to explain that now. I've only got one phone call, and Sheriff Tucker's standing over me like a warlord. Listen, I need you to come bail me out."

"Bail you out?"

"Don't sound so worried, honey, I've been in jail before."

"You didn't tell me that before we were married."

"You didn't ask." He seemed to find her concern amusing.

"Are you all right?" Her knees were weak with an overwhelming sense of relief.

"You mean other than being half-starved, half-frozen, and plumb out of luck?"

"Yeah?"

His voice lowered. "I'm fine, other than . . ." He hesitated.

"Yes?" Worry rang in her own ears.

"Damn, but I missed you, woman."

"I . . . I missed you, too."

"Good." He sounded cheered by that. "I want you to know I intend to make it up to you. Now hurry before Tucker decides to throw the book at me."

Travis felt good. Damn good. The wolf wouldn't be a problem any longer, thanks to Larry's tracking skills and a fair amount of luck. Too bad their good fortune hadn't held, but he didn't have a whole lot to complain about. They'd found the wolf, trapped it themselves, and then with a good deal of ceremony turned him over to the U.S. Fish and Wildlife Service headquarters. The department head was not amused, nor had he found them particularly clever. In fact, he was furious. No more than five minutes after their arrival, he'd phoned the sheriff and had the three arrested. Travis, like Larry and Rob, knew they were taking a chance and might possibly get stuck with a hefty penalty, but they figured any fair-minded judge would see matters their way. That was the best they could hope for. All three were aware of the risks when they'd started this little adventure.

"Poor Travis," Larry said from the bottom bunk of the holding cell when Travis returned. He was on his back, his hands cradling his head. "One phone call, and I'd guess you chose to call the little woman. Got to check in home now that you're married, don't you?"

Travis grumbled but didn't rise to the bait.

"Now me," Larry said with an air of superiority, "I'm not wasting my phone call checking in with no wife. No siree, I'm calling my attorney. He'll have me out of here lickety split. Meanwhile Travis is going to be stuck in the cell twiddling his thumbs until Mary decides to forgive him."

Sheriff Tucker came for Rob next. Rob made his phone call and returned scowling. "Problems?" Larry demanded.

Rob shook his head. "My attorney's in court this morning. His secretary said she'd let him know as soon as he's back in the office, but it probably won't be until late this afternoon."

"In other words, we're stuck here until your man shows?" Larry cried, bolting upright. He seemed to have forgotten he was in a bunk and bonged his head against the springs. A rush of swear words purpled the air.

"You got a problem back there, Larry Martin?" Tucker shouted as he strolled back toward their cell. He looped his thumbs into his waist and rocked back onto his heels. It seemed to Travis that the lawman was enjoying this a bit too much.

"Yeah, I changed my mind. I want to make that call after all."

"Fine." The sheriff unlocked the cell door and led Larry out to the front, where he could place his own call.

No more than a couple of minutes passed before Larry was back. "Who'd you call?" Rob wanted to know.

"Logan Anderson. He might be new in town, but at least that's where he is, in town."

"Is he any good?"

"Hell if I know. All I care about is getting out of here. I don't know about you two, but I could do with a hot meal and bath."

"Is Anderson coming?" Rob pressed.

"I don't know."

"What do you mean you don't know?"

"I talked to his secretary," Larry explained. "But apparently he hasn't shown up at the office yet."

"Ten o'clock in the morning and he hasn't even bothered to come in to work. It's no wonder these city folks are all soft. He's probably still in bed."

"I would be, too," Larry muttered, sagging onto the bottom bunk, "if Tilly Lawrence showed half as much interest in me."

"What did Anderson's secretary say?"

"She promised she'd have him come over to the jail as soon as he arrived."

Rob stretched out his long legs and crossed them at the ankles. "It looks like we're all gonna be stuck here until this afternoon. God only knows how much time it'll take Mary to bail out Travis."

"I bet she'll chew your hide all the way home."

Travis shrugged, uncaring.

"She'll probably make him sleep on the sofa for a week," Larry added, and the two men guffawed loudly, apparently thinking it was fitting punishment.

"Poor Travis," Rob crooned.

"Poor Travis," Larry echoed.

"Travis Thompson." The door opened and Sheriff Tucker stepped into the jail area. "Mary's here. She's put up the money for your bail."

Rob's and Larry's laughter slowly faded. In shocked silence they watched, eyes wide and disbelieving, as Tucker brought out the keys and opened the holding cell. No sooner was Travis on the other side than Mary raced into the room and catapulted into his embrace.

With her arms wrapped around his neck, she spread hot, branding kisses over his face. Travis tasted the salt of her tears and knew she'd been frantic with worry. He wished he could have spared her that, but there'd been no way of contacting her. With his arms wrapped around her slender waist, he half lifted her from the floor. Tenderly she brushed the hair from his face and gazed into his eyes with undisguised love.

"You all right?" he asked.

"I am now," she told him, and kissed him

once more. She raised her head and seemed self-conscious all of a sudden. "Your friends," she whispered, nodding toward Larry and Rob.

Travis turned and found his partners in crime standing on the other side of the jail cell, their hands wrapped around the bars, their faces sharp with envy as they studied him from the other side of freedom.

"Should I have gotten the money to bail them out, too?" Mary whispered.

"No," Travis said, grinning broadly at his friends, "they've already made arrangements with their attorneys. Isn't that right, boys?" He released Mary but couldn't bear to be separated from her, so he wrapped his arm around her shoulder and kept her close to his side. They were ready to leave the jail area when he turned around as if he'd forgotten something and smiled to his friends. "See you later, boys."

"Later," Larry muttered.

Travis nearly laughed out loud. The way he figured, it would be a good long while before either of them consoled him about his sorry lot in life again.

Travis couldn't remember a time the Triple T looked more appealing. Once inside the house, he gripped Mary by the waist and dragged her back into his arms. It didn't matter how many times he held her or how often they kissed, it wasn't near enough to satisfy him. "It seems to me I've got two nights' worth of lovin' to make up for."

"Travis!"

"Hmm. I need you, woman. You aren't going to give me an argument now, are you?"

"It's broad daylight," Mary protested, but he noted the words didn't carry any conviction as she raised her mouth to his.

Sweet heaven, he loved her mouth. He'd never kissed a woman as warm and loving as Mary. Certainly none who had a more powerful effect on him. He cherished her vulnerability. Her soft, wet kisses drove him wild. Without taking his lips from hers, he removed her coat. His hands brushed against her breasts and he groaned when he felt her nipples go taut.

"Aren't you hungry?" Mary asked breathlessly.

He nodded. "You're going to feed me, aren't you?"

"You're cold."

Once again he nodded. "You're going to warm me, aren't you?"

"Travis!"

"That's my name."

"Take a bath and I'll cook you some breakfast, and when you're finished we'll discuss making up for lost time."

He groaned, but he knew she was right. "You drive a hard bargain, Mary Thompson." There wasn't any need to rush into bed, not when they had a good portion of the day left to themselves. Besides, he must smell as bad as sheep dung.

"I'll take a shower," he told her, letting her go reluctantly. "And be right back."

Mary nodded. They backed away from each

other like war-torn lovers. "I'll cook you breakfast," she whispered.

"Make it big. I'm half-starved."

"I will," she promised.

There wasn't any need to hurry through his shower, but Travis did, jealous of every minute spent apart from his wife. He found himself singing, belting out a raunchy cowboy song he'd learned in his youth. His mood improved when he stepped out from under the hot spray to the most delectable smells wafting in from the kitchen. Sausage, eggs, pancakes, he guessed. He was hungry enough to eat a bear in one sitting.

As soon as he'd finished his meal he was bedding his wife, he promised himself. With that in mind, it didn't seem necessary to dress. He wrapped a towel around his waist for decency's sake and donned his boots and hat.

He kinda figured Mary would get a kick out of his attire.

"Oh, Mary," he called out in a seductive, singsong voice, before stepping out into the kitchen.

"Travis . . ."

"I'm coming, sweetcakes." Hands on his hips, he ambled into the kitchen wearing a ten-gallon grin.

And froze.

"Good morning, Travis Thompson," Clara Morgan greeted him warmly. A lazy smile coaxed the edges of her mouth. "I thought I'd drop by to be certain you were safe and sound. I can see that you are very well indeed."

Where warm blood had flowed through his veins seconds before, now there was stale well water. Travis's gaze flew to Mary, hoping she could rescue him from this embarrassment. Naturally if he was going to make a fool of himself, it would be in front of his former schoolteacher. By tomorrow morning the news of him traipsing about the house wearing little more than a loincloth, hat, and boots would be all over town. With his luck the Ladies Missionary Society would make his behavior a prayer concern at their next gathering.

"It was very kind of you to drop by, Mrs. Morgan," Mary said, coughing in a damn poor attempt to disguise a laugh.

"It looks like you're no worse off for your adventure, Travis."

He nodded. His jaw was clenched so tight, his teeth ached. He gripped hold of the towel from behind to prevent any further risk of embarrassment.

"I'll be on my way, then," Mrs. Morgan said cheerfully. "I will see you in church on Sunday, won't I, Travis?"

Travis frowned. This was out-and-out blackmail if ever he heard it. He wasn't going to give in to such a blatant attempt to manipulate his freedom. He'd attended church services with Mary that first Sunday, but there wasn't any need to overdo religion.

"I will, won't I?" Clara Morgan prompted once more.

The old biddy hadn't changed much, Travis

mused darkly. He seemed to remember her being just as dictatorial during his school days. "I'll be there," he agreed under his breath.

"I thought you would. Now, I'll be on my way and leave you two to your . . . reunion."

"Thank you for getting the children off on time for me this morning," Mary said, steering the older woman toward the back door.

"Any time, Mary, all you need to do is ask."

That too was directed at Travis, for his refusal to accept help when the kids first came to live with him. Mrs. Morgan's spirits were certainly chipper, he noted, especially when it was at his expense. She raised her hand and toddled out the door, humming gleefully to herself.

"You might have warned me," Travis muttered as soon as the older woman had gone.

"I didn't get a chance. Besides, how was I to know you were going to come traipsing out looking like . . . that?"

"Go ahead and laugh."

"Oh, Travis, you do make such an adorable sight."

He growled at her. "You're going to have to pay for that comment, my delectable wife, and pay dearly." He purposely dropped the towel and started after her.

Mary squealed with delight and took off at a full run. He didn't know if it was by accident or design that they ended up in the bedroom. But he did know it was the appropriate room for what he had in mind.

* * *

Mary was humming softly to herself as she stripped away the old wallpaper from Beth Ann's bedroom walls. The weather was miserable, and Travis had stuck around the house since lunch. At first he'd changed the oil in the truck, but when he'd come inside for coffee, he'd stayed.

The next thing Mary knew, he was working alongside her. She welcomed his company and this rare time alone together. In addition, he was much stronger and more accustomed to working with tools, so he could strip away twice as much paper as she could.

Apparently, however, he didn't find the task much easier than Mary did, even if he was stronger. Every now and again he'd let lose with an angry cuss word when the paper wasn't cooperating.

Beth Ann was excited with the prospect of a "new" room. The boys tried to make light of it, but they were eager for Mary to do something with their room as well. Especially Scotty, who wanted wallpaper with airplanes on it.

"Mary."

Travis muttered a curse, and this time she sensed a frustrated, angry note to it. He dropped his tool and swung around.

"Travis?"

He was clenching his thumb, holding a white handkerchief over it. Blood had already soaked through.

"You hurt yourself." Her concern was immediate. "What happened?"

"I'm all right," he said, glancing her way suspiciously as if to say he really wasn't. "I was hoping you'd kiss it and make it all better."

She ignored his teasing and steered him by the elbow toward the bathroom. He seemed more eager to have her investigate his injury in their bedroom, but she guided him to her first choice. Using her hands against his shoulders, she forced him to sit against the edge of the bathtub while she cautiously removed the makeshift bandage.

Losing patience with her, Travis gripped her about the waist and lowered her onto his lap. "I already told you it's nothing."

"I'll be the judge of that," she returned tartly. Now wasn't the time for heroics. With that much blood lost he was surely going to need medical attention.

"You're going to have to kiss me senseless to make up for the pain." He edged his free hand into her blouse and cupped her breast.

"Travis, stop that this instant."

"Stop what?"

"You know what!"

"This?" He flicked his thumb over her nipple, and traitor that her body was, she responded immediately.

"Travis Thompson," she muttered with mock irritation as she examined his injured thumb, "this is little more than a paper cut."

"I told you it wasn't anything to worry about." His teeth caught her earlobe and nibbled on it greedily.

"The blood."

"From another cut earlier when I was working on the truck. You know what I'm thinking?"

It was fairly obvious what he had in mind. "Travis, what's gotten into you lately?" The man was insatiable. Mary loved having such a demanding husband, but there were limits. "The kids . . ."

"How long before they'll be home from school?"

"Another hour."

"Ah," he whispered, sounding pleased. "That's plenty of time."

"But . . ."

"The next time you're in town," he whispered, turning her head toward his and pressing his mouth hungrily to hers, "I want you to buy bras that snap in the front. Understand?"

"But . . ." His thumb flecked over her taut nipple, and her breast tightened even more. "Okay," she agreed, knowing he'd quickly overpower any objections she offered.

The phone pealed in the distance, sounding far away. Much too far away to worry herself with. "I . . . should get that," she protested.

"Let it ring."

"Travis, really . . . it might be important."

"Aren't I?"

"Yes, but you can wait . . . can't you?"

He released her, not the least bit pleased. Mary was grinning by the time she reached the phone. It surprised her that she was able to speak clearly into the receiver.

"Mrs. Thompson, this is Mr. Moon from the school."

Mary's heart skipped into overdrive. "Beth Ann . . ."

"None of the children are hurt. Forgive me, I didn't mean to alarm you."

He was apologetic, but not overly so, Mary noted. "There's a problem with one of the children?"

"Yes, I'm afraid so," the school principal continued. "We're going to need you or your husband to come down to the school. Jim was caught stealing."

"Jim wouldn't do that," she flared angrily.

"I'm afraid the teacher found him with her purse. He doesn't deny it."

Mary placed her hand over her eyes to blot out the image of Jim's look that morning. He'd been sullen and angry. He'd done a poor job of his chores, but Mary had covered for him when Travis had asked. It had been wrong, she knew it even as she was making excuses for him, but it'd seemed a small price to pay to keep the peace.

"What's wrong?" Travis asked when she slowly set the receiver back into the cradle.

Mary didn't turn around, needing time to collect her thoughts. "It was the school."

"Jim?"

She nodded. "Mr. Moon is suspending him."

"What's he done?"

Mary kept her gaze lowered and shook her head.

"Tell me!" he demanded. Moments earlier he'd been whispering sweet nothings in her ear, and in the space of a few moments he was shouting at her.

"He was caught taking money from a teacher's purse."

Travis's calm acceptance surprised her. "Is the school calling in the police?"

"He . . . he didn't say. I don't think so."

"Pity. Time in juvenile hall might teach Jim a good lesson."

The tension between Travis and Lee's oldest hadn't lessened, and this latest incident was sure to cause even more problems. "You're talking about a twelve-year-old boy," Mary felt obliged to remind him.

"I'm talking about a thief," Travis snapped. He headed toward the door, grabbed his coat and hat.

"Where are you going?"

Travis shot her a disgusted look. "Where else? The school."

"I'm going with you." She reached for her own coat and purse, pleased that Travis didn't argue with her.

Nineteen

Logan slipped into the booth at Martha's and waited. Tilly watched him out of the corner of her eye. He was patiently waiting for her to deliver a menu and a glass of water with the warm, eager smile she usually gave him.

Not anymore.

The decision to break off the relationship with Logan had been one of the most painful of her life. She wasn't going back on her word now. Second thoughts were too damn costly.

It was too much to hope that Logan would calmly accept her word. He insisted he wasn't responsible for the accident that killed the Thompsons. Because she so desperately wanted to believe him, Tilly had wavered. That had been her first mistake, but she was determined not to make more. He'd phoned twice, but she'd let the answering machine screen her calls. Logan must have figured it out because he'd stopped phoning. Tilly should have known he wouldn't make this easy.

She tucked the menu under her arm and delivered a glass of water to his table. She pulled the small green pad from her apron pocket. "What can I get for you?"

"Hi, Tilly."

"Would you like me to list the specials?"

"Can we talk?" he asked.

"In case you haven't noticed, I'm working."

"I don't mean now. Later, when you're free."

"No thanks."

"You don't believe me, do you?" Logan asked tightly, displaying the first bit of impatience. "Apparently the fact I love you and have for months doesn't count for a damn thing."

"Pumpkin pie's the special of the month. Martha ordered pumpkin-flavored ice cream as well. Do you want to give it a try?"

"I'd like to try strangling you. I don't know when anyone's frustrated me more."

Tilly felt the blood drain from her face.

"I didn't mean that the way it sounded. Damn it, Tilly, you've got me so tied up in knots I don't know what to do anymore."

His face was tight with pain. She couldn't look at him and not hurt. His eyes pleaded with her, telling her he was miserable. She was miserable, too, but more than that she was afraid she was throwing away the best thing that had ever happened to her.

"I don't know what I can say or do to convince you of the truth." There was a tortured quality to his voice that tugged at her resolve.

She didn't dare listen for fear he'd change her mind. She started to turn away, but Logan caught her arm and held her there. "Hear me out. This one last time, that's all I ask. Will you do that for me?"

Unable to speak, she nodded.

"I don't blame you for thinking I'm the one responsible. I probably would have reached the same conclusion. I'll say it again, just one last time. I had nothing to do with the accident that killed Lee and Janice Thompson. Frankly, I don't blame you for not believing me. I'm not sure I would either in like circumstances."

This was much harder than Tilly had expected it would be.

"I love you, Tilly, I have from almost the first. I wish I'd done things differently. In the beginning you wouldn't even date me, remember? Then you assumed I was attracted to you for one thing and one thing only. Dear God, when I think back . . ." He paused and rubbed his hands over his eyes, then shook his head as if to dislodge the memory. "When I arrived in Grandview, I was an emotional wreck. You know, the divorce and all . . . and, well, the whole thing was like a festering boil.

"Then I met you. You were so warm and generous. Not once did you ask anything of me. I couldn't get over it. I'd never met a woman who didn't expect something from me. At first I found it refreshing. It seemed too good to be true."

It had felt that way for Tilly, too. She'd been scared and battle weary when she'd first met Logan. They'd needed each other, and that was what had drawn them together.

"The sex . . . dear sweet heaven, I've never known it could be so good. By the time the divorce was final, Kathe had stripped away my pride, my self-esteem, and my manhood. When I met you, I'd given up the idea of ever being able . . . you know, to please a woman in bed."

Tilly looked at him in disbelief. "But . . ."

"I know," he said with a halfhearted laugh. "It was different with you. It's always been incredible, because that was the way you made me feel about myself. We seemed to get stuck there, at the sex part. I never intended to have an affair with you. I wanted to date you the way I would any other woman I was attracted to. I planned on taking you out to dinner and the movies, to treat you to a night in Miles City. I'm proud of who and what you are, Tilly, I always have been. I never wanted what we shared to remain behind closed doors.

"Something dawned on me recently regarding our relationship. Sex was all a man's ever given you. You've never been valued for the warm, wonderful woman you are. You made the mistake of believing I was like the others, but I'm not. I'd give just about anything to have figured this out sooner. Now, it might be too late." He reached inside his suit pocket and set a velvet jeweler's box on the faded Formica tabletop.

Tilly stopped breathing for a long moment.

"You can do what you want with this ring, Tilly. It's yours to keep no matter what you decide. If you want to cash it in, I'll understand. If you want to stuff it in a drawer, that's fine, too. But if I see you wearing it, I'll know."

Her eyes were mesmerized by the plush box. She'd never owned any expensive jewelry that didn't come out of a pawnshop. "What will you know?"

"That you've agreed to be my wife."

"Your wife?" Of all the men she'd slept with, of all the men she'd loved, not one had asked her to marry him, at least not when they were sober.

"I didn't come here for anything to eat," Logan said, handing her back the menu. She accepted it with numb fingers. "I came because I love you. I want us to build a life together. Someday I'd like us to have children. If that's what you want, too, let me know."

Tilly continued to stare at the ring case. "You don't need to buy my silence. I already told you I wouldn't tell anyone, and I meant it."

The cutting pain that flashed into his eyes was so strong and so sharp, Tilly felt it herself. She longed to yank back the words, but she couldn't. His pain was followed by a restrained but savage anger. His body tensed, and his eyes snapped. "I can't force you to believe me, but for the love of God, don't insult me. If you want to throw my proposal back in my face, fine, but don't degrade what prompted it."

"What am I supposed to think?" she demanded.

"I don't know, Tilly. Honest to God, I don't know. Maybe that for once in your life you've got a man who genuinely loves you. Don't you believe you've found someone who wants more than to sneak around behind closed doors? Oh, I get it," he said with biting sarcasm. "If it isn't sullied and dirty, you're not interested. Think about what you want, Tilly, reason it out, because I won't ask you again." He scooted out of the booth as if he couldn't get away fast enough. He stalked across the restaurant and out the door, not looking back.

Tilly didn't know what she should do. She picked up the jeweler's case and slowly, almost fearfully, opened the lid. On a thick bed of black velvet was a beautiful diamond ring. The stone was bright and clear and beautiful. It sparkled and gleamed at her.

Her heart was pounding hard and fast, but it felt as though she were hollow inside. The temptation to slip it on her finger was so strong, she had to snap the lid closed. She stuffed the ring in her pocket and carried it with her the rest of the day as though it had been a generous tip. And in a way, it had been.

It assured her silence.

"Jim, I don't understand," Mary said patiently, glancing to Travis as they drove back to the Triple T. "You had your allowance with you. Why did you need money?"

Travis easily saw through her doubts. She blamed herself for this latest in a long line of problems with Jim. Personally, he wasn't falling prey to that mumbo-jumbo fault-finding crap the school principal had attempted to feed them. By the time they'd left the school office, everyone right down to the city garbage collector was to blame for Jim's problems.

As far as Travis was concerned, it was all a load of worthless talk. The boy was caught taking money out of a teacher's purse. It didn't get much plainer than that. No one had stood over him with a gun and demanded he do it. Of his own free will, Jim had wrongfully taken what belonged to someone else. That was the way Travis intended to treat it. As for the bull about Mary and him making an appointment with a child psychologist, well, he wanted no part of that. He'd listened with more patience than most. A few months earlier he would have had it out then and there with Mr. Moon. For Mary's sake he'd held his tongue, knowing a scene would embarrass her.

All the talk about a dysfunctional family. Hell, Travis mused, he'd like to see a functional one. Every family had problems, some more than others.

Jim was suffering from—what was it Moon had called it?—unresolved aggression. Travis strongly suspected that was another word for plain, old-fashioned belligerence. Anyone who'd ever lived dealt with it at one time or another. A man worked aggression out of his system with hard toil. If Jim worked hard, played hard, and studied hard, then he wouldn't have time to be stirring up trouble.

"I just don't understand," Mary repeated, softly this time, speaking more to herself.

Travis feared she'd blindly swallowed the bull Moon had been dishing out. By the time they left, her shoulders had started to droop and she was close to tears. That was when Travis finally put an end to it. He wasn't going to let any man make Mary feel like that. If Moon wanted to stir up trouble, they could do it man-to-man, the same way he intended to deal with the boy. If Jim was suffering from unresolved aggression, Travis could guarantee a full psychological recovery by the time he was finished with the twelve-year-old.

As if reading his uncle's thoughts, Jim squirmed on the seat. The youth was sandwiched between Travis and Mary on the front seat of the truck, and some sixth sense must have told him what was coming.

Jim hadn't spoken more than a handful of words since they'd picked him up at the school. It wasn't a regretful, remorseful silence, Travis noted, but the sullen, brooding kind Jim carried with him so much of the time.

Mary had made excuses for Jim on the drive to the school; she'd tried to cover for the boy over the matter of chores, too, but Travis would have no more of that. He and the boy were going to have this out once and for all.

This could be touchy with Mary, Travis realized with some regret. They'd already gone one round with this discipline thing. But if it came to round two, so be it. He wasn't going to have her soft heart bleeding all over what needed to be done.

Travis turned off the highway and down the long dirt road that led to the Triple T. A thick trail of dust settled over the truck as he eased to a stop.

"I want to talk to Jim," Travis said, looking pointedly at Mary. He braced his hands against the steering wheel, expecting an argument.

"I think we should," Mary agreed, and climbed out of the truck. Jim leaped onto the ground after her.

"I mean alone." Travis met her gaze over the hood. "Man-to-man."

Jim whirled around, and his eyes raced from Travis to Mary, looking for her help.

Travis waited, wondering if she was going to intervene. He read the struggle, the indecision, in her. Her teeth worried her lower lip before she nodded and turned toward the house. She hesitated on the top step, her stance filled with reluctance.

"I don't have anything to say to you," Jim shouted at Travis with open hostility. "Mary," he pleaded, "you aren't going to let him take me in the barn, are you?"

Travis waited, half expecting her to challenge him, to demand that she be a part of this. He couldn't allow it, not this time. What he had to say to Jim was between the two of them. It didn't involve her.

"So you're looking to hide behind a woman's skirts now." Travis made sure his words were thick with sarcasm. "That's exactly what I'd expect from a boy who steals money from a teacher's purse."

Jim whipped around and tried to slug Travis. His arm sliced through the air with such force, he nearly lost his balance. Travis grabbed him by the back of his coat.

"This won't take long," Travis assured his wife as he half dragged Jim into the barn. From the corner of his eye he noticed Mary start toward him, then stop, halfway down the steps. He was grateful she chose to let him handle this.

He walked inside the shadow-filled barn and closed the door. They were close to the tack room, and that seemed as good a place as any. Travis steered the boy there.

"I hate you." Jim's eyes were filled with venom. "I've always hated you."

"Good," Travis said brightly. "Now we're getting somewhere. You hate me. Why's that?"

"You should have died. Not my dad. You."

"It didn't happen that way, though, did it. It was your father who was killed that night, not me. That wasn't my choice, boy, so you're stuck with me. Now either we settle what's eating you, or we spend the next ten years doing stupid things to hurt each other. Personally, I'd rather we had this out right now."

"You going to spank me?" Jim made it sound as if he'd get a kick out of Travis trying.

Travis rubbed the side of his jaw as though giving

the idea some consideration. "Seems to me you're too big for a lickin', although it's tempting."

This last comment infuriated Jim, who clenched his fists and brought them up in front of his face. "We'll fight it out, then."

It would've been a mistake to laugh, Travis realized, so he swallowed his amusement. "Fighting's not going to settle this."

"You don't think I can beat you, do you?" Jim taunted.

"Well, boy, since you asked, I'd say you haven't got a prayer."

"I don't care, I don't care." With a wild shout, the twelve-year-old came at him, fists flying, taking Travis by surprise. There wasn't any chance Jim could hurt him, although he was certainly trying. A few blows struck him, but none that would do him any real harm.

Gripping hold of Jim by his belt, Travis lifted him from the ground, arms and legs kicking out furiously. He let Jim struggle until he'd tired himself out enough to listen to reason.

"You ready to talk?" Travis asked.

"I hate you."

"So you said earlier."

"You promised . . . you promised me and Scotty and Beth Ann that you'd find whoever killed Mom and Dad. I believed you, and now . . . now it's like you don't care anymore."

Travis sank onto a bale of hay, removed his Stetson, and wiped his forearm across his forehead. "I haven't given up, and I won't."

Jim spat on the ground. "You're letting them get away with it."

Travis stood up, gripped the boy by the upper arms, and shook him with more force than he intended. The words struggled to escape from between his clenched teeth. "That's not true. No one wants justice more than I do. No one needs it more than you kids. I know that."

"Then do something."

"What?" Travis cried. "The sheriff's office closed the investigation. I've contacted three private investigators, and not one of them is willing to come all the way into Grandview without a huge retainer. All my money's tied up right now. I've tried to do as much as I can on my own."

"Like what?"

"Listen, Jim, I'm not going to stand here and make excuses. There are only so many hours in a day, and I can't afford to donate as much time as I'd like to tracking down the person responsible. I've got a ranch and a family now, and that takes up most of my energy. Eventually whoever was responsible is going to make a mistake. One small slip. They're going to make an innocent remark and think no one will notice. But I will. I'm determined to be patient. It isn't easy, because I'd like nothing better than to see the bastard in jail."

Jim lowered his head, and Travis suspected he was close to tears. He recalled his own battle with his emotions and the struggle he had to keep them bottled inside. When he was finally able to release them it had been like water gushing over the sides of a hydroelectric dam. If it hadn't been for Mary, he didn't know what he would have done.

Now it was Jim's turn.

"Your father was a good man."

"Better than you," Jim spat.

Travis grinned. "You won't get an argument from me."

"He never got in trouble at school."

"You're right," Travis said. "I was the one who raised cain around these parts. If you're trying to live up to my reputation, then you've got quite a ways to go. I suggest you take a shortcut."

"What do you mean?" Jim's gaze was centered on his shoes, and he wiped the sleeve of his jacket under his nose.

"Save yourself some grief and a whole lot of trouble and don't buck the system. You're going to be in school another six years, so you might as well make the effort to get along with the authorities right now."

"You didn't get along with them."

"Yeah, and I paid for it, too. Don't make the same mistakes I did, son." The last word slipped from his mouth before he could stop it. Before he could judge the wisdom of it.

Jim jerked his head up and scrutinized Travis closely.

"You don't have to say it," Travis muttered.

"Say what?"

"You don't need to remind me you're not my son. It's what you were thinking just now, wasn't it?"

Jim lifted one shoulder in a halfhearted shrug.

"You're my nephew, but you're far more than that. I wish I knew a way to explain it better. I was with your dad, pacing the hospital corridor, the night you were born. After we saw your mother and made sure she was recuperating, your dad and I went out celebrating. I guess I was more thrilled than I realized because I lost a boot in the shrubs outside the Logger. Best damn pair of boots I ever owned. Never did find it, either."

Jim seemed to find a bit of humor in that. A smile cracked his lips. "You lost a boot?"

"Yeah. Until you were born, it was just your father and me. You were the first addition to the Thompson family in over twenty years. I was damn pleased Janice had seen fit to give birth to a boy so he could carry on the family name. I never thought I'd marry, so it was up to my brother."

A suspicious sheen brightened Jim's eyes. He knotted his hands into fists and rubbed his eyes.

"Your mother insisted I hold you. Right there in the hospital with everyone looking. Don't take offense, but you were dog ugly. Everyone was saying how cute you were. I didn't see it."

Jim half sobbed, half laughed.

"But even then I saw the man you'd become. I thought about the three of us through the years. Of course there was no telling Scotty was coming or that your dad was going to be killed. Those were just a couple of the unexpected things life threw our way."

"What else did you see?"

"A time when you'd feel like I was important to you, too," Travis admitted solemnly. He hadn't expected to say these things, to bare his soul this way. He'd intended to lay into the boy, read him what his dad used to call the riot act. He wanted it plain as creek water that if Jim ever pulled a stunt like this again, there'd be hell to pay. Life's lessons didn't come cheap, and Travis wasn't there to issue any discount coupons.

"I . . . don't blame you for not wanting us," Jim whispered.

"Not want you?" he challenged. "Who the blazes said something like that?"

The boy shrugged noncommittally.

"All I know is that I was going to move heaven or hell, whichever the state decreed necessary, to make damn sure the four of us stayed together. It's true I hadn't counted on raising you kids, but it wasn't anything I'd ever back away from. You're the only family I've got."

"You don't like me . . . I don't blame you, because sometimes I don't like myself."

Travis chuckled. "You got an attitude, kid, but that's all right because most of us get one sometime in our lives. Generally we outgrow it, like big ears."

"You didn't, at least not until Mary came."

Travis examined the statement, looking for the truth in it, and figured Jim was probably right. He guessed that was what home-cooked meals, regular sex, and a woman's tenderness did for a man.

"It's all right to miss your parents, Jim. Not a day passes that I don't think about Lee. It's like a hole in my gut that doesn't go away. I don't imagine it will until we find whoever was responsible for the accident."

"Men don't cry."

Travis exhaled slowly, gauging his words carefully. "Sometimes it's for the best to let out our emotions. It isn't comfortable. It feels like someone stuck a fistful of cow chips down your throat, but you'll feel better afterward. I did."

Jim hung his head, and Travis waited for him to speak. He didn't do it with words; instead a tear splashed against the floor. He reached for the boy and brought him close and held him. The young body broke into silent sobs that shook his shoulders. Travis felt his throat thicken as Jim raised his arms and hugged his middle.

"It's all right, son. Everything's going to be all right."

And for the first time it felt like that to Travis.

They emerged from the barn ten minutes later. Travis had his arm draped across Jim's shoulders. They'd crossed important ground together, forged a bond that wouldn't easily be broken.

He happened to glance up and saw Mary. His Mary. She was standing on the porch steps, leaving Travis to wonder if she'd spent the whole time there. The sun was setting and seemed to settle over the gentle curve of her shoulders. His steps faltered momentarily as his gaze found hers. She looked so damn beautiful, standing there with her hand over her heart, her eyes soft and as blue as anything he'd ever seen.

Life was good. Travis couldn't recall a time he'd ever thought that before or believed it was possible.

Tilly knocked against the front door and waited. No one answered, and then she realized she would probably need to ring the bell. Pride dictated that if she'd come this far, she'd be a fool to turn away because she was afraid to push a stupid button. She used her thumb to hold down the buzzer and kept it there for several ear-shattering seconds.

"All right, all right," Logan snapped impatiently as he threw open the door. He froze when he saw Tilly. Apparently he'd come straight from the shower; he was all wrapped up in a thick robe.

"Hello, Logan."

He looked at her as if she were an apparition, as if he were certain she'd vanish right before his eyes any second. "You came."

She smiled and nodded. "I thought about what you had to say about things . . . and realized you were right. I never believed you'd want to marry me. I still don't. My life hasn't been any pristine walk through the park, if you know what I mean."

"That doesn't matter to me, Tilly, it never has." He reached for her hands and drew her inside. When he noticed the diamond ring on her finger, he closed his eyes as if to issue a silent prayer of gratitude.

"There are things you should know before you

decide you want to marry me. Things I should have told you a long time ago. I'm no bargain."

"Don't say that again," he told her sternly. "None of it matters, you hear? You're the woman I love." He gathered her in his arms and kissed her with a hunger that left them both weak with longing.

"I didn't dare hope you'd come," Logan whispered, rubbing his lips over hers.

"I tried to stay away. I told myself it'd be a mistake to believe you really meant everything you said, but I couldn't do it. You don't have to marry me, even now you don't."

"Our children might appreciate it later on, though, don't you think?"

"You really meant that, about raising a family?"

"With all my heart. As long as you're willing." His eyes were filled with an expectant love.

Tilly nodded eagerly.

"I don't know how you're going to feel about this, but I was thinking it might not be such a good idea for us to make love for a while."

"Why not?" Tilly demanded. He was right, she didn't like this decree one bit. It was a little late to play the role of the virgin. She'd given that up at fifteen on the backseat of a Dodge convertible.

"Because I want everything to be right between us with no questions, no doubts."

"I certainly hope you intend to make this a short engagement."

Logan's smile was broad and full of love. "Damn short. Just enough time for us to make all the proper arrangements. We'll let Martha cater a reception."

"You want a reception?"

"Of course."

"You must have told your dad."

Logan grinned again. "A few days ago."

"How'd he take it?"

Logan laughed, and Tilly swore she'd never heard a more beautiful sound. "He said I was old enough to marry whoever I damn well please, and Tilly Lawrence, you please me."

"You know, I'm not a bad cook, or at least I'm not completely inept in the kitchen. Mary Thompson will teach me to sew, I know she will. Before long—Oh, my goodness." She stopped and pressed her hands to her lips. "Next thing you know, I'm going to be a regular housewife with kids and a husband."

"So you cook." Logan kissed the end of her pert nose. "Good. Why don't you see what you can rustle up for dinner while I get dressed?"

A frenzied exchange of kisses nearly routed Tilly into the bedroom, but she laughingly reminded him of their agreement. Logan looked sorry for ever having said anything, which made her love him all the more.

Bragging about her expertise in the kitchen might have been a mistake. She examined his cupboards and found them as empty as her own. A box of raisin bran, two cans of tunafish, and a sack of potatoes would take more imagination than she had.

The freezer on top of the refrigerator netted her a half gallon of ice cream that looked as if it had been left over from the Fourth of July.

Thinking he might keep a larger freezer in the garage, she opened the door leading from the house. Her guess proved to be accurate. Turning on the light switch, she scooted past the blue car to the upright freezer against the wall. She found two T-bone steaks and a bag of frozen hash browns and was carrying them back into the kitchen when she saw it.

If ever there had been a moment Tilly wanted to die, it was then. Die, because if she were dead, she wouldn't feel this terrible pain.

The sense of betrayal cut far deeper than the lies. Everything Logan had said to her had been a lie. He didn't love her. He only wanted to marry her for legal reasons. According to the law, a wife couldn't testify against her husband, or so she'd heard.

The proof of his deceit sat directly in front of her. Logan's car. The dented front, the scrape of paint along the side the same color as Lee Thompson's car.

This was the vehicle Logan had told her he'd traded in for a new one shortly after his arrival in Grandview. The same car Travis Thompson had been searching for in the parking lot the night of the Harvest Moon Festival.

The car that was responsible for the deaths of Lee and Janice Thompson.

Twenty

Mary stood naked in front of the fog-smudged bathroom mirror, squinting, seeking a glimpse of herself. A woman was supposed to know these things. Especially a married woman.

Tilly had been the first one to put the notion she might be pregnant into her head. Pregnant. Mary flattened her palm over her abdomen.

If she'd suffered from the more classic symptoms, she could have been sure. But not once had she been queasy. If anything, she was more fit than ever. Her appetite was good, better than average, and she felt wonderful. A pregnant woman generally felt just the opposite, or so she'd heard.

At first Mary had brushed off Tilly's suggestion as sheer nonsense. Then, after consulting a number of books on pregnancy and childbirth, she'd acknowledged that if anyone was being foolish, it was she, and quite possibly Travis. They'd never given birth control a second thought, while they'd repeatedly enjoyed the delights of their marriage.

No longer able to ignore the possibility, Mary had made an appointment with Doc Anderson. His nurse had squeezed her in late in the afternoon, but waiting even another few hours seemed unreasonable now. She wanted to know. Needed to know, because keeping even the possibility to herself was becoming increasingly difficult.

Tears glazed her eyes as she tried to imagine what she would have been like if she'd never answered Travis's newspaper ad. The dull, lifeless existence as Petite's librarian seemed so far removed from the woman she was now. It was more difficult to accept that Travis and the children hadn't always been a part of her life.

Mary finished dressing and stuck a load of jeans in the washing machine. When she finished she rewarded herself with a call to her longtime friend.

"Georgeanne," Mary said into the telephone receiver, "it's me, Mary."

"Mary . . . oh, Mary, it's so good to hear from you!" Georgeanne's happy chatter cheered her instantly. "Oh, my goodness, I've missed you so much. I can't tell you the number of times I've wanted to call, but you seem to be so busy, and I . . . Mary, your letters are so full of your joy. You're happy, really happy, aren't you?"

Mary's smile was warm as she watched the morning blossom softly over the hill. With it came a remarkable, unrestrained joy she'd never dreamed would be hers. Being plain and small had been obstacles enough, but intelligence had killed any chance of romance in her small town. She'd been discarded, rejected, overlooked. A left-over girl. That was what her own grandmother had called her once. But no longer.

"I am happy," she admitted.

"I never dreamed this crazy marriage of yours would work. I hope you'll forgive me, Mary, for being so selfish. I should never have said the things I did."

"Georgeanne, don't fret." Mary was unwilling to pay long-distance rates to hear her friend whine over her misgivings. No woman in her right mind would have left the only home she'd ever known to marry a stranger. That was, unless she was desperate. As her best friend, Georgeanne had had every right to be concerned.

"I'm calling because, well, because I think I might be pregnant," Mary explained a bit sheepishly.

"Mary! How wonderful! Are you taking care of yourself?"

"Of course I am."

"You make sure Travis doesn't let you lift anything heavier than a—"

"Travis doesn't know."

Georgeanne clucked her disapproval. "Why in heaven's name doesn't he? The dear man's going to be a father!"

"I can't say anything to Travis until everything's confirmed. I feel giddy, Georgeanne, I'm so happy. Every time I think about a baby tears come to my eyes."

"What's Travis going to say?"

Mary laughed. She'd put a lot of thought into that same question. Her guess was that he'd never given the matter a second thought. "He'll be ecstatic." Stunned, but delighted, Mary decided.

"You'll let me know the minute you get home from the doctor, won't you?"

"Of course," Mary promised.

Tilly sat on the easy chair in her living room all night. She hadn't slept. Hadn't eaten. Nor had she cried since she'd found the damaged car in Logan's garage. One more piece of the puzzle neatly in place. That explained why he'd bought a new car when his old one was perfectly good. It was crazy that she hadn't connected Logan's purchase with the Thompsons' accident.

Come sunrise, she knew what she had to do. Packing was easy, she'd done it so often. Grandview had been her fresh start in life, yet she'd made the same mistakes, lived the same old lies. When was she going to learn? Probably never.

Logan's diamond ring was clenched tightly in the palm of her hand. He'd insisted she keep it, and she had, although she wasn't sure why. Possibly as a reminder of what a fool she was. A reminder of how close she'd come to living the impossible dream.

Her fist ached so badly, and still she didn't relax her hand. Not even when her arm started to throb. Nor did she weep. She was empty. Numb. Dead to all the lonely tomorrows.

As she had countless times in the past, she'd survive. One day at a time. One hour at a time. And for now, minute to minute.

Not once did she allow her mind to dwell on Logan or the shocked, sick look that had come over him when he'd found her in his garage. He hadn't tried to explain or offer her an excuse. For that much she was grateful. As she'd walked past him, he'd reached out and touched her arm, lightly, without pressure, and told her she could keep the diamond.

Tilly didn't know how she was going to be able to report for work. Somehow she'd make it through her shift, and when she was through she'd pull out of Grandview, Montana. There was nothing left for her here except heartache and a whole lot of memories she'd rather forget. It was the same reason she'd left Idaho. At this rate, she could work her way across fifty states, dying a little more each stop along the way.

By ten everything of value she owned was loaded in the trunk of her Chevy Impala. She hoped Martha would forgive her for leaving her in a crunch, but that was only a small worry. Tilly doubted she would manage to forgive herself. Not for running, that was second nature to her. But for swallowing the truth, keeping it to herself when she should have gone straight to the sheriff's office. Her last gift to Logan was her silence.

"What's the matter with you, kid?" Martha said

when she walked through the cafe kitchen. "You look awful."

"I'm giving my notice," Tilly said without emotion, steeling herself for the confrontation. "It's time I moved on."

Martha handed her spatula to the assistant chef and followed Tilly. "What in tarnation are you talking about, girl? This is your home now. You fit in here better than me, and I was born and raised in Grandview. The customers love you."

"I'm leaving, Martha." Unwilling to argue, Tilly reached for a pencil and wrote down the specials for the day on the back of her pad.

"Leaving?" Martha cried, hands braced against her hips. "I thought you were smarter than that."

"So did I," Tilly murmured, "but I can't stay. I won't stay."

Martha mulled over her words. "It's Doc's boy, isn't it?"

Tilly didn't answer the question. "You've been a good friend. Sally, too. I'm going to miss you both."

"All right," Martha muttered, throwing her hands into the air. "I can see you've already made up your mind. I don't know why it is, but every time I find myself a decent waitress, she falls in love. That's the beginning of the end."

Tilly felt much the same. Love was the beginning of the end for her, too, only she kept repeating the same, senseless mistake. She'd convinced herself with each new relationship that it was going to be better or different. With Logan she'd been so sure, but then she'd felt that way about the others, too.

She tied her apron around her waist and walked onto the floor to relieve Susan, a housewife who worked part-time.

She hadn't taken two steps when she saw Logan. For several unguarded moments she soaked in the sight of him. He looked as bad as she felt. That offered her no comfort. He must have sensed her presence because he turned toward her.

Her first instinct was to walk away. But he wouldn't allow that. His gaze held her as effectively as a policeman's grip.

"Hello, Tilly." She noticed how he glanced at her bare ring finger. A flicker of pain flashed into his eyes but was quickly gone.

"Logan."

"Give me twenty-four hours."

"For what?" The man was arrogant beyond belief.

"That's all I'm asking."

"Sorry," she said with a flippant laugh. "That's sixteen hours too long. As soon as my shift is over, I'm leaving Grandview."

He nodded. Slowly he raised his hand to her face and caressed the line of her jaw with his finger.

Tilly swayed but caught herself in time and jerked away.

"I'll be right there, Pete," she said to the feed store manager, who took a seat at the counter. She practically raced to pour him a cup of coffee.

Logan turned and walked out the door.

Tilly's hands were shaking so badly, she nearly scalded herself. The physical pain felt good. It helped her remember she was alive.

Five minutes after Logan left, Travis Thompson wandered into the cafe and straddled a seat at the counter.

"Tilly, has Mary been here?"

"Haven't seen her," she said, unable to look him in the eye. Travis and Mary were another reason she had to leave town. They were her friends, and she was betraying that friendship, leaving Travis and the children to the agony of the unknown.

"She's got to be someplace in town."

"If she stops in, I'll tell her you're looking for her," Tilly said, pulling down Pete's order from the kitchen. She delivered it and refilled his coffee.

"Doc Anderson's nurse called and canceled her appointment this afternoon. Hell, I didn't even know she had one." Travis set his Stetson on the counter. "I'll take a cup of that coffee," he said, scratching the side of his head. "What would Mary have a doctor's appointment for?"

Tilly brought him his coffee. "Is Beth Ann's cast ready to come off?"

"Not yet. Besides, the appointment was for Mary."

"Travis," Tilly said, out of patience with all men, especially one who could be so damned obtuse, "think about it."

"About what?" he snapped.

"Why does a woman generally see a doctor?"

"If I knew that, I wouldn't be pumping you for information, now, would I?"

"Did it ever occur to you that Mary might be pregnant?"

"Pregnant!" Travis bellowed, spewing out a mouthful of hot coffee. He reared up out of his seat and grabbed his hat, slamming it down on his head. "Pregnant," he repeated, sinking onto the stool as if his legs had lost their strength. "Why, that's . . ." He paused when Tilly moved in front of him. "Why, that's entirely possible," he admitted.

"Hello, is anyone here?" Mary stood in the middle of Doc Anderson's empty waiting room. Generally an empty seat was a rare commodity at Doc's.

At the receptionist's desk, she set down her purse and rummaged through it for her appointment book, certain she'd written down the time correctly.

A noise, the sound of breaking glass, startled her. "Hello," she called again, "is anyone here?"

Silence.

"Hello," she said a bit louder this time, stepping into the long hallway toward Doc's office. "It's Mary Thompson. Is Doc Anderson here?"

"Mary." The hoarse sound of her own name greeted her as she discovered Doc sitting at his desk. His eyes were wild and his face twisted. In one hand he held a whiskey bottle and in the other a small handgun.

"Doc?"

"Mary . . . sweet Mary Thompson." He fortified himself with a long swallow of the whiskey.

"Doc, what's wrong?" she asked, eyeing the gun.

"Leave." He waved the weapon at her. "Get out of here."

Mary tensed. Every instinct demanded she turn and run. Either her fear paralyzed her or her intuition. Doc wasn't planning on hurting her. He wouldn't demand she leave if that were the case.

"You've been drinking," she said softly.

He sobbed and stood, slouching against the wall.

"Doc, please listen to me. There's help for you—"

"Not anymore," he said, cutting her off. "Leave, Mary, for the love of heaven, just leave me alone."

"If I do," she argued, "you're going to do something stupid."

"I already have."

Mary didn't know if she should continue to reason with him or not. "This town needs you," she told him. "People respect and love you."

"Tell them I'm sorry," he cried, and staggered forward. "It was an accident . . . I never meant to hurt anyone. Tell . . . tell the children for me."

"Doc, you're not making any sense. Give me the gun and then we can talk this whole thing out. No one's going to hate you."

Mary thought she heard something behind her, but she didn't dare divert her attention from Doc.

"You'll know soon . . . enough."

"Doc, please."

"Hate myself . . . tell Travis I'm sorry . . . I never meant to kill anyone," he cried again. "Lee and Janice were good people . . . they shouldn't have died. I'm so sorry . . . tell Travis."

"You're going to have to tell me that yourself, old man," Travis's steel tones announced from behind her.

Twenty-one

"*Get behind me,*" *Travis instructed*, doing his best to jockey himself between Mary and the pistol Doc Anderson was holding. His eyes were trained on the older man.

"You killed Lee and Janice," he said calmly, edging his way around Mary. He prayed she had sense enough to slip away while he kept Doc occupied. Instead she stayed glued to his back. He tried to push her farther back but couldn't do much without attracting Doc's attention.

"What am I going to do now?" Doc cried, waving the weapon in their direction.

"First you're going to give me the gun," Travis said, extending his arm.

"No," Doc returned forcefully. "I'll end up in prison. I couldn't take that." He staggered a few steps forward, pointing the gun toward Mary.

Travis froze, all senses heightened until the

slightest sound was magnified in his ears. He could smell Doc's fear. And his own.

Then, slowly, cautiously, he stepped toward Doc.

"Stop right there."

"Put down the gun," Travis encouraged. "You don't want to do this."

"I . . . can't. I won't hurt you, I left . . . a letter. One to you and the other to Logan. Oh, God, Logan . . . my only son. He wanted to help me . . . instead I ruined him. . . . He tried so hard. I was never a good father to him. . . ." He was sobbing uncontrollably now.

Travis advanced another step.

"Stay back."

The barrel of the gun loomed before him like the huge gaping mouth of a cannon. Mary was behind him, which at this point was small comfort. He couldn't trust her to do the sane, sensible thing, like sneaking away and calling the sheriff. It was obvious Doc was psychotic, driven mad with booze and guilt.

"I didn't want to hurt you . . . never meant to."

"I know."

"Did you suffer?" Doc dropped the bottle. He wavered a couple of steps. "Were you in terrible pain? I thought about that. Dear, sweet Jesus, why wouldn't you let me sleep?"

"What are you talking about?"

"The night I killed you," Doc shouted impatiently.

Travis paused, then said evenly, "No, I didn't suffer. Neither did my wife." He edged toward the doctor, taking one minuscule step at a time.

The slightest abrupt movement might topple the man's precarious hold on sanity.

"I . . . suffered, too . . . every day since, every night. No sleep, drugs didn't help . . . not even whiskey."

"I know how sorry you are," Travis said.

"You do?"

Travis nodded. "Janice forgives you, too."

"The children . . . I couldn't look at those children, knowing I had killed their parents."

"Janice and I know it was a terrible accident. You didn't mean to hurt us."

Doc's shoulders heaved with the force of his sobbing. "I . . . I drove you off the road and didn't stop. I'm a physician . . . and I didn't stop. That's the worst part, knowing . . . I might have saved you if I hadn't been so scared. You must hate me . . . I hate myself."

"It was an accident," Travis repeated.

"I . . . I stopped drinking. I promised myself and God, and I didn't touch it again . . . not for weeks." His gaze fell to the discarded, empty bottle on the floor. "I need it," he shouted. "I hate it . . . I didn't want to drink, but I had to have something to get me through the day."

"Dad."

Logan Anderson's calm voice sounded from behind Travis.

"Logan . . . go away."

"Give me the gun."

"No . . . no. Got to finish what I started."

"Dad, you don't realize what you're doing.

You're not well. I'll take care of everything." Logan eased past Travis and continued on toward his father.

"Not anymore . . . no one can. I deserve to die. . . ." Doc lifted the gun to his head.

"Dad, no!" Logan shouted as he rushed forward.

Everything happened in slow motion for Travis. Logan flung himself at his father, and it seemed he flew through the air. He gripped hold of Doc's arm with both hands.

The gun exploded, and the force of it knocked Travis, who hadn't realized he was so close to Doc, against the wall.

Mary screamed in panic and called for him.

"No . . . no!" Doc's hysterical wail blended with hers, and he sagged, his features contorted.

Logan gripped his shoulder, and a dark glistening stain spread through his shirt and coat. Instinctively he gripped the wound and stumbled backward, catching himself against the wall. He slid down it until he was in a sitting position on the floor. Trickles of blood seeped through his splayed fingers and over his hand. His gaze sought out his father's, but Travis noticed his eyes were blank. Then he went slack and slumped onto his side.

Travis removed the gun from Doc's hand.

"My son, my son . . . I've killed my son." Doc's knees crumpled slowly and he pitched forward.

"Travis." His name was little more breath than sound. He turned in time to see his wife, as pale as alabaster, sink to the floor like a sack of potatoes.

*   *   *

Tilly sat patiently by the hospital bed. She'd been there from the moment she'd heard Logan had been shot and his father arrested for the deaths of Lee and Janice Thompson. She still wore her pale pink uniform from Martha's, and had a wad of damp tissue clenched in her hand.

Logan had been in surgery when Tilly arrived. She'd paced the hospital corridor, awaiting the outcome, not knowing if he'd survive. When she'd learned Logan would recover, she'd broken down. For the last few hours she had been content to sit by Logan's bedside, surround him with her love, and wait.

He was pale; he was so deathly pale. Chalky shadows marked his face, and a film of moisture dampened his upper brow. Tilly worried he was burning up with fever. She longed to touch him, to run her hand down his precious face, to hold him in her arms again. Only hours earlier she'd been determined to walk away from him, but nothing on this earth was powerful enough to force her from his side now that she knew the truth.

She took comfort in the steady rise and fall of his chest, willing him to rest in comfort, free from pain.

Sometime later, how long Tilly didn't know, she discovered that his eyes were open and he was studying her. He continued to stare as if he weren't sure he could trust she was actually there.

"Hello," she whispered.

"Tilly?"

"You damn well better not be thinking I'm some other women, bub," she teased. She would have preferred him to mistake her for an angel, but she doubted that many of God's messengers had blotchy red faces and pink uniforms. "How do you feel?" she ventured.

Logan moistened his lips. "Like I've got a hole the size of Kansas in my shoulder."

"Why didn't you tell me?" Tilly said. "Why'd you let me believe you were responsible?"

Logan's eyes drifted shut, and Tilly knew it was wrong of her to demand an explanation when he was so weak. There'd be plenty of time for that later.

"Dad had taken my car and returned hours later in a panic, drunk and badly shaken. I knew something was wrong, and when he broke down and told me, I lost it. I hadn't had a drink in years. I thought I was beyond ever needing one again. It's a disease, Tilly, cunning and powerful. That was the night I came to you, remember?"

Tilly nodded.

"It was also the night I realized I'd fallen in love with you. You were the one person I could turn to when it seemed the whole world was exploding in my face."

"It's all right, you don't need to tell me now. Rest."

"I'm an attorney . . . I should have known protecting him was wrong."

"He's your father."

"He's sick, Tilly."

"I know."

"He's been an alcoholic for years, even while I was growing up. God only knows how he was able to hide it. He never drank at the office, and by every outward appearance his life was in order. He'd been living a lie for so long, he didn't know how to deal with the truth. The accident forced him to face up to his problem."

Tilly's hand reached for his. "You would have let me walk away?"

"I . . . had no choice. I talked with Dad countless times, pleaded with him, and each time he'd promise to turn himself over to the authorities, but he kept finding excuses. We had terrible fights about it. I threatened a hundred times to turn him in, but I couldn't make myself do it. Not my own father."

Tilly massaged the inside of his wrist with her thumb.

"I couldn't tell you, Tilly, couldn't put that burden on you. I went to Dad, explained about us. I thought it would prompt him to do the right thing. Instead it drove him over the edge."

"You can't blame yourself for what happened."

"On a conscious level I don't, but in another way I do. Matters should never have gone this far. When you talked about trying to fix things for me with Travis, that's what I was doing with Dad. I should have known better. Taking care of my own problems is all I can handle. I can't help my father any longer, not that I ever was helping him. I just assumed because it was costing me so much, it must be doing him some good. I was wrong. Because of that everything nearly blew up in my face."

"I wanted to believe you so much, but I couldn't let myself."

"I don't blame you, baby. I appreciated your strength."

"My strength. You're wrong. I'm the weak one. I always have been. I had a baby, Logan," she whispered, "and gave him up for adoption. I wanted to tell you that for a long time. He's three now."

"Shhh." Logan's hand gripped hers. "It doesn't matter, Tilly. None of it matters. You did what was best for you and your child."

"I know, it's just that I thought you should know what you're getting." Tilly looked away, unable to believe she'd found such a man.

"I've always known, Tilly, and I don't want you any different than you are."

"Why didn't you tell me about your dad?" she whispered.

"Would you have believed me? Think about it, baby. All the evidence pointed to me. You saw me drunk the night of the accident. It was my car Dad was driving. All I could tell you was that it wasn't me and leave it at that."

"The engagement ring?"

"It wasn't a bribe," he said, and his eyes darkened with his sincerity. "I meant every word. I love you, I want us to be together."

"It's a good thing because this ring isn't coming off my finger again. Not for anything. You'd better concentrate on recovering because we've got lots of lost time to make up for. I don't intend this engagement to be a long one."

His eyes met hers, and when he smiled, it was full and sexy. "You can count on it."

"I am. Furthermore, you should probably know, I've thrown away my birth control pills."

Logan's grin grew wider. "Give me a day or two, that's all I'll need to fulfill your wish."

Tilly sniffled and rubbed her hand across her face.

"Baby, don't cry."

"I can't help it. I'm so damn happy."

"Good. Let's both stay that way for the next fifty years."

"Why the hell didn't you leave? Couldn't you see Doc had gone crazy?" Travis demanded the minute they were outside Sheriff Tucker's office. They'd spent hours answering questions and a bunch of other nonsense Tucker seemed to think was necessary. Travis's patience had long since been used up.

His unreasonable anger was directed at Mary, but he couldn't seem to stop himself. He helped her inside the truck, but her hand on his arm stopped him.

"Hold me," Mary asked in a small voice.

Travis brought her into his arms, absorbing the miracle of her, warm and alive. His hands were in her hair, and her breath was soft and sweet against his skin. She smelled of roses and violets.

"I was so scared."

Travis's arms tightened. This was his woman, and he'd just lived through one of the worst hours of his life. All he'd known when he'd confronted Doc holding the gun on her was that he wasn't going to lose her. Mary would walk away from this no matter what it took, even if it meant his own life. When she'd fainted, he'd lost a good five years to fear, thinking she somehow had been hit, too. It took several moments before he'd realized she'd passed out.

"Let's go home," he said on the tail end of a sigh.

He waited until she was comfortably situated on the seat before he shut the door. When he climbed in beside her, he started the engine. Holding her had assuaged some of his anger. His hands tightened around the steering wheel.

"You might have said something," he blurted out.

"Travis, I'm sorry, I truly am. It was wrong of me to have misled you. I probably should have said something much sooner."

"You're damn right you should have."

She paled at the vehemence with which he spoke, but Travis couldn't help that. He was going to be a father, and it seemed everyone in town had known it except him.

"Being a rancher's wife . . . if I'd told you sooner, you and the children might not have chosen me, and I—"

Travis swore savagely. "What the hell are you talking about?"

"My aversion to the sight of blood. That's why I fainted. What are *you* talking about?"

"I thought you were pregnant." He shifted gears with unnecessary force.

"You know about that?"

"You mean you were planning on keeping it a secret?"

"Of course not. Travis, I don't think we should discuss this until you're rational."

"Unfortunately, that may take a hell of a long time." Travis sped ahead, uncaring that they'd left the minivan in town. They'd come back for it later. What was important was getting Mary home and in his arms and in his bed again. Only then would his fear recede. It wasn't until he'd shifted gears again that he noticed his hands were shaking. Delayed reaction, he realized. His heart hadn't fully recovered even now. He was a rancher and a hell-raiser, and he'd lived on the hard edge of life, flirting with danger, even death, but he'd done it without a trace of fear.

Fear, Travis decided, was seeing an insane doctor holding a gun on his wife. He trembled with it hours later, knowing how terribly close he'd come to losing Mary.

"I was keeping the news as a surprise."

"When did you plan to tell me? On the delivery table?"

"Don't be silly."

Travis grumbled under his breath and chanced a look in her direction. She sat, her backbone straight as a bookcase, her hands folded primly in her lap, looking very much like the frumpy librarian who'd taken his life by storm.

"Well?" she asked with an exaggerated sigh, as though she were impatient about something. "What do you think about us having a baby? Are you pleased?"

Most husbands probably said something poetic and mushy at times like these. Things about being so overwhelmed with joy that his heart forgot to beat and his lungs didn't need to breathe. Mary deserved to hear those fanciful words. He felt her scrutiny and knew she was waiting for his answer.

"Tilly was the one who told me. I damn near choked to death on a mouthful of coffee, if knowing that pleases you."

Mary laughed softly, and he turned and smiled at her. Damn, but he loved this woman. She was foolish and stubborn, but she was one hell of a wife, about all the woman he ever hoped to handle.

It was hard to keep his eyes on the road, she was so pretty. Her cheeks were rosy and her blue eyes were twinkling up at him. A breeze ruffled and teased her hair, blowing it this way and that.

"I knew you'd be shocked. I hoped you'd be as delighted as I am. Are you?"

Travis nodded. "Hell, Mary, as soon as Tilly said it, I figured it had to be true, and then I realized how much I wanted it to be true. I remembered how Lee was after Janice first told him she was pregnant with Jim. He came over and he was so damn excited. He got this funny look on his face. When I asked him about it, he just chuckled.

"I've missed my brother. He was more to me than just my brother, he was my friend, too. Ever since he's been gone, it's felt like there's a giant emptiness right here." He slammed his fist against his heart. "That space filled up when I learned you were pregnant. For the first time since Lee's been gone I felt his presence far stronger than his absence. Yes, Mary, I'm pleased you're going to have our baby. Nothing on this earth could make me happier."

"Could twins?"

"Twins," he blurted out. "You're teasing, I hope."

"Well, it's much too soon to be sure, but they run in my family. My mother was a twin, and—"

Travis drove to the side of the road, put the truck in neutral, and reached for her. She came into his embrace like a magnet, wrapping her slender arms around him.

"God knows, I love you."

"I love you, too."

He'd never thought it would be possible to find such happiness with the frumpy old maid who'd stepped off the plane, but that was before she'd bulldozed her way into his heart. Now he couldn't live without her any more than he could go without air or water. Mary was his window, his light, his love.

Mary nestled in his embrace and yawned. "I'm so tired. I don't know about you, but I've had an exhausting day."

"You might say that I have, too." Travis smiled at the understatement. He switched gears, and within minutes they were home.

The instant they pulled into the yard, Jim, Scotty, and Beth Ann raced down the back steps. Travis climbed out of the pickup and helped Mary out.

"Listen, kids, we've got something to tell you."

"You mean about Doc Anderson?" Scotty asked. "We already know. Billy Jenkins called and said Doc is going to a mental hospital and Logan got shot and that Mary fainted and you were bossing everyone around and telling them what to do."

"Billy said you wouldn't let anyone take Mary out of your arms."

"How the hell did Billy Jenkins hear all that?"

"His mother told him and Hester Johnson told her. I don't know who told her."

"Come on inside," Travis urged. Mary ushered the two younger children in ahead of them. Jim lingered behind with Travis.

"You were right," Jim said, stuffing his hands in his pockets.

The way Travis figured things, it might be a good ten or fifteen years before he heard those same words out of Jim's mouth again.

"It all came out on its own," Jim elaborated.

"Doc's a sick man. I don't think we could ever punish him as much as he has himself."

Jim nodded. "Mom and Dad wouldn't have wanted us to hate him."

Travis lingered at the bottom of the stairs. "There's something else. Mary may be pregnant."

The way news traveled around these parts, Jim probably knew about his baby before he did.

"Really?"

Travis grinned and nodded.

Jim placed his foot on the bottom step and shook his head. "I remember when Mom was pregnant with Beth Ann. I've got to be honest with you, Uncle Travis, I don't know if I can go through this again."

Travis suppressed a smile, and with his arm around Jim's shoulders the two walked into the house. Already Mary had gotten Scotty and Beth Ann organized. She was at the sink, washing potatoes for their dinner.

Travis removed his hat and coat and stood behind her. He wrapped his arms around her middle and laid his hand flat against her stomach. Mary's hand covered his.

"Are you two going to get mushy?" Scotty demanded.

"Wait until you hear what Uncle Travis told me," Jim said from behind him.

Mary twisted her head around to look up at him. "You told Jim?"

He nodded. "I was surprised he didn't already know. Most everyone else did." Chuckling, he turned his wife into his arms and watched as their two separate shadows became one.

Travis Thompson had found his peace at last.

EATING
for LIFE

EATING
for LIFE

One Simple Diet for Total Health

Michael Mogadam, M.D.

Clinical Associate Professor, George Washington
University School of Medicine, Washington, D.C.

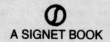

A SIGNET BOOK

SIGNET
Published by New American Library, a division of
Penguin Group (USA) Inc., 375 Hudson Street,
New York, New York 10014, U.S.A.
Penguin Books Ltd, 80 Strand,
London WC2R 0RL, England
Penguin Books Australia Ltd, 250 Camberwell Road,
Camberwell, Victoria 3124, Australia
Penguin Books Canada Ltd, 10 Alcorn Avenue,
Toronto, Ontario, Canada M4V 3B2
Penguin Books (N.Z.) Ltd, Cnr Rosedale and Airborne Roads,
Albany, Auckland 1310, New Zealand

Penguin Books Ltd, Registered Offices:
80 Strand, London WC2R 0RL, England

First published by Signet, an imprint of New American Library,
a division of Penguin Group (USA) Inc.

First Printing, January 2004
10 9 8 7 6 5 4 3 2 1

PUBLISHER'S NOTE
Every effort as been made to ensure that the information contained in this
book is complete and accurate. However, neither the publisher nor the author
is engaged in rendering professional advice or services to the individual
reader. The ideas, procedures, and suggestions contained in this book are not
intended as a substitute for consulting with your physician. All matters regarding your health require medical supervision. Neither the author nor the publisher shall be liable or responsible for any loss or damage allegedly arising
from any information or suggestion in this book.

Contents

CONTENTS

Introduction

Let's face it. We are a nation of disease-oriented, not prevention-minded, people. We wait and do very little until people have heart attacks; then we pounce all over them with everything at our disposal. Yet despite our sophisticated and expensive medical technology and a vast number of modern "life-saving" drugs, one and a half million Americans suffer a heart attack each year, of whom a third die, and a large number of others experience long-lasting cardiovascular complications or disabilities. The majority of these deaths and disabilities should never happen; coronary artery disease and heart attacks are mostly preventable!

Consider another example: In the U.S., two out of thee adults, and one out of three children and adolescents, have a weight problem, and half of these have moderate to severe obesity. (And contrary to a common misconception, children and adolescents do *not* outgrow their weight problem; more than 80 percent track it to adulthood.) Most of these people are affected by at least one weight-related disease, such as diabetes, hypertension, abnormal blood cholesterol, coronary artery disease, liver dysfunction, degenerative joint disease, or breast and colon cancer.

The prevalence (number of individuals per thousand) of diabetes among Americans has increased by more than 200 percent in the past fifteen years, and by more than 500 percent in the past thirty years! Today, an estimated twenty million Americans suffer from diabetes and an equal number have an undetected, early form of the disease. Ten years ago type II diabetes was unheard of among children and adolescents—after all, this was supposed to be the disease of mature people, past their forties. But today, type II diabetes is one of the fastest growing epidemics. Yet, like heart disease, diabetes is almost always preventable!

Table 1
ESTIMATED NUMBER OF AMERICANS
WITH PREVENTABLE CHRONIC DISORDERS

Disorder	Millions
Weight problems	130
Abnormal blood cholesterol	100
Hypertension	65
Osteoporosis	60
Metabolic Syndrome*	50
Diabetes	35
Alcoholism & Other (Non-tobacco) Drug Addictions	30
Coronary Artery Disease	30
Cancers of the Breast, Colon, Lungs & Prostate	5
Chronic Bronchitis & Emphysema (Smoke-Related)	5
Liver Diseases (Hepatitis B & C, Alcohol-Related)	3
Vascular (Stroke-Induced) Dementia	3
TOTAL	**516****

* Metabolic syndrome is another new epidemic disease characterized by a moderate to severe weight problem, a sedentary lifestyle, an abnormal blood cholesterol level, hypertension, and insulin resistance or frank diabetes. It affects 1 out of 4 adult Americans!

**Obviously there are some overlaps; i.e., the same person may have several disorders.

Coronary artery disease and diabetes are only two examples among a large number of preventable chronic diseases (table 1) that we do very little or nothing at all to prevent. People don't go to bed one night and wake up in the morning with a weight problem, diabetes, coronary artery disease, or breast and colon cancers. The common bond among all the listed diseases is that they are principally caused or aggravated by nutritional and lifestyle miscues over many years. And there lies the problem: Aside from vaccinations for certain infectious diseases, there are no shortcut solutions to long-term (chronic) diseases. So what should we do?

Clearly it would be an impossible and unmanageable task if we had to adopt one set of dietary or lifestyle changes to prevent heart attacks, another plan to lose weight, another to prevent diabetes, yet another to reduce the risk of various cancers, or directed at preventing a host of other chronic disorders. But what if a single nutritional and lifestyle plan could dramatically reduce your risk of experiencing any of these chronic diseases or cancers? Even more importantly, what if such a plan was user-friendly and didn't make you feel deprived, bored, or frustrated to the point of giving up? Welcome to *Eating for Life*!

Chapter One

Why Do We Have So Many Chronic Diseases?

We have a paradox. On one hand, we have made enormous progress in medicine and nutritional sciences, and have a vast number of life-saving drugs and medical technology. On the other hand, we are in the midst of multiple, simultaneous epidemics including weight problems, diabetes, hypertension, coronary artery disease, osteoporosis, and a large number of cancers, as shown in table 1. *Why do we have so many chronic diseases when we are supposed to be so healthy?*

1. Longevity. About 150 years ago, the average life span in America was about forty-seven years. Today, it is about eighty years for women, and seventy-five years for men. A similar, dramatic change in longevity has occurred in nearly all developed countries. Clearly this is not due to any change in our genes; such changes take one or two million years. Rather, what accounts for our

Table 2
THE 20 MAJOR CORONARY RISK FACTORS

Risk Factor	Relative Risk*
1. Low birth weight	2
2. High blood pressure	2
3. Abdominal obesity	2
4. Elevated blood C-reactive protein **(due to chronic inflammations, or infections with c. pneumoniae)**	2
5. Elevated blood fibrinogen level	2
6. Abnormal blood platelets	2
7. Too many red blood cells (hematocric >48)	2
8. Elevated blood homocrysteine level	2
9. Elevated blood triglycerides	2
10. Smoking	3
11. Sedentary lifestyle	3
12. Negative affect (depression, anger, hostility)	3
13. Elevated LDL cholesterol	3
14. Elevated lipoprotein (a)	3
15. Low HDL cholesterol (<40 in men, <50 in women)	3
16. Atherogenic diet (a typical Western diet)	3
17. Diabetes	3
18. Age: >45 for men, >55 for women**	3
19. Premature coronary artery disease in close family members <55 years of age	10
20. personal history of a coronary event	20

increasing life span is improvements in our public health infrastructure, food and water safety, vaccinations, and various advances in medicine and surgery. But as we live longer, we are exposed for many years to numerous risk factors for various chronic diseases and cancers. Regrettably, many of us take our health for granted and pay very little or no attention to these, in particular cancer or cardiovascular risk factors (table 2). *The consequence of our collective neglect is the vast number of chronic diseases listed in table 1.*

The risk of cardiovascular diseases, cancers, and a host of other chronic disorders among older persons is more than a thousand times greater than in young people. However, this huge generational inequity is not an inevitable or mandatory consequence of aging. When we subject our bodies to flawed nutritional and lifestyle practices for many years, we slowly undermine our health, and predispose ourselves to the detrimental impact of carcinogens and to numerous risk factors for various chronic diseases. Positive and disease-free aging is possible provided *we, the public,* adopt preventive measures and sustain them for many years.

---

* Relative risk measures the impact of a risk factor in an individual compared with another person who does not have that particular risk factor.

> = Greater than, < = Less than

** Relative risk for age >65 is 8 times higher, and for age >79 is 34 times higher, than for age <35.

For comparison, the relative risk of lung cancer in a long-term heavy smoker is 10 times higher than in a nonsmoker.

2. Habit. Most of our entrenched dietary and lifestyle practices as adults are carried over from our childhood and adolescence (see chapter 6). Look at our school cafeteria foods (and our school lunch programs), which are loaded with saturated fat and trans-fatty acids. Look at the popularity of fast-food items, which are more of the same. And look at what our youngsters eat at home.

The five staples of school cafeterias are as follows.

1. Hamburger patties, ground beef for chilies, and hot dogs: They contain more than 30 percent fat (in fact more than 80 percent of calories in a hot dog comes from fat).
2. Processed cheeses: They contain more than 30 percent fat, half of which is saturated.
3. Cooking fats: They contain about 30 percent saturated fat and 20 percent or more trans-fatty acids. All of these are highly undesirable and indeed may be toxic (see chapter 2).
4. Pizza, which contains loads of cheese, pepperoni, and other greasy meats.
5. Chips, cookies, cakes, pies, donuts, and other pastries: They are loaded with trans-fatty acids, are highly energy-dense, and often replace other nutritious meals.

We are alarmed when our adolescents smoke a cigarette or drink a beer, but where is our sense of outrage when we knowingly feed our children and adolescents foods and snacks that will increase their future risk of cardiovascular diseases, diabetes, or various cancers? We strictly prohibit foods if our child is allergic to peanuts or any other food, because we anticipate an immediate allergic reaction that is unpleasant or even dangerous. But what we don't see and does not cause immediate symptoms still unleashes the cascade of cellular events that become quite evident and symptomatic ten, twenty, or thirty years later. We must think ahead!

3. Conflicting messages. There is a deep and irreconcilable conflict between the health promotion messages to eat *less* fat, carbohydrates, and calories, and the food industry's unceasing campaign to eat *more* of everything. Diet foods and diet drinks, diet snacks and diet packs, diet pills and diet supplements, diet books and diet cookbooks, diet centers, diet counselors, diet gurus and personal trainers—all sell us short-term (and often sham) solutions for long-term problems. We have light this thing or lite the other, low this and lower something else, fat-free, cholesterol-free, sugar-free, salt-free, and nutrition-free "foods," drinks, and snacks. And to replace the nutrients lacking in these pseudofoods, we are inundated with power foods, power drinks, power packs, power vitamins, power minerals, and power proteins.

The message of the food supplements manufacturers is always the same, whether they promote nutrient-deficient or nutrient-rich foods, drinks, snacks, or supplements: The more the better! (Because they think of their own bottom line, not your health or your life!)

4. Misconceptions. For decades we have mistakenly approached weight problems as a constantly renewable cosmetic or aesthetic "market" and not as what it is, a medical disorder. Let me ask you a question: Do you consider severe weight problems, diabetes, cholesterol disorders, hypertension, heart attack and stroke, or various cancers trivial matters? Of course not! So why do we allow unqualified, self-appointed diet gurus to trivialize our health issues and our lives with such nonsense as grapefruit, cabbage, or "eight-week cholesterol cure" diets, high "carbs" or no "carbs," low fat or high fat, this fruit but not that one, this zone or the other, this herb or that supplement, this fad or that hook or gimmick? Choosing foods for your health and your life should not be random or indiscriminate, and certainly not based on current fads. Nor should it be based on the fear of something bad in every bite, forcing you to embark on a mission to avoid a huge number of foods because they happen to be carbs or fats.

5. Misinformation? People have been misled by flawed recommendations that to reduce the risk of heart attack and stroke, they should reduce dietary fat and cholesterol. Yet reducing dietary fat and cholesterol, on average, may lower blood cholesterol by only 5 to 10 percent. Reducing your blood cholesterol of 280 milligrams per deciliter by 10 percent lowers it to 250 (the normal level should be less than 180). That's like being eight feet underwater rather than ten—it hardly makes a difference when you're drowning!

There are an estimated three million Americans who are strict vegetarians, i.e., they do not eat any animal flesh or products; therefore, their diet is cholesterol free. (Cholesterol is present in animal flesh and products only. No part of any plant contains cholesterol.) Do you think all these vegetarians have zero blood cholesterol levels? Of course not. In fact many have elevated blood cholesterol, and some, with or without elevated cholesterol, develop coronary artery disease like the rest of us. That is because more than 70 percent of blood cholesterol is made in-house, by the liver and other organs, from carbohydrates, and the contribution of dietary cholesterol is relatively minor. Furthermore, elevated blood cholesterol is only one of twenty major risk factors for coronary artery disease and heart attack (see table 2). Leaving the other nineteen "foxes in the chicken coop" is hardly an effective means of curbing the epidemic of heart attacks.

Where Do You Get Your Nutrition Information?

For most of us it is annoying and impractical to be constantly on guard against certain nutrients, or try to figure out how much of what ingredient is present in a particular food. Moreover, we cannot assume that all proteins, fats, or carbohydrates are alike; there are huge differences among different types of the same nutrient. Very few people are biochemists, nutrition experts, or food technologists. So where and how can we find adequate information?

Recently researchers at Case Western Reserve Medical Center in Cleveland, Ohio, analyzed data from a study of 138 physicians during 3,475 patient visits. Overall only about a quarter of patients received any nutritional or lifestyle counseling during their visits. *We know* that the vast majority of chronic diseases can be prevented by nutritional and lifestyle modifications. Yet *the study found that, incredibly, physicians spent an average of less than one minute on nutrition or lifestyle counseling!*

Nutrition information labels on prepackaged foods and snacks provide some helpful but often deceptive data. For example, *nearly all food manufacturers in the U.S. deliberately hide the trans-fatty acids in their products, bundling them with polyunsaturated fats on nutrition information labels.* As a result of this *industry-wide deception*, consumers will never know how much of these toxic fats they consume.

A vast number of foods, snacks, and drinks contain fructose, a simple sugar, usually in the form of high-fructose corn sweeteners (HFCSs). But here, too, the information about fructose and HFCSs is hidden in the middle of the fine print listing the ingredients on food packages, where few bother to read it, and even fewer pay any attention to it when they do see it.

Serving sizes are another annoying and confusing nuisance for the public. There is no standard serving size for anything in the U.S. The manufacturer decides what a serving size for a particular product is, and may change it for a particular market. Thus the serving size of snacks, pizzas, or hamburgers made by different food manufacturers vary quite confusingly. This is particularly true for snacks, and restaurants or fast-food menus (see tables 40–62).

What about fast foods? *The total U.S. spending on fast foods in 2002 was estimated at 115 billion dollars (or approximately 400 dollars per year per person)!* Given the pervasive nature of fast foods, shouldn't there be some oversight to make sure this mega-industry's products do not endanger the public's health and safety? Unless there is an outbreak of E coli or other foodborne infections, the U.S. government and its various agencies have no jurisdiction over the fast-food industry. Although we all hear or read disparaging remarks about the fast-food industry, the public really has no way of knowing what they eat or feed their children at these establishments.

These are only a few examples of the fragmented, inadequate, outdated, confusing, or deceptive nutrition information the public faces. Yes, there are countless books, pamphlets, and charts that show the fat and cholesterol content, calorie and carbo counts, and grams of fiber or salt in certain foods. However, there is no single source that provides a full account of all major ingredients in common foods and their total health impact. Shouldn't you have access to such a comprehensive resource? *The Total Health Impact (THI) Diet* and the scoring system I will introduce in chapter 4 fill this void, and provide you with an incredibly easy way to see the total health impact of thousands of foods.

The bottom line is that for four decades both consumers and health care providers have been inundated with a hodgepodge of fossilized, useless, contradictory, wrong, or even harmful nutritional and lifestyle recommendations! *Eating for Life: The Total Health Impact Diet* is a state-of-the-science plan founded on the most recent developments in medicine, nutrition, and health sciences. It introduces you to a novel nutritional and lifestyle plan that can dramatically reduce your risk of cardiovascular diseases, diabetes, premature aging, and dementia. It will also enable you to reduce your risk of breast, colon, lung, and prostate cancer by 90 percent! And it provides you with a safe and comprehensive blueprint for weight loss and long-term weight management that is doable. Just as important, it shields you from the pervasive fad-of-the-day peddlers.

Look at table 1 again. *The lifetime risk of one or more of these diseases for an adult American is more than 70 percent! But none of these diseases or the deaths and disabilities they cause is inevitable.* Cardiovascular diseases, diabetes, osteoporosis-related complications, and cancers of the breast, colon, lungs, and prostate account for more than 80 percent of all deaths in the U.S., and most developed countries. Incredibly, *the majority of these deaths, and a vast number of related disabilities, can be prevented by practical nutritional and lifestyle modifications!* Even if we are saddled with one or more disease-promoting genes, they, too, are modifiable. But *effective prevention requires long-term intervention.* Giving up, letting nature take its course, thinking "It's in my genes so I can't do anything about it" or conversely "It won't happen to me, because no one in my family has it," are all mistaken and self-destructive attitudes. In subsequent pages, I'll guide you through the easy steps that will enable you to prevent most of these chronic diseases.

The centerpiece of the plan is the *Total Health Impact Index,* a unique food counter that makes choosing healthy food simple and more accurate than ever. But first let's look at the two areas of nutrition that seem to cause the most confusion: fats and carbohydrates.

Chapter Two

The Many Faces of Dietary Fats

Fat is the most vilified nutrient in our diet. This is based on an unfortunate misunderstanding, since in fact the right kind of fat can dramatically reduce the risk of coronary artery disease, heart attack, stroke, dementia, diabetes, kidney disorders, and breast, colon, and prostate cancers. Why the blanket "damnation" of all fats?

- Each gram of fat contains 10 calories, two and one-half times more than proteins or carbohydrates.

- We digest and absorb fats very efficiently, and waste very few calories in the process. In fact, when traveling from the mouth to the stomach, the intestine, and eventually the bloodstream, fats lose (burn) only 2 percent of their total caloric value, compared to 8 percent for carbohydrates and 20 percent for proteins. In other words, when we eat 100 calories of fat, it delivers 98 calories, while the same amount of carbohydrates provides 92 calories, and proteins give us only 80 calories. (So the next time someone tells you that calories are calories no matter where they come from, you'll know better: *Fat calories are 18 percent "richer" than protein calories and 6 percent more than carbohydrates*).

• Contrary to a common misconception, recent studies have shown that *dietary fats produce a shorter period of satiety than proteins or carbohydrates*. Until recently, it was thought that dietary fats make us feel full longer by slowing the emptying of the stomach, However, new studies have shown that *hunger returns much faster after a fatty meal* than after a meal of carbohydrates and proteins with the same amount of calories.

• Since our tissues and organs prefer to use carbohydrates (glucose) first and proteins second for their energy needs, adults need (and burn) very little fat. Thus, in a normal diet,* up to 90 percent of dietary fat can be stored in fat

---

* Fasting, and very low-calorie or very low-carbohydrate diets, decrease the availability of glucose and proteins as energy sources. Under these circumstances the body turns to fat as an alternative energy source. This shift to fat as fuel explains why carbohydrate restriction can be an effective short-term approach to weight management, provided it is not deficient in proteins or, as with some fad diets, not loaded with various harmful fats.

cells. The remarkable absorption efficiency of dietary fat, and the availability of billions of fat cells eager to store the unused fat, make it easy to see how a high intake of dietary fat can be a major culprit in weight problems (see chapter 8).

• *Does the Type of Fat Matter?*

Perhaps it seems logical, then, that for decades health care professionals and nutritionists have habitually blamed fats for everything from heart attacks, strokes, and cancers to diabetes and weight problems. For over forty years the American Heart Association and the National Institute of Heart and Lung Diseases insisted that we should cut down dietary fat to less than 20 percent of our daily calories, *without any evidence that such recommendations were safe, effective, or necessary.* But in late August 2002, the U.S. Institute of Medicine and the National Institutes of Health finally revised the guidelines, stating that *for most people the right kinds of dietary fats can be increased to 35 percent of total daily calories (quite a turnaround!).*

Note the phrase "the right kinds" of fat. For although certain fats are indeed unhealthy, not all fats behave similarly. For example, *omega-3 fatty acids from seafoods, and monounsaturated fat* from hazelnut oil (84 percent monounsaturated), olive oil (74 percent mono), and canola oil (58 percent mono) *burn about 10 percent to 15 percent more efficiently than saturated fats or partially hydrogenated fats* in margarine, shortenings, and cooking fats.

Two recent studies showed that *monounsaturated fats*, such as olive oil, but not saturated or polyunsaturated fats, increase the activity of *Uncoupling Protein (UP)* in the muscles. *UP* is a compound inside muscle cells that regulates the burning of calories by muscles. High concentrations of *UP* encourage the muscles to burn more calories and convert them to heat, which is then dissipated (see appendix).

This new discovery further supports the findings of previous studies that showed monounsaturated fats result in much less weight gain than

- polyunsaturated fats, such as corn, safflower, or sunflower oils,

- saturated fats, present in high concentrations in palm and cottonseed oil, beef tallow, marbled red meats, sausages, hot dogs, butter, cream, and cheeses (including pizzas),

- trans-fatty acids, present in large quantities in most stick margarines, shortenings, and cooking fats, as well as all foods prepared with them. Some of these include deep-fried foods such as fried chicken or shrimp, French fries, potato or corn chips, and most pastries, cookies, cakes, pies, donuts, croissants, and less expensive chocolates (the more expensive ones are made with butter).

Monounsaturated fats, and specifically extra-virgin olive oil (first pressing), have a host of other benefits. For example, they lower the blood level of the bad LDL cholesterol and raise the good HDL cholesterol. Eggs prepared with olive oil are far less likely to raise the bad LDL cholesterol than those with which margarine or butter is used. This is because unlike saturated fats and trans-fatty acids, monounsaturates *esterify* (attach to) cholesterol particles as soon as cholesterol is absorbed. Esterified cholesterol particles signal the liver to produce more LDL receptors and bring in more LDL cholesterol particles from the bloodstream, a process that <u>*lowers the blood cholesterol level*</u>. More importantly, *monounsaturates reduce the oxidization* of LDL cholesterol*. It is the oxidized LDL cholesterol, not the native or nonoxidized LDL, that damages the wall of the arteries and contributes to heart attack and stroke. Monounsaturated fats also reduce the risk of diabetes and

---

* *What is oxidization?* The interaction of a molecule with oxygen. When you peel an apple or skin a potato, within a short time it turns brown. That browning is due to oxidization. The rust on a nail is also due to the oxidization of the iron. Oxidization of LDL cholesterol and other compounds in the bloodstream or inside the lining of the arteries and various organs is a major contributing factor to many chronic diseases including those listed in table 1, as well as skin cancers and aging.

cancers of the breast, colon, and prostate by about 30 percent.

In contrast to monounsaturated fats, *trans-fatty acids* in margarines, shortening, and cooking fats raise the "bad" LDL cholesterol, lower the "good" HDL cholesterol, and *increase oxidization of LDL cholesterol*. Trans-fatty acids also increase the risk of a number of cancers, including breast and colon cancers. They may also have contributed heavily to our epidemic of diabetes and fatty liver. If nothing else, increased oxidization of the LDL cholesterol and other fat deposits in our bodies enriched with trans-fatty acids is a compelling reason to avoid these unhealthy fats.

Saturated fats raise the LDL cholesterol level in the bloodstream, increase the risk of heart attack and stroke, and also contribute to weight problems. However, unlike trans-fatty acids, they *do not increase oxidization of the LDL cholesterol and other fats*, or the risk of diabetes, liver damage, or any cancer.

For several decades the producers of vegetable fats have promoted the notion that because they are "100 percent natural and 100 percent cholesterol free," they are healthful. *They are not!* Most margarines, shortenings, and cooking fats (solid vegetable fats) sold in the U.S. contain high concentrations of saturated fat. In addition, some may have as much as 25 percent to 30 percent trans-fatty acids, making them even worse than the butter and the cream they are intended to replace (see tables 8 and 9). The undesirable effects of trans-fatty acids make switching from butter to stick margarines or cooking fats like jumping from the frying pan into the fire. (Newer soft spreads such as Benecol, Brummel & Brown, Promise, Smart Balance, and Take Control do not have trans-fatty acids and, therefore, do not pose the same risks.)

A small serving of French fries, or an occasional donut, or a piece of cake on someone's birthday, will not capsize the world. However, *frequent, long-term use of trans-fatty acids* in the form of deep-fried foods, chips, donuts, and other pastries or confectionery snacks *contributes to abdominal obesity, insulin resistance and diabetes, coronary artery disease, heart attack and stroke, fatty degeneration of the liver, which in some cases may result in liver failure, and possibly cancers of the breast, colon, and prostate.* In a recent long-term Harvard study, researchers estimated that trans-fatty acids might be responsible for over thirty thousand deaths in the U.S. each year from cardiovascular diseases alone.

The long-term, widespread use of these unhealthy fats may explain in part the global epidemic of obesity, diabetes, and coronary artery disease, even among developing nations. In spite of horrendous malnutrition, type II diabetes is now one of the fastest spreading epidemics in the Indian subcontinent, where cooking (vegetable) fats have been the main source of dietary fat for the past thirty years.

Dietary Fat Extremism

The very high-fat with very low-carbohydrate diet (Atkins) versus the very low-fat with very high-carbohydrate diet (Ornish)

Dietary extremism is not new. Only the fad, the hook, and the niche vary from diet to diet, and from one dietary guru to the next. Because the thirty-five-billion-dollar diet industry has a massive, renewable client base, it is easy to see why there is a free-for-all race to capture some of this huge market. Dietary fat is currently among the most prominent nutritional controversies, especially as it relates to weight loss regimens and cardiovascular health. Although everyone seems to have an opinion about dietary fat, very few opinions are evidence based or credible.

For example, on one side, the *Atkins camp* forbids nearly all carbohydrates (even fruits!), but encourages you to eat loads of fatty foods, including proteins from various fatty meats and cheeses. On the other side, the *Ornish camp* declares dietary fats and all meats (even poultry and fish) evil, and demands that you increase your dietary carbohydrates to more than 60 percent of your energy intake. These two camps are 180 degrees apart. How could they both be right? They're not. Both are dead wrong!

Here are some clarifications to convince you why *both of these extreme diets are harmful.*

Very high-fat with very low-carbohydrate diets (Atkins and others): The believers in these flawed diets promote the notion that very high fat intake (70 percent of calories coming from fat) produces early satiety, leading you to eat less and, therefore, lose weight. Wrong! Although some people initially lose weight on these diets, the weight loss is not all due to loss of fat, not due to eating fat, and not sustainable. Here's why:

- Since *humans cannot burn fats efficiently*, we produce a good amount of fat by-products (ketones and other acidic compounds) in our bodies on a high-fat/carbohydrate restricted diet. For several hours after eating a high-fat meal (65 percent to 70 percent of the calories from fat), blood levels of these compounds increase by more than 300 percent, creating a chemical overload called *ketosis*. In the first two or three weeks on these diets, ketosis increases water loss through the urine and may cause a 10-to-15-pound weight loss due to dehydration. With rehydration, most of this weight reappears.

- Recent studies have shown that *dietary fat does not produce satiety* any earlier or longer than a diet containing proteins and carbohydrates. In fact, dietary proteins are the most satiating nutrients, followed by carbohydrates. However, long-term ketosis contributes to nausea and decreased appetite.

The dehydrating effect of ketosis and the high protein intake may also cause fatigue, constipation, increased calcium loss in the urine, and kidney stones. We *know* that frequent ketosis is toxic in diabetics and pregnant women. Since *there is no study to show that long-term exposure to high levels of ketones is safe, in the absence of such safety data, we should "err" on the side of safety and avoid ketogenic diets.*

- *The principal reason for weight loss with very high-fat diets is not the high fat, but the extremely low carbohydrates!* Carbohydrates provide 55 percent to 60 percent of the calories in the average Western diet. By reducing your intake of carbohydrates to less than 15 percent, as is required with Atkins-type diets, you slash your total caloric intake by 40 percent to 50 percent, or an average of 1,000 to 1,200 calories a day. On this carbo-calorie restricted diet, you can be expected (at least theoretically) to lose 1 pound every three days (each pound equals 3,500 calories), 2 pounds a week, 8 pounds a month, and about 25 pounds in three months. *But you can achieve all this weight loss by reducing your carbohydrate intake alone, without increasing your dietary fat by a single gram!* In fact the extra calories from the high fat content in these diets slow down your weight loss and are counterproductive.

In two recent randomized studies, an Atkins-type diet was compared with a modestly low-fat diet (about 30 percent fat versus the usual 35–38 percent US intake). Nearly one-half of those on the Atkins-type diet dropped out of the studies (could not stay with it). Although in the first three months the low-carb diet induced, on average, 7–10 pounds more weight loss than the relatively low-fat diet, there was no difference between the two diets after six to twelve months. In fact, the authors of these two studies made it clear that the slightly greater weight loss with the low-carb diet was due to a lower overall daily calorie intake and not due to the low-carb diet itself. Importantly, the majority of these cases had severe to extreme obesity for whom a 7-to-10-pound additional weight loss (in the first three months) had no significant clinical benefit. Moreover, since a weight problem is a chronic, relapsing, lifelong disorder, it cannot be treated with *any* intervention that most people find difficult to adhere to even for three to six months. The myopic promoters of these diets focus on the short-term response but ignore the long-term nature of the disease.

Almost *two out of three people who go on these diets have coexisting cholesterol problems, cardiovascular diseases, or diabetes.* The promoters of these diets make the frivolous argument that when you lose weight, you increase your HDL cholesterol (but only slightly), and therefore reduce your cardiovascular risk. However, they neglect to mention that the trans-fatty acids of these diets oxidize both the HDL (making it ineffective) and the LDL cholesterol (which makes these particles highly toxic to the lining of the arteries). Moreover, this kind of diet-induced weight loss, even 20 to 30 pounds, offers very little protection against coronary artery disease, heart attack, or stroke, and does even less to protect you against various cancers or other diseases listed in table 1.

Although a short-term high-fat, very low-carbohydrate diet may be safe in young and otherwise healthy overweight people, it may very well have a long-lasting negative cardiovascular impact on others. For most adults with cardiovascular risk factors, very high-fat, high-cholesterol diets, even for a few months, defy sense. Increasing the future risk of a catastrophic cardiovascular event or the other side effects alluded to here is too high a price for losing 10, 20, or even 30 pounds, especially since you can lose weight more effectively, and certainly safely, with the *Total Health Impact Diet*.

There is nothing wrong with eating a piece of lean beef, veal, lamb, or pork. Extra-lean ground beef contains 7 percent fat, one-third of which is made up of saturated fats; a serving of ¼ pound (4 ounces or 120 grams) of extra-lean ground beef, sirloin, or London broil gives you no more than 3 grams of the "bad" saturated fats. No one can hassle you about 2 or 3 grams of saturated fat. But how many people do you know who eat the extra-lean versions and in such small quantities? Very few! As you can see, *these simple, basic calculations have escaped the proponents of all-you-can-eat, high-fat, high-protein, and very low-carbohydrate diets.*

Very low-fat, cholesterol-free, and very high-carbohydrate diets (Ornish, Pritikin, and others): These cholesterol-free and extremely low-fat diets (less than 7 percent to 10 percent of the diet as fat) became fashionable several years ago with the release of the findings of a single study. The study was a five-year follow-up of a very small number (twenty-two) of older men with severe coronary artery disease and various major coronary risk factors. The study subjects were enrolled in a rigid program, including regular exercises, smoking cessation, vigorous treatment of high blood pressure and diabetes, regular twice-weekly stress management sessions, and a daily low-dose aspirin. They were also placed on a rigid vegan diet with no red meat, poultry, seafoods, dairy products (except for a small amount of skim milk), nuts, alcohol, tea, coffee, sugar, or chocolate (leaving me wondering what's left).

After five years of follow-up, the researchers reported a 50 percent reduction in the risk of another coronary event, which has become the basis for promoting the diet. But this study was based on a very small number of (highly selected) older men with *severe coronary artery disease*, not several thousand men and women of different age groups, or with less severe coronary disease.

Incredibly, the researchers also totally misinterpreted their own findings! For example, one low-dose aspirin alone (81 milligrams per day) would reduce the risk of a coronary event by 30 percent; smoking cessation, by at least 50 percent; treatment of high blood pressure, by 50 percent; regular exercises, by 50 percent; stress management, by at least 50 percent; controlling diabetes, by at least 50 percent. **With all these interventions, the subjects should have had at least a 250 percent risk reduction, not a meager 50 percent!** In other words, almost surely their rigid, very low-fat, vegan diet not only deprived the patients of enjoyable meals, but also held them back, countering the expected benefits they should have had from the other interventions. Even more puzzling, the researchers misattribute this 50 percent benefit to the restrictive diet, not all the other risk factor modifications.

> ***Recent studies have shown that very low-fat diets can increase the risk of stroke by 50 percent.*** This significant and unacceptable high risk is due to the fact that smaller brain arteries require an adequate amount of fat to maintain their integrity, so that they won't rupture and cause bleeding into the brain. This is even more relevant in older persons with multiple coronary risk factors, who have a much higher risk of stroke. On the other hand, a diet with high levels of monounsaturated fats significantly reduces this risk, while at the same time reduces the risk of heart attack and various cancers.

What You Should Do

Some saturated fats and all trans-fatty acids contribute to coronary artery disease, heart attack, stroke, and the risk of diabetes. Trans-fatty acids can also contribute to the development and progression of fatty liver (which is present in more than 70 percent of people with abdominal obesity or a severe weight problem). Fatty liver in nearly one out of five people will progress to cirrhosis, an end-stage disease. Trans-fatty acids can also aggravate your weight burden unless you dramatically reduce your other sources of calories.

Very high-fat diets (Atkins and others)—especially those that encourage eating large amounts of fatty meats (fresh or processed), cheeses, butter, creams, and partially hydrogenated vegetable fats, such as margarines, shortening, or cooking fats used for deep-frying—are dreadfully imbalanced, have no redeeming features, and may increase the risk of cardiovascular events. Their opposite, the very low-fat, very high-carbohydrate diets (Ornish and others), are just as nonsensical—they are too rigid and, far from being cardioprotective, may negate the benefits of other coronary risk reductions.

What kind of fats should you use? As noted previously, *monounsaturated fats* (olive oil, hazelnut oil, or canola oil) have a vast number of health benefits. Use them for all your cooking needs. Eating 1 or 2 ounces of nuts with high concentrations of monounsaturates, such as almonds, hazelnuts, pistachios, and walnuts, (but not Brazil nuts, cashews, or peanuts), several times a week can also reduce the risk of diabetes and coronary artery disease by 30 percent.

Omega-3 fatty acids in the form of three or four seafood meals a week (provided they are not cooked with partially hydrogenated fats, such as margarines, shortenings, or cooking fats) reduce your risk of a heart attack by 40 percent. Even more importantly, they'll reduce the risk of a sudden cardiac death (due to extremely rapid heart rates) by 70 percent. No medicine in the world today can offer such a robust cardioprotective benefit! The omega-3 fats in seafoods also reduce the risk of stroke, dementia, diabetes complications, and cancers of the breast, colon, and prostate. Since the benefits of seafoods are primarily due to their omega-3 fat, fatty fish are even more desirable than very lean seafoods (see tables 3 and 4).

Table 3
FATTY-ACID COMPOSITION OF SHELLFISH*
3.5 oz/100g

Shellfish	Fat	SFA	MUFA	Omeg A-3 Pufa	Cholesterol
Clams	1.2	0.2	0.2	0.4	36
Crab	1.1	0.2	0.3	0.6	60
Lobster	1	0.2	0.2	0.3	90
Mussels	2	0.2	0.2	0.4	67
Oysters	2.6	0.7	0.5	0.9	72
Scallops	0.9	0.3	0.2	0.3	35
Shrimp	1.7	0.4	0.5	0.5	157
Squid	1.8	0.7	0.4	0.6	280

SFA = saturated fatty acids, MUFA = monounsaturated fatty acids, Omega-3 PUFA = omega-3 polyunsaturated fatty acids

All shellfish have very low to only trivial amounts of saturated fat. With the exception of squid (which has a high concentration of cholesterol), all other shellfish are wonderful alternatives to poultry or red meats. They also do not raise blood cholesterol levels because they have extremely low levels of saturated fats.

Table 4
FATTY-ACID COMPOSITION OF SEAFOOD*
3.5 oz/100g

Fish	Fat	SFA	Mufa	Omega-3 Pufa	Cholesterol
Anchovies	4.8	1.3	1.2	1.5	60
Bass, freshwater	2	0.4	0.7	0.8	60
Bass, striped	2.3	0.5	0.7	0.8	80
Bluefish	4.5	1	2	1	59
Catfish	3	0.8	0.9	0.5	58
Caviar (½ oz)	2.6	0.6	0.6	1	84
Cod	0.7	0.1	0.1	0.3	43
Croaker	3.1	1	1.2	0.2	61
Flounder or carp	1	0.2	0.3	0.4	46
Grouper	1.1	0.2	0.2	0.3	37
Haddock	0.7	0.1	0.1	0.2	58
Halibut	2.3	0.3	0.7	0.4	32
Herring	9	2	3.8	1.8	60
Mackerel, Atlantic	13	3.3	5.4	2.7	70
Mackerel, Pacific	8	2.2	2.6	1.6	47
Mahimahi	2.1	0.2	1.1	0.2	73
Monkfish	1.5	0.4	0.3	0.3	25
Mullet	3.8	1.1	1	0.4	49
Orange Roughy	1.8	0.7	0.5	0.5	54
Perch	1	0.2	0.2	0.4	76
Pike	1.2	0.3	0.3	0.4	86
Pollack	1	0.2	0.2	0.5	71
Pompano	1.4	0.3	0.4	0.6	61
Rockfish	1.5	0.4	0.5	0.4	44
Sablefish	15	3.5	8	1.7	50
Salmon, Atlantic	6.3	1	2	1.6	55
Salmon, Chinook	10.5	2.5	4.5	1.7	66
Salmon, Chinook (smoked) (lox)	4.3	1	2	0.5	23

Table 4
FATTY-ACID COMPOSITION OF SEAFOOD*
3.5 oz/100g (cont.)

Fish	Fat	SFA	Mufa	Omega-3 Pufa	Cholesterol
Salmon, Coho	6	1.3	2.2	1.5	45
Sardines (canned in oil)	11.4	1.5	3.9	1	142
Sea bass	2	0.5	0.4	0.4	42
Shark	1.9	0.3	0.4	0.5	44
Snapper	1.4	0.3	0.3	0.3	38
Sole	1.2	0.3	0.4	0.2	50
Spot	4.9	1.5	1.3	0.7	60
Sturgeon	4	0.9	1.9	0.3	60
Swordfish	4	1.1	1.6	0.3	39
Trout, Rainbow (farm raised)	5.4	1.6	1.5	1	59
Trout, Rainbow (lake)	3.4	0.7	1.2	0.6	60
Trout (sea)	3.6	1.2	1.8	0.9	64
Tuna, Bluefin	6.6	1.7	2.2	1.7	60
Tuna, Yellowfin	1	0.2	0.2	0.25	45
Whitefish	5.8	1	2	1.6	60

FAT = total amount of fat, SFA = saturated fatty acids, MUFA = monounsaturated fatty acids, Omega-3 PUFA = omega-3 polyunsaturated fatty acids

*The fat content of various species of the same fish (for example, Pacific versus Atlantic salmon, or different types of tuna) may vary significantly. Canned tuna (in water, not in oil) offers one of the best and most affordable sources of omega-3 fat, provided you do not defeat the purpose by adding mayonnaise or margarine to it. However, depending on the type, and where the tuna was caught (Pacific or Atlantic Ocean), the fat content may differ by more than 500 percent. So always look for cans of tuna in water with a total fat content per serving of 3 grams or higher (instead of 0.5 to 1 gram per serving). Also, wild fish usually have more omega-3 fat than farm-raised varieties. Since more than 30 percent of the fat in seafoods is the desirable omega-3 fat, fish or shellfish with a high fat content are preferable. Smaller (younger) fish often have less fat than larger (older) ones of the same type.

Chapter Three

Dietary Carbohydrates: Facts and Controversies

Dietary carbohydrates come in two forms, simple and complex. Simple carbohydrates consist of three edible sugars: fructose, glucose, and galactose. Plants are major sources of simple carbohydrates, including table sugar or sucrose (an equal amount of fructose and glucose), corn-derived sweeteners (fructose), and grapes, raisins, and other fruits (glucose or fructose). Some plants also store carbohydrates as a substance made of hundreds of glucose molecules called starch. Grains (breads, cereals, pastas, and rice) and potatoes are all rich sources of starch, which is rapidly digested and broken down to glucose in the intestine. In a way, eating these starchy foods is not that much different from eating a handful of sugar cubes. On the other hand, complex (nonstarchy) carbohydrates (legumes, and vegetables other than potatoes or sweet potatoes) are highly desirable because they are broken down very slowly in the intestine so they do not raise the blood sugar or cause an insulin surge.

Carbs are the ideal fuel for muscles and nearly all our vital organs. After a meal, our tissues use all the carbohydrates, simple and complex, for their fuel, and later on when the supply of carbs runs low, they will extract proteins from the bloodstream or the muscles for fuel. This preferential process often leaves very little need for dietary fat. When the fuel need of our tissues is satisfied with carbohydrates, proteins, and a small portion of dietary fat, the unused fat is deposited in fat cells or in nonfatty tissues including the muscles, the heart, and the liver. In a way, *carbohydrates and proteins have a fat-sparing (or fat-saving) effect.*

What Happens to the Excess Carbohydrates We Eat?

Humans do not store carbs as starch but as *glycogen* in the liver and the muscles. After we burn all the carbohydrates our tissues need, a portion of the unused carbs is stored as glycogen in the muscles and the liver. However, we can store no more than 1 kilogram (2.2 pounds) of glycogen, unlike fat, of which up to a few hundred pounds can be deposited in our fat cells. We can deplete our glycogen store by doing moderate-intensity activities for several hours, and in even fewer hours with more intensive exercises.

But if we eat too much carbohydrates and live a sedentary lifestyle, where can those carbs go? We convert as much as 20 percent of our dietary carbohydrates into fat. This "coerced" conversion is a factor in most people's weight problems. Excessive intake of carbohydrates (more than 50–55 percent of daily calories), especially those that have high glycemic indices (see page 36), is a major risk factor for weight gain, type II diabetes, an increase in blood triglycerides, and lower levels of the good HDL cholesterol. A high carbohydrate intake also *increases* the number of *small LDL cholesterol particles*, which are far more harmful than the larger particles.

After we convert some of those excess carbs into fat, the liver and many other organs take another portion of carbs and break it down into much smaller subunits. Some of these pieces are then reassembled to make cholesterol. In fact, dietary (ingested) cholesterol accounts for only 30 percent of blood cholesterol; the other 70 percent is made "in-house" through this reassembling process. This explains why strict vegetarians, who do not eat any animal products, may have high blood cholesterol levels. Cattle, too, grazing on grass (complex carbohydrates) can grow to well over 1,000 pounds, a fourth of which is composed of fat and cholesterol.

Glycemic Index of Carbohydrates

Simple carbs (the three sugars—fructose, galactose, and glucose), and starches (white flour/bread/pasta, potatoes, and rice) tend to quickly raise our blood sugar level, which causes an insulin surge. In contrast, complex carbs in vegetables and legumes have a significantly lower impact on these reactions. This blood sugar–raising property of carbohydrates is called the *glycemic response*, or more commonly the *glycemic index*. The glycemic index of rapidly digested and quickly absorbed complex carbohydrates, such as starchy foods, is only slightly less than that of sugars (see tables 5 and 6). This is in part because breads, pastas, cereals, rice, and potatoes are readily broken down in the intestine into glucose.

A glycemic index of more than 70 is *HIGH,* and less than 50 is *LOW.* Glycemic indices between 70 and 50 are moderate but behave similarly to the low items.

The long-term, frequent consumption of foods with high glycemic indices has a number of undesirable effects. For example, calorie for calorie, *high glycemic index foods contribute to a far greater insulin surge than low glycemic foods.* Over time, this will contribute to *insulin resistance.* Insulin resistance is an early stage of diabetes in which the muscles and many organs, especially the liver, require a lot more insulin to break down dietary carbohydrates and fats. The problem is that an excessive amount of insulin is toxic to many tissues, especially the arteries of the heart, the brain, the kidneys, and the eyes. The long-term consequences of this toxicity include high blood pressure, coronary artery disease and heart attack, stroke, kidney failure, and retinal bleeding.

Many factors can alter the glycemic index of the same food. For example, the very small amount of acids added to dough to make sourdough bread lowers its glycemic index compared with white bread made from the same dough without the added acid. Physical characteristics also change the glycemic index. You will find a higher glycemic response with flours that are bleached, low in fiber, or composed of a smaller particle size. Toasting bread, adding jam or marmalade to bread, or syrup to waffles, baking a potato as opposed to boiling or sautéing, or eating the same potato without the skin—all increase the glycemic indices of these foods. On the other hand, eating a lot of fiber or some fat along with a carbohydrate lowers it glycemic index by slowing the stomach's emptying (another good reason to eat lots of fruits and vegetables!).

In contrast to the low glycemic–index carbohydrates, *high glycemic carbs stimulate fat cells to enlarge and accumulate more fat*. These activated fat cells have the potential to overproduce and release into the bloodstream a toxic, inflammation-provoking protein called *interleukin-6.* High blood levels of interleukin-6 not only can contribute to insulin resistance (and the risk of diabetes), but also stimulate the liver to produce another substance called *C-reactive protein (CRP). High levels of CRP are associated with a twofold higher risk of coronary artery disease, heart attack, and stroke.* People who are more than 40 to 50 pounds overweight have CRP levels that are almost three times higher than in people with normal weight. Why make a bad situation worse by eating high glycemic carbs?

High glycemic–index carbohydrates have other undesirable effects. For example, *of sixteen recent studies in humans, fifteen found lower satiety, more hunger, and more calorie consumption after high, compared with low, glycemic-index meals.* In another study, obese children who ate high glycemic–index instant oatmeal at breakfast and lunch ate 53 percent more calories during the rest of the day than did children who had low glycemic–index regular oatmeal.

Thus, *high glycemic–index foods*

- cause our insulin to surge and may contribute to insulin resistance and diabetes,

- stimulate our fat cells to enlarge and accumulate more fat (in other words, they are "obesogenic"),

- stimulate the fat cells to produce *interleukin-6,* which in turn signals the liver to overproduce *C-reactive protein* (high levels of interleukin-6 and C-reactive protein significantly increase the risk of coronary artery disease, heart attack, stroke, diabetes, and degenerative joint disease often present in overweight people),

• do not make us feel as full as complex carbohydrates, proteins, or even fats, and therefore promote overeating.

What You Should Do

The first thing you should do is not to jump to the conclusion that all carbohydrates are bad for you and avoid them at all cost. Carbohydrates are essential for the proper function of nearly every organ, including your heart, brain, liver, kidneys, and muscles. Thus there is no rational reason to go on a long-term crusade to avoid all carbohydrates. In the short term, a significant reduction in dietary carbohydrates to less than 20 percent to 30 percent of your total daily energy intake is safe (on average, carbohydrates provide about 55 percent of the daily calories of Americans and most people in Western societies). It can also help you lose a significant amount of weight by reducing your total caloric intake, and by burning off stored fat as a fuel substitute.

Unfortunately, if you go overboard and reduce your carbohydrate intake too drastically and for too long, in addition to burning the fat for fuel, your body also extracts proteins from your muscles, including the heart muscle, for fuel. Minor, short-term protein (muscle) wasting associated with severe carbohydrate restriction may not be clinically significant. However, long-term carbohydrate deprivation is an inappropriate solution to weight management or cardiovascular health, and may result in skeletal and cardiac-muscle wasting, at times with catastrophic and even fatal consequences.

In general, try to cut back your intake of high glycemic carbs by at least 50 percent. Some of these less desirable carbohydrates include table sugar, all-natural (usually corn) sweeteners, honey, sweet fruits such as dates and raisins, candies, fig bars, cookies, cakes, pies, chocolates, donuts, muffins, white flour/bread/pasta, all sugar or frosted cereals, potatoes, and white rice, all of which quickly turn into sugar when they reach your intestine (see tables 5 and 6).

High fructose corn sweeteners (HFCS) are now present in nearly any food or snack that in the past used the more expensive sugar. Practically everything from sodas, candies, cookies, cakes, and other snacks to ketchup and pasta sauces and canned fruits have HFCS. From 1980 to 2000, the use of HFCS in the U.S. increased from 19 to 64 pounds per person per year, a 240 percent increase. Unfortunately, fructose is broken down rapidly in our body and by-products are reassembled into fat molecules and stored in our fat cells. In other words, even though we think we are

Table 5
GLYCEMIC INDEX OF GRAIN PRODUCTS AND DAIRIES

Bread Products	Index		Index
Bagel, most without glazing	100	Crispix	125
Bread, French, Italian, roll	100	Golden Grahams	110
Bread, hamburger bun	95	Grape-Nuts	105
Bread, multigrain	80	Life	100
Bread, pumpernickel	80	Mini-Wheats (unfrosted)	83
Bread, rye	95	Nutri-Grain or Product 19	94
Bread, sourdough	80	Oat bran	85
Bread, whole wheat	80	Puffed wheat	110
Croissant	100	Quick oats	93
Kaiser roll	105	Rice Chex	130
Melba toast	105	Rice Krispies	120
Potato bread	105	Shredded Wheat (frosted)	105
Waffles	110	Shredded Wheat or	
Cakes		Special K	80
Angel food	105	Team	120
Banana	80	Total	110
Pound	85	**Grains**	
Sponge	100	Corn	80
Donuts	115	Rice, basmati	85
Most other cakes	110	Rice, brown	85
Cereals		Rice, high amylose	90
All-Bran	65	Rice, low amylose	125
Bran Buds or Raisin Bran	90	Rice cake	120
Bran Chex	90	Whole wheat	65
Cheerios	110	**Dairy**	
Coco Pops	110	Cheeses (processed)	40
Corn Chex	120	Ice cream	95
Cornflakes	120	Milk, chocolate	50
Cream of Wheat	95	Milk, skim	46
		Milk, whole	45
		Yogurt (plain)	20
		Yogurt (with fruit)	46

eating a carbohydrate, we are increasing our body fat and blood cholesterol, and our risk of diabetes, fatty liver, and cardiovascular diseases. Thus you should avoid HFCS much the same as saturated or trans-fatty acids.

"Carbo busting" very high-fat/high-protein diets, or very low-fat, cholesterol-free diets, or any other rigid diet, may work for a few weeks for some people without posing a significant risk. But weight problems, cardiovascular diseases, diabetes, and various cancers are not short-term processes to respond to or be prevented by short-term, sham diets. In subsequent chapters, I'll offer you a safe and scientific alternative that will effectively protect you against these diseases.

The glycemic index (GI) is not very precise and may vary by 10–20 units for the same type of foods. Some of this variance is due to physical characteristics, processing, cooking technique, added dietary fiber, fat, sugars or other sweeteners, and chemical composition of the food item, such as the low-amylose content of rice (which increases the GI of some types of rice compared with high-amylose rice).

Table 6
GLYCEMIC INDEX OF FRUITS, VEGETABLES, MEATS, AND MISC.

Fruits	Index		Index
Apple	52	Kidney beans	45
Apple juice	58	Lentils	42
Apricot	45	Lima beans	50
Banana	80	Pinto beans	55
Cantaloupe	80	Red beans	40
Cherries	32	Soybeans	30
Fruit cocktail	80	Split peas	45
Grapefruit	36	**Vegetables**	
Grapes	62		
Kiwi	80	Carrot	100
Orange	65	Corn chips	103
Orange juice	75	Peas, dried	32
Peach	40	Peas, green	55
Peach, canned in heavy syrup	83	Popcorn	80
Peach, canned in natural juice	43	Potato, baked	120
Pear	52	Potato, French fries	110
Pineapple	94	Potato, mashed	105
Plum	34	Potato, sweet	85
Raisins	91	Potato chips	105
Watermelon	103	Sweet corn	80
Legumes		Other vegetables	<40
		Other	
Black-eyed peas	60		
Butter beans	45	Beef, pork, lamb	50
Canned beans	57	Poultry & seafoods	<50
Chickpeas	48	Pasta (less for whole wheat)	80
Dried beans	50	Desserts & sweet snacks	>110
Green beans	45		

Chapter Four

The Total Health Impact Diet

The **Total Health Impact Diet** introduced here is based on the commonsense principle that with very few exceptions (such as sugar or sugar cubes), foods contain several major ingredients including various fats, proteins, carbohydrates, salt, and dietary fiber, as well as a vast number of *micronutrients,* such as vitamins, minerals, and antioxidants. Each of these ingredients may have a distinct health impact, either helpful or harmful. Thus we cannot single out one nutrient (such as cholesterol, saturated fat, or carbohydrate) among the many ingredients of foods and dismiss or totally ignore the health impact of all the other ingredients.

Several years of research and review of well over four thousand recent scientific works in medicine, nutrition, and food technology helped me develop a novel formula by which to calculate the

Total Heath Impact (THI) of ten major nutrients in foods, not just one or two. I have computed and listed the *THI* scores of thousands of foods and snacks so you no longer have to worry about how much or what kinds of fat, or how much cholesterol, sugar/fructose, salt, calories, or fiber, are present in this or that food. All you have to do is to make sure your total daily scores for all your foods and snacks remain below +30 points. It is as simple as that!

Table 7
THI SCORING SYSTEM

Nutrient	Amount	Score
Salt	each 1,000 mg	+1
High glycemic carbohydrates	each 10 g	+1
Cholesterol	each 100 mg	+1
Omega-6 PUFA	each 5 g	+1
Trans-fatty acids	each 1 g	+2
Saturated fat	each 1 g	+2
Fruits & vegetables	each 2 servings	-1
Unsaturated fat	each 2 g	-1
Omega-3 PUFA (plant source)	each 2 g	-1
Omega-3 PUFA (from seafoods)	each 1 g	-3

PUFA = poloynsaturated fatty acids, MG = milligram, G = gram, # A serving of fruit and vegetables is usually 100 grams (3.5 ounces) of edible portions.

The formula for the *THI scores* is presented for your interest only. However, the copyrighted formula is a novel tool for other researchers interested in public health, nutrition, and preventive medicine.

The score of a given food or snack is the sum of all its ten ingredients. This single score provides an instantaneous understanding of the total nutritional impact of a given food, instead of an isolated or unbalanced focus on cholesterol, saturated fat, or carbohydrates. The lower your total daily score is, the easier it is to lose weight or prevent weight regain, and protect yourself against diabetes, cancers, and cardiovascular diseases. The goal is to keep the total scores of all your foods and snacks under +30 points per day, and preferably closer to +20. *Don't start looking for any loopholes; I'll close them for you in the next chapter!*

Table 8
THI SCORES OF OILS AND FATS per 2 tablespoon.

Coconut [A]*	+48	Chicken fat*	+14
Palm kernel [A]*	+44	Cottonseed*	+14
Vegetable shortening*	+26	Turkey fat*	+14
Butter [A]*	+25	Safflower [B]*	+8
Palm*	+23	Sunflower [B]*	+8
Beef tallow*	+22	Corn [B]*	+6
Lamb tallow*	+21	Soybean*	+6
Some stick margarines*	+17	Peanut*	+5
Mayonnaise*	+17	Sesame	+3
Lard*	+17	Olive [C]	-2
Some soft margarines*	+15	Canola [C]	-3
Duck fat*	+15	Hazelnut [C]	-5

* AVOID

A-Coconut oil, palm kernel oil, and butter have the highest percentage of saturated fats, 86 percent, 81 percent, and 62 percent, respectively.

B-Safflower, sunflower, and corn oils contain the highest percentage of omega-6 polyunsaturated fats, 77 percent, 69 percent, and 61 percent, respectively.

C-Hazelnut, olive, and canola oils are the richest sources of healthful monounsaturated fats, containing 78 percent, 72 percent, and 56 percent, respectively.

Table 9
THI SCORES OF MARGARINES
per 2-tablespoon serving +

All fat-free margarines	0	Land O Lakes*, stick	+13
Benecol Spread++	+1	Land O Lakes, fresh buttery*	+12
Blue Bonnet	+13	Land O Lakes, spread*	+12
Blue Bonnet, Home Style*	+7	Mazola*	+18
Brummel & Brown Spread++	+4	Mazola, diet 100% corn oil imitation	+5
Canoleo from canola oil	+2	Mazola, unsalted*	+18
Country Crock, churn style*	+8	Mrs. Filbert's 100% corn oil*	+14
Country Crock, spread*	+8	Mrs. Filbert's golden*	+17
Country Crock, stick*	+17	Mrs. Filbert's soft golden*	+15
Empress, soft*	+14	Mrs. Filbert's whipped margarine*	+15
Empress, stick*	+18	Mrs. Filbert's whipped spread*	+11
Fleischmann's, squeezable*	+6	Parkay*, stick	+15
Fleischmann's, stick*	+11	Parkay Squeezable*	+8
Fleischmann's, light++	+4	Parkay Calcium Plus	+3
Fleischmann's Move Over Butter*	+15	Parkay Light*	+11
Fleischmann's Premium Blend*++	+7	Parkay Spread*	+8
Fleischmann's Today's Choice*	+6	Promise*++, stick	+10
I Can't Believe It's Not Butter*	+14	Promise, Buttery Light++	+4
I Can't Believe It's Not Butter, light*	+8	Promise, fat-free	0
I Can't Believe It's Not Butter, spread++	+4	Promise, spread*++	+8
I Can't Believe It's Not Butter, sweet cream & calcium	+4	Smart Balance, soft++	+5
		Smart Beat, spread++	0
		Take Control, spread++	+1
I Can't Believe It's Not Butter, sweet cream buttermilk*	+6	Weight Watchers Extra Light, stick	+5
Imperial, soft*	+12		
Imperial, stick*	+15		

* AVOID

+ Because of variability in the trans-fatty acid content of different samples, a plus or minus 2-point variation in THI scores may occur in different batches.

++ All these products are free of trans-fatty acids.

Table 10
THI SCORES OF EGGS, MILK, AND MILK PRODUCTS
per 3.5 oz/100 g unless otherwise noted

Egg, 2 (hard, soft cooked, or poached)	+8
Egg, 2 (omelette cooked in butter)*	+11
Egg, 2 (omelette cooked in butter with ½ oz added cheese)*	+13
Egg, 2 (scrambled with added milk & margarine)*	+10
Egg, 2 (scrambled with olive or canola oil)	+6
Egg, 2 (sunny-side up cooked with margarine)*	+10
Egg, whites	0
Egg, yolk (1 large)	+4
Eggnog*	+7
Buttermilk	+1
Canned milk, skim, evaporated	0
Canned milk, whole, evaporated*	+21
Chocolate milk, 1% fat	+2
Chocolate milk, 2% fat	+2
Chocolate milk, regular*	+6
Evaporated, condensed, & sweetened*	+18
Evaporated, condensed & sweetened, (1 cup)*	+45
Milk, skim, no fat	0
Milk, 1% fat	1
Milk, 2% low fat	+2
Milk, 4% fat whole*	+4
Milk shake (8 oz)*	+9
Cocoa & chocolate powder in nonfat milk	+3
Cocoa & chocolate powder in whole milk*	+12
Dried, nonfat milk	0

* AVOID

All low-fat dairy products provide high-quality protein, and can significantly reduce the risk of insulin resistance in overweight people. Eggs prepared with olive oil or canola oil have lower THI scores than those with butter or margarines.

Table 11
THI SCORES OF CHEESES AND OTHER DAIRY PRODUCTS
cheeses 1 oz. slice or portion—
other dairy products 3.5 oz., unless noted

American*	+11	Mozzarella*	+8
American spread (2 tbs)*	+7	Mozzarella, part skim	+6
Blue*	+10	Muenster*	+11
Brie*	+9	Parmesan, grated (2 tbs)	+4
Camembert*	+7	Parmesan, hard*	+7
Cheddar*	+12	Pimento*	+11
Cheddar, shredded (½ cup)*	+23	Provolone*	+8
Colby*	+11	Ricotta (2 tbs)	+4
Cottage, 1% (½ cup)	+2	Ricotta, part skim (2 tbs)	+3
Cottage, 2% (½ cup)	+3	Romano*	+10
Cottage, creamed (½ cup)	+6	Roquefort*	+12
Cream cheese (2 tbs)*	+12	Swiss*	+10
Cream cheese, fat free	0	Swiss, low fat	+5
Cream cheese, light (2 tbs)	+5	Ice cream, regular,	
Cream cheese, olive & pimento		11% fat*	+13
(2 tbs)	+6	Ice cream, rich, 16% fat*	+19
Cream cheese, Rondele (2 tbs)*	+11	Ice cream, soft, 3% fat	+5
Edam, regular or smoked	+8	Sherbet, 2% fat	+4
Feta (2 tbs)*	+8	Yogurt, frozen, fat free	+2
Goat*	+8	Yogurt low-fat milk, plain	+2
Gorgonzola*	+9	Yogurt, nonfat milk	0
Gouda*	+10	Yogurt, low-fat milk, fruit	+2
Havarti*	+13	Yogurt, whole milk	+3
Jarlsberg*	+10	Yogurt, whole milk (8-oz	
Monterey*	+9	container)*	+7

* AVOID

Although the THI scores of nearly all other processed cheeses is between +8 to +12 per each 1-ounce portion, an occasional piece of any cheese, or an ounce tossed in your salad, has no negative health impact.

Table 12
THI SCORES OF PREPACKAGED CHEESES
per 1-oz. serving or as otherwise noted

KRAFT

American	+4
Cheddar Jack, with Jalapeño (¼ cup*)	+10
Classic Melt, 4 Cheeses (¼ cup)*	+10
Classic Melt, Cheddar & American (¼ cup)*	+12
Classic Melt, Mexican (¼ cup)*	+10
Deli Deluxe American*	+7
Deli Deluxe, Hearty Taste*	+11
Deli Deluxe, Deli Thin, Aged Swiss	+4
Deli Deluxe, Deli Thin, Mozzarella*	+8
Deli Deluxe Mild Cheddar*	+15
Deli Deluxe Old English*	+14
Deli Deluxe Provolone*	+10
Deli Deluxe Skim Swiss*	+11

KRAFT FAT FREE

Mexican Taco (¼ cup)*	+10
Mild Cheddar (¼ cup)*	+12
Mozzarella (¼ cup)*	+7
Mozzarella, 2% fat	+5
Mozzarella & Parmesan (¼ cup)*	+8
Parmesan Italian (¼ cup)	+2
Sharp Cheddar	+4
Singles, American*	+7

Singles, Pepper Jack, 2%	+4
Singles, Swiss, 2% fat	+4
Velveeta*	+9
Velveeta, light	+5
Velveeta, Mexican*	+9

KRAFT CRACKER BARREL

Baby Swiss*	+12
Extra Sharp*	+14
Extra Sharp, 2% milk*	+8
New York Aged Sharp*	+14
Sharp Cheddar*	+12
Sharp White*	+12
Vermont Sharp White*	+12

KRAFT CUBES (per 8 cubes)

Cheddar & Monterey Jack*	+13
Colby & Monterey Jack*	+13
Mild Cheddar*	+13
Sharp Cheddar*	+13

KRAFT STRIPS (per 1 strip)

Polly-O String-Ums	+7
Polly-O Superlong*	+8
Polly-O Twisfun	+5
Rip-Ums*	+8

* AVOID

Always try to choose among lighter cheeses with lower THI scores. However, here, too, an occasional piece of cheese, or any food containing cheeses, with a higher THI score is not an unpardonable sin! On the other hand, putting 2 or 3 slices of cheddar, American, or Swiss cheese on your turkey or ham sandwich, or drowning your baked potato on melted cheese, converts your healthy lunch into an unhealthy one. Similarly you should avoid "cheese lovers' " pizzas and casseroles overburdened with multiple cheeses.

When in doubt, always use the THI scores!

Table 13
THI SCORES OF OTHER PREPACKAGED CHEESES
per ¼ cup or as noted

SARGENTO	
Cheddar Jack*	+9
Double Cheddar*	+9
Fancy Mild Cheddar*	+9
Fancy Monterey Jack*	+9
Fancy Parmesan	+2
Fancy Sharp Cheddar*	+9
Fancy Swiss*	+8
Italian 6 Cheese*	+7
Italian with Garlic*	+8
Light Mexican	+6
Light Mozzarella	+5
Mexican 4 Cheese*	+11
Mild Cheddar*	+9
Mild Cheddar, light	+6
Mozzarella	+6
Mozzarella, light	+5
Nacho & Taco*	+9
Parmesan, Mozzarella, & Romano*	+8
Pepper Jack*	+9
Pizza*	+8
Stringsters (1 stick)	+7

* AVOID

There are well over 350 varieties of cheeses, from the familiar cheddar and Parmesan to exotic handmade (and very expensive) ones. But there are literally thousands of brand names, regional brands, store brands, or country-specific cheeses. The THI scores of nearly all of these products are very similar to those listed in tables 11 through 13.

Although processed cheeses have relatively high concentrations of calcium, they are actually poor sources for this mineral. The reason is that they also have high concentrations of (added) salt. As the excess salt (sodium) is excreted through the kidneys, it drags the calcium with it into the urine, which essentially defeats the purpose. Better choices are dairy products such as low-fat milk, yogurt, or cottage cheese, all of which have very low sodium content. Furthermore, low-fat milk and other dairy products can reduce the risk of colon cancer by nearly 30 percent.

Table 14
THI SCORES OF POULTRY
per 3.5 oz./100 g

Chicken, Fried

Breast without skin (½)	+3
Breast without skin with batter (½)	+5
Breast without skin with flour (½)	+4
Breast with skin (½)	+7
Drumsticks without skin (2)	+5
Drumsticks without skin with batter (2)*	+8
Drumsticks without skin with flour (2)	+7
Drumsticks with skin (2)	+7
Drumsticks with skin & batter (2)*	+10
Drumsticks with skin & flour (2)*	+9
Leg without skin (1)	+5
Leg without skin with batter (1)*	+8
Leg without skin with flour (1)	+6
Leg with skin (1)*	+10
Leg with skin with batter (1)*	+13
Leg with skin with flour (1)*	+11
Thigh without skin (2)	+6
Thigh with skin (2)*	+10

Chicken, Roasted

Breast without skin (½)	+3
Breast with skin (½)	+5

Drumsticks without skin (2)	+3
Drumsticks with skin (2)	+5
Leg without skin (1)	+3
Leg with skin (1)	+5
Thigh without skin (2)	+5
Thigh with skin (2)*	+8

Other Poultry

Cornish hen with skin, roasted	+6
Duck without skin, roasted	+6
Duck with skin, roasted*	+15
Pheasant without skin, roasted	+2
Pheasant with skin, roasted	+5
Turkey, breast (sliced)	+2
Dark meat without skin	+4
Dark meat with skin	+6
White meat without skin	+3
White meat with skin	+5

* AVOID

Table 15
THI SCORES OF BEEF AND BOVINE ORGAN MEATS
3.5 oz/100g

Boneless chuck, trimmed*	+16	Porterhouse steak, choice*	+25
Chopped sirloin, or sirloin steak, extra lean	+7	Rib roast without bone, choice*	+28
Chuck, ground, extra lean*	+11	Round steak, lean*	+10
Chuck, ground, lean*	+16	Rump roast, choice*	+20
Chuck, rib roast*	+28	Short ribs*	+30
Chuck roast, choice (without bone)*	+24	Sirloin steak, choice*	+20
Chuck roast, lean*	+13	T-Bone steak, choice*	+25
Chuck steak, choice (without bone)*	+24	Tenderloin, lean, not marbled	+6
Chuck steak, lean*	+13	Beef brain*	+22
Corned beef, cooked*	+23	Beef heart	+5
Corned beef hash (with potato)*	+10	Beef liver	+7
Ground beef, extra lean, 10% fat	+8	Beef tongue*	+14
Ground beef lean, 20% fat*	+17	Beef tongue, lean	+8
Ground round, extra lean, 7% fat	+6	Chicken heart	+5
Ground round, lean*	+12	Chicken liver	+8
Ground rump, regular*	+21	Chicken liver pâté (1 oz)	+5
London broil, flank steak, choice	+6	Duck liver	+8

* Avoid

Remember, the problem is not the red meat, but the white fat. Even more important, remember that the listed THI scores are for 3.5-ounce portions, not 16- or 20-ounce steaks!

Table 16
THI SCORES OF LAMB, PORK, AND VEAL PRODUCTS
3.5 oz/100 g unless otherwise noted

Lamb

Chop, 1 lean, broiled or grilled	+8
Chop, 1 lean loin, broiled or grilled	+9
Chops, 2, lean meat only	+9
Chops, 2 average loin chops, untrimmed*	+21
Chops, 2 average size, not trimmed*	+24
Chops, 2 small, lean loin meat only	+6
Leg, roasted	+10
Leg, roasted, lean meat only	+4
Rib, roasted*	+20
Rib, roasted, lean meat only	+8
Shoulder, roasted*	+14
Shoulder, roasted, lean meat only	+7

Pork

Bacon, 3 slices	+4
Canadian bacon, 2 slices	+2
Ham, canned	+3
Ham, leg, roasted, lean meat only	+4
Ham, leg, roasted, trimmed	+4
Ham, lunch meat, 2 slices	+3
Ham, roasted, lean meat only	+5
Ham, roasted, trimmed	+5
Pork chop, broiled or grilled	+9*
Pork chop, lean meat only	+4
Pork chop, pan fried*	+14
Pork chop, pan fried, lean meat only	+6
Pork ribs, roasted*	+14
Pork ribs, roasted, lean meat only	+8
Pork shoulder, roasted*	+14
Pork shoulder, roasted, lean meat only	+6
Spare ribs, roasted or broiled*	+19

Veal

Chop, broiled, grilled, untrimmed	+8
Chop, lean meat only	+4
Cutlet, lean	+4
Rib, roasted, untrimmed*	+9
Rib, lean meat only	+4

Venison

Steak	+3

Table 17
THI SCORES OF FISH*
per 3.5oz./100 g

Anchovies	-1	Pollack	0
Bass, Freshwater	-1	Pompano	+1
Bass, Sea	0	Rockfish	-1
Bass, Striped	-1	Sablefish	-2
Bluefish	-2	Salmon, Atlantic	-1
Catfish	-2	Salmon, Chinook	-4
Caviar (per tsp)	+1	Salmon, Chinook, smoked (lox)	-2
Cod	0	Salmon, coho	-3
Croaker	-2	Sardines (canned in oil)	-1
Flounder or Carp	0	Shark	-1
Grouper	0	Snapper	-1
Haddock	0	Sole	0
Halibut	-1	Spot	+1
Herring	-1	Sturgeon	0
Mackerel, Atlantic	-5	Swordfish	-1
Mackerel, King	0	Trout, Rainbow (farm raised)	-2
Mahimahi	-2	Trout, Rainbow (lake)	-1
Monkfish	0	Trout, Sea	-1
Mullet	-2	Tuna, Bluefin	-2
Ocean Perch	0	Tuna, Skipjack	0
Orange Roughy	-2	Tuna, Yellowfin	-1
Perch	0	Whitefish	-2

* THI scores of some fish such as tuna (fresh or canned), salmon, or rainbow trout may be higher or lower depending on the fish's habitat and the species of the same fish (for example, Pacific, coho, or Atlantic salmon). Also, almost always the concentration of healthful omega-3 fats is higher in the wild fish compared with the farm raised.

Although predator fish such as sharks, mackerel, and swordfish may have slightly higher levels of mercury, the amount present in other fish is negligible to undetectable.

Table 18
THI SCORES OF OTHER SEAFOODS
per 3.5 oz./100 g

Tuna & Salmon, Canned in Water[a]

Bumble Bee, pink salmon	-2
Bumble Bee, red salmon	-2
Bumble Bee, tuna, chunk white	-1
Bumble Bee, tuna, solid white	-1
Chicken of the Sea, salmon	-2
Chicken of the Sea, tuna, chunk white	-1
Chicken of the Sea, tuna, solid white	-1
StarKist, tuna, chunk light	-1
StarKist, tuna, solid white	-2

Tuna, Canned in Olive or Canola Oil

Bumble Bee, chunk white	+1
Bumble Bee, solid white	-1
Chicken of the Sea, chunk light	-1
StarKist, chunk white lunch	-1
StarKist, lunch kit	-1
StarKist, solid white	0

Shelfish

Clams	0
Crabs, Alaska King	0
Crabs, Dungeness	0
Crayfish	0
Lobster	+1
Mussels	0
Octopus	0
Oysters	0
Scallops	0
Shrimp	+1
Snails	0
Squid	+2

Table 19
THI SCORES OF NUTS, VEGETABLES & FRUITS

Nuts (1 oz)			
Almonds, dried or dry roasted	-1	Sesame seeds roasted or toasted	+2
Almonds, oil roasted	-1	Sunflower kernels	+4
Beechnuts, dried or roasted	+1	Walnuts, dried or roasted	-2
Brazilnuts, dried or roasted*	+7	**Fruits & Vegetables (3.5 oz. 100 g)**	
Butternuts, dry roasted	+2		
Cashew nuts, dry roasted	+2	All Fruits except avocado, dates, olives, and raisins	-1
Chestnuts, roasted or dried	0		
Coconut, dry meat*	+17	Avocado (1 medium), or olives (8)	-2
Coconut, dried, shredded*	+17		
Coconut, raw meat, 2" X 2" piece*	+26	Dates (2) or raisins (one oz)	+1
Filberts, dried, roasted	-4	All vegetables except potato	-2
Ginko nuts, dried	0		
Hickory nuts, dried	+1	Potato and sweet potato (1 medium)*	+4
Macadamia nuts, dried or roasted	-3		
Mixed nuts, dry roasted	+1	Popcorn, 94% fat free (½ bag)	+1
Peanuts, dried or roasted	+2		
Peanut butter (2 tbsp)	+4	Popcorn, light butter (½ bag)*	+3
Pecans, dried or roasted	-2		
Pine nuts, dried or roasted	+3	Popcorn, butter, honey butter, cheddar, movie or toffee*	+5
Pistachio nuts, dry roasted	-1		
Pumpkin kernels	+4		

* AVOID

In general, dark or deep-colored fruits (all berries, black grapes, cherries, figs, nectarines, peaches, and plums, etc.), and dark vegetables (broccoli, chives, collards, herbs, kale, lettuce, parsley, tomato, watercress, etc.) have more cardioprotective and anti-carcinogen compounds than their lighter counterparts.

Table 20
THI SCORES OF BREAD PRODUCTS

Bagel	+4
Bread crumbs (1 cup)	+4
Bread stuffing (1 cup)*	+8
Cracked wheat (1 slice)	+1
Dinner roll	+2
English muffin	+3
French or Austrian, ⅓ baguette	+3
Hard roll	+3
Hoagie/submarine roll, small	+4
Hot dog or hamburger roll	+3
Italian, ⅓ of a baguette	+3
Mixed grain (1 slice)	+3
Oatmeal bread (1 slice)	+2
Pita (1 medium)	+3
Pumpernickel (1 slice)	+3
Raisin (1 slice)	+3
Rye (1 slice)	+2
Wheat (1 slice)	+2
Whole wheat (1 slice)	+2
White (1 slice)	+3
Other European breads, rustic, etc. (1 slice)	+2

* Avoid

There are countless varieties of breads—national, regional or ethnic—both in the U.S. and abroad. By and large, they have THI scores ranging from 0 to 4 per serving. Which ones should you avoid, if any? The answer is that fresh, crunchy French or other European breads are heavenly morsels, but must be enjoyed in moderation. Keep in mind that the THI scores listed above are per serving, not for the whole baguette or the loaf!

You should also guard against the practice of spreading a pound of butter or margarine(!) on a slice of bread. However, a touch of extra-virgin olive oil, or a thin spread of some of the soft margarines without trans-fatty acids (see table 9), is not unreasonable. A better option is to eat your bread without any added fat/calories.

Bleached white flour, and therefore white bread (including most pita, Italian, or French breads) and pasta, all have high glycemic indices (see table 5). You should opt for whole wheat, rye, or even sourdough flour products.

Table 21
THI SCORES OF KELLOGG'S CEREALS
AND OTHER PRODUCTS

Cereals (per bowl)			
All-Bran, Bran Buds	+2	Pokemon	+2
All-Bran, Extra Fiber	+1	Product 19	+2
All-Bran, Original	+1	Raisin Bran	+2
Apple Jacks ·	+2	Raisin Bran Crunch	+3
Cinnamon Crunch Crispix	+2	Rice Krispies	+4
Cocoa Rice Krispies	+2	Smacks	+3
Complete Oat Bran Flakes	+1	Smart Start	+2
Complete Wheat Bran Flakes	+1	Special K	+2
Corn Flakes	+2	**Cereal Bars (per bar)**	
Corn Pops	+2	Apple Cinnamon	+2
Cracklin' Oat Bran	+2	Blueberry	+2
Crispix	+2	Cherry	+2
Disney Buzz Blasts	+2	Mixed Berry	+2
Disney Hunny B'S	+2	Raspberry or Strawberry	+2
Disney Mickey's Magix	+2	Special K Bars	+3
Disney Mud and Bugs	+2	**Nutri-Grain Products**	
Froot Loops	+2	Blueberry Yogurt Bar (1)	+2
Frosted Flakes	+2	Strawberry Yogurt Bar (1)	+2
Honey Crunch Corn Flakes	+2	Vanilla Yogurt Bar (1)	+2
Just Right Fruit & Nut	+3	Minis, Apple Cinnamon	
Marshamallow Froot Loops	+2	(1 pouch)	+3
Mini-Wheats, Frosted Bite Size	+4	Minnis, Blueberry (1 pouch)	+3
Mini-Wheats, Frosted Original	+4	Minis, Strawberry (1 pouch)	+3
Mini-Wheats, Honey Frosted Bite Size	+4	Twists, Apple Cobbler (1)	+3
Mini-Wheats, Raisin	+3	Twists, Cappuccino &	
Mini-Wheats, Strawberry	+3	Créme (1)	+3
Mueslix	+3	Twists, Strawberry Cheesecake	
		(1)	+3

Table 21
THI SCORES OF KELLOGG'S CEREALS AND OTHER PRODUCTS *(cont.)*

Rice Krispies Treats (per 1)			
Apple Cinnamon*	+4	Double Chocolatey Chunk*	+5
Caramel Chocolatey Chunk*	+4	Original	+2
Chocolatey Peanut Butter*	+5	Single Serve*	+4

* AVOID

Table 22
THI SCORES OF QUAKER CEREALS, OATMEALS, AND GRITS

Oatmeals (per serving)		Cereals	
Baked Apple (1 packet-instant)	+2	Cap'n Crunch	+2
Banana Bread (1 packet)	+2	Life	+1
Brown Sugar (1 packet)	+2	Quaker Oatmeal Cereal	+1
Cinnamon Roll (1 packet-instant)	+2	Quaker Squares, brown sugar	+2
Crystal Wedding Oats (½ cup)	+3	Quaker Squares, cinnamon	+2
Dinosaur Eggs (1 packet)*	+7	Quisp	+2
Express Instant Oatmeal (1 packet)	+2	**Instant Grits (per serving or packet)**	
French Vanilla (1 packet)	+3	American cheese	+2
Honey Nut (1 packet)	+3	Cheddar cheese blend	+3
Instant Oatmeal, Maple & Brown Sugar	+3	Country bacon	+2
Instant oatmeal, raisin cinnamon swirl (1 packet)	+4	Ham n' cheese	+3
		Original	+1
Instant oatmeal, regular (1 packet)	+1	Real butter	+2
Instant oatmeal, strawberries & cream (1 packet)	+3	Real cheddar Cheese	+1
		Red eye gravy & country ham	+2
Multigrain oatmeal (½ cup)	+2	3 cheeses	+1
Nutrition for women, golden brown sugar (1 packet)	+3		
Oat bran hot cereal (½ cup)	+2		
Sun Country iron-fortified (½ cup)	+3		

* AVOID

Table 23
THI SCORES OF GENERAL MILLS CEREALS
per bowl

Apple Cinnamon Cheerios	+1	Multi Grain Cheerios	0
Basic 4	+1	Nature Valley Low Fat	
Boo Berry	+1	Fruit Granola	+3
Cheerios	0	Nesquik	+2
Cinnamon Grahams	+1	Oatmeal Crisp, Almond	+4
Cinnamon Toast Crunch	+2	Oatmeal Crisp, Apple Cinnamon	+3
Cocoa Puffs	+1	Oatmeal Crisp, Raisin	+3
Cookie Crisp	+1	Para Su Familia Cinnamon Stars	+2
Corn or Rice Chex	+2	Para Su Familia Frutis	+2
Count Chocula	+2	Para Su Familia Raisin Bran	+3
Country Corn Flakes	+2	Raisin Nut Bran	+2
Fiber One	+1	Reese's Peanut Butter Puffs	+3
Franken Berry	+1	Sunrise, Organic	+2
French Toast Crunch	+2	Total Brown Sugar & Oats	+2
Frosted Cheerios	+1	Total Corn Flakes	+2
Golden Grahams	+2	Total Raisin Bran	+2
Gold Medal Raisin Bran	+2	Total Whole Grain	+2
Harmony	+3	Trix	+2
Honey Nut Cheerios	+1	Wheat Chex	+2
Honey Nut Chex	+2	**Wheaties**	
Honey Nut Clusters	+3		
Kaboom	+2	Breakfast of Champions	+1
Kix & Berry Berry Kix	+2	Frosted Wheaties	+2
Lucky Charms	+2	Wheaties Energy Crunch	+3
Multi Bran Chex	+3	Wheaties Raisin Bran	+3

Various bran cereals made by nearly all manufacturers contain more sugar and total carbohydrates than other (frosted) cereals. The obvious reason for overburdening bran products with sugar or corn sweeteners is to make these sawdust-tasting products more acceptable. Another problem with wheat bran products is that they are not digested in the small intestine. So when they reach the large intestine (colon), they are partially fermented by the colon's abundant bacteria, and contribute to gas and bloating in some people.

Even though there are some minor differences in the nutrient content of cereals and other packaged foods made by the same company in various countries, these differences are minor, and do not alter their THIs significantly.

Table 24
THI SCORES OF BUDGET GOURMET FROZEN ENTRÉES
per meal

Beef Cantonese	+6	Roasted Chicken Breast	
Beef Sirloin Salisbury Steak*	+5	with Herb Gravy	+4
Cheese Manicotti with Meat Sauce*	+22	Scalloped Noodles &	
Chicken Marsala*	+9	Turkey*	+21
Chinese Style Vegetables & Chicken	+4	Shrimp Mariner	+5
Fettuccini Alfredo with 4 Cheeses*	+26	Sirloin Tips with Country	
Glazed Turkey	+4	Style Vegetables*	+11
Herbed Chicken Breast with		Spaghetti with Chunky To-	
Fettuccini*	+9	mato & Meat Sauce	+7
Italian Sausage Lasagna*	+18	Special Recipe Sirloin Beef	+6
Italian Style Vegetables & Chicken	+4	Spicy Szechuan Style	
Linguini with Tomato Sauce &		Vegetables & Chicken	+5
Italian Sausage*	+10	Stuffed Turkey Breast	+5
Macaroni and Cheese*	+12	Swedish Meatballs*	+32
Mandarin Chicken	+3	Three Cheese Lasagna*	+21
Orange Glazed Chicken Breast	+3	Wide Ribbon Pasta with	
Oriental Beef*	+10	Ricotta & Chunky	
Penne Pasta With Chunky		Tomatoes*	+17
Tomatoes*	+10	Yankee Pot Roast	+5
Pepper Steak	+6		
Rigatoni in Cream Sauce with			
Broccoli & Chicken	+7		

* AVOID

Table 25
THI SCORES OF HEALTHY CHOICE FROZEN MEALS
per meal

Bowl Creations		Salisbury steak & mashed	
Cheese tortellini*	+8	potatoes	+6
Chicken alfredo	+7	Sirloin beef tips & rice	+5
Chicken teriyaki with rice	+6	Slow roasted turkey & potato	+5
Chili with beans	+6	**Medleys**	
Colonial style chicken pie	+7	Beef teriyaki*	+8
Country chicken bake*	+8	Beef tips & spiral pasta	+6
Orange beef with noodles*	+9	Chicken breast & vegetables	+5
Roasted potatoes with ham	+5	Chicken carbonara	+6
Roasted pepper chicken & rice	+7	Chicken fettuccini alfredo	+6
Shrimp & vegetables	+6	Chicken piccata	+6
Southwestern chicken & pasta	+7	Country roasted turkey	+5
Spicy beef/broccoli with rice	+7	Glazed chicken	+5
Sweet and sour chicken/rice	+3	Grillied chicken Sonoma	+4
Thai curry chicken	+7	Mandarin chicken	+3
Turkey divan	+7	Meat lasagna*	+8
Duos		Oriental style chicken	+4
		Rigatoni with broccoli &	
Baked chicken breast	+5	chicken	+6
Beef with BBQ sauce	+6	Sesame chicken	+6
Grilled chicken with mashed		**Solos**	
potatoes	+5		
Grilled chicken breast &		Beef macaroni	+6
pasta	+6	Cheddar broccoli potato*	+8
Breaded chicken breast strips with		Cheese ravioli parmigiana*	+8
macaroni & cheese	+5	Cheesy rice and chicken	+7
Herb-breaded pork patty	+6		

Table 25
THI SCORES OF HEALTHY CHOICE FROZEN MEALS
per meal (cont.)

Chicken enchilada	+6	Blackened Chicken	+6
Chicken óle	+3	Charbroiled Beef Patty*	+8
Fettuccini alfredo	+5	Chicken Broccoli Alfredo	+7
Homestyle chicken & pasta	+7	Chicken Enchilada Supreme	+7
Lasagna with meat sauce*	+8	Chicken Parmigiana*	+8
Macaroni & cheese	+7	Chicken Teriyaki	+6
Manicotti with 3 cheeses*	+9	Country Breaded Chicken*	+8
Santa Fe rice & beans	+6	Country Herb Chicken*	+8
Spaghetti & beef	+7	Grilled Turkey Breast	+7
Tuna casserole	+5	Herb-Baked Fish	+6

Mixed Grills

		Honey-Glazed Chicken	+6
Beef teriyaki*	+8	Lemon-Pepper Fish	+5
Chicken, ginger dip sauce	+7	Mesquite Beef with Barbecue	
Chicken, barbecue dip sauce	+7	Sauce*	+8
Chicken, roasted		Mesquite Chicken Barbecue	+6
red pepper*	+9	Oven Roasted Beef	+7
Chicken garlic tomato		Roasted Chicken Breast	+7
dip sauce	+6	Sesame Chicken	+7
Steak with zesty steak sauce	+7	Stuffed Pasta Shells with Bread	

Meals To Go

		Stick	+5
All meals to go items	+5	Sweet and Sour Chicken	+7
Ice creams (per ½ cup)		Traditional Beef Tips Portabella*	
All no-sugar-added			+9
ice creams	+2	Traditional Meatloaf*	+9
All other ice creams	+4	Traditional Salisbury Steak*	+10
		Traditional Turkey Breasts*	+8

Healthy Choice Meals

		Yankee Pot Roast*	+9
Beef Stroganoff*	+8		

* AVOID

Many items among Healthy Choice and Lean Cuisine products are quite reasonable nutritionwise (but not necessarily in their taste or "personality"). However, just because they are Healthy Choice or Lean Cuisine does not mean they all are healthful. For example, among the 25 items listed in this table, 11 should be avoided.

Table 26
THI SCORES OF LEAN CUISINE FROZEN FOODS
per meal

Café Classics	
Baked Chicken	+4
Baked Fish	+7
Beef Peppercorn	+5
Beef Portabello*	+8
Beef Pot Roast	+5
Bow Tie Pasta & Chicken	+3
Cheese Lasagna with Chicken Scaloppine	+6
Chicken À l'Orange	+2
Chicken & Vegetables	+6
Chicken Carbonara	+5
Chicken in Peanut Sauce	+4
Chicken Mediterranean	+2
Chicken Parmesan	+4
Chicken Piccata	+5
Chicken with Almonds	+2
Chicken with Basil Cream Sauce	+6
Chicken, Fiesta Grilled	+6
Chicken, Glazed	+3
Chicken, Grilled	+3
Chicken, Herb Roasted	+3
Chicken, Honey Mustard	+4
Chicken, Honey Roasted	+5
Glazed Turkey Tenderloins	+4
Honey Roasted Pork	+5
Meat Loaf & Whipped Potatoes*	+9
Orange Beef	+5
Oriental Beef	+3
Oven Roasted Beef*	+8
Roasted Garlic Chicken	+4
Roasted Turkey Breast	+2
Salisbury Steak*	+10
Sesame Chicken	+4
Shrimp & Angel-hair Pasta	+3
Southern Beef Tips	+6
Sweet & Sour Chicken	+2
Teriyaki Chicken	+4
Thai-Style Chicken	+6

Everyday Favorites	
Alfredo Pasta Primavera*	+8
Angel-hair Pasta	+3
Baked Chicken Florentine	+4
Cheese Cannelloni	+5
Cheese Lasagna Casserole*	+8
Cheese Ravioli*	+8
Chicken Chow Mein	+3
Chicken Enchilada	+5
Chicken Fettuccini	+7
Chicken Florentine Lasagna	+6
Five Cheese Lasagna*	+9
Deluxe Cheddar Potato*	+8
Fettuccini Alfredo*	+8
Hunan Beef & Broccoli	+4
Lasagna with Meat Sauce*	+9
Macaroni & Cheese*	+9
Mandarin Chicken	+3
Oriental Style Pot Stickers	+5
Penne Pasta with Tomato-Basil Sauce	+3
Roasted Chicken with Lemon-Pepper Fettuccini	+5
Roasted Potatoes with Broccoli	+7
Santa Fe Style Rice & Beans	+5

Table 26
THI SCORES OF LEAN CUISINE FROZEN FOODS
per meal (cont.)

Spaghetti with Meatballs	+5	Roasted Turkey Breast	+3
Spaghetti with Meat Sauce	+3	Salisbury Steak*	+10
Stuffed Cabbage	+5	**Skillet Sensations**	
Swedish Meatballs	+7		
Teriyaki Stir-Fry	+2	3-Cheese Chicken	+5
Three-Bean Chili	+5	Beef Teriyaki & Rice	+3
Vegetable Eggroll	+4	Chicken Alfredo	+6
Family Style Recipes		Chicken Oriental	+2
		Chicken Primavera	+2
Chicken Florentine Lasagna	+4	Chicken Teriyaki	+3
Five Cheese Lasagna	+6	Garlic Chicken	+4
French Bread Cheese Pizza*	+9	Herb Chicken & Roasted	
French Bread Deluxe Pizza*	+8	Potatoes	+2
French Bread Pepperoni	+6	Roasted Turkey	+3
Dinnertime Selections		**Café Classic Bowls**	
Beef Steak Tips Dijon	+7	3-Cheese Stuffed Rigatoni*	+9
Chicken Fettuccini*	+9	Chicken Fried Rice	+4
Chicken Florentine	+6	Chicken Teriyaki	+3
Glazed Chicken	+3	Creamy Chicken &	
Grilled Chicken & Penne Pasta	+7	Vegetables	+7
Grilled Chicken Tuscan	+4		
Jumbo Rigatoni with Meatballs*	+8		
Oriental Glazed Chicken Teriyaki	+2		
Roasted Chicken	+3		

* AVOID

Table 27
THI SCORES OF FROZEN SEAFOODS
per 3.5 oz/100g unless otherwise noted

Gorton's		Healthy Treasures Fish	
Breaded Fish Sticks	+6	Sticks	+2
Crunchy Golden Fish Fillets*	+8	Light Filets, Flounder	+3
Garlic & Herb Fish Fillets*	+8	Sea Pals (Fish Shapes)	+2
Hot & Spicy Fish Fillets*	+9	**Van De Kamp's**	
Mrs. Paul's		Batterd Fish Portions*	+8
		Breaded Butterfly Shrimp	+6
Breaded Fish Sticks	+3	Breaded Fish Sticks	+5
Crispy Crunchy Filets	+5	Breaded Popcorn Shrimp	+6
Crispy Crunchy Fish Sticks	+3	Crisp & Healthy Fish Fillets	+3
Deviled Crabs	+5	Crisp & Healthy Fish Sticks	+2
Deviled Crab Miniatures	+6	Fish Fillets in Batter	+4
Fried Clams	+2	Ministix	+6
Healthy Treasures Fish Filets	+1		

*AVOID

Table 28
THI SCORES OF STOUFFER'S FROZEN MEALS
per meal or as listed

Stouffer's Entrées		Macaroni & Cheese (9 oz)*	+16
Cheddar Cheese & Chicken Bake*	+17	Macaroni & Cheese	
Cheesy Spaghetti Bake*	+18	(12 oz)*	+15
Chicken Pot Pie (10 oz)*	+39	Penne Pasta & Chicken	
Creamed Chipped Beef (11 oz)*	+11	Bake*	+9
Five-Cheese Lasagna*	+14	Spaghetti with Meatballs*	+10
Lasagna Bake (1½ oz)*	+17	Spaghetti with Meat Sauce*	+12
Lasagna with Italian Sausage*	+21	Stuffed Peppers (16 oz)*	+9
Lasagna with Meat		Turkey Pot Pie (10 oz)*	+39
& Sauce (10 oz)*	+17	Vegetable & Chicken Pasta	
		Bake*	+10

Table 28
THI SCORES OF STOUFFER'S FROZEN MEALS
per meal or as listed (cont.)

Vegetable Lasagna*	+15		Beef Stroganoff*	+14
Welch Rarebit (10 oz)*	+9		Breaded Boneless Pork	
Family Style Recipes			Cutlet*	+9
Chicken & Broccoli			Chicken in Mushroom	
Pasta Bake*	+18		Gravy*	+15
Chicken Cordon Bleu Pasta*	+12		Chicken Fettuccini*	+10
Chicken Enchiladas*	+15		Chicken Parmigiana*	+10
Chicken Lasagna*	+11		Chicken Tenders in	
Escalloped Chicken &			BBQ Sauce*	+21
Noodles	+9		Fish Fillet with Macaroni &	
Grandma's Chicken &			Cheese	+13
Vegetable Rice Bake*	+15		Fried Chicken Breast*	+16
Hashed Brown Potato			Green Pepper Steak	+5
Casserole*	+14		Meatloaf*	+24
Lasagna with Meat			Roast Chicken & Stuffing	+17
& Sauce*	+10		Roasted Pork*	+12
Macaroni & Cheese*	+18		Roast Turkey Breast*	+10
Meatloaf in Gravy*	+12		Salisbury Steak*	+18
Potato Pot Roast Bake*	+25		Veal Parmigiana*	+12
Vegetable Lasagna	+14		**Homestyle Dinners**	
French Bread Pizza			Baked Chicken	+6
Cheese*	+13		Beef Pot Roast*	+15
Deluxe*	+13		Chicken & Fettuccini*	+9
Extra Cheese*	+15		Chicken Monterey*	+18
Five Cheese*	+21		Country Fried Beef Steak*	+25
Grilled Vegetable*	+11		Meatloaf*	+26
Pepperoni*	+15		Pork & Roasted Potatoes*	+14
Pepperoni 7 Mushroom*	+15		Roast Turkey Breast*	+14
Sausage*	+15		Salisbury Steak*	+21
Sausage & Pepperoni*	+17		Veal Parmigiana*	+12
Three Meat*	+19			
White*	+15			
Homestyle Entrees				
Baked Chicken Breast*	+14			
Beef Pot Roast*	+10			

* AVOID

Table 29
THI SCORES OF OTHER STOUFFER'S PRODUCTS
per serving

Stouffer's Entrées		Harvest Apples	+5
Cheese Manicotti*	+18	Potatoes Au Gratin*	+8
Cheese Ravioli*	+15	Spinach Soufflé	+5
Chicken À la King*	+10	Whipped Potatoes & Gravy	+8
Chicken Oriental	+3	**Skillet Sensations**	
Escalloped Chicken & Noodles*	+11	Beef Stroganoff*	+9
Fettuccini Alfredo*	+27	Broccoli & Beef*	+10
Macaroni & Beef*	+12	Chicken Alfredo*	+12
Macaroni & Cheese with Broccoli*	+13	Grilled Chicken &	
Stuffed Pepper (10 oz)*	+10	Vegetables*	+12
Swedish Meatballs*	+22	Homestyle Beef*	+14
Tuna Noodle Casserole*	+11	Homestyle Chicken &	
Turkey Tetrazzini*	+17	Noodles	+8
Oven Sensations		Savory Chicken & Rice	+4
		Teriyaki Chicken	+5
Baked Chicken*	+15	**Slowfire Classics**	
Beef, Roasted Potatoes, &			
Peppers	+4	Beef Stew*	+10
Chicken & Dumplings*	+10	Cheesy Pizzatini*	+14
Chicken, Stuffing, &		Hearty Chicken &	
Gravy*	+11	Vegetables*	+13
Yankee Pot Roast*	+10	Homestyle Chicken &	
Cheddar Potato Bake*	+12	Noodles*	+10
Corn Soufflé	+5	Steak & Mushroom*	+9
Creamed Spinach*	+17		

* AVOID

When I asked a spokesperson for Stouffer's why do they not publish nutritional information on the Internet, I was told, "Sir, if you're concerned about the nutritional value of our products, then you should choose among Lean Cuisine items. People who eat our products are not interested in nutrition information!" (Lean Cuisine is another division of the parent company of Stouffer's.)

As you can see from tables 29 and 30, very few frozen entrées produced by Stouffer's have a THI index low enough to make them edible! Your best bet is to look elsewhere, such as Lean Cuisine and Healthy Choice, and avoid Stouffer's altogether.

Table 30
THI SCORES OF WEIGHT WATCHERS FROZEN ENTRÉES
per meal

Angel-hair Pasta	+3
Broccoli & Cheese Baked Potato	+3
Chicken Broccoli & Cheddar	+5
Chicken Enchilada Suiza	+4
Deluxe Combo Pizza*	+7
Fettuccini Alfredo	+5
Fiesta Chicken	+1
Garden Lasagna	+3
Grilled Chicken Sandwich	+5
Grilled Salisbury Steak	+5
Ham & Cheese Pocket Sandwich	+6
Honey Mustard Chicken & Sauce	+1
Italian Cheese Lasagna	+6
Lasagna Florentine	+3
Lasagna with Meat Sauce	+5
Lemon Herb Chicken Piccata	+3
Macaroni & Cheese	+5
Pasta Portofino	+3
Ravioli Florentine	+3
Reuben Pocket Sandwich	+5
Three Cheese Rotini	+5
Stuffed Turkey Breast	+5
Swedish Meatballs*	+8
Tuna Noodle Casserole	+5

* AVOID

For those with a weight problem the items listed above and other Weight Watchers products are nutritionally sound. However, as is the case with nearly all frozen foods, the limited variety is pretty boring and cannot be the basis or even a major component of long-term dietary practices.

Table 31
THI SCORES OF OTHER FROZEN ENTRÉES
per meal

Banquet		Honey Roasted Chicken	+4
Beef Pot Pie*	+17	Roasted Chicken	+3
Charbroiled Beef Patties*	+8	**Swanson**	
Chicken Nugget Meal*	+11	Beef Pot Pie*	+19
Chicken Pot Pie*	+16	Chicken Pot Pie*	+19
Country Fried Chicken*	+12	Fish & Chips*	+32
Fried Chicken*	+12	Fried Chicken*	+21
Fried Chicken Meal*	+20	Hungry-Man Beef Pot Pie*	+28
Gravy & Sliced Turkey	+4	Hungry-Man Chicken Pot Pie*	+26
Salisbury Steak*	+11	Hungry-Man Salisbury Steak*	+29
Salisbury Steak with Gravy*	+9	Hungry-Man Sirloin Beef Tips*	+15
Skinless Fried Chicken	+7	Hungry-Man Turkey*	+12
Turkey & Gravy	+6	Hungry-Man Turkey Pot Pie*	+26
Turkey Pot Pie*	+17	Hungry-Man Yankee Pot Roast	+7
Tyson		Salisbury Steak*	+12
		Turkey	+5
Chicken Marsala	+4	Turkey Pot Pie*	+19
Chicken Mesquite*	+8	Veal Parmigiana*	+14
Chicken Piccata	+4	Yankee Pot Roast*	+10
Grilled Chicken	+4		

* AVOID

Table 32
THI SCORES OF PROGRESSO SOUPS
per 1 cup

Beef & Baked Potato	+3
Beef & Mushroom Portobello	+3
Beef & Vegetable*	+4
Chicken & Wild Rice	+1
Chicken Barley	+1
Chicken Noodle	+1
Creamy Mushroom*	+13
French Onion	+2
Grilled Chicken Italiano with Vegetables & Penne	+2
Grilled Steak with Vegetables & Penne	+3
Hearty Tomato	+2
Homestyle Chicken with Vegetables & Pearl Onion	+1
Lentil	+1
Manhattan Clam Chowder	+1
Minestrone	+1
New England Clam Chowder*	+11
Potato Chowder with Broccoli & Cheese*	+5
Roasted Chicken Rotini	+1
Roasted Chicken with Garden Herbs	+1
Southwestern Style Corn Chowder	+1
Tomato Rotini	+2

* AVOID

The THI scores of all other commercial soups, including store brands, are similar.
Although a serving of soup (1 can or ½ can, depending on brand) as a lunch is reasonable, you still need to be selective by avoiding those with THI scores greater than +4. Also, keep in mind that serving sizes for various soups are not the same. When in doubt use THI scores.

Table 33
THI SCORES OF CAMPBELL'S CONDENSED SOUPS
per cup (prepared)

Healthy Request		Chicken & Dumplings	+3
Bean with Ham & Bacon	+3	Chicken & Stars	+2
Chicken & Rice	+3	Chicken Gumbo	+2
Chicken Noodle	+3	Chicken Noodle	+2
Chicken Vegetable	+2	Chicken Noodle O's	+3
Cream of Broccoli	+3	Chicken with Rice	+2
Cream of Celery	+3	Chicken with Vegetables	+2
Cream of Chicken	+3	Chicken with Wild Rice	+2
Cream of Chicken & Broccoli	+3	Cream of Asparagus*	+5
Cream of Mushroom	+3	Cream of Broccoli*	+5
Healthy Request (cont.)		Cream of Broccoli & Cheese*	+5
Hearty Pasta & Vegetables	+1	Cream of Celery*	+5
Minestrone	+1	Cream of Chicken*	+5
Tomato	+2	Cream of Chicken & Broccoli*	+6
Vegetable	+1		
Vegetable Beef	+2	Cream of Chicken Dijon*	+6
Regular		Cream of Chicken Mushroom*	+6
Bean with Bacon	+4	Cream of Chicken with Herbs	+4
Beef Noodle	+3	Cream of Mushroom*	+5
Beef with Vegetable & Barley	+3	Cream of Mushroom with Garlic	+3
Beefy Mushroom	+3		
Black Bean	+1	Cream of Onion*	+5
California Style Vegetables	+1	Cream of Potato	+4
Cheddar Cheese*	+9	Cream of Potato with Shrimp*	+5
Chicken Alphabet with Vegetable	+3		

Table 33
THI SCORES OF CAMPBELL'S CONDENSED SOUPS
per cup (prepared) (cont.)

Creamy Chicken Noodle*	+5	Noodle & Ground Beef*	+5
Curly Chicken Noodle	+3	Old-Fashioned Tomato Rice	+2
Double Noodle in Chicken		Old-Fashioned Vegetables	+2
Broth	+3	Oyster Stew*	+8
Fiesta Chili Beef with Beans*	+5	Pepper Pot	+4
Fiesta Nacho Cheese*	+8	Scotch Broth	+3
French Onion	+2	Southwestern Chicken	
Fun Shapes Pasta with		Vegetable	+1
Chicken	+1	Split Pea with Ham*	+5
Golden Mushroom	+2	Tomato	+1
Green Pea	+3	Tomato Bisque	+3
Hearty Vegetable with Pasta	+1	Tomato Noodle	+1
Homestyle Chicken Noodle	+3	Tomato with Garlic &	
Italian Tomato with		Herbs	+1
Basil/Oregano	+1	Turkey Noodle	+3
Manhattan Clam Chowder	+1	Turkey Vegetables	+2
Mega Noodle in Chicken		Vegetables	+1
Broth	+2	Vegetable Beef	+1
Minestrone	+2	Won Ton	+1
New England Clam Chowder	+2		

* AVOID

Table 34
THI SCORES OF CAMPBELL'S READY-TO-SERVE SOUPS
per 1 can or as noted

Healthy Request

Chicken Noodle	+2
Chicken Vegetable	+1
Creamy Potato with Garlic	+2
Hearty Chicken with White & Wild Rice	+1
Hearty Country Vegetables	+1
Hearty Vegetable	+1
Hearty Vegetable Beef	+2
New England Clam Chowder	+1
Split Pea with Ham	+2
Tomato Ravioli with Vegetables	+3

Classic

Bean & Bacon	+4
Chicken Noodle	+3
Chicken with Rice	+2
Creamy Tomato*	+5
Minestrone	+2
Tomato	+2
Vegetable with Beef Stock	+2

Select

Bean & Ham	+3
Chicken & Potato with Garlic	+2
Chicken & Rice	+1
Chicken Vegetable	+2
Chicken with Egg Noodles	+3
Country Mushroom Rice	+2
Country Vegetables	+2
Creamy Potato with Roasted Garlic*	+6

Fiesta Vegetable	+2
Grilled Chicken with Sundried Tomatoes	+2
Italian Style Chicken with Vegetables	+3
New England Clam Chowder*	+12
Old World Minestrone	+3
Oriental Noodles with Vegetables	+2
Roasted Chicken with White & Wild Rice	+2
Savory Lentil	+1
Split Pea with Ham	+3
Tomato Garden	+2
Tuscany Style Minestrone	+4
Vegetable Beef	+2

Soup at Hand

Blended Vegetable Medley*	+5
Classic Tomato	+3
Cream of Broccoli*	+5
Creamy Chicken*	+6

Simply Home

Chicken Vegetable Pasta	+2
Chicken Noodle	+2
Chicken with White & Wild Rice	+4
Country Vegetable	+2
Minestrone	+2
Vegetable Garden	+3

Table 34
THI SCORES OF CAMPBELL'S READY-TO-SERVE SOUPS
per 1 can or as noted (cont.)

98% Fat Free Cream of Broccoli	+3	Hearty Chicken with Vegetables	+3
98% Fat Free Cream of Celery	+3	Herb Roasted Chicken with Potato	+3
98% Fat Free Cream of Mushroom	+3	Honey Roasted Ham with Potatoes*	+4
Chunky Soups (per ½ can)		Old Fashioned Potato Ham Chowder*	+11
Baked Potato with Steak & Cheese*	+9	Old Fashioned Vegetable Beef*	+4
Baked Potato with Bacon & Chives*	+5	Pepper Steak	+3
Baked Potato with Bacon & Cheese*	+7	Salisbury Steak with Mushrooms*	+7
Beef with Country Vegetables*	+4	Savory Chicken with White & Wild Rice	+2
Beef with White & Wild Rice*	+5	Seasoned Beef with Potatoes & Herbs	+3
Cheese Tortelilni with Chicken & Vegetables	+3	Sirloin Burger with Country Vegetable*	+9
Chicken Broccoli Cheese & Potato*	+9	Slow Roasted Beef with Mushrooms	+3
Chicken Corn Chowder*	+11	Split Pea 'n' Ham	+3
Chicken & Dumplings*	+5	Steak 'n' Potato	+2
Clam Chowder Manhattan-Style	+3	Tomato Cheese Ravioli with Vegetable	+5
Classic Chicken Noodle	+3	Vegetable	+3
Grilled Chicken with Vegetables & Pasta	+2		
Grilled Sirloin with Hearty Vegetables	+3		

* AVOID
Note that the THI scores of Chunky soups are half the container (or 1 cup).

Table 35
THI SCORES OF CANNED PASTA ENTRÉES AND BEANS
3.5 oz/100 g

Campbell's		Meat Tortellini	+4
Baked Barbecue Beans#	0	Mini Ravioli in Tomato & Meat Sauce	+7
Baked Beans, brown sugar, bacon-flavored	+3	Pasta with Mini Meatballs	+7
		Spaghetti & Meatballs*	+8
Baked Beans, New England Style	+2	Teenage Mutant Ninja Turtles	+7
Pork N' Beans	+2	Tic Tac Toe	+4
		Tic Tac Toe with Meatballs	+7
Chef Boyardee		**Franco-American**	
Beefaroni	+7		
Beef Ravioli (all varieties)	+7	Garfield Ravioli in Meat Sauce*	+9
Cheese Ravioli	+4	SpaghettiOs in Cheese Sauce	+5
Cheese Tortellini	+4		
Chomps-A-Lot Bite Size Beef Rovioli	+4	SpaghettiOs in Cheese Sauce Teddyos	+5
Chomps-A-Lot Bite Size Lasagna	+4	SpaghettiOs with Meatballs (all varieties)*	+9
Dinosaurs	+4		
Fettuccini in Meat Sauce	+7	SpaghettiOs with Sliced Franks*	+10
Lasagna*	+8		

* AVOID
\# The THI scores of hundreds of beans, peas, and other legumes without the added sugar, meats, or fat is between -1 and 0. They provide a good amount of protein, complex, low-glycemic-index carbohydrates, plenty of dietary fiber, and various vitamins, minerals, and antioxidants. Their only drawback is that many individuals, especially with irritable bowel syndrome or some other digestive disorders, may experience gas and bloating when they eat these products.

Table 36
THI SCORES OF BOXED PASTA ENTRÉES
per cup, cooked

Rice-A-Roni		Lipton Noodles N' Sauce	
Angel Hair Pasta with Parmesan Cheese	+5	Alfredo*	+11
		Beef	+6
Corkscrew Pasta with 4 Cheeses	+6	Chicken	+5
		Creamy Chicken*	+7
Fettuccine	+5	Mild Cheddar Bacon	+5
Fettuccine Alfredo	+6	Parmesan*	+9
Fettuccine with Romanoff Sauce	+7	Romanoff	+6
		Stroganoff	+5
Linguini with Chicken & Broccoli Sauce	+5	**Lipton Pasta & Sauce**	
Penne Pasta, Herb & Butter	+4	Cheddar Broccoli	+4
Rigatoni with White Cheddar & Broccoli	+6	Creamy Garlic	+4
		Tini Primavera	+5
Rice-A-Roni		**Lipton Golden Sauté**	
Tenderthin Pasta with Parmesan Sauce	+6	Angel Hair with Chicken N' Broccoli	+3
Hamburger Helper		Penne Pasta, Herb with Garlic	+5
		Rice & Vermicelli with Chicken Flavor	+5
Beef Noodle	+2	
Cheeseburger Macaroni	+5	**Kraft Macaroni & Cheese**	
Italian Rigatoni	+4	Dinomac (all varieties including Rugrats & SpongeBob)	+4
Lasagna	+4	
Pizza Pasta	+4	Original	+5
Stroganoff	+2	Super Mario	+6
Tuna Helper, Cheesy Noodles	+4		
Zesty Italian	+2		

* AVOID

Table 37
THI SCORES OF PROCESSED FOODS
per slice

Butterball		Bologna (thin sliced)	+4
		Corned Beef (thin sliced)	+1
Roasted Chicken	+1	Hard Salami	+2
Roasted Turkey (breast or white		Healthy Favorites	+4
turkey)	+1	Light Beef Bologna	+1
Roasted Turkey Breast	+1	Oven Roasted Chicken	+1
		Oven Roasted Turkey	+1
Healthy Choice		Pastrami	+2

Oscar Mayer Lunchables
(per package)

Healthy Choice		Oscar Mayer Lunchables (per package)	
Baked Cooked Ham	+1	Bologna with American	
Bologna, Turkey	+1	Cheese*	+28
Smoked Turkey Breast	+1	Chicken with American	
Turkey	+1	Cheese*	+20
Hebrew National		Lean Chicken with Monterey	
Beef Bologna*	+6	Jack*	+20
Beef Salami*	+6	Lean Ham with American	
Louis Rich		Cheese*	+20
Bologna*	+6	Lean Ham with Swiss	
Cooked Turkey Salami	+2	Cheese without Dessert*	+18
Roasted Turkey Breast	+1	Lean Turkey with Cheddar	
Salami	+4	Cheese & Reese's Cup*	+20
Smoked Turkey	+1	Lean Turkey with Cheddar	
Turkey Bologna	+5	Cheese & Trail Mix*	+26
Turkey Pastrami	+1		
White Turkey	+1		
Oscar Mayer			
Beef Bologna*	+8		
Bologna*	+8		

* AVOID

Table 38
THI SCORES OF SALAD DRESSINGS
per 2 tablespoons

Hidden Valley	
Bacon*	+4
Blue Cheese	+3
Honey Dijon	+3
Ranch Italian	+3
All Reduced-calorie varieties	+2
All Low-fat/reduced-calorie	0

Ken's Steak House	
Balsamic & Basil Vinaigrette*	+4
Blue Cheese*	+6
Caesar Lite	+2
Creamy Parmesan Lite	+3
Raspberry Walnut Vinaigrette	+2
Red Wine Vinegar & Olive Oil	-1
Sweet Vidalia Onion	+3
Thousand Island*	+5

Kraft	
Blue Cheese*	+6
Caesar Ranch*	+4
Catalina*	+4
Classic Caesar*	+5
Coleslaw*	+4
Creamy Italian*	+6
Creamy Parmesan Romano*	+5
Cucumber Ranch*	+5
Deliciously Right Catalina	+2
Deliciously Right Italian	+2
Deliciously Right Ranch*	+4
Deliciously Right Thousand Island	+2
French*	+4
Greek Vinaigrette	+3

Honey Dijon*	+5
Italian, Olive Oil*	+4
Peppercorn Ranch*	+5
Ranch*	+5
Ranch Sour Cream & Onion*	+5
Salsa Zesty Garden	+2
Tangy Tomato Bacon	+3
Thousand Island*	+4
Zesty Italian*	+4

Newman's Own	
Balsamic Vinaigrette	+2
Caesar	+3
Creamy Caesar*	+6
Light Italian	+3
Olive Oil & Vinegar	+3
Parisienne Dijon Lime	+1
Parmesan	+1
Parmesiano Italiano	+3
Ranch	+3

Wish-bone	
all fat-free varieties	0
Chunky Blue Cheese*	+5
Creamy Caesar*	+5
Deluxe French	+3
Italian	+2
Italian, Robusto	+2
Just 2 Good! Italian	0
Ranch*	+5
Russian	+3
Thousand Island*	+4
Vinaigrette, all varieties	+1

* AVOID

Table 39
THI SCORES OF SAUCES
per ½ cup = 120 ml or as listed

Classico

4 Cheese	+3
Mushrooms & Ripe Olives	+2
Onion & Garlic	+2
Spicy Red Pepper	+2
Sweet Peppers & Onions	+2
Tomato & Basil	+3

Healthy Choice

Chunky Garlic & Onions	+1
Chunky Mushroom	+1
Extra Chunky Mushroom	+1
Flavored with Meat	+1
Garlic & Herb	+1
Traditional	+1

Newman's Own

Sockarooni	+1
Venetian with Mushroom	+1

Prego

Three Cheese	+2
Diced Onion & Garlic	+2
Flavored with Meat	+3
Fresh Mushroom	+3
Garden Combination	+2
Low Sodium	+2
Mushroom & Diced Onion	+3
Mushroom & Diced Tomato	+2
Mushroom & Green Pepper	+3
Sausage & Green Pepper*	+5
Tomato & Basil	+2
Tomato, Onion, & Garlic	+3
Traditional	+4
Zesty Basil	+4
Zesty Garlic & Cheese	+4
Zesty Mushroom with Cheese	+3

Other Sauces (per 4 tbs)

Alfredo*	+16
Barbeque	+2
Béarnaise*	+8
Gravy*	+4
Gravy, low fat	+2
Hollandaise	+3
Ketchup	+1
Marinara (tomato based)	0
Mustard Sauce	0
Salsa	-1
Seafood cocktail sauce	+2
Spaghetti with meat	+1

Table 39
THI SCORES OF SAUCES
per ½ cup = 120 ml or as listed (cont.)

Spaghetti with meatballs	+1	Light Garden Harvest	+1
Soy sauce	+1	Light Tomato & Herb	+1
Tartar	+4	Old World Style Traditional	+2
Worcestershire (1 tbs)	0	Old World Style with Meat	+3
Ragu		Thick & Hearty Mushroom	+2
		Thick & Hearty Tomato & Herb	+2
Chunky Gardenstyle	+2	Thick & Hearty with Meat	+2
Chunky Gardenstyle Super Mushroom	+2	**Pastas+**	
Chunky Gardenstyle Mushroom & Green Pepper	+3	Most pastas without sauces, meats, fats or cheeses	+3
Chunky Gardenstyle Vegetable Primavera	+2	Pasta with 3.5 oz serving of Prego Tomato & basil sauce	+5
Homestyle Flavored with Meat	+3	Above with 2 medium-size Ground Round meatballs	
Homestyle with Mushroom	+2	(3.5 oz)*	+17
Homestyle with Tomato & Herb	+2	Pasta with Alfredo sauce & cheese*	+25

* Avoid the added meats, creamy/buttery sauces, and cheese-based pastas.
+ For THI scores of pastas with sauces, cheeses, or meats, you should add up the THI scores of all the ingredients with the pasta.

Table 40
THI SCORES OF CHIPS & PRETZELS
per serving size or pieces

Doritos:		Terra	
Baked Nacho Cheese (15)	+3	Blues (15)*	+4
Cool Ranch (14)*	+7	Red Bliss (12)*	+6
Four Cheese (14)*	+7	Red Bliss Olive Oil/Garlic	
Nacho Cheese (12)*	+7	(13)	+2
Spicier Nacho (11)*	+7	Stix (50)*	+7
3 D Jalapeno (27)*	+6	Sweet Potato (17)*	+8
3 D Nacho Cheese (27)*	+6	Vegetable Chips (10)*	+7
3 D Maximum Cheddar (27)*	+7	Yukon Gold (8)*	+6
Lays		**Tostitos**	
Baked Masterpiece (11)	+2	Bite Size (24)*	+6
Baked Original (11)	+2	Crispy Rounds (13)*	+7
Bistro Gourmet/Applewood (12)*	+8	Scoops (13)*	+6
Bistro Gourmet/Garlic (15)*	+8	White Corn (13)*	+5
California Cool Dill (17)*	+10	White Lime (13)*	+5
Classic (20)*	+10	**UTZ (per 20 pieces)**	
Classic Russets (20)*	+7	Bar-B-Q*	+8
Hickory BBQ (13)*	+8	Crisp, All Natural*	+7
Masterpiece (15)*	+9	Ripples*	+8
Original (11)*	+10	Sour Cream & Onion*	+9
Sour Cream & Onion (17)*	+10	Wavy Crisp*	+7
Robert's Amer. Gourmet		Wavy Honey Bar-B-Q	+8
Original Flyers (1½ oz bag)	+2	**Pretzels**	
Original Veggie Chips (1½ oz)	+2	**Rolled Gold**	
Pirate's Booty Chips (1½ oz)	+3	Classic Thins (9)	+3
Smart Puffs with Cheddar (1½ oz)	+3		

Table 40
THI SCORES OF CHIPS & PRETZELS
per serving size or pieces (cont.)

Hard Sourdough (1)	+2	Nibblers (16)	+2
Honey Mustard (13)	+2	Old Thyme (30)	+2
Sticks (40)	+2	Rods (3)	+2
Tiny Twists (17)	+3	Sourdough Hard (1)	+2
Twist, Braided (8)	+2	Sourdough Specials (6)	+2
Snyder's		Snaps (24)	+2
		Sticks (28)	+2
Jalapeno, or Cheese (½ cup)*	+4	Thin (11)	+2
Mini (20)	+2		

* = AVOID

WOW and all other fat-free chips have THI scores of +1 per serving.

Since the serving size of chips varies from item to item, even from the same manufacturer, you should always check the serving size on the packet.

THI scores of all other generic and store brands of chips and pretzels are similar to those listed above.

Table 41
THI SCORES OF CRACKERS

Pepperidge Farm Goldfish

Baby Goldfish (90)	+3
Cheddar (55 pieces or 1 oz)	+3
Cheese Trio (58)	+3
Pizza (14)	+3
Pretzel (41)	+2
Snack Mix (½ cup)	+4
Snack Sticks (5)	+4

Nabisco Crackers

Better Cheddar (22)	+4
Better Cheddar, Reduced Fat (25)	+3
Ritz Jalapeño Cheddar (33)	+3
Ritz Mini Cheddar or Original (33)	+3
Ritz Reduced Fat (5)	+2
Ritz Regular or Low Sodium (5)	+2
Sociables (5)	+1
Teddy Grahams BearWiches (pack)	+3
Triscuit (7)	+2
Triscuit Reduced Fat (7)	+1
Triscuit Deli-Style Rye (7)	+2
Triscuit Garden Herb (6)	+2
Triscuit Thin Crisps (14)	+2
Wheat Thins, Crispy Thins, Ranch (10)	+1
Wheat Thins, multigrain (7)	+2
Wheat Thins, reduced fat (16)	+2
Whole Wheat, reduced fat (5)	0

Sunshine Crackers

Big Baked Snack Crackers (13)	+3
Cheddar Jack (26)	+3

Cheese It, Baked Crackers (14)	+4
Cheese It, Club Mini Sandwiches (14)*	+5
Cheese It, Mini Sandwiches (14)*	+5
Cheese It, Reduced Fat (29)	+2
Cheese It, White Cheddar (26)	+3
Original Krispy Mild Cheddars (5)	+1
Original Krispy Saltine (5)	0
Parmesan & Garlic (26)	+3

Keebler Crackers

Cinnamon Crisp Grahams (8)	+3
Chocolate Grahams (8)	+3
Club, Mini Sandwiches (1 package)*	+7
Club, Reduced Fat (5)	+0
Harvest Bakery Crackers (2)	+1
Honey Grahams (8)	+3
Honey Grahams, Low Fat (9)	+1
Town House (5)	+1
Wheatables, 7 Grain (17)*	+5
Wheatables, Honey or Low Fat (17)	+2
Wheatables, Original (15)	+3

Stella D'oro

Breadsticks (1)	+3
Fat-Free Breadstick (1)	+1
Sesame Breadstick (1)	+3

Table 42
THI SCORES OF HERSHEY'S CHOCOLATE PRODUCTS

5th Avenue (1)	+4	Milk Chocolate Eggs (4)*	+6
Almond Joy, small size (1)*	+5	Milk Chocolate with	
Almond Joy, regular size (1)*	+8	Almonds (7)*	+7
Caramello (1)*	+5	York Peppermint Pattie (9)	+4
Heath Bar (1)	+3		
Kisses (4)*	+8	**Hershey's Miniatures (1 piece)**	
Kisses with Almond (4)*	+7	Krackel	+3
Kit Kat Wafer Bar (1)	+3	Milk Chocolate	+3
Krackel Chocolate Bar (1)*	+6	Mr. Goodbar	+3
Milk Chocolate Bar (1)*	+7	Special Dark	+3
Milk Duds (7 pieces)	+3	**Hershey's Nuggets (1 piece)**	
Mounds (1)*	+9	Cookies 'n' Creme	+3
Mr. Goodbar (1)	+4	Dark Chocolate with Almonds	+3
Reese's Cups (1)	+2	Milk Chocolate	+4
Reese's Eggs (1)	+4	Milk Chocolate with Almonds	+3
Reese's Nutrageous (1)	+4	Milk Chocolate with	
Rolo Caramels in Milk		Almonds & Toffee	+3
Chocolate (1)	+4	Milk Chocolate with Raisins	
Sixlets (3 8-ball tubes)*	+7	& Almonds	+3
Symphony Chocolate Bar (1)*	+7	**Hershey's Sweet Escapes (1 bar)**	
Whatchamacallit (1)*	+7		
Whoppers (9 pieces)*	+7	Caramel & Peanut Butter	+3
York Peppermint Pattie (1)	+4	Crispy Caramel Fudge Bar	+3
Zagnut, snack size (1)*	+7	Crunchy Peanut Butter	+3
Hershey's Bites		Triple Chocolate Wafer Bar	+4
Almond Joy (8)*	+7		
Cookies 'n' Creme (8)*	+6		

* AVOID

Although the THI scores of some chocolate products are high, total abstention is not necessary. An alternative is to eat less than the manufacturer's serving size listed in all these tables. Chocolates contain some antioxidants. Alas, with regular and heavy consumption, the undesirable impact of their saturated fats and trans-fatty acids negates the minor role of their antioxidants.

* There are an estimated 35,000 different kinds of chocolate and nonchocolate snacks worldwide. With a few exceptions, their THI scores are very close to the items listed in tables 44-47.

Table 43
THI SCORES OF HERSHEY'S OTHER PRODUCTS
per serving as listed

Classic Caramels Creme (3)*	+5	**Hershey's Grocery Products**	
Classic Caramels Soft & Chewy (3)	+4	Candy Coated Sprinkles (1 tbs)*	+5
Crispy Rice Snacks, Peanut Butter (1)	+2	Caramel Sundae Syrup (1 tbs)	+2
Good & Plenty (1 box)	+1	Chocolate Fudge (1 tbs)*	+5
Good 'n Fruity	+1	Chocolate Syrup (2 tbs)	+2
		Chocolate Syrup, Lite (2 tbs)	+1
Hershey's Tastetations Candies		Cocoa (1 tbs)	+2
Butterscotch (3)	+3	Double Chocolate (1 tbs)	+2
Caramel (3)	+3	European Style Cocoa (1 tbs)	+2
Jolly Rancher Candies (3)	+1	Fat Free Chocolate Syrup (1 tbs)	+2
Jolly Rancher Lollipop (1)	+1	Hot Fudge Syrup (1 tbs)	+3
Payday (1 bar)	+1	Reese's & Milk Chocolate (1 tbs)*	+5
Rainblo Bubblegum Balls (2)	0	Strawberry Syrup (2 tbs)	+2
Reese's Pieces (2)	+1	Whoppers Malt Syrup	+2
Robin Eggs		**Hershey's Bake Shoppe**	
Mini (10 pieces)*	+5	Butterscotch Chips (1 tbs)*	+5
Medium (4 pieces)*	+5	Milk Chocolate Chips (1 tbs)*	+6
Large (2 pieces)	+4	Mini Chocolate Chips (1 tbs)*	+6
		Mini Kisses (1 tbs)*	+7
Twizzlers		Premier White Milk Chocolate	
Cherry Candy (1)	+1	Chips (1 tbs)*	+7
Chocolate Candy (1)	+1	Raspberry Chips (1 tbs)*	+6
Licorice Candy (1)	+1	Reese's Peanut Butter Chips (1 tbs)*	+5
Nibs Cherry or Licorice (9)	+1	Semisweet Chocolate Chips (1 tbs)*	+6
Pull 'n' Peel (1)	+1	Semisweet Mini Chips (1 tbs)*	+6
Strawberry (1)	+1	Skor, English Toffee Bits (1 tbs)*	+6
Zero Candy Bar (1)	+1		

* AVOID

One or two candies here and there do not have a negative impact on anyone's health. The problem is that most people do not exercise any dietary restraint, so that often they snack on far more than 1 or 2 candies, cookies, or any other available morsels. So instead of total avoidance, let reason, sensibility, and your health guide you, not your eyes or taste buds.

Table 44
THI SCORES OF MARS PRODUCTS

M&M'S Snacks (per serving)		Milky Way	
M&M's Milk Chocolate, large bar (1.7 oz)*	+15	Fun Size, 2 bars*	+9
M&M'S Milk Chocolate, Fun Size*	+6	Large bar, 1 bar*	+13
M&M'S Peanut, large*	+12	Miniatures, 5 pieces*	+9
M&M'S Peanut, Fun Size	+5	Midnight, 1 bar*	+12
M&M'S Peanut Butter, large*	+20	**Snickers**	
M&M'S Almond (1.3 oz)*	+9	Large (1 bar)*	+13
M&M'S Crispy, large pack (1.5 oz)*	+13	Fun Size (2 bars)*	+9
M&M'S Crispy, Fun Size (3 packs)*	+13	Miniatures (4 pieces)*	+9
M&M'S Mini (1-oz tube)*	+13	Cruncher, Fun Size (3 pieces)*	+11
DOVE Dark Chocolate (1 piece) (6 g)	+3	**Other Candy Bars**	
DOVE Milk Chocolate Caramel 1 piece	+2	Almond Joy, large bar*	+20
		Baby Ruth, large bar*	+21
DOVE Milk Chocolate, 1 piece	+3	Butterfinger, large bar*	+15
		Kit Kat, Big Kat*	+23
3 Musketeers		Mounds, large bar*	+22
Chewlicious Candy, 1 bar	+3	**Starburst**	
Fun Size, 2 bars*	+7	Fruit Chews, 1 Pack (2 oz)	+4
Large Bar, 1 bar*	+13	Fruit Chew Pop, 1 Lollipop	+1
Miniatures, 7 pieces*	+9	Hard Candy (1)	+1

* AVOID

Table 45
THI SCORES OF CANDY
1 ounce unless otherwise noted

Butterscotch	+3	Peanut brittle	+4
Caramel, plain	+4	Yogurt-coveerd nuts	+1
Caramel with chocolate*	+5	Yogurt-Covered raisins	+2
Caramel with nuts	+3	Other candies without milk,	
Chocolate, bittersweet*	+12	fat, or chocolate	+2
Choclate, milk, plain*	+8	**Nestle**	
Chocolate, milk, with		Assorted Miniatures (5)*	+16
almonds*	+7	Butterfinger (small) (4)*	+10
Chocolate, milk, with peanuts*	+7	Chocolate Raisins (1 oz)	+4
Chocolate, semisweet*	+8	Crunch (¼ bar)*	+14
Chocolate-coated almonds*	+5		
Chocolate-covered raisins*	+6	**Russell Stover**	
Chocolate fudge*	+5	Dark Chocolate Assortment	
Chocolate fudge with nuts	+5	(2)*	+12
Chocolate fudge with walnuts	+4	Jellies (5)	+1
Coconut center	+3	Rocky Mellow (1/8 piece)*	+5
Peanut bar*	+5	**Whitman's Sampler (3)***	+12

*AVOID

Table 46
THI SCORES OF COOKIES

Archway Cookies (per cookie)	
Apple 'n Raisin*	+5
Chocolate Chip & Toffee*	+6
Date-Filled Oatmeal*	+7
Dutch Cocoa*	+8
Frosty Lemon*	+6
Fat-Free Oatmeal Raisin*	+5
Fat-Free Fruit Bar	+3
Fat-Free Granola	+3
Golden Oatmeal	+3
Oatmeal	+3
Old-Fashioned Molasses*	+6
Rocky Road*	+6

Keebler	
Chocolate Chip, Original (1)	+3
Chocolate Lovers, Chips Deluxe (1)*	+6
Club Mini Sandwiches (1 package)*	+7
Coconut, Chips Deluxe (10)*	+6
Country Style Oatmeal & Raisins (2)	+3
Frosted Animals Cookies (1 pack)*	+20
Fudge Shoppe Clusters, Double Fudge 'n Caramel (2)*	+8
Fudge Shoppe Clusters, Peanut (1)*	+6
Fudge Shoppe Deluxe Grahams (3)*	+10
Fudge Shoppe Fudge Stripes (3)*	+10
Fudge Shoppe Fudge Stripes, reduced fat (3)*	+7
Fudge Shoppe Grasshopper (4)*	+9

Fudge Shoppe Fudge Sticks (3)*	+9
Mini Fudge Shoppe Stripes (4)	+3
Mini Fudge, Chips Deluxe (4)*	+7
Peanut Butter Fudge Sticks (3)*	+3
Peanut Butter, Chips Deluxe (1)	+4
Rainbow, Chips Deluxe (1)	+4
Sandies Chocolate Chip & Pecan (1)	+2
Sandies Mini Pecan Shortbread (4)*	+5
Sandies Pecan Shortbread (1)	+1
Sandies Simply Shortbread (1)	+4
Soft 'n Chewy, Chips Deluxe (1)	+2
Vienna Fingers (4)*	+8

Mrs. Fields (per cookie)	
Macadamia*	+9
Milk Chocolate*	+10
Semi-Sweet Chocolate(	+10
Oatmeal With Nuts & Raisins	+7

Nabisco	
Chips Ahoy! (3)*	+3

(*continued on next page*)

Table 46
THI SCORES OF COOKIES
(cont.)

Chips Ahoy! Candy Blast (1)	+2
Chips Ahoy! Chocolate Chewy (3)*	+6
Chips Ahoy! Chunky (1)	+4
Chips Ahoy! CremeWiches (2)*	+6
Chips Ahoy! Peanut Butter (1)	+3
Chips Ahoy! reduced fat (1)	+4
Ginger Snaps (4)	+2
Grahams, all varieties (28)	+3
Grahams, Dora Explorer (8)	+3
Mini Oreo, Bite-Size (9)	+3
Mini Oreo, Chocolate Creme (9)	+3
Newtons, Apple, Fig, or Berries (2)	+1
Nutter Butter (1 package)*	+5
Oreo (3)	+4
Oreo Cookie Bar (1)*	+15
Oreo Double Delight (2)	+4
Oreo Double Stuf (4)*	+7
Oreo Fudge (1)	+3
Oreo Fudge Mint (1)	+3
Pinwheels, Pure Chocolate (1)*	+6

Nabisco SnackWell's

Chocolate Chip Bite Size (6)	+2
Chocolate Sandwich (2)	+2
Creme Sandwich (2)	+2
Devil's Food, fat free (1)	+1
Ginger Snaps (4)	+2

Mint Creme (2)	+3
Sugar Free Chocolate Chip (3)	+2
Sugar Free Chocolate Sandwich (3)	+3
Sugar Free Lemon Creme (3)	+2
Sugar Free Oatmeal (1)	+1

Nabisco, Other Snacks

Treasures, Chocolate Creme (3 pieces)*	+14
Treasures, Peanut Butter (3 pieces)*	+13
Treasures, Toasted Coconut (3 pieces)*	+18

Pepperidge Farm

Bordeaux (4)*	+6
Brussels (3)*	+7
Chantilly (2)	+3
Chessmen (3)*	+7
Crème Magnifique (2)*	+6
Decadent Chocolate (2)*	+8
Delectables (3)*	+8
Dessert Bliss (3)*	+7
Geneva (3)*	+8
Ginger Man (4)	+3
Golden Orchard (5)*	+5
Lemon Nut (3)*	+5

Lido (2)*	+6
Milano (3)*	+8
Milano, Endless Chocolate (3)*	+11
Milano, Milk Chocolate (3)*	+8
Pirouettes (2)*	+8
Salzburg, Chocolate Mocha (2)*	+5
Shortbread (2)*	+5
Spritzers (5)	+4
St. Tropez (2)*	+6
Verona (3)*	+5

Pepperidge Farm Soft Chocolate Chunks (1)

Caramel*	+5
Chesapeake*	+6
Chesapeake Dark Chocolate*	+6
Laredo*	+5
Nantucket*	+7

Nantucket Dark Chocolate*	+6
Nantucket Double Chocolate*	+7
Santa Cruz	+3
Sausalito*	+7
Sausalito Milk Chocolate Macademia*	+6
Sedona*	+5
Tahoe*	+7

Others

Chocolate Chip Cookies with Butter* (1)	+9
Chocolate Chip Cookies with Shortening*	+8
Fig Bars (1)	+2
Gingersnaps (3)	+3
Oatmeal Cookies with Raisins (3)	+4
Raisin Cookies (3)	+3
Sugar Wafers (3)	+3

* AVOID

Table 47
THI SCORES OF CAKES
per 1/16 of cake

Angel Food	+3
Caramel, no icing (made with butter)*	+8
Caramel, no icing (made with vegetable shortening)*	+8
Caramel, with icing (made with butter)*	+11
Caramel, with icing (made with vegetable shortening)*	+10
Carrot, with cream cheese frosting*	+9
Cheesecake*	+20
Chocolate, no icing (made with butter)*	+10
Chocolate, no icing (made with vegetable shortening)*	+9
Chocolate, with icing (made with butter)*	+22
Chocolate, with icing (made with vegetable shortening)*	+21
Coffee Cake, no icing (made with vegetable shortening)*	+6
Coffee Cake, with Icing*	+8
Fruitcake (made with butter)*	+6
Fruitcake (made with vegetable shortening)	+5
Gingerbread (made with butter)*	+9
Gingerbread (made with vegetable shortening)*	+8
Marble Cake*	+6
Marble Cake, with icing*	+8
Plain (yellow), with chocolate icing (made with butter)*	+11
Plain (yellow) with chocolate icing (made with vegetable shortening)*	+10
Plain (yelllow), (made with vegetable shortening)*	+7
Pound Cake (made with butter)*	+8
Pound Cake (made with vegetable shortening)*	+7
Sponge Cake*	+5
Caramel icing (2 tbs)	+3
Chocolate-fudge icing (2 tbs)*	+6
Chocolate icing (2 tbs)*	+6
Coconut icing (2 tbs)*	+6
Chocolate syrup (2 tbs)*	+6
Chocolate syrup, fat free (2 tbs)	+2

* AVOID

Table 48
THI SCORES OF PIES
per 1 regular slice or ⅛ of pie

Apple*	+10	Coconut Custard*	+12
Apple, 1 small slice*	+5	Coconut Custard, 1 small slice*	+6
Banana Custard*	+8	Custard*	+7
Banana Custard, 1 small slice	+4	Custard, 1 small slice	+3
Blackberry*	+10	Lemon Chiffon*	+8
Blackberry, 1 small slice*	+5	Lemon Chiffon, 1 small slice	+4
Blueberry*	+10	Lemon Meringue*	+9
Blueberry, 1 small slice*	+5	Lemon Meringue, 1 small slice	+4
Cherry*	+10	Peach*	+8
Cherry, 1 small slice*	+5	Peach, 1 small slice	+4
Chocolate Chiffon*	+11	Pecan*	+8
Chocolate Chiffon, 1 small slice	+5	Pecan, 1 small slice	+4
Chocolate Meringue*	+12	Pineapple*	+9
Chocolate Meringue, 1 small slice*	+6	Pineapple, 1 small slice*	+5
Pumpkin*	+10	Walnut, 1 small slice	+3
Pumpkin, 1 small slice*	+5	Apple for pie filling (½ cup)	0
Raisin*	+8	Applesauce pie filling (½ cup)	0
Raisin, 1 small slice	+4	Cherry for pie filling (½ cup)	0
Strawberry*	+8	Cranberry for pie filling	
Strawberry, 1 small slice	+4	(jelly/whole, ½ cup)	+1
Sweet Potato*	+9	Libby's Pumpkin Pie Filling (½ cup)	0
Sweet Potato, 1 small slice	+4	Mincemeat pie filling (½ cup)	0
Walnut*	+5		

* AVOID

Most pies and cakes are made with partially hydrogenated vegetable fats or short-ening, which makes them possibly carcinogenic, and even more coronary-unfriendly than if they were made with butter. Even so, an occasional small slice of cake or pie has no negative health impact.

Table 49
THI SCORES OF DUNKIN' DONUTS
per 1 Donut or 3 Munchkins

Apple Crumb*	+7	Jelly Filled	+4
Apple Fritter*	+7	Jelly Stick*	+7
Apple N' Spice	+4	Lemon Donut*	+5
Banana Kreme*	+5	Maple Frosted Coffee Roll*	+7
Bismark Chocolate Iced*	+10	Maple Frosted Donut*	+5
Black Raspberry*	+5	Marble Frosted Donut*	+5
Blueberry Cake*	+8	Old Fashioned Cake Donut*	+7
Blueberry Crumb*	+8	Plain Cruller*	+7
Boston Kreme*	+5	Powdered Cruller*	+7
Bow Tie Donut Ring*	+11	Powdered Cake Donut*	+7
Chocolate Coconut Cake*	+8	Strawberry Filled Donut	+4
Chocolate Frosted Coffee Roll*	+5	Strawberry Frosted Donut*	+5
Chocolate Glazed Cake*	+8	Sugar Cruller*	+7
Chocolate Kreme Filled*	+8	Sugar Raised Donut*	+7
Cinnamon Bun*	+12	Toasted Coconut*	+12
Cinnamon Cake*	+7	Vanilla Frosted Coffee Roll*	+7
Coconut Cake*	+11	Vanilla Frosted Donut*	+8
Coffee Roll*	+7	Whole Wheat Glazed Donut*	+9
Double Chocolate Cake*	+9		
Dunkin' Donut*	+7	**Munchkins (per 3)**	
Eclair*	+7		
Glazed Cake*	+7	Chocolate Glazed*	+5
Glazed Chocolate Cruller*	+8	Butter Nut*	+7
Glazed Cruller*	+8	Cinnamon*	+7
Glazed Donut	+4	Coconut*	+8
Glazed Fritter*	+7	Glazed*	+5
		Plain*	+7
		Powdered*	+7

Table 49
THI SCORES OF DUNKIN' DONUTS
per 1 Donut or 3 Munchkins (cont.)

Munchkins (per 3) (cont.)		Coffee Cake Muffin*	+24
Sugar Raised*	+7	Corn Muffin*	+12
Toasted Coconut*	+7	Cranberry Orange Muffin*	+14
Yeast, Glazed*	+5	Honey Bran Raisin Muffin*	+12
Yeast, Jelly Filled*	+6	Maple Walnut Scone*	+13
Yeast, Lemon Filled	+4	Raspberry White Chocolate Scone*	+17
Yeast, Sugar Raised*	+6		
Muffins, Danish, & Scones		Reduced Fat Blueberry Muffin*	+20
Apple Danish*	+7	Strawberry Cheese Danish*	+8
Banana Nut Muffin*	+16	**Cookies**	
Blueberry Muffin*	+16	Chocolate Chunk*	+16
Blueberry Scone*	+12	Chocolate Chunk with Walnut*	+14
Cheese Danish*	+10		
Chocolate Chip Muffin*	+25	Oatmeal Raisin Pecan*	+12
		White Chocolate Chunk*	+16

* AVOID

In addition to having an extremely high THI score, 1 Chocolate Chip Muffin has 590 calories, and a Coffee Cake Muffin is even worse: It carries 710 calories, the equivalent of a main meal.

Table 50
THI SCORES OF KRISPY KREME DOUGHNUTS
per 1 doughnut

Apple Cinnamon Sugar*	+7	Glazed Yeast*	+7
Blueberry Powdered Sugar*	+9	Honey Bun*	+14
Cake Glazed Cruller*	+8	Old Fashioned Honey & Oat*	+7
Chocolate Enrobed*	+17	Old Fashioned Sour Cream*	+7
Chocolate Enrobed Mini Cake*	+20	Plain Mini Cake*	+9
Chocolate Iced, Creme Filled*	+12	Powdered Raspberry Filled*	+10
Chocolate Iced, Custard Filled*	+10	Powdered Strawberry Filled*	+9
Chocolate Iced, Glazed*	+8	Powdered Sugar Cake*	+7
Cinnamon Bun*	+9	Powdered Sugar Mini Cake*	+7
Cinnamon Twist*	+7	Sugar Doughnut*	+7
Cranapple Crunch Filled*	+11	Traditional Cake Doughnut*	+7
Glazed Blueberry*	+9	Traditional Chocolate Iced*	+8
Glazed Cherry*	+10	Vanilla Iced Cake with Sprinkles*	+8
Glazed Cinnamon*	+7	Vanilla Iced, Custard Filled*	+9
Glazed Creme Filled*	+12	Vanilla Iced, Creme Filled*	+12
Glazed Custard Filled*	+9	Yeast, Chocolate Iced with Sprinkles*	+8
Glazed Devil's Food*	+12	**PIES (one)**	
Glazed Doughnut*	+7		
Glazed Lemon Filled*	+10	Apple*	+15
Glazed Mini Cruller*	+8	Cherry*	+15
Glazed Pumpkin Spice*	+14	Coconut Creme*	+15
Glazed Raspberry Filled*	+10	Peach*	+18
Glazed Twist*	+7		

* AVOID

The problem with all snacks and sweetened drinks is that they are less satisfying than solid foods. Thus the calories and the fat or carbohydrate content of these items is added to our regular intake, but they are often not taken into account. A better choice is snacking on fruits (fresh or dried) or sugar-free and low-fat snacks. This is even more important if you already have a weight problem, diabetes, raised blood levels of LDL cholesterol and triglycerides, or low levels of HDL-cholesterol.

Table 51
THI SCORES OF KELLOGG'S POP-TARTS AND EGGOS

Pop-Tarts Pastry Swirls (per 1)

Apple Cinnamon*	+9
Cheese*	+8
Cheese & Cherry*	+8
Cinnamon & Creme*	+9
Strawberry*	+9

Pop-Tarts Snak-Stix (per 1)

Frosted Berry*	+5
Frosted Caramel Chocolate*	+5
Frosted Cookies & Creme*	+6
Frosted Double Chocolate*	+6
Frosted Strawberry*	+5

Pop-Tarts (per 1)

Apple Cinnamon	+3
Blueberry	+3
Chocolate Chip*	+5
Frosted Blueberry*	+5
Frosted Brown Sugar Cinnamon	+3
Frosted Cherry*	+4
Frosted Chocolate Vanilla Creme*	+4
Frosted Grape*	+4
Frosted Raspberry	+3
Frosted S'Mores*	+4
Frosted Strawberry*	+4
Frosted Wild Berry*	+4
Frosted Wild Magiburst*	+4
Frosted Low Fat Brown Sugar Cinnamon	+3
Frosted Low Fat Chocolate Fudge	+3
Frosted Low Fat Strawberry	+3

Eggo Waffles (per 2) and Pancakes (per 3)

Apple Cinnamon, Banana Bread, Blueberry, & Waf-Fulls Waffles	+4
Buttermilk, Chocolate Chip, Homestyle, Minis, & Strawberry Waffles*	+5
Cinnamon Toast Waffles*	+7
Special K Waffles	+2
Buttermilk Pancakes*	+5

* AVOID

Table 52
TH1 SCORES OF SWEET SNACKS

Hostess	Serving Size	
Fruit Pie, Apple	1*	+22
Fruit Pie, Blueberry	1*	+23
Fruit Pie, Cherry	1*	+24
Fruit Pie, Lemon	1*	+26
Ho Hos	3 pieces*	+26
Mini-Muffins, Banana	3 pieces*	+5
Mini-Muffins, Blueberry	3 pieces*	+5
Mini-Muffins, Brownie	3 pieces*	+8
Mini-Muffins, Cinnamon Apple	3 pieces*	+6
Mini-Muffins, Chocolate Chip	3 pieces*	+7
Twinkies	1 piece	+4
Twinkies, Chocolate Cake	1 cake*	+5
Twinkies, Ding Dongs	2 cakes*	+22
Twinkies, Low Fat	1 cake	+2
Twinkies, Sponge Cake	1 cake	+2

Tastykake		
Butterscotch Krimpets	3 cakes*	+6
Cherry Pie	1 pie*	+9
Chocolate Cupcakes	3 cakes*	+7
Chocolate Iced Tasty Klair	1 pie*	+16
Chocolate Kandykakes	2 pieces*	+10
French Apple Pie	1 piece*	+6
Frosted Mini-Donuts	2 pieces*	+9
Ghostly Goodies	2 pieces*	+16
Jelly Krimpets	2 pieces*	+1
Koffee Kakes	2 cakes*	+7
Koffee Kakes, Low Fat	2 cakes	+2

Table 52
THI SCORES OF SWEET SNACKS
(cont.)

Kreepy Kakes	2 cakes*	+5
Lemon Pie	1 pie*	+7
Snak Bar Chocolate Chip	1 bar*	+10
Iced Fudge	1 bar*	+7
Oatmeal Raisin	1 bar*	+17
Witchy Goodies	2 pieces*	+16
Quaker Chewy Granola		
Caramel Apple Bar	1	+5
Chocolate Chip Granola Bar	1	+5
Quaker Chewy Granola		
Peanut Butter Bar	1*	+6
Trail Mix Granola Bar	1*	+5
Others		
Brownies with butter*	1.5*	+8
Brownies with nuts*	1.5*	+7
Coconut bar*	3 pieces	+8
Danish, small plain*	1	+8
Danish, small with fruit*	1	+7
Donut, chocolate covered*	1	+11
Donut, with custard inside*	1	+12

* AVOID

Although the THI scores of many snacks per serving are quite high, total abstinence is not necessary. Instead, smaller "doses" allow enough flexibility to enjoy a morsel here and there, and minimize frustration. For example, an occasional piece of After Eight or a piece of chocolate, instead of the manufacturers' recommended serving size, is not a sin!

Table 53
THI SCORES OF STARBUCKS AND OTHER SOFT AND ALCOHOLIC BEVERAGES

Starbucks Beverages	
Caffè Americano, Black	0
Caffè with Cream & Sugar	+3
Caffè Latte	+3
Caffè Mocha*	+4
Cappuccino*	+4
Caramel Macchiato	+3
Espresso	0
Espresso con Panna	+3
Espresso Macchiato	+2
Mocha Valencia	0
Vanilla Latte	+3

Frappuccinos	
Caramel*	+4
Chocolate Brownie*	+4
Coffee	+2
Espresso	0
Mocha*	+4
Mocha Coconut*	+5
Mocha Malt*	+4

Crème-Frappuccinos	
Chocolate Malt*	+4
Coconut Crème*	+5
Vanilla Crème*	+4

Tazo Tea-Frappuccinos	
Tazoberry	-1
Tazoberry Crème*	+4
Tazo Citrus	-1
Tazo Citrus Crème*	+4
Tazo Chai Crème*	+4

Coffee Alternatives	
Caramel Apple Cider*	+4
Children's Special	+2
Hot Chocolate*	+5
Tazo Chai	+2
Tazo Hot Tea	-1
Vanilla Crème*	+4

Other Beverages (8 oz)	
Apple juice	+1
Cranberry juice (unsweetened)	-1
Grape juice	+1
Grapefruit juice	-1
Lemonade	+1
Orange juice	0
Soft drinks (per can)*	+4
Soft drinks, sugar free (per can)	0

Table 53
THI SCORES OF STARBUCKS AND OTHER SOFT AND ALCOHOLIC BEVERAGES
(cont.)

Alcoholic Beverages			
Beer (can or bottle)	+3	Drambuie	+1
Beer, light (can or bottle)	+2	Gin & Vodka	0
Wine & dry vermouth (4 oz)	+1	Godiva*	+4
Wine, sweet (4 oz)	+3	Grand Marnier	+1
Liquor & Liqueur (2 oz)		Kahlúa	+2
		Mozart*	+4
Amaretto	+2	Rum	+1
Benedictine	+1	Sherry	+1
Chambord	+2	Tequila	+1
Cognac	0	Tia Maria	+2
Crème De Minthe	+2	Whiskeys	+1

* AVOID

Table 54
THI SCORES OF BURGER KING

Breakfast

Biscuit*	+ 8
Biscuit with Egg*	+12
Biscuit with Sausage*	+20
Biscuit with Sausage, Egg & Cheese*	+30
Cini-minis (without icing)*	+12
Croissan'wich with Sausage & Cheese*	+26
Croissan'wich with Sausage, Egg & Cheese*	+33
French Toast Sticks (5)*	+25
Hash Browns, small*	+19
Hash Browns, large*	+35

Sandwiches/Side Orders

BK Broiler Chicken*	+14
BK Broiler Chicken without mayo*	+11
BK Big Fish*	+34
Chicken Whopper*	+11
Chicken Whopper without mayo*	+7
Chicken Tenders (4)*	+7
Chicken Tenders (5)*	+9
Chicken Tenders (8)*	+15
Big Veggie Burger	+4
French Fries, small*	+12
French Fries, medium*	+18
French Fries, king*	+26
Onion Rings, medium*	+15
Onion Rings, large*	+22
Onion Rings, king*	+25

Burgers

Bacon Cheeseburger*	+20
Bacon Double Cheeseburger*	+35
Big King*	+36
Cheeseburger*	+18
Double Cheeseburger*	+33
Double Whopper*	+45
Double Whopper, without mayo*	+42
Double Whopper with Cheese*	+53
Double Whopper with Cheese, without mayo*	+54
Hamburger*	+13
Whopper*	+28
Whopper without mayo*	+25
Whopper with Cheese*	+37
Whopper with Cheese, without mayo	+34
Whopper Jr.*	+20
Whopper Jr., without mayo*	+17
Whopper Jr., with Cheese*	+23

Table 54
THI SCORES OF BURGER KING
(cont.)

Burgers *(cont.)*		Chocolate Shake, medium*	
Whopper Jr., with Cheese with mayo*	+21		+12
		Strawberry Shake, small*	+9
Desserts/Drinks		Strawberry Shake, medium*	+11
Dutch Apple Pie*	+13	Vanilla Shake, small*	+9
Chocolate Shake, small*	+9	Vanilla Shake, medium*	+11

* AVOID

The scores of some newer "Super Size" versions being test-marketed are 10 to 15 points higher, making them even less healthful. To its credit, Burger King is the only large fast-food chain to list the trans-fatty acid content of its menu in its nutritional information tables. Incredibly, its large fries and hash browns have the highest concentrations of trans-fatty acids at 7 and 8 grams per serving, respectively. These are higher than a prudent diet should have for 1 whole month!

Table 55
THI SCORES OF DENNY'S
per meal

Breakfast		Other Breakfast Items	
Big Texas Chicken Fajita*	+42	Belgian Waffle(1)	+6
Breakfast Dagwood*	+84	Buttermilk Hotcakes (3)	+3
Country-fried Steak & Eggs*	+29	Country-fried Potatoes*	+13
Egg Beaters	+2	Fabulous French Toast (3)*	+36
Egg Breakfast (2)*	+39	Hashed Browns	+8
Farmer's Slam*	+48	Moons Over My Hammy*	+51
French Slam*	+48	**Sandwiches**	
French Slam (2)*	+59	Albacore Tuna Melt*	+27
Grand Slam Slugger*	+32	Bacon-Cheddar Burger*	+39
Ham, Grilled (per slice)	+3	Bacon Lettuce & Tomato*	+18
Ham & Cheddar Omelette*	+22	BBQ Chicken*	+20
Lumberjack Slam (2)*	+47	Big Texas BBQ Burger*	+49
Meat Lover's Skillet*	+58	Boca Burger*	+11
Oatmeal N' Fixins	+6	Buffalo Chicken*	+24
Original Grand Slam*	+35	Classic Burger*	+28
Sausage (4 Links)*	+14	Classic Burger with Cheese*	+39
Shamrock Slam*	+52	Club*	+16
T-bone Steak & Eggs*	+70	Double Decker Burger*	+71
Ultimate Slam*	+32	Garlic/Mushroom/Swiss Burger*	+30
Veggie-Cheese Omelette*	+31	Grilled Chicken	+8

*AVOID

Table 55
THI SCORE OF DENNY'S (cont.)

Salads, Soups, & Sides

Clam Chowder* (It has 34 g of saturated fat & 1,174 g of sodium!)	+65
Cream of Broccoli* (It has 34 g of saturated fat & 1,474 g of sodium!)	+65
Deluxe Caesar Salad with Grilled Chicken*	+20
Deluxe Garden Salad with Beef*	+16
Deluxe Garden Salad with Chicken Breast*	+10
Deluxe Garden Salad with Fried Chicken Strips*	+12
Deluxe Garden Salad with Tuna*	+16
Deluxe Garden Salad with Turkey & Ham*	+15
Side Caesar Salad with Dressing*	+13
Side Caesar Salad without Dressing	+2
French Fries, seasoned*	+9
French Fries, unsalted*	+14
Onion Rings*	+12

* AVOID

As you can see, the majority of the items on the Denny's menu should carry a warning similar to those for tobacco products and alcohol; i.e., they are hazardous to your health! Some of the items are just outright ridiculous. For example, on the breakfast menu, the Farmer's Slam contains 80 grams of fat (24 grams of which is saturated), 704 milligrams of cholesterol, and more than 3,200 milligrams of sodium. French Slam 2 has even more total fat (82 grams), saturated fat (26 grams), and cholesterol (825 milligrams). Worst of all, Breakfast Dagwood has 90 grams of fat (38 grams of which are saturated), but incredibly, it has more than 800 milligrams of cholesterol, and 3,600 milligrams of sodium! Why do they do this to us? (The amount of saturated fat and cholesterol in each of these items is greater than what a prudent diet should contain in 2 full days!)

Table 56
THI SCORES OF McDONALD'S

Breakfast		French Fries	
Bacon, Egg & Cheese Biscuit*	+28	Small*	+17
Biscuit*	+6	Large*	+20
Breakfast Burrito*	+20	Super Size*	+26
Egg McMuffin*	+13	**Burgers/Sandwiches**	
English Muffin	+3		
Hash Browns*	+6	Big Mac*	+19
Hotcakes*	+11	Big N' Tasty*	+27
Hotcakes with margarine & syrup*	+22	Big N' Tasty with Cheese*	+31
Sausage*	+9	Cheeseburger*	+12
Sausage Biscuit*	+17	Crispy Chicken Deluxe*	+14
Sausage Biscuit with Egg*	+27	Fish Filet Deluxe*	+14
Sausage McMuffin*	+22	Grilled Chicken Deluxe*	+10
Sausage McMuffin with Egg*	+25	Hamburger	+7
Scrambled Eggs*	+14	Quarter Pounder*	+17
Chicken McNuggets		Quarter Pounder with Cheese*	+25
Chicken McNuggets (4)*	+8	**Salads & Dressings**	
Chicken McNuggets (6)*	+11	Caesar Salad with Grilled Chicken	+3
Chicken McNuggets (9)*	+18	Chef Salad*	+8
Chicken McGrill*	+9	Garden Salad	+4
Chicken McGrill without mayo	+6	Caesar Dressing (1 package)	+4
Crispy Chicken*	+12	Ranch (1 package)	+4
		Red French (1 package)	+2

Table 56
THI SCORES OF McDONALD'S
(cont.)

Desserts			
		Hot Caramel Sundae*	+15
Baked Apple Pie*	+10	Hot Fudge Sundae*	+17
Butterfinger McFlurry*	+35	Strawberry Triple Thick Shake*	+32
Chocolate Chip Cookie (1)*	+18	Vanilla Triple Thick Shake*	+32

* AVOID

Although a THI score of +8 to +10 for the main entrées may be acceptable, you should always try to keep the THI scores of side dishes or desserts to less than +3 to +5. Just think: A Strawberry Triple Thick Shake or a Super Size serving of fries has a higher THI score than a Quarter Pounder with Cheese!

The scores of some newer "Super Size," "double," or "triple," versions that are being test-marketed are 10 to 15 points higher, making these product lines even less healthful.

Since fast-food eateries are not in business to promote public health (nor should we expect them to be), you should protect yourself by avoiding their high-THI items. Just as important is your role in steering your young children and adolescents away from these items.

Table 57
THI SCORES OF TACO BELL

Border Wraps		Nachos & Sides	
Chicken Fajita*	+12	3 Cheese Sauce (serving)	+4
Chicken Fajita Supreme*	+16	Nachos*	+16
Steak Fajita*	+12	Nachos Bellgrande*	+22
Steak Fajita Supreme*	+16	Nachos Pintos 'N Cheese*	+8
Veggie Fajita*	+9	Nachos Supreme*	+17
Veggie Fajita Supreme*	+12	Mexican Rice*	+8

Breakfast		Gorditas & Quesadillas	
Burrito*	+22	Gordita Baja Beef*	+12
Fiesta Burrito*	+12	Gordita Baja Chicken*	+9
Gordita*	+17	Gordita Baja Steak*	+9
Quesadilla*	+19	Gordita Nacho Cheese-Beef*	+9
Quesadilla, Bacon*	+24	Gordita Nacho Cheese-	
Quesadilla, Cheese*	+20	hicken*	+9
Quesadilla, Sausage*	+22	Gordita Nacho Cheese-Steak	+7
Quesadilla, Steak*	+20	Gordita Supreme-Beef*	+13

Burritos		Gordita Supreme-Chicken*	10
		Gordita Supreme-Steak*	+11
Bean	+8	Quesadilla, Cheese*	+25
Chili Cheese*	+18	Quesadilla Cheese Extreme*	+24
Fiesta, Beef*	+12	Quesadilla, Chicken*	+24
Fiesta, Chicken	+8	Quesadilla, Steak*	+25
Fiesta, Steak	+8		

		Chalupas	
Grilled Stuft, Beef*	+21		
Grilled Stuft, Chicken*	+16	Baja Beef*	+14
Grilled Stuft, Steak*	+17	Baja Chicken*	+13
Supreme, Chicken or Steak*	+12	Baja Steak*	+14

Table 57
THI SCORES OF TACO BELL
(cont.)

Nacho Beef or Steak*	+13	Mexican Pizza*	+22
Nacho Chicken*	+10	Southwest Steak Bowl*	+22
Supreme Beef*	+17	Taco Salad with Salsa*	+30
Supreme Chicken or Steak*	+14	Taco Salad with Salsa, without shell*	+22
Tacos		Tostada*	+9
Enchirito, Beef*	+19	Zesty Chicken Border Bowl without dressing*	+21
Enchirito, Chicken	+15		
Enchirito, Steak*	+16		
Mexican Melt*	+15		

* AVOID

The scores of some "Super Size" or "4-D" versions being test-marketed are 10 to 15 points higher. Even though an occasional taco is not detrimental to anyone's health, frequent fast foods such as tacos, pizzas, Whoppers, etc., are clearly harmful to your health.

Table 58
THI SCORES OF KENTUCKY FRIED CHICKEN

Crispy Strips (3 strips)		Sandwiches	
Colonel's Strips*	+14	Original Roast with Sauce*	+14
Spicy, Honey BBQ, or Blazin' Strips*	+12	Original Roast without Sauce*	+10
Extra Crispy		Tender Roast with Sauce*	+8
Breast*	+20	Tender Roast without Sauce	+5
Drumstick*	+8	**Other Sandwiches**	
Thigh*	+18	Twister*	+31
Whole Wing*	+10	Honey BBQ Flavored	+4
Hot & Spicy Chicken		Triple Crunch without Sauce*	+18
Breast*	+20	Triple Crunch Zinger without Sauce*	+16
Drumstick	+6	**Sides**	
Thigh*	+20	Biscuit (1)*	+5
Whole Wing*	+8	Cole Slaw	+4
Original Recipe Chicken		Corn on the Cob (without butter)	0
Breast*	+16	Mashed Potatoes*	+5
Chicken Pot Pie*	+28	Mean Greens	+3
Drumstick	+7	Potato Salad*	+7
Thigh*	+18	Potato Wedges*	+10
Whole Wing*	+8	**Desserts**	
Popcorn Chicken & Wings		**Double Chocolate Chip Cake***	+10
Individual Popcorn Chicken*	+18	**Parfait, Fudge Brownie***	+9
Kid's Popcorn Chicken*	+10	Parfait, Lemon Creme*	+17
Large Popcorn Chicken*	+27	Pecan Pie*	+10
Honey BBQ Wings*	+22		
Hot Wings*	+22		

* AVOID

Table 59
THI SCORES OF SUBWAY

Classic Sandwiches:

B.L.T.	+8
Cold Cut Trio*	+14
Italian BMT*	+17
Seafood, light mayo*	+9
Seafood, regular mayo*	+15
Tuna, light mayo*	+9
Tuna, regular mayo*	+21

6 Grams Fat or Less (6")

Ham	+4
Roasted Beef	+5
Roasted Chicken Breast	+5
Subway Club	+5
Turkey Breast	+4
Turkey Breast & Ham	+4
Veggie Delite	+3

6" Select

Chipotle Southwest Steak & Cheese*	+15
Chipotle Southwest Turkey & Bacon*	+11
Dijon Horseradish Melt*	+17
Honey Mustard Ham	+4
Red Wine Vinaigrette Club	+8
Sweet Onion Chicken Teriyaki	+4

Extreme Sandwiches

Dijon Horseradish Melt*	+18

Southwestern Onion Chicken Teriyaki	+7
Southwestern Turkey & Ham*	+13
Vinaigrette Club*	+9

Double Meat Sandwiches

Chicken Breast	+8
Cold Cut Trio*	+28
Ham	+7
Italian BMT*	+31
Meatballs*	+35
Roast Beef	+8
Seafood & Crab*	+15
Steak & Cheese*	+16
Subway Club*	+9
Subway Melt*	+21
Tuna*	+19
Turkey Breast	+7
Turkey & Ham	+7

Salads

BLT*	+8
Chicken Taco*	+14
Italian BMT*	+13
Veggie Delite	0

* AVOID

BMT stands for "biggest, meatiest, and tastiest!" (according to Subway officials)
Subways as well a many other fast food chains have certain regional, or test-marketing items that may not be available throughout their restaurants.

Table 60
THI SCORES OF PIZZA HUT PIZZAS
per 2 slices

Beef Topping			
Hand Tossed*	+31		
Pan*	+28		
Stuffed Crust*	+32		
Thin n' Crispy*	+20		
Big New Yorker			
Cheese*	+36		
Pepperoni*	+28		
Supreme*	+40		
Veggie Lover's*	+22		
Cheese			
Hand Tossed*	+22		
Pan*	+25		
Stuffed Crust*	+32		
Thin n' Crispy*	+18		
Chicago Dish			
Meat Lover's*	+24		
Pepperoni*	+18		
Supreme*	+20		
Veggie Lover's*	+16		
Ham			
Hand Tossed*	+19		
Pan*	+15		
Stuffed Crust*	+22		
Thin n' Crispy*	+13		
Italian Sausage			
Hand Tossed*	+22		
Pan*	+24		

Stuffed Crust*	+31		
Thin n' Crispy*	+25		
Meat Lover's			
Hand Tossed*	+24		
Pan*	+23		
Stuffed Crust*	+44		
Thin n' Crispy*	+29		
Pepperoni			
Hand Tossed*	+17		
Pan*	+17		
Stuffed Crust*	+29		
Thin n' Crispy*	+16		
Personal Pan (per pizza)			
Cheese*	+21		
Pepperoni Lover's*	+24		
Supreme*	+26		
Pork			
Hand Tossed*	+21		
Pan*	+21		
Stuffed Crust*	+29		
Thin n' Crispy*	+25		
Super Supreme			
Hand Tossed*	+19		
Pan*	+21		
Stuffed Crust*	+34		
Thin n' Crispy*	+21		
Supreme			
Hand Tossed*	+21		

Table 60
THI SCORES OF PIZZA HUT PIZZAS
per 2 slices (cont.)

Pan*	+20	Cavatini Pasta*	+12
Stuffed Crust*	+32	Cavatini Supreme*	+15
Thin n' Crispy*	+20	Cherry Dessert	+4
Veggie Lover's		Garlic Bread	+2
		Ham & Cheese Sandwich*	+15
Hand Tossed*	+12	Hot Buffalo Wings (4)*	+6
Pan*	+15	Mild Buffalo Wings (5)*	+8
Stuffed Crust*	+24	**Spaghetti**	
Thin n' Crispy	+9		
Other		Spaghetti with Marinara	+4
		Spaghetti with Meatballs*	+20
Apple Dessert	+4	Spaghetti with Meat Sauce*	+12
Bread Stick (1)	+2		
Breadstick Sausage	0		

* AVOID

The problem with all pizzas is that most people eat more than 2 slices at a time, making them even more problematic. Still, an occasional slice or two of any pizza will not do irreparable harm to anyone.

Table 61
THI SCORES OF PAPA JOHN'S PIZZAS
per 2 slices, and side orders per serving

	6 CHEESE	ALL THE MEATS	CHEESE	GARDEN SPECIAL	PEPPERONI	SAUSAGE	SPINACH ALFREDO	THE WORKS
ORIGINAL CRUST	+30*	+30*	+17*	+13	+21*	+21*	+33*	+25*
THIN CRUST	+46*	+39*	+17*	+17*	+21*	+25*	+38*	+30*
SIDE ORDERS	BREAD- STICKS	CHEESE- SAUCE	CHEESE STICKS	CHICKEN STRIPS	GARLIC SAUCE	HONEY MUSTARD	PIZZA SAUCE	RANCH SAUCE
	+2	+8*	+6*	+2	+6*	+6	0	+5*

* AVOID

As you can see, the THI scores of Papa John's pizzas are just as high as Pizza Hut's, and quite comparable to other national or regional brands, with minor variations. Often people assume the thin-crust versions are "better" or less unhealthy. Regrettably, that is not always the case. For example, as you can see, the THI score of 2 slices of Papa John's Thin Crust, Six Cheese is +46. (And if you happen to be among those who eat 4 slices, the THI score of that single meal is +92, which exceeds 3 days' allowance!) Considering the very high THI scores of all pizzas, you should opt for 1 or 2 slices, and certainly no side orders, even if they come with your order or you have the coupons for them.

The THI scores of nearly all frozen pizzas are the same as those of their fresh counterparts. Freezing does not alter nutrients in foods, especially their fat, cholesterol, salt, carbohydrate, or calorie content. So the next time you unwrap that 16-inch frozen pizza, remember each slice is loaded with plenty of saturated fat, cholesterol, carbohydrates, calories, and sodium. Go easy!

Table 62
THI SCORES OF WENDY'S

Fresh Stuffed Pitas		Salads	
Chicken Caesar*	+10	Caesar with one packet dressing*	+7
Classic Greek*	+15	Honey Mustard Dressing*	+9
Garden Ranch Chicken*	+8	Mandarin Chicken	+4
Garden Veggie	+6	Oriental Sesame*	+7
Pita Dressings		Spring Mix with Cheese*	+12
Caesar Vinaigrette	+3	Taco Supremo Salad*	+21
Garden Ranch Sauce	+3	**Salad Dressings/Garnish**	
Potatoes		Blue Cheese*	+13
Baked Potato, plain	+7	Creamy Ranch or Honey Mustard*	+9
Potato with Bacon & Cheese*	+20	Creamy Ranch, reduced fat	+4
Potato with Broccoli & Cheese*	+15	French	+3
Potato with Cheese*	+15	Honey Roasted Almonds or Pecans	+1
Potato with Chili & Cheese*	+18	House Vinaigrette*	+7
Potato with Sour Cream & Chives*	+15	Sour Cream*	+7
Potato with Whipped margarine*	+11	**Sandwiches**	
Nuggets, Chilies, & Fries		Big Bacon Classic*	+27
Chicken Nuggets (4)	+6	Breaded Chicken Fillet*	+9
Chicken Nuggets (5)	+7	Cheeseburger, Kids' Meal	+11
Chili, Small	+6	Chicken Club*	+10
Chili, Large*	+9	Grilled Chicken	+5
Chili with Shredded Cheddar	+7	Hamburger, Kids' Meal	+7
French Fries, medium*	+13	Jr. Bacon Cheeseburger*	+16
French Fries, Biggie*	+15	Jr. Cheeseburger*	+11
Desserts		Jr. Cheeseburger Deluxe*	+14
Chocolate Chip Cookie*	+12	Jr. Hamburger	+7
Frosty, Junior (6 oz)*	+6	Plain Hamburger*	+11
Frosty, Small (12 oz)*	+12	Hamburger with Everything*	+16
Frosty, Medium (16 oz)*	+17	Spicy Chicken	+8

* AVOID

The scores of some of the newer "Super Size" products being test-marketed are 10 to 15 points higher. Avoid them to the best of your ability!

Chapter Five

How to Use the THI Scores

Let's set a single ground rule: If you are serious about losing weight or preventing diabetes, coronary artery disease, premature aging, and various cancers, or improving your overall well-being, *you must part with your old dietary ways*. Although you don't have to raise your right hand, you must pledge to abide by this simple and single ground rule without making a U-turn!

Even though we are a nation of dieters, supplement users, and medicine takers, contrary to our erroneous perception, *we are not a healthy nation!* Just look at table 1, and you'll see why. *Although we have a vast number of modern, "life-saving" (albeit expensive) medicines and medical technology, they are mostly directed at and are used for the treatment of diseases, not their prevention.* For example, there are well over one hundred different drugs currently available for the *treatment* of diabetes and some of its complications. But in spite of all these wonder drugs, *more than 80 percent of people with diabetes eventually die from cardiovascular complications of their diabetes.* We have well over one thousand cardiovascular drugs, yet there are 130 million Americans with abnormal blood cholesterol, 65 million with high blood pressure, and 40 million with coronary artery disease. What is missing—glaringly—is prevention, not available treatments.

It is now universally accepted that our epidemics of cardiovascular diseases, weight problems, and diabetes, and a vast number of cancers and other chronic diseases, are the consequence of many years of dietary and lifestyle miscues that are now catching up with us. The good news is that most of these chronic diseases are preventable!

For example, in a recent Harvard study, 42,504 male health professionals were followed up for twelve years. The participants were forty to seventy-five years of age at entry into the study and free from diabetes. Over the course of the study *the risk of developing diabetes was 1,100 percent higher in those who were moderately to severely overweight and sedentary, and continued to eat a typical Western diet!* This study and three other large ones (two from the U.S. and one from Finland) of men and women also showed that a prudent diet (similar to the THI Diet presented here), along with moderate, regular exercise, *reduced the risk of diabe-*

tes by 60 percent in men, and by an astounding 90 percent in women.

We are also in the midst of another epidemic. Each year one and a half million Americans, many in their thirties, forties, and fifties, suffer a heart attack. The annual death toll from all cardiovascular diseases in the U.S. is one million, with at least twice as many suffering related complications and disabilities. So *unless we adopt a different nutritional and lifestyle plan, the current generations of ten-, twenty-, and 30-year-olds will have a similar future,* riddled with cardiovascular death and disabilities. But *it is doable!*

We do not develop coronary artery disease suddenly as we reach the age of forty or fifty. Coronary artery disease starts early, often in childhood and adolescence. A heart attack is due to a sudden and often unpredictable tear in the wall of a coronary artery, resulting in a clot that blocks the flow of blood to a portion of the heart muscle. However, this dramatic and sometimes fatal event is the culmination of years of neglecting various coronary risk factors (remember table 2), which cause a smoldering inflammation in the wall of the arteries. When Richard Cheney, the U.S. vice president, had his first heart attack at the age of thirty-four, it wasn't because of something that happened the previous day, month, or even year. He was developing coronary artery disease when he was an adolescent. Just look at table 63.

Table 63
PERCENTAGE OF YOUNG AMERICANS WITH EARLY CORONARY ARTERY DISEASE

| Age | White | | African-American | |
	Males	Females	Males	Females
15–19	24	7	24	18
20–24	28	15	32	12
25–29	39	21	42	25
30–34	51	32	49	38

Based on autopsy data of 2,876 subjects who had died of external, noncardiac causes.

Prevention of coronary artery disease is achievable if we start controlling or modifying all major coronary risk factors (table 2) early and consistently. (For more on this, see my book *Every Heart Attack is Preventable: How to Control the Twenty Major Coronary Risk Factors and Save Your Life*.) Here, too, nutritional and lifestyle miscues are at the core of multiple coronary risk factors.

> Contrary to a common misconception, heart attacks are not mainly the disease of middle-aged or post-middle-aged men. Every year for the past sixteen years, more women in the U.S. have died of cardiovascular diseases than men. The problem is that we have done very little to prevent coronary artery disease in men, and even less in women.

In the U.S. Nurses' Health Study, 84,129 women thirty to fifty-five years old were followed up for twelve years. Among those who followed a "prudent" diet, did not smoke, and engaged in moderate, regular exercises, the risk of a coronary event was 82 percent lower than among those who did not follow these dietary and lifestyle practices. Dietary and lifestyle modifications are the cornerstone of controlling or minimizing the impact of the twenty major coronary risk factors listed in table 2. *Incredibly, only 3 percent of American women and about 8 percent of American men follow such dietary and lifestyle practices!* Do you now wonder why we have an epidemic of coronary artery disease?

More than eighty percent of cancer deaths in the U.S. are from cancers of the breast, colon, lungs, and prostate. No matter what genetic predispositions we are saddled with, *we can still dramatically reduce our risk of breast, colon, and prostate cancer by nearly 90 percent, and the risk of lung cancer by more than 90 percent.* What is tragic is that most of the deaths and a vast number of the disabilities caused by these cancers can be prevented by diet and lifestyle as presented here (see chapter 6).

At the 2002 Congress of the European Society of Cardiology, Swedish researchers presented data showing that at least one-half of men and women with heart attacks have diagnosed or undiagnosed diabetes. As noted previously, the risk of diabetes among people with a moderate to severe weight problem and a sedentary lifestyle (more than 30 percent of the U.S. adult population) is 1,100 percent greater than for physically active adults with a normal weight. The incidence of abnormal blood cholesterol, hypertension, and cancers of the breast, colon, and prostate is also far greater among these subjects. In other words, *the common bond* among weight problems, diabetes, cholesterol disorders, cardiovascular diseases, and most common cancers is that *they are mostly the consequences of our nutritional and lifestyle behaviors, not our inevitable genetic destiny.*

We have gone through forty years of the American Heart Association (AHA) diets: step one, two, or three, with 30 percent, 20 percent, and 10 percent fat and 300 milligrams, 200 milligrams, and 100 milligrams cholesterol in the diet, respectively. Yet each year more Americans have died from cardiovascular diseases than the year before! For decades the American Diabetes Association has promoted the low-sugar, low-carbohydrate diet for the prevention and treatment of diabetes, only to witness a fast expanding epidemic of diabetes among Americans of all ages, including children and adolescents. The U.S. Department of Agriculture offered us the Dietary Guideline for Americans, the Food Pyramid, and the Healthy Eating Index. *Recent data have shown only trivial reduction in the risk of cardiovascular diseases, and no risk reduction of various cancers, with the Food Pyramid scheme.* Why?

As shown in table 2, *cardiovascular diseases are*

the consequence of long-term exposure to multiple risk factors. Reducing one's blood cholesterol by ten or twenty points (the average result on the AHA diet) leaves many "foxes in the chicken coop." Diabetes is not caused by simple carbohydrate excess, to be treated by avoiding these nutrients. Cancers, too, are multifactorial (see chapter 6); therefore, we cannot expect to prevent them by eating two or three additional servings of fruit and vegetables here and there. It would have been marvelous if these simplistic assumptions were correct. But they are not! These ineffective dietary recommendations were all based on inadequate and antiquated information dating back forty years. They were also never more than a start; it was inevitable that they would change. We have since made great strides in medicine and food and nutritional sciences. Shouldn't we have access to current information?

I have extracted and incorporated data from more than four thousand recent scientific works and discoveries in medicine, nutrition, and health to provide you with the *Total Health Impact nutritional and lifestyle plan,* a state-of-the-science blueprint to prevent and modify a basket of chronic diseases. Since the THI scoring system is *qualitative,* it should not be used as a quantitative (mathematical) number. For example, you cannot assume that the low THI score of a seafood dinner can somehow counterbalance the load of saturated fats and trans-fatty acids in the rich dessert that follows. That is because trans-fatty acids (and omega-6 polyunsaturated fats) in vegetable oils, margarines, shortenings, or cooking fats compete and interfere with the entry of seafood's omega-3 fat into various cells, including white blood cells and cells of the plateletes, heart muscle, breast, and colon. In addition, a high intake of saturated fats and high glycemic carbohydrates (rich, fat-laden meals, desserts, or snacks) cannot be counteracted by a tablespoon of olive oil in your salad dressing and a small side salad. So there are *ten commandments* when you use the THI nutritional system, five DON'Ts and five DOs. You should abide by them!

The Ten Commandments of the THI Diet

The purpose of these "commandments" is to simplify and streamline your options, so you have a broad understanding of *how to choose healthful foods and avoid the unhealthy traps*, both at home and away from home.

Here Are Five DON'Ts

1. *Don't eat high glycemic carbohydrates.* This is particularly true for foods that contain sugar, honey, and high-fructose corn sweeteners. The majority of sweet snacks are also burdened by a large amount of hidden fats, mostly saturates or trans fats, sugar and high fructose corn sweeteners.

*See tables 5 and 6

You are well familiar with all of them: candies, cookies, cakes, pies, pastries, donuts, chocolate, muffins, croissants, and the like. Complex carbohydrates with relatively high glycemic indices, such as white bread, pasta, potatoes, and rice, quickly break down in the intestine and are converted to sugar. The end result is almost the same: a rapid rise in blood insulin level with all its drawbacks (see chapter 3).

> *Eliminating all high glycemic carbohydrates* may be difficult and not necessary. However, as a long-term approach to weight management, you should cut them down by at least half.

Instead of using two slices of white bread for your turkey, ham, chicken, or roast beef sandwich, use half a small whole wheat pita bread. Stuff the pocket with all kinds of vegetables or salsa, but please, *no mayonnaise or other fat-laden sauces*. If you have to have a roll, a bagel, or a piece of a baguette, empty it of the soft mushy inside dough and use the crusty shell as above (even if you love that soft inside dough!). Instead of French fries, share a baked potato (with the skin) with someone, or just eat half of it with chives or salsa, but without the melted cheese, butter, margarine, or bacon.

Pasta with olive oil or tomato-based sauces (without greasy meat or cheeses) are reasonable choices provided you don't fill up the plate and go for seconds. Instead, have a large plate of your favorite salad with (or for) your lunch and dinner, provided you use low-calorie dressings, and preferably olive oil and vinegar. White rice is often problematic, so use half as much as you have used in the past, and eat it as infrequently as you can. Although wild rice is a more reasonable option (partly because the portion sizes are much smaller), it is more expensive and may not be as adaptable to various recipes.

Since finding a nonsugared cereal is more difficult than finding a pearl in your next oyster dish, you just need to use it sparingly. Always add some fruit—fresh, canned (not in syrup), or dried—to your cereal.

Desserts are often very calorie-rich, and contain a good deal of undesirable, high glycemic carbohydrates and trans-fatty acids, butter, cream, or all of the above. In most instances they contain more calories than your main entrée. Why eat two meals instead of one? Alas, using a sugar substitute in your coffee cannot offset the negative impact of a piece of pastry, cake, or pie.

If you have a sweet tooth, bypass the low-fat or fat-free cookies; they are loaded with sugar calories. Instead choose among the numerous *fat-free and sugar-free* custards, puddings, ice creams, frozen yogurts, candies, or various fruits or fruit cocktails, or enjoy all kinds of berries with or without a sprinkle of sugar or a thin swirl of chocolate syrup. If you are an ice-cream enthusiast, ½ cup of very low-fat brands such as Healthy Choice, with a *THI* score of +3, will not derail your other good deeds. Make sure to choose a low-sugar, low-fat version, not something billed as light (or lite) ice cream; it may have 20 percent to 30 percent less sugar or fat, but it is still calorie-rich. On the other hand, three scoops of regular ice cream, for example, contain 600 to 800 calories (depending on how generous the scoop is), with a *THI* score of +11 to +15. Adding them to a piece of pie or cake (*THI* scores of about +22) increases the total calories to over 1000 and gives you a total THI score of +33 to +37! So opt for berries, other fruit, or the low-fat, sugar-free ice creams, yogurts, or sorbets.

2. Don't eat any hard or stick margarines, shortenings, and cooking fats. They account for 95 percent of the trans-fatty acids in the American diet. This means you should stay away from deep-fried anything (such as French fries, fried chicken, deep-fried onion rings and mushrooms, potato or corn chips, donuts, etc.). Also, as noted previously, most pastries, cookies, cakes, pies, donuts, croissants, muffins, chocolates, and other sweet snacks made in the U.S. are made with partially hydrogenated vegetable fat, which contains trans-fatty acids.

Newer "designer" soft margarines such as Benecol, Brummel & Brown, Fleischmann's Premium Blend, Promise Spread, Smart Balance, and Take Control do not have any trans-fatty acids. They can safely replace other margarines or butter as a spread. Also, they are suitable for high-heat cooking.

In many restaurants, including the expensive ones, cooks often brush the fillet of fish, chicken, or even red meat with an unhealthy dose of melted cooking fat before, during, and after grilling or broiling it. Once they transfer the meat (white or red) to a plate, they add insult to injury by pouring some of the same horrible fat (with or without melted butter) on top of your meal. This practice turns a healthy food into an energy-dense, coronary-unfriendly, and carcinogenic one and defeats your good intentions of ordering seafood or other healthful dishes. So in restaurants, always make it a habit to let your server know that you cannot have any butter, cream, mayonnaise, margarine, shortening, or cooking fat. Instead, always ask your server to have your dish prepared either with olive oil or without any butter, cream, or vegetable fat.

High glycemic carbohydrates that are deep-fried, or processed and cooked at high temperature have an additional problem. Cooked at high heat, starchy foods such as potato and corn products (especially potato or corn chips), cereals, breads and even some baby foods and barbecue sauces (containing sugar or corn sweeteners) have a potential carcinogen called acrylamide. Nearly all public health agencies of Western European countries, the World Health Organization, and belatedly, the U.S. Food and Drug Administration (FDA) are in agreement that acrylamide is "a serious concern." Even some food processors and manufacturers have taken the (unusual) voluntary step of joining in a consortium to study the health impact of acrylamide, and how to minimize or eliminate it from processed foods or snacks.

Acrylamide is formed at high temperature by a reaction between a harmless amino acid (a simple protein) called asparagine, and a sugar derived from carbohydrates. Once digested, acrylamide (which itself is not carcinogenic) is converted to a potent (test tube) carcinogen called glycinamide. The U.S. FDA has set the safe level of acrylamide in foods at less than 0.1 milligram per kilogram of edible parts, hundreds of times lower than levels found in some deep-fried or processed foods.

Among potato chips the highest levels of acrylamide are found in Pringles, Wavy Lay's Original, and Utz's Home Style Kettle-Cooked varieties. Popeye's, Fuddruckers', Arby's, Wendy's, and Kentucky Fried Chicken's French fries have higher levels of acrylamide than French fries from other fast food chains. Many cereals (such as General Mills Cheerios), breads (such as Arnold Bakery's 100% whole wheat, or Schmidt's Old Tyme Split-Top wheat), and even some baby foods (such as

Gerber's Tender-Harvest Organic Sweet potatoes, or Beech Nut's Stage 2 Vegetables and Chicken) have unacceptably high levels of acrylamide.

Of course what is a carcinogen in a test tube or in rodents is not necessarily a human carcinogen (See chapter 6). Even if acrylamide proves to be a true human carcinogen, it would require frequent exposure to high doses over an extended period of time to cause any human cancer. As such, eating a small serving of French fries, Pringles potato chips, or a piece of barbecued chicken or ribs, no matter how much acrylamide or other carcinogens they have, will not start the process of carcinogenesis in anyone. Still the prudent course is to avoid these items as much as possible.

What about monounsaturated fats (such as olive oil, canola oil, or hazelnut oil)? Since all of these oils have very low *THI* scores, can you use them with impunity? The short answer is yes! For cardiovascular health, and for reducing the risk of diabetes or various cancers, they are the oils for all people. However, overdosing with any fat when you are trying to lose weight is not very helpful. Our fat cells don't quibble over the type or the source of dietary fat, and will gladly receive and store any surplus fat, anytime.

Still, even for those with a weight problem, there are two extenuating circumstances that tend to reduce the caloric impact of these oils. *First,* these oils contain high concentrations of monounsaturated fats. As noted in chapter 2, monounsaturates burn more quickly and efficiently than saturated or trans fats; hence they are *less "obeso-genic."* In other words, they are less likely to add to your weight burden. So for those who wish to dramatically cut down their dietary carbohydrates, cooking (lightly) with these oils is a reasonable alternative to using butter, cream, margarine, shortening, or other cooking fats. *Second,* unlike saturated fats and trans-fatty acids that are often hidden in processed foods and snacks, olive oil, canola oil, or hazelnut oil is *added* to foods we cook or eat. So we have some control.

> Given the choice between rich, buttery/creamy sauces and olive oil– and tomato-based sauces, always choose the latter.

Since low-fat diets reduce the blood level of the "good" HDL cholesterol, and increase the risk of a stroke by more than 50 percent, especially among those with one or more major cardiovascular risk factors (table 2), you should consider using olive oil or canola oil for all your cooking and baking needs, including muffins, cakes, or cookies.

3. *Don't skip meals!* It is the wrong answer no matter what the question is! A recent study by the U.S. Food and Drug Administration and the National Heart, Lung, and Blood Institute showed that in the U.S. 20 percent of men and women, and 50 percent of female high school students (and 20 percent of male students), skip breakfast on a regular basis. Often people skip breakfast because they get up too late and rush to get out of the house to go to school or work, or to take care of children or the elderly. Some people claim they just aren't hungry or their stomach doesn't feel right when they wake up, or they just don't have the time to grab a bite for lunch, etc. But a large number of people skip breakfast or lunch intentionally, thinking (incorrectly) that meal skipping is a good way to cut calories or lose weight. It is not!

Numerous studies in laboratory animals and humans have consistently shown that eating *fewer meals per day leads to weight gain, not weight loss*. One reason for this apparent paradox is that when you skip a meal, during the next feeding you have plenty of digestive enzymes to break down the food and absorb the nutrients more efficiently. Consequently, much smaller portions of food remain undigested and pass through the intestine unabsorbed. Another reason is that people who skip breakfast or lunch tend to eat a big dinner, followed by frequent snacks until bedtime. In fact, the total twenty-four-hour caloric intake of many meal skippers equals or exceeds the average intake of three or four meals. Even more importantly, the shift from daytime to dinnertime calorie loading has an additional disadvantage of burning fewer calories at night, with a greater potential for calorie surplus and weight gain (see chapter 8).

The 130 million Americans with abnormal blood cholesterol levels have another reason not to skip meals. Liver cells have certain designated receptors (or landing sites) for the "bad" LDL cholesterol particles. LDL receptors trap cholesterol particles from the bloodstream and use them to make bile or other compounds. The more LDL receptors we have, the less likely it is that we have elevated blood cholesterol levels. In fact, 70 percent of people with high blood cholesterol levels have an inadequate number of functional LDL receptors. Feeding stimulates the liver cells to produce more LDL receptors, whereas meal skipping deprives you of this natural cholesterol-lowering function of the liver. Don't do it.

Quite often people who skip breakfast because they aren't hungry or feel queasy in the morning have an upper-digestive-tract disorder such as acid reflux disease or gastritis caused by H pylori germs. Either way, instead of ignoring it, you should really see your health care provider to find out if you have a coexisting digestive disorder. Meal skipping is not the answer!

---

4. *Don't make dinner your biggest meal.* The time of day makes a significant difference in the body's handling of foods. The French, for example, eat nearly 60 percent of all their calories by two p.m., whereas the amount is less than 40% for Americans. Many other populations eat their main meal at lunch and a small dinner at night.

Numerous studies have shown that humans

burn calories eaten in the morning at a much greater rate (about 10 percent to 15 percent more) than nighttime calories, and about 5 percent more than lunchtime calories. Although burning an additional 5 percent to 10 percent of calories may have no appreciable short-term benefit, over time it may help your weight loss efforts.

> *Why do we burn more calories in the morning than we do at night?* Even when we are not physically very active in the morning, our muscles, heart, lungs, brain, liver, and kidneys emerge from their nocturnal rest with a heightened need for fuel. This is even truer as we go to work and engage in our daily activities. On the other hand, when we eat a large meal at night, and then, as most Americans tend to do, rest in a comfortable chair or sofa and soon sink into sleep mode, we simply do not burn as many calories. Also, in the morning various hormones (especially adrenaline-like hormones) are more plentiful, further increasing our metabolic rate.

Clearly, the practice of eating a big dinner followed by dessert and frequent postdinner snacks (usually high glycemic and calorie-rich chips, candies, or cookies) adds up to plenty of unnecessary calories and very high *THI* scores. Couple this with a slower nighttime metabolism, and it is easy to see why you'd have a hard time losing weight.

This diurnal variation in energy handling (metabolism) is another reason why the French and Southern Mediterranean peoples have less abdominal obesity, diabetes, and coronary artery disease than northern Europeans or Americans.

5. *Don't let your eyes or taste buds dictate how much you eat.* No big meals, buffets, smorgasbords, two-for-ones, all-you-can-eats, double this, or extra-large that, particularly at fast-food eateries! *Large food portions and uninhibited eating,* especially at night, are huge factors in creating energy surplus, weight gain, and many weight-related disorders.

Fast Foods

Whether we like it or not, fast foods and fast-food eateries are here to stay. In fact, most burger and pizza chains nowadays have a worldwide presence. With a fast-food restaurant at almost every corner, they are unavoidable, especially for those who have young children, are too busy to cook, have very little time, or want and like the predictability of these eateries. So what should we do?

Some entrées at fast-food chains have *THI* scores that are so unhealthful that, like alcohol or tobacco products, they *should be forced to carry a health warning!* For example, one Double Whopper with Cheese at Burger King has *67 grams of fat*

(100 percent of the total daily fat requirement), *26 grams of saturated fat* (more than 100 percent of an average daily intake), and nearly *3,000 milligrams of salt* (60 percent of the average daily requirement). Overall, the *THI* score of this atrocious concoction is +53. By the time you add a king-size French fries (+26 points), and a Dutch Apple Pie (+13), your total *THI* score climbs to + 92! This is more than the allowed *THI* score of all meals for three whole days!

> Burger King's breakfast hash browns are not food; they are "hazardous material"! A large order of hash browns contains 8.4 grams of trans-fatty acids, more than an average week's intake (and probably more than I consume in six months!)

The offerings of McDonald's, Wendy's, and Taco Bell have also become bigger and more energy-dense, and pack in much higher *THI* scores than a few years ago. Among the big fast-food chains, only Wendy's resisted the trend for a while, but they, too, have recently succumbed to the notion that bigger is better. For example, they have introduced the Cheddar Lover's Bacon Cheeseburger, a dreadful combination with about 50 grams of fat, nearly half of which is saturated, and more than 3,000 milligrams of salt.

Everyone assumes that salads are quite healthy meals. You'll have to throw out that assumption if you choose Wendy's Taco Supreme Salad or Chicken BLT and Honey-Mustard Dressing with *THI* scores of +21 and +23, respectively. On the other hand, the scores of its Deluxe Garden Salad and Grilled Chicken Salad are quite reasonable at +3 and +5, respectively.

Kentucky Fried Chicken has transformed the harmless chicken into a coronary-unfriendly meal by deep-frying it in cooking fat loaded with saturated fat and trans-fatty acids. For example, while the chain's Tender Roast Breast without skin has a healthful score of +4, the Twister has a THI score of +31. If you order Potato Wedges (+10), and a Lemon Creme Parfait dessert (+17), your THI score reaches +58, twice your "allowance" for two days.

Look at the horrifying items in the Denny's menu listed in table 57. Denny's Breakfast Dagwood contains 90 grams of fat (greater than one full day's allowance), 38 grams of which is saturated (more than two days' allowance), 802 milligrams of cholesterol (almost three days' allowance), and 3,600 milligrams of sodium (greater than an entire day's requirement). The French Slam 2 breakfast contains even more cholesterol, 825 milligrams! Certainly some if not most of such horrendously unhealthy offerings should carry labels, very much like tobacco products or alcohol, informing consumers that *these items are hazardous to your health.*

Subway sandwiches are another example of good and bad all mixed up. For example, a Subway Double Meat Meatballs has a *THI* score of +37, and a Double Meat Italian BMT has a score of +31, each eight to nine times higher than the *THI* scores of the chain's Turkey Breast or Ham (with *THI* scores of +4), and more than six times higher than its Roasted Beef or Chicken (*THI* score of +5).

What about pizza? Pizza Hut and nearly all other pizzerias, both national and regional, are just as bad. For example, most people associate the term *vegetarian* with nutritious and healthy foods. At pizzerias, *vegetarian* no longer means what it implies. Instead, it has made a U-turn, and means a greasy cheese or margarine-laden concoction with a few slivers of onions, green peppers, mushrooms, or occasionally black olives. The *THI* scores of all of these pizzas are very high, especially since most people tend to eat more than one or two pieces. For example, the *THI* score of four pieces of Pizza Hut's Stuffed Crust with beef (or cheese) topping is +64, and for the Veggie Lover's

---

When you order your pizza, ask for thin dough, very little cheese, and no meat, but lots of mushrooms, peppers, onions, olives, tomatoes, and any other vegetables or fruits, such as pineapple. Avoid the Meat Lover's, Cheese Lover's, and Veggie Lover's pizzas, or variations thereof.

Stuffed Crust Pizza, it is a disheartening +48. Even if you are among those who eat only two slices, your scores for the two pizzas listed above are +32 and +24 respectively.

How about a 20-ounce rib roast at a steak house? Do you really want to know? Well, it sets you back by four days, and that's assuming that you won't order an appetizer or dessert! Here, the problem is not the red meat but the white fat that comes with it, and the portion size.

To various degrees all fast-food eateries contribute to our epidemics of coronary artery disease, diabetes, osteoporosis, and cancers of the breast, colon, and prostate. They focus unceasing advertisements and promotional campaigns primarily on children and adolescents to ensnare a new generation of loyal customers. Although their actions represent "legitimate" business and profit-driven decisions, they are just as dangerous to public health as the "legitimate" business decisions of tobacco manufacturers promoting their "legitimate" products.

As if the existing entrées of many fast-food restaurants were not bad enough, the chains are all involved in active campaigns to promote bigger, fatter, and more caloric entrées. Over the past twenty years the size and energy density of many sandwiches at most fast-food restaurants has doubled, and they are climbing higher and higher. For example, during the same period, the size and calorie content of a typical Coke and order of French fries at fast-food eateries has tripled! Even

Recent studies have shown that consumption of fat that has been used for deep-frying in fast-food restaurants impairs the ability of the arteries to dilate properly. This is because *repeatedly heated cooking fats have a 400 percent higher concentration of oxidized fatty product than fresh fats have*. Thus, fried items at fast-food restaurants put consumers in double jeopardy: too much fat with very high **THI** scores, and too much oxidized fat by-products. Although McDonald's recently announced that they intend to change their cooking fat to a new one with less trans-fatty acids, this is no more than a smoke screen. What they failed to mention is that the caloric content of foods prepared with these fats remains unchanged, and the repeated heating of this new cooking fat still produces the same undesirable oxidized fatty by-products.

the smaller fast-food eateries have joined the "bigger is better" competition. For example, in December 2002, Jack in the Box announced that they would increase the meat in their burgers by 66 percent, which doubles the fat content of their burgers.

What Should You Do as a Consumer?

Although you may not be able to escape fast-food restaurants altogether, especially if you have kids, try to avoid them as much as possible. When you go to any of these eateries, look at the *THI* scores of the menus beforehand (tables 54 through 62), so you can choose among the healthier items. To reduce the *THI* score and caloric content of any item, ask the server to leave out sauces, mayonnaise, margarine, fried onions, mushrooms, bacon, and cheese. Grilled chicken, roast beef, or turkey sandwiches without the above items are usually reasonable choices. Ordering a baked potato instead of French fries is another way of cutting down on trans-fatty acids and added calories. Even more important, resist the pressure from your young children and take them to these restaurants as infrequently as possible. Remember, the reason these eateries promote their foods to youngsters is to turn them into long-term adult customers.

Since the impact of a single meal, whether it is a fast food or any other food, does not last more than a few hours, there is no justification for a rigid or deprivational approach to eating. The total prohibition of any food, except for people with specific food allergies, makes eating unnecessarily inflexible, especially when eating out or visiting friends and relatives. Follow the five DON'Ts for all your meals, but don't fret about your occasional dietary infractions.

And the Five DOs

1. *Eat three to four seafood meals per week.* But remember, cooking your seafood with vegetable oils (such as corn, safflower, soybean, or sunflower oil) and vegetable fats defeats the purpose of eating seafood. That's because their omega-6 fatty acids and the harmful trans-fatty acids in margarines, shortenings, and cooking fats interfere with the entry of seafood's beneficial omega-3 fat into various cells. Instead, sauté your favorite seafood in olive oil or canola oil. If you prefer, you can broil, bake, or poach it, using the same oils. Since the main reason for eating seafood is its cardioprotective omega-3 fat, avoid grilling—you'd waste that desirable fat in the drippings. Eating three to four seafood meals per week can reduce your risk of a heart attack by 40 percent. It also displaces other (energy-dense) meals that you would've eaten otherwise. That is why taking a fish oil supplement (instead of eating seafood) is not a good alternative.

Given the choice between a fatty or nonfatty fish, which one should you choose? The answer is the fatty fish. This is because approximately 35 percent of seafood's fat is omega-3, and more than one-half of the remainder is monounsaturates. As you can see in tables 3 and 4 (chapter 2), most fish, and in particular shellfish, have very low concentrations of fat. In contrast, a T-bone steak or regular ground beef is 30 percent fat, a large proportion of which is undesirable saturated fat, but has no omega-3 fatty acids. The darker the flesh of the fish, the more omega-3 it has, and the better it is. Thus salmon, tuna, and mackerel have more omega-3 than white fish such as cod, flounder, perch, or rockfish. In general, ounce for ounce, seafoods provide one-half the calories of choice red meats and a third less than chicken or turkey. In other words, seafoods are neither energy-dense nor "obesogenic."

The total fat per serving (35 percent of which is omega-3 fat) in canned tuna fish can vary tenfold. For example, premium albacore (Bumble Bee, Chicken of the Sea, or StarKist) may have 0.5, 1, 3, or 5 grams of fat per serving. Why such a difference? This is because not all tunas are alike. A tuna caught in the Pacific Northwest is different from the same tuna caught off the coast of the Carolinas. So when you look for canned tuna, look at the nutrition information on each can. Always choose cans with the highest fat content (remember the purpose of eating fish is primarily the omega-3 fat).

2. *Try to make breakfast and lunch your bigger meals.* This will reduce the likelihood that you'll eat most of your calories at night. In case you forgot, breakfast and lunch are metabolized about 10 percent to 15 percent faster than dinner meals. This means that your 1,000-calorie dinner counts as 1,150 calories. Since dietary *disinhibition* (over-

eating) is more common at night, make a committed effort to shift most of your eating to lunchtime or breakfast, when overeating is less likely.

3. *Eat tons of dark fruits and vegetables*. Darker varieties have higher concentrations of various vitamins, minerals, and antioxidants. Examples include all kinds of berries, nectarines, peaches, plums, and red or black grapes, and all herbs, asparagus, broccoli, kale, spinach, tomatoes, watercress, or whatever else you like.

A typical Western diet contains a high level of organic acid, which is eliminated through the kidneys. This aciduria drags calcium with it and, over time, contributes to our epidemic of osteoporosis. Because of their abundant potassium, a high intake of vegetables and fruit reduces aciduria and calcium loss, thereby decreasing the risk of osteoporosis.

Recent studies suggest that lengthy cold-storage of fruits such as apples and pears, can significantly reduce the antioxidant activity of these fruits. At 6 months, the antioxidant potency of apples can be reduced by more than 60%.

Fresh (or fresh frozen) ripe fruit and vegetables have more taste, flavor, vitamins, antioxidants, and anticarcinogens than the unripe, plasticlike versions sold at many supermarkets. However when not in season, use what is available. Some fruits and vegetables ripen after picking, but most may soften or change color without ripening (table 66). Dried fruits (various berries, figs, peaches, plums, raisins) fresh frozen berries, or canned fruits (in light fruit juice and not in heavy syrup) are almost as healthful as their fresh counterparts. This is equally true for most vegetables.

Table 64
FRUIT & VEGETABLES THAT DO OR DON'T RIPEN AFTER PICKING

Ripen after picking	Do not ripen after picking
Apples	All berries
Bananas	All citrus fruits
Guavas	All melons
Kiwis	Apricots
Mangoes	Avocados
Papayas	Cherries
Passion fruits	Eggplants
Pears	Figs
Persimmons	Grapes
Plantains	Nectarines, peaches, plums
Quinces	Pineapples
Tomatoes	Pomegranates

Vegetables including various herbs, asparagus, broccoli, Brussels sprouts, collards, kale, lettuce, onions, potatoes, spinach, watercress, zucchini, and others are equally healthful as "baby" versions of mature ones. In fact, some sprouts such as bean or broccoli may have more anticarcinogens than their mature versions.

Try to eat fruit with breakfast instead of drinking juice, so you won't be hungry by ten o'clock in the morning. If possible, eat large servings of vegetables or a side plate of salad (low-calorie dressing) with lunch and dinner. Instead of raiding the pantry for snacks at night, eat a couple of servings of fruit.

Once a week (twice a week if you have a moderate to severe weight problem) eat only salad for dinner. Fix a big plate of baby spinach, romaine lettuce, florets of broccoli, a bunch of watercress, a few red onion rings, and mushrooms, or any other vegetables you like. You can add a bit of goat cheese or fresh Parmesan, and toss it with a small amount of fat-free, low-calorie salad dressing. Or make your own dressing with a small amount of balsamic vinegar and lemon juice, salt, pepper, a touch of Dijon mustard, dry oregano or basil, crushed garlic or garlic powder, and 1 tablespoon of extra-virgin olive oil (add a tablespoon of dry white wine if desired). This not only provides you with a filling and hopefully satisfying dinner; it'll save you several hundred calories that you would've otherwise had. Always choose fruits and vegetables you like, not what you think may have less calories.

Taste and Distaste for Fruits and Vegetables

Nearly everyone knows that eating plenty of fruits and vegetables is an essential component of a healthy diet. So why is it that in the U.S. and many developed countries very few people eat adequate amounts of fruits and vegetables?

Recent data suggest that our genes have something to do with it. Almost one-third of us are genetically extra sensitive to certain tastes, such as bitter and tart. Individuals who shy away from strong-tasting vegetables like broccoli, spinach, peas, and watercress, or various berries, are called *supertasters*. Former president George H. Bush, who made "I hate broccoli!" one of his lasting legacies, and his son President George W. Bush (who also doesn't like broccoli) are two examples of supertasters.

The rest of the population is made up of *normal tasters*, who are somewhat discriminating, and *nontasters*, who eat anything and everything. Of course besides genetic predisposition, our cultural and culinary experiences in childhood and adolescence also influence our likes and dislikes as adults. However finicky you are, keep trying fruits and vegetables until you find a few that you enjoy. Don't force yourself to eat something you can't stand.

4. *Make whatever you eat pleasant-appearing and pleasant-tasting.* One of the joys of life is to eat and enjoy what we eat. Don't treat your meals and mealtime with disdain and impatience, or tell yourself and the world, "I just want to get it over with." Instead of feeling coerced and resentful, you should keep your head up, take pride in, and embrace the changes you have made. After all, you are trying to improve your health and save your life!

Add some fresh herbs (such as basil, chives, oregano, parsley, savory, thyme, or watercress), spices, chopped green onions, slivers of carrots, or whatever else you fancy to your meals. In addition to adding taste, flavor, and color to foods, herbs and spices contain a vast number of vitamins, minerals, and cancer-protective compounds (see chapter 6). These simple culinary touches can enhance the presentation and personality of your meals, and reduce your chance of relapsing to your old ways.

5. *Make sure you get enough fluids, vitamins, and minerals.* Traditionally, diets have almost always focused on solid foods, disregarding liquids. However, fluids have a major role in our health and well-being.

Adequate intake of fluids, especially water, has a number of health benefits. For example, by momentarily filling the stomach, water creates a short-lived sensation of satiety, and helps prevent overeating. A high intake of water can also reduce the risk of heart attack, strokes, kidney stones, and kidney and bladder cancers.

Water. In a six-year study of more than thirty-four thousand Seventh-Day Adventists, *men who drank five or more glasses of water daily had a 51 percent lower risk of a fatal heart attack* than those drinking fewer than two glasses per day. *Women who drank more than five glasses of water daily had a 35 percent lower risk.* Even after adjusting for other coronary risk factors, these remarkable differences persisted. Just as important, both men and women who drank more than five glasses of water daily had a 44 percent lower risk of fatal strokes. In a Swedish study, men and women fifty to sixty-nine years old who had lived in hard-water counties (where water contains more calcium and magnesium), had a 30 percent lower risk of fatal heart attacks.

One likely reason water is cardioprotective is that it dilutes the blood, making it less viscous and therefore less likely to cause clot formation and clog up the arteries (and the veins). Also, in a well-hydrated bloodstream, platelets are less likely to stick together to form tiny nuclei of blood clots, where a snowballing effect can progressively increase the size of the clots. In addition, a well-hydrated person passes a good deal of (diluted) urine. Since certain clotting factors (humans have at least twelve clotting factors) are eliminated in the urine, a high urine output reduces the concentration of these clotting factors. As an added bonus, dilute urine reduces the likelihood that calcium oxalate will form a sediment and start a kidney stone, and washes away carcinogens in the urinary tract, thereby reducing the risks of kidney/bladder cancers.

Both *calcium and magnesium* in hard waters also play a significant role in reducing the risk of severe cardiac-rhythm irregularities, which account for at least half of all fatal heart attacks. These observations cast doubt on whether bottled waters, which are mostly filtered and devoid of calcium, magnesium, fluoride, iodine, zinc, and selenium, are as healthful as good old city water. This is not a trivial matter, especially for those who exercise vigorously and might deplete their magnesium and potassium through perspiration. Men and women, as well as children and adolescents, need calcium, magnesium, and fluoride, and should not follow the fad of carrying commercially bottled water with them everywhere they go. Instead, *bottle your own from the tap!*

Admittedly, the taste and smell of some local waters leave a lot to be desired. In such communities, you can always use faucet-mounted filters, which are very effective in removing the chlorine and 95 percent of organisms, but will not remove all the minerals. On the practical side, if for whatever reason, you don't bottle your own, drinking bottled water is far better than dehydration.

At present, there are over nine hundred brands of bottled water in the U.S., with annual sales exceeding four billion dollars. Among the many regional and national brands, only Mendocino and Trinity have an adequate and balanced amount of calcium and magnesium without going overboard with sodium. Evian is a distant third.

Soft drinks. Although an occasional soft drink is harmless, drinking several cans or bottles a day is problematic. One major disadvantage of carbonated beverages is that they often increase the rate of acid reflux into the esophagus. The large percentage of people with weight problems who also have acid reflux disease will aggravate their problem by drinking soda. Also, as the air bubbles travel through the intestine, they invariably contribute to more bloating, gaseousness, and abdominal cramps, especially among those with irritable bowel syndrome, colitis, or diverticulosis. Also, one regular soda, on average, has about 40 grams of sugar with a THI score of +4, almost equal to the THI score of a prudent breakfast. Drinking water or iced tea may be better alternatives.

The availability of sodas everywhere, including at schools, coupled with their ceaseless advertisements, affects adolescents more than other segments of the population. Caffeinated sodas can cause significant sleep and mood disorders in this age group. Recently researchers from Harvard University evaluated the effects of drinking carbonated beverages, and colas in particular, in 460 high school girls. Overall, *girls who frequently drank carbonated beverages had a three-fold (300 percent) greater likelihood of having a bone fracture than those who drank very little or no soda.* Even more alarming, girls who were more physically active and participated in sports (hence were exposed to various traumas) had a fivefold (500 percent) risk of fracturing a bone! Why?

One reason for these disturbing findings is that colas (with or without caffeine) may be replacing milk (a wonderful source of balanced calcium and phosphorus) in the girls' diet. Also, most sodas contain phosphoric acid, which can contribute to bone loss. A genuine concern is that this generation of young people may grow up to produce a massive number of middle-aged or post-middle-aged men and women with premature osteoporosis.

Tea: Next to water, people all over the world drink *tea* more than any other beverage. Very much as with wine, the taste, flavor, aroma, and various cardioprotective and anticarcinogenic properties of tea are affected by the tea master's expertise and creativity, the soil conditions and the climate where the tea is grown, the amount of rainfall, and the type of tea plants.

Black tea, which is the fermentation by-product of green tea leaves, contains various antioxidants that can reduce the risk of cardiovascular diseases. Recent data from the Boston Area Health Study showed that among men and women with no previous history of coronary artery disease, *those who habitually drank tea had a 45 percent lower risk of developing a heart attack than tea nondrinkers*. In another study, from the Netherlands, the risk of stroke during a fifteen-year period was

70 percent less in men who drank an average of over four cups per day than in those who drank less than two cups. In a joint study, researchers from Boston University, and the Linus Pauling Institute at Oregon State University, showed that both short-term and long-term tea drinking improved the function of coronary artery among men and women with pre-existing coronary artery disease.

> These and a vast number of other studies provide robust and evidence-based data that long-term tea consumption of tea significantly reduces the risk of cardiovascular diseases.

Green tea seems to offer cardiovascular benefits similar to black tea. Although green tea has been promoted as a possible anticarcinogen, recent studies (including some from Japan, which has one of the highest rates of stomach cancer) have shown that *green tea has no protective role against stomach, colon, or other cancers*. Whether larger amounts such as eight or ten cups per day may have some anticarcinogenic benefit is not known. But drinking ten cups of green tea every day for an illusionary benefit is not a practical idea.

Still, green or black tea (regular or iced) provides a healthy alternative to coffee. Tea contains certain compounds that act like diuretics. By increasing the urine volume, tea can reduce the risk of kidney stones. It also reduces the exposure of the bladder to carcinogens by diluting and washing them away.

Adding milk or cream to your tea may well defeat the purpose of drinking tea. That's because at high temperatures (about 220 degrees Fahrenheit), the antioxidants and other healthful phenolic compounds in tea may bind to milk's calcium phosphate or lactalbumin, making them unabsorbable.

Coffee. Two or three cups of coffee per day have no significant effect on any system of the body, positive or negative. Some (usually younger) people may occasionally feel jittery or have minor changes in their sleep pattern or heart rate after even one or two cups of coffee. Several cups of regular coffee per day may increase our metabolic rate by 3 to 5 percent, but this is too small to be of value in weight management.

Excessive coffee (more than five to six cups per day) may also contribute to irregular heart rate and osteoporosis (particularly in smokers). Although coffee does not increase (or decrease) the risk of any cancers, unfortunately many heavy coffee drinkers are also heavy smokers, therefore at a high risk for various tobacco-related cancers, including tongue, throat, esophagus, and particularly lung (*90 percent of all lung cancers are tobacco-related*).

Paper filters remove the two cholesterol-raising compounds in coffee, Cafestol and Kahweol. However, drinking more than five or six cups of coffee may raise the blood homocysteine level, which is one of the major cardiovascular risk factors (table 2). The compounds responsible for raising homocysteine are caffeine and chlorogenic acid, both of which readily pass through filter papers.

If you are among millions of Americans who enjoy two or three cups of coffee a day, don't deprive yourself. Remember, we do a lot of things such as wearing nice clothes, jewelry, and makeup, or going to movies and concerts, not because they enhance our health, but because we like them. However, if you really have no preferences between tea and coffee, opt for a nice cup of tea!

Fruit juices. Most fruit juices contain a combination of glucose and fructose (simple sugars) and on average about 110 calories per 8-ounce glass. However, fruit and vegetable juices are rich sources of many vitamins, especially vitamin C and folic acid (which reduces the blood homocysteine level); minerals, especially potassium (which helps lower the blood pressure); and antioxidants. Most nonsweetened juices have a THI score of +1 per eight ounces, compared with +4 for sodas. *A recent study showed that eating two or more oranges a day (or drinking two to four glasses of orange juice) could increase the blood level of HDL cholesterol by about 10 percent.* (However, this is not appropriate for diabetics.) Given the choice between pulp-free and "lots of pulp" orange juice, always choose the latter, preferably fortified with calcium.

Numerous studies have clearly established that regular consumption of fruits and vegetables (or their juices) reduces the risk of heart attack and stroke by 30 percent, and the risk of colon and prostate cancer by 40 percent.

Tomatoes and tomato products contain high levels of *lycopene,* a potent antioxidant. Several recent studies have shown that regular consumption of tomato products can significantly reduce the risk of lung and prostate cancers, especially among African Americans (in whom low intake of tomato products may contribute to lycopene deficiency). Since lycopene is a fat-soluble antioxidant, it is better absorbed from tomato sauces, tomato pastes, and ketchup with meals containing some fat (as compared with drinking a glass of tomato or V8 juice in the morning with a low-fat breakfast).

Grapefruit and grapefruit juice are a bit tricky when you take them along with certain medicines, especially heart medications and blood thinners. The reason is that a compound in grapefruit (and Seville oranges) or their juice deactivates an enzyme system in the wall of the small intestine.

Contrary to a common misconception, supplemental fiber *by itself* has no protective value against cardiovascular diseases, diabetes, or various cancers. Thus taking fiber supplements is a poor substitute for eating several servings of fruits and vegetables every day. Fruits and vegetables (more than their juices) provide you with the right kind of fiber, which may improve bowel function, add cardioprotective and anti-carcinogenic compounds to your diet, and as a bonus, especially for those who wish to lose weight, have a filling effect and replace other calorie-rich foods and snacks.

This enzyme (called cytochrome P3A4) partially breaks down many drugs, making them less available for absorption into the bloodstream. When cytochrome P3A4 is deactivated, the breakdown of various drugs in the intestine does not occur. Consequently, a higher proportion of these drugs can be absorbed, increasing their potential to cause side effects. To be safe, do not drink grapefruit juice (or eat grapefruit) for two or three hours before you take your medicines.

Alcohol and alcoholic beverages. Alcohol, also a carbohydrate, is enjoyed (and sometimes abused) by billions of people worldwide. Like a liquid Dr. Jekyll and Mr. Hyde, it has a number of health benefits when used properly, and deadly side effects when it is abused. As a carbohydrate, theoretically each gram of alcohol should generate

4 calories. In practice, its yield is much lower. That's because nearly one-third of alcohol is metabolized (broken down) in the stomach before it ever reaches the bloodstream. The liver extracts and breaks down a substantial part of the alcohol once it is absorbed from the intestine. However, unlike with other carbohydrates, the muscles and other organs are neither interested in nor metabolize alcohol to any extent. So the calories of alcohol are mostly wasted, and cannot be counted in the same manner as other carbs.

A number of other factors can affect alcohol's energy delivery. For example, the caloric yield of each gram of alcohol is less in men than in women, less in the active versus the sedentary, less in slim as opposed to heavy people, and less with food than during the happy hour.

One ounce of 100-proof vodka (which is 50 percent alcohol) contains 15 grams of a carbohydrate (alcohol), which theoretically (and in a test tube) should deliver about 60 calories. However, it actually delivers half as many calories in our body. On the other hand, the same 1 ounce served in orange juice or in a cocktail mixer can deliver two or three times more calories than if it were drunk straight or in a calorie-free soda (the extra calories are from the juice or the mixer). Similarly, a can of beer has an equivalent amount of alcohol as an ounce of vodka, but twice as many calories (due to other carbohydrates in the brew). Sweet wines also deliver more calories than dry (nonsweet) wines.

A modest amount of alcohol (one or two drinks per day with a meal) reduces insulin resistance and the risk of diabetes, increases the metabolism, causes dilatation of the arteries hence lowering the blood pressure, increases the good HDL cholesterol level (which accounts for 50 percent of the cardiovascular benefit), and reduces the risk of clot formation inside the arteries for several hours (accounts for 30 percent of the benefit). It also reduces the risk of colon cancer and dementia (table 65). *All alcoholic beverages (beer, wine, and liquor) share these properties.*

Wine, however, has some added benefits due to the presence of certain antioxidants and other phenolic compounds. During the crushing of dark or black grapes in preparation for wine-making, hundreds of phenolic compounds seep through the grapes' skin, some of which account for wine's additional cardiovascular benefits. So which wine is better, red or white?

Since more than 80 percent of the benefits of alcoholic beverages are due to the alcohol, and most of the phenolic compounds (which account for another 10 percent to 20 percent of the benefits) are similar in red and white grapes, the overall benefits of any kind of wine are pretty similar. Tannins in red wines (especially the young ones, in which the tannins have not had enough time to separate and form a sediment at the bottom of the bottle) may reduce the absorption of some phenolic compounds from red wines. On the other hand, a recent study from the London School of

Table 65
Alcohol's Health Impact

Benefits of ≤2 drinks per day 3 to 5 days a week)	Increases the good HDL level by 10% Reduces clot formation inside arteries Reduces the risk of heart attack by 40% Reduces the risk of dementia by 40% Reduces the risk of macular degeneration (the most common cause of adult blindness) Reduces the risk of kidney stone formation Reduces insulin resistance & the risk of diabetes Reduces the risk of colon cancer by 30% *IS ENJOYABLE!*
Side effects of ≥4 drinks per day (even if 2 or 3 times a week)	Increases the risk of irregular heart rhythm, heart attacks, & stroke, especially in women Damages the heart muscle, pancreas, brain, & liver (a common cause of liver cirrhosis) Increases the risk of breast cancer in women and cancer of larynx and pancreas in men Increases the risk of violence & accidents (is a factor in ⅔ of all fatal motor vehicle accidents, or 26,000 deaths) Increases depression Increases abdominal obesity Causes testicular atrophy & impotence Is addictive & tears families apart Costs the U.S. more than $150 billion annually

Medicine showed that red wine, but not white, significantly reduces the production of endothelin-1 in the wall of the arteries. Endothelin-1 is a potent compound that, when produced at high concentrations, can injure the lining of the arteries and promote the development of tiny clots inside the arteries, which may grow into larger clots. Ordinary red table wines (or, if you prefer, the more expensive, vintage red wines) are seven times more potent in reducing the production of endothelin-1 than red grape juice. However, two or three glasses of Concord or other black grape juices daily can significantly reduce the oxidization of LDL cholesterol, and reduce the risk of cardiovascular events.

In a recent Harvard study of more than thirty-eight thousand health professionals over a period of twelve years, those who drank fewer than three drinks a day three to five times a week had a 40 percent lower risk of heart attack or other cardiovascular events. Similar results were reported by Australian researchers, suggesting that *it is the frequency (per week) of drinking small amounts of alcohol that provides cardioprotection*. In fact, large amounts of alcohol, even once or twice a week, increase the risk of a heart attack by 200 percent. These and other studies also show that the beverage most widely consumed by a given population (whether it is beer, liquor, or wine) is the one most likely to offer cardioprotection.

Most benefits of alcohol occur with the first drink. After the second or third one, the benefits decline and are progressively overwhelmed by the side effects. Also, the doubling of calories in beer, cocktails (in mixers), and sweet wines becomes counterproductive. As Edward Rowland (1841–1887) put it, "First the man takes a drink, Then the drink takes a drink, Then the drink takes the man!"

Antioxidants, Vitamins, and Minerals

Inside each living cell, an endless number of ultrafast biological reactions takes place continuously. Some of these reactions may take no more than milliseconds. Although these hectic processes are necessary for the metabolism and life of each cell, they also produce a number of supercharged chemical compounds that are called *free radicals* or *oxygen-free-radicals,* which are commonly referred to as *oxidants.* Oxidants can wreak havoc in a cell, transform it into something entirely different such as a fat cell or a cancerous cell, or just degenerate and kill the cell altogether.

Examples of oxidant damage include most cardiovascular diseases, especially heart attacks, and strokes; many cancers; complications of insulin resistance and diabetes including peripheral vascular disease; retinal changes and blindness; kidney failure; and fatty liver. Aging, and a host of degenerative disorders including sun-damaged skin are other examples of oxidant damage.

Fortunately, *all human cells* and those of almost all animals and plants contain various antioxidants, which *can effectively neutralize nearly all the oxidants more than 99 percent of the time*. If there were no rational balance between oxidants and antioxidants, we wouldn't be around to talk about them! Only when the oxidant load overwhelms intracellular antioxidants do cells sustain damage.

Excessive energy intake (i.e., overeating) increases the oxidant load. Why? Because our cells produce oxidants as they burn proteins, fats, and carbohydrates. The more calories we eat and burn, the more oxidants we produce.

In moderately to severely overweight people (who often consume excessive calories), this high oxidant load coupled with the unavailability of sufficient antioxidants contributes to significantly higher rates of many weight-related chronic diseases and some cancers, including those of the breast, colon, and prostate. *Postmenopausal women with abdominal obesity are particularly at risk;* in addition to the high oxidant load, their abdominal fat cells also produce a large amount of an enzyme called *aromatase*. Aromatase converts some of the normally present steroids into an estrogen-like compound that is carcinogenic for breast tissues.

Does cutting down on calories reduce the oxidant load? It does, but this is a slow process. Even with a sustained calorie reduction for weeks or even months, our bodies continue to produce an excessive amount of oxidants, because it takes time for various cells, including our fat cells, to cut back (downregulate) their oxidant production. In addition, a low-carbohydrate diet makes things worse. *Recent studies have shown that dietary fat increases the oxidant load for several hours, as compared with an hour or two for carbohydrates or proteins. Thus a fat-for-fuel diet is associated with a more sustained increase in the oxidant load in various tissues.* As noted in chapter 2, a long-term switch to fat for fuel (in very low-carbohydrate, high-fat, high-protein diets) has a number of other undesirable consequences. By increasing the already high oxidant load in people who are overweight, these diets are even more undesirable and illogical.

How much and what kind of antioxidants, vitamins, or minerals do we need? Theoretically, antioxidant supplements can counteract oxidants, but that is just in theory! Oxidants and antioxidants can be compared to germs and antibiotics. You cannot assume that no matter what kind of infection you have, you take the same dose of the same antibiotic, and presto, your infection is gone! No. What kinds of infection, in which organ, what germs or viruses, how severe, and in whom determine which antibiotic(s), how much, how often, how long, by mouth or intravenously, and so forth. Similarly, not all oxidants are the same, or respond to the same antioxidants. Moreover, some oxidants (free radicals) have a potency that is six or more orders of magnitude (thousands of times) greater than, for example, vitamin E. You see the problem?

The simplest way to reduce your oxidant load is to lower your total calories, especially fat calories from saturated fats and trans-fatty acids from margarines, shortenings, and cooking fats. In other words, you should avoid anything that's made with these vegetable fats, including all deep-fried foods and snacks (see chapter 2).

As you reduce your caloric intake, especially if you are attempting to lose weight, you can take *vitamin C (500 milligrams), vitamin E (400–1000 milligrams), and selenium (200 micrograms)* daily. This combination provides a mix of both fat- and water-soluble antioxidant vitamins, along with a potent antioxidant mineral.

Vitamin B family. All humans have a complex protein compound in their bloodstream called *homocysteine*. Approximately 15 percent of Americans (and Western Europeans) have one or more genetic abnormalities in the enzymes that break down this compound into a harmless protein. One consequence of these genetically programmed dysfunctions is that homocysteine accumulates in the bloodstream. (Normal blood homocysteine level is less than 9 millimol/liter.

Elevated blood homocysteine increases the risk of coronary artery disease, heart attack, and stroke by 300 percent, and the risk of dementia by more than 200 percent (see table 2). Numerous studies have shown that a combination of vitamin B_6, folic acid, and vitamin B_{12} can significantly lower and normalize blood homocysteine levels. The dosage of folic acid ranges from 1,000 to more than 5,000 micrograms per day, and often depends on the extent of genetic mutations in various enzymes responsible for handling homocysteine. The doses of vitamin B_6 and B_{12} are usually 100 to 300 milligrams and 1,000 to 2,000 micrograms respectively per day.

Folic acid has a vast number of other benefits. For example, it can reduce the risk of breast and colon cancers by 50 percent (see chapter 6). In pregnant women, it can dramatically reduce the risk of neurological abnormalities in their babies. The effective dose of folic acid for these benefits is usually about 1,000 to 2,000 micrograms per day. However, a recent Canadian study of 336,963 women showed that following the mandatory fortification of breakfast cereals with folic acid in 1998 (which provided on average only an additional 100 to 200 micrograms of folic acid per day), the rate of fetal neural-tube defects still decreased by 50 percent.

Vitamins C and E. Although these vitamins are potent antioxidants, there is no compelling evidence to show that they have a significant protective role against cancers of the breast, colon, lungs, or prostate. However, among adults, long-term use of these vitamins may lower the risk of cardiovascular disease by 30 percent.

Chromium. Chromium (a trace mineral) reduces insulin resistance and the risk of diabetes by increasing the number of insulin receptors in the muscles and the liver, and acts like a safe "insulin helper." This is particularly relevant to those who are moderately to severely overweight, or have abdominal obesity and a fatty liver. A study by the U.S. Department of Agriculture showed that daily supplementation with chromium (200 micrograms two or three times a day) improved blood sugar levels in type II diabetes. Some recent studies also suggest that chromium can lower the "bad" LDL cholesterol level by about 10 percent while at the same time it can raise the "good" HDL cholesterol by 5 percent to 7 percent. In general, doses beyond 400 to 600 micrograms per day are not necessary.

Although chromium has been promoted as a weight loss aid, its impact beyond the benefits listed above should not be oversold. One caveat: Since vitamin C interferes with the absorption of chromium, the two should not be taken together.

Selenium. Several studies over the past few years have shown that selenium, a trace metal and a potent antioxidant, can significantly reduce the risk of prostate, and possibly colon and pancreatic, cancers. The average dose is usually 200 to 400 micrograms per day (one or two tablets).

Chapter Six

Nutrition, Lifestyle, and Cancer

The breasts, colon, lungs, and prostate are now the most common sites of human cancers, accounting for almost 90 percent of all cancer deaths in adult Americans and most Western societies. Because of the vast improvement in treatment options, death rates (deaths per one thousand affected persons) from these cancers have steadily declined over the past three decades. However, because of a significant increase in the size of our population, especially of those forty-five and older (who are at higher risk), the annual number of new cases of these cancers, and the deaths from them, has risen considerably. *Incredibly, the majority of these cancers are preventable!*

Nutritional and lifestyle modifications are the foundation of cancer prevention. The idea of cancer prevention through diet has enormous appeal, and you may be one of the many people who avidly follow the news on any aspect of the diet-cancer relationship. Unfortunately, quite often the information provided by the news media and especially the Internet may be preliminary, fragmented, based on animal experiments, or in conflict with other reported studies. Quite often pharmaceutical companies through their "advertorials," advertisements packaged in popular magazines to look like real articles, feed consumers sound bites about this or the other new "breakthroughs" in cancer therapy. And quite often, their aim is self-serving and focused on pumping up their Wall Street appeal and higher share prices. They often sell consumers hope and hoax, not information.

Most foods have carcinogens (cancer-causing ingredients) as well as anticarcinogens, cancer promoters (which enhance the growth and spread of a cancer that has already started) and antipromoters. But when subjected to stomach acid and all the digestive enzymes in the intestine, most (though certainly not all) carcinogens change, break down, or are destroyed. *So what is a carcinogen or an anticarcinogen in a test tube or in rats is often neither in humans.*

Another common misperception is that a carcinogen is a compound or chemical substance that causes cancer in humans. In fact the carcinogenic potential of chemical compounds, including drugs and foods, is tested on single cells such as bacteria or cultured animal cells, and occasionally in rodents. These experiments do not take into account the endless number of biochemical reactions within the human digestive tract, or the vast number of redundant systems in the human body for dealing with a carcinogen after it is absorbed from the intestine.

Setting aside the role of polyunsaturated fats (such as vegetable oils) or trans-fatty acids (in margarines, shortenings, cooking fats, deep-fried foods, or pastries), our daily exposure to dietary carcinogens is trivial and of little or no consequence; otherwise we wouldn't be around to talk about it. So what is carcinogenic to a rat or a mouse in laboratory experiments, and at daily doses fifty to one hundred times greater than what we would ever be exposed to, is not relevant to humans.

Even fruits and vegetables contain test-tube carcinogens. Potatoes, for example, have several carcinogens, but as with all other foods these carcinogens are present in such small quantities that you'd need to eat about fifty to seventy potatoes daily for several months before getting a significant dose of them. Even then, the human digestive tract and liver would deactivate nearly all of these carcinogens on a continuous basis, reducing them to trivial levels.

We are often warned about the nitrites in processed meats such as bacon or sausages. Yet human saliva contains more nitrites than an average serving of these foods. The human stomach, too, produces nitrites at concentrations much higher than are present in any food. Some "cancer in every bite" zealots scare the daylights out of people by claiming that food additives are potent carcinogens. In fact, 98 percent of food additives consist of sugar, corn sweeteners, and salt. The highest risk for any cancer from a *lifelong exposure* to a food additive such as dye 19 is approximately one in nine million. If we apply this purely theoretical number to the current U.S. population of 285 million, over the next eighty years dye 19 may cause approximately thirty-five cancers. Of course, this assumes a daily intake of dye 19 from birth to the age of eighty in all Americans, a most unlikely scenario. By comparison, tobacco-related deaths over the same eighty years will exceed thirty-five million, assuming that only about 25 percent of adults will remain smokers (which is the current rate). You see how sometimes people take things out of context, or focus on a single tree, not the forest?

How Do We Get Cancer?

Humans have approximately thirty-five thousand pairs of genes in every cell. These genes are like microscopic switches that turn on or off various functions of our cells. Among these genes, there are fifty pairs that reduce the susceptibility of our cells to various carcinogens, or quickly repair any cell damage done by carcinogens. They are called cancer-protective genes. Unfortunately, sometimes carcinogens can damage (cause muta-

174

tions in) these cancer-protective genes, rendering them ineffective. In the absence of functional cancer-protective and repair genes, carcinogens—whether physical (such as ultraviolet rays or radiation), chemical (such as ingredients in tobacco smoke, or other chemical compounds), or viral (see box)—can damage our cells and set in motion the transformation of a normal cell into a wild and out-of-control cancer cell.

We know that *certain cancers are provoked or caused by viruses*. Some examples include certain acute leukemias (cancers of red or white blood cells), lymphomas (cancers of lymph nodes), liver cancer (caused by hepatitis viruses B and C), cancer of the uterine cervix (caused by herpes viruses), and Kaposi's sarcoma (caused by the AIDS virus). In the U.S. and most developed countries, viral cancers account for less than 10 percent of all human cancers. A few other cancers, such as those of the brain, bones, kidneys, and pancreas, are still enigmas that we have not solved.

So, Is There a Diet-Cancer Connection?

The answer is a strong affirmative. On the one hand, long-term nutritional and lifestyle intervention enables us to block the start or "initiation" of cancer cells by preventing damage to our cancer-protective genes. On the other hand, long-term exposure to dietary carcinogens and a sedentary life-style significantly decrease the ability of our various tissues, especially breast, colon, lung and prostate tissues, to mount an effective defense against carcinogens or to repair the damage. This is an enormously important point to keep in mind because once a cell makes its transformation into a cancerous cell, nutritional and lifestyle modifications can do very little to reverse what has already taken place. However, we may still be able to alter the speed with which these cancer cells grow or spread to other sites.

The 90 Percent Solution

Over five hundred thousand Americans die each year of various cancers, 90 percent of which are in four sites; the breast, colon, lungs, and prostate. *Incredibly, 90% preventable!* The problem is that we are a nation of disease-oriented, not prevention-minded, people. What we must do is to change our mind-set of focusing all our resources and fund-raising activities on the treatment of cancers, and think of preemption and prevention. *Here is what you can do.*

Breast cancer. A large number of studies have shown that adding *omega-6 polyunsaturated* fatty acids (omega-6 PUFA) and trans-fatty acids (TFA) to the diet of laboratory animals *can significantly increase the risk of chemically induced breast cancer.*

176

For example, in a recent study, 80 percent of rats given a breast carcinogen and fed a chow enriched with corn oil (mostly omega-6 PUFA) developed breast cancers, compared with 20 percent of similarly treated animals that were fed a mix of monounsaturates and saturated fats. Moreover, the corn oil group had 300 percent more tumors than the other group.

Other studies have shown that a diet enriched with omega-6 PUFA (vegetable oils and fats) promotes the growth and spread (metastasis) of experimentally induced breast cancers in rodents. Cancer's invasive nature is caused by a significant increase in the activity of certain enzymes within the cells. These enzymes dissolve adjacent structures, enabling the cancer cells to invade blood vessels, enter the bloodstream, and travel to and grow at other sites. *Omega-6 PUFA and TFA increase the activity of these enzymes, whereas omega-3 PUFA (from seafood) decrease it.*

What about human breast cancer? A large body of evidence over the past decade points to transfatty acids and omega-6 PUFA as major culprits in human breast cancer. In a recent study, biopsies of fatty tissues of the buttocks were obtained from seven hundred postmenopausal women with breast cancer and women of the same age without breast cancer. Women with the highest levels of TFA in their buttocks had a 40 percent higher risk of breast cancer than women with the lowest levels. These findings were confirmed in another large study. (Since fatty tissues represent a stable reservoir that reflects the long-term use of various fats including TFA, they provide a more accurate record than dietary history, which is subject to recall errors.)

Numerous studies over the past fifteen years have shown that a high intake of dietary omega-6 PUFA not only increases the risk of breast cancer, but it can potentially enhance its progression and distant metastasis. In contrast, recent studies from the U.S., Spain, Italy, Greece, and Sweden have shown that a high dietary intake of monounsaturated fats such as olive or canola oil significantly reduces the risk of breast cancer. For example, in a recent Swedish study, more than sixty-one thousand women forty to seventy-six years of age were observed for an average of four and a half years. *A high dietary intake of monounsaturated fats was associated with a 20 percent lower risk of breast cancer, whereas women with a high intake of omega-6 polyunsaturated fats had a 20 percent higher risk.* In other words, there was a 40 percent difference between the monounsaturated group and the group consuming high levels of omega-6 PUFA. The available data suggest that monounsaturates improve the resistance of breast tissue against the damaging effects of carcinogens and the oxidants they produce.

Olive oil, with its abundant antioxidants and flavonoid compounds, may have a small additional anticancer benefit beyond its monounsaturated fat. In a recent Italian study, 2,569 women with breast cancer were compared with 2,588 age-matched women who did not have breast cancer. Women with the highest olive oil consumption had a 30 percent lower risk of breast cancer, a slightly higher protection (an additional 10 percent) than was shown in the Swedish study. *Numerous studies have also shown that high consumption of seafood (omega-3 PUFA) is associated with a consistent and strong protective role against breast cancer.*

What other nutritional and lifestyle factors can impact the risk of breast cancer? Heavy alcohol consumption (more than two drinks per day) can increase the risk of breast cancer by more than 20 percent, more so in smokers. A high intake of calories per day and abdominal obesity also increase the risk by nearly 30 percent. On the other hand, as noted in chapter 7, regular vigorous exercises

---

*Thus a woman who follows **the Total Health Impact Diet,** is physically active, does not have significant abdominal obesity, is a nonsmoker, drinks lightly, and eats very little vegetable oil, margarine, shortening, cooking fats, or foods and snacks prepared with these fats, but eats three or four seafood meals a week, uses olive oil for all her cooking or baking needs, eats plenty of dark fruits and vegetables, and takes a folic acid supplement of 1 to 2 milligrams per day can slash her risk of breast cancer by more than 90 percent! These doable preventive measures are even more compelling if you have a family history of breast, ovary, or colon cancer. (See tables 66 and 67 below)*

Table 66
Impact of Weight and Physical Activity on Cancer Rates

Cancer	Overweight % Increased Risk	Physical Activity % Decreased Risk
Breast	25 to 30	30 to 40
Colon	15 to 30	40 to 70
Lung	5 to 10	30 to 40
Prostate	5 to 10	10 to 30

can reduce the risk by 50%. In addition, 1 to 2 milligrams a day of folic acid, can also reduce the risk by more than 50 percent.

(For a discussion of the fears and the facts of hormone replacement therapy and its possible contribution to breast cancer risk, please see my book *Every Heart Attack Is Preventable*.)

Colon Cancer. In experimental studies, *omega-6 PUFA and TFA* consistently increase the risk of colon cancer in laboratory animals. However, *human* studies have not shown a consistent or robust link between omega-6 PUFA and the *initiation* of colon cancer. On the other hand, a large number of studies suggest that heavy consumption of *these fats can promote the growth and metastasis of colon cancers*. Omega-6 PUFA and TFA reduce the ability of certain scavenger (defensive) cells in the liver, called *Kupffer cells*, to adhere to and gobble up metastatic cells that reach the liver via the bloodstream. Thus some cancer cells can settle and multiply in the liver or move to other organs. *Monounsaturated fat and seafood omega-3 fats reduce the unregulated overgrowth of colon cells, the primary event in polyp formation and its subsequent progression to cancer.*

Red meat and colon cancer. An extensive review of more than one hundred recent reports suggests that *heavy consumption* of read meat (beef, pork, and lamb) may increase the risk of colon cancer. It is not clear, however, if this is due to factors other than the red meat or any ingredients therein. The high-temperature grilling, frying, or broiling of red meats produces compounds called *heterocyclic amines (HCAs)*, which some studies have suggested can damage the DNA of colon cells and

Seventy percent of us have an enzyme system in our bodies called a *slow-acetylator* system, and the other 30 percent have a *rapid-acetylator* system. Only those with the rapid-acetylator system can activate HCAs, whereas the slow acetylators cannot, and therefore would not be at risk at all no matter how much red meat they eat. (The acetylator status can be determined by blood test through most reputable laboratories.) Unless you happen to know that you have the slow-acetylator type, preheat your steak in a microwave oven for one to two minutes before cooking to substantially reduce the meat's creatine, the amino acid that is an important building block of HCAs.

initiate carcinogenesis. However, fish and chicken cooked at high heat also produce high levels of HCAs, but they do not increase the risk of colon polyps or cancer. It turns out that the amount of HCAs produced during cooking is nearly one thousand times smaller than the dose necessary to cause colon cancer in animals. Gastrointestinal enzymes also denature a large proportion of these HCAs. Yet among forty-eight recent studies, *high consumption* of red meat was associated with an average 35 percent increase in the risk of colon cancer, whereas *white-meat and fish consumption reduced the risk.*

So why does high consumption of red meats increase the risk of colon cancer? Aside from HCAs in people with a rapid-acetylator system, one other explanation is that consumption of red meat and processed meats such as hot dogs and sausages increases the production of carcinogenic nitrites in the colon (by bacterial action on the meat proteins that pass into the colon) by 300 percent to 500 percent compared with white meats.

Another important finding among heavy red-meat eaters is that they frequently eat very little fruit, vegetables, or seafood, depriving themselves of the antioxidant and anticarcinogenic benefits of these nutrients. For example, although the consumption of red meat in the United Kingdom fell by 28 percent from 1970 to 1990, the incidence of colon cancer actually rose by 15 percent. However, during the same period, consumption of green leafy vegetables fell by 28 percent and fresh fruit by 9 percent. In effect, the high intake of red meat is often a surrogate or marker for other unhealthy dietary practices.

In a recent study by the U.S. National Cancer Institute, 33,971 adults without colon polyps or cancer were compared with 3,591 who had one or more colon polyps/cancer. The risk of colon cancer was 30 percent less among those with the highest fruit and vegetable consumption than among those with the lowest intake.

What other nutritional and lifestyle factors can impact colon cancer? A large number of studies have shown that *dairy products, especially milk and yogurt,* significantly reduce the risk of colon cancer. This protective role is in part due to a balanced mix of calcium and phosphates in dairies, and the desirable organisms (such as lactobacillus bacteria) in yogurt that would populate the colon. *Light to moderate alcohol intake* (less than three drinks per day) and *a low-dose aspirin* (81 milligrams per day) are also associated with a 30 percent risk reduction each. *Folic acid, at 1,000 to 2,000 micrograms per day (1 to 2 milligrams), can also reduce the risk by an additional 50 percent.* Calcium supplements can lower the risk of colon cancer by a small 7 percent to 10 percent, but neither vitamin C nor E has been shown to have a significant protective role against colon (or other major) cancers.

Finally, of all cancers, the most definitive evidence for the effectiveness of regular exercise in preventing cancer exists for colon cancer. Of fifty-

> Thus, *following the nutritional and lifestyle changes presented here, taking a low-dose (81 milligram) aspirin daily, folic acid (1 to 2 milligrams per day), and selenium (200 micrograms per day), with or without one to two drinks a day, and having regular colon examinations (colonoscopies) to remove any polyps reduces your risk of colon cancer by 90 percent!*

one studies conducted to date on the link between colon cancer and exercise, forty-three demonstrated *a robust risk reduction averaging 50 percent, and in some studies up to 70 percent!*

Lung Cancer. The risk of lung cancer in a long-term heavy smoker (about one pack or more per day) is 1,000 percent greater than in a nonsmoker. Since more than 90 percent of lung cancers are tobacco-related, a single act of self-defense—quitting the habit—can reduce your risk by 90 percent! Although the reduction in lung cancer risk requires seven to ten years of staying "clean," the cardiovascular risk reduction starts within a week of quitting the habit. Either way, you win! In addition to not smoking, you should also adhere to my previous recommendations to protect yourself against other cancers and chronic diseases.

You can get additional protection from *increasing tomato products* in the diet, and taking *supplemental lycopene (the most important anticarcinogen in tomatoes), 20 milligrams per day*, but these are not substitutes for quitting the habit. (Also see tables 67 and 68.) Note that in two large long-term studies of smokers, vitamins C and E supplementation not only had no benefit; they actually *increased* the risk of lung cancer.

Prostate cancer. Both experimental and human studies have suggested that trans-fatty acids and omega-6 PUFA increase the risk of prostate cancer, but the data are not as robust as those for breast cancer. Numerous studies suggest that supplemental *selenium, a mineral, 200 to 400 micrograms per day, may reduce the risk of prostate cancer by more than 50 percent. Folic acid and lycopene can also reduce the risk by more than 30 percent each.* Thus, collectively, the combination of *THI* nutritional and lifestyle modifications suggested previously, along with selenium, folic acid, and lycopene, should reduce the risk of prostate cancer by 90 percent! *To achieve these high success rates, start all these preventive measures early; don't wait until you are in your late fifties or sixties.* (Also see tables 66 and 67.)

Table 67
Impact of Various Nutrients on Human Cancers

NUTRIENT	BREAST	COLON	LUNG	PROSTATE
SFA	0	0	0	0
Omega-6 PUFA	+++	++	0	++
TFA	+++	++	0	++
Omega-3 PUFA	—	—	0	—
MUFA	—	—	0	—
F & V	—	—	0	—
Folic Acid	—	—	0	-
Selenium	—	—	0	—
Lycopene	0	—	—	-
Vitamins C & E	0	—	+	-
Calcium	0	-	0	0
Dairies	0	-	0	0

SFA = saturated fatty acids   PUFA = polyunsaturated fatty acids
TFA = trans-fatty acids   MUFA = monounsaturated fatty acids
F & V = fruits & vegetables   0 = no effect   + = increases the risk
- = decreases the risk

Chapter Seven

Thirty-four Reasons to Exercise

In the past decade, numerous studies have reaffirmed what everyone intuitively knows: Vigorous, regular exercise has a vast number of health benefits (see table 68). In contrast, a sedentary lifestyle contributes to a vast number of chronic diseases. **The U.S. Centers for Disease Control and Prevention attributes more than 250,000 deaths each year to lack of regular physical activity.** Regular exercise is not just for healthy young people. It is even more important for adults of all ages, including older persons, with or without weight problems, diabetes, abnormal blood cholesterol, coronary artery disease, high blood pressure, osteoporosis, or a predisposition to various cancers. According to a new report from the U.S. Department of Health and Human Services, sedentary lifestyles associated with the overweight or obesity cost about 120 billion dollars annually.

A large number of studies across all ethnic groups and ages, men and women, the overweight and the healthy-weight, and people with and without coexisting health problems have shown that *better physical and cardiorespiratory fitness is associated with greater longevity and positive aging*. The link between survival and physical fitness is almost linear. For example, in a recent Stanford University study, 6,213 men with an average age of fifty-nine were divided into two groups: 3,679 who had abnormal exercise electrocardiograms (EECGs) indicative of various cardiovascular diseases, and 2,534 who had normal EECGs and no cardiovascular disease. In both groups, *those with the highest cardiovascular or physical fitness had survival rates that were two to three times higher than persons with very low physical fitness*.

A recent study by researchers at the Harvard School of Public Health showed that long-term sedentary behaviors, especially TV watching, were associated with a significantly elevated risk of obesity and type II cardiovascular diseases and Type II diabetes. For example, each two-hour/day increment in TV watching increased the risk of obesity by 23 percent and the risk of diabetes by 14 percent. Each two-hour/day increment in sitting at work increased the risk of obesity and diabetes by 5 percent and 7 percent respectively.

Several studies in the past few years have shown similar benefits in women, with or without a weight problem or cardiovascular disorders. In a long-term Harvard study of more than eighty thousand female nurses, regular physical activity along with some dietary modification reduced the rate of diabetes by 91 percent compared with sedentary lifestyles and a western-type diet. *Numerous studies have also shown that regular exercises reduce the risk of breast cancer by 50 percent, colon cancer by 40 to 70 percent, and prostate cancer by 30 percent.* In other words, physical fitness means more disease-free years of life and positive aging.

Many exercise enthusiasts and self-appointed exercise gurus overplay and highly exaggerate the weight-reducing benefits of exercise. Although rigorous and sustained exercises such as jogging, basketball, racquetball, and cross-country skiing can significantly increase the amount of calories we burn, let's be realistic. How many overweight people do you know who engage in these activities on a regular basis? Furthermore, a large number of people with weight problems also have various physical limitations such as osteoarthritis of the hips or knees, or lack of cardiorespiratory fitness, all of which make such exercises impractical or even dangerous. And regrettably, there are also people who just don't like to exercise!

If you have a weight problem, exercising alone

Table 68
34 Reasons Why You Should Exercise
on a Regular Basis

System	Benefits of Regular, Vigorous Exercise
	Decreases
Cardiovascular	-Risk of heart attack by 50%
	-Risk of stroke by > 35%
	-"Bad" LDL cholesterol by 10–15%
	-Triglycerides by 20–30%
	-Abdominal obesity
	-Risk of diabetes by 60% in men & 90% in women
	-Blood pressure
	-Blood fibrinogen (a potent clotting factor)
	-Insulin resistance
	-Number of small, harmful LDL particles
	Increases
	-"Good" HDL cholesterol by 10–20%
	-TPA (A potent clot buster) in the blood by >20%
	Decreases
Anticancer	-Risk of breast cancer by 50%
	-Risk of colon cancer by 50%
	-Risk of prostate cancer by > 30%
	-Risk of lung/ovary/pancreas/uterus cancers by 10–20%
	Decreases
	-Risk of premature aging
	-Weight regain after weight loss
	-Risk of depression & anxiety disorders
	-Risk of various infections
	-Muscle wasting

System	Benefits of Regular, Vigorous Exercise
	Decreases *(cont.)*
Other	-Osteoarthritis
	-Osteoporosis
	-Chronic fatigue syndrome
	-Risk of dementia
	-Constipation and irritable bowel
	Increases
	-Stamina
	-Well-being
	-Sexual functioning
	-Self-esteem
	-Muscle tone
	-Lean body mass
	-Healthful longevity
	-Immune system functioning

won't help you lose a significant amount of weight. You still need to cut down your total caloric intake, in particular the portion that comes from starches, vegetable fats (margarines, shortenings, and cooking fats), and saturated fats from greasy red meats, butter, cream, and processed meats and cheeses. When you lose weight, only 60 percent of the weight loss is from body fat; 30 percent is due to the loss of lean body mass (all tissues except fat), and another 10 percent is water. Regular exercise helps minimize muscle wasting, tones up the muscles to give you a trimmer and more physically fit body, and prevents weight regain and weight cycling.

The Vulnerable "Weekend Athlete"

The quote "He who rests, rots!" is attributed to Arthur Fiedler, the late conductor of the Boston Pops. Unfortunately, we are a nonexercising nation! Incredibly, only 8 percent of American men and 3 percent of American women engage in regular, vigorous physical activities and follow a healthy, prudent diet. Many Europeans are just as sedentary, and the problem is now widespread among the more affluent people in less developed countries, contributing to their epidemics of diabetes and cardiovascular diseases.

Some people occasionally "get out to get the oxygen going." They often act on impulses triggered by the "right" mood, weather, or opportunity. Unfortunately, *occasional bursts of exercise not only are useless, but may also be harmful*. Weekend athletes and occasional exercisers suffer more aches and pains, pulled muscles, shin splints, hairline fractures of arms and legs, and fasciitis of the soles of their feet than regular exercisers. They also take an unacceptably high risk of suffering a catastrophic cardiovascular event, such as a fatal or nonfatal heart attack.

To be sure, the risk of an exercise-induced heart attack in fit persons is extremely low. But people who are moderately to severely obese, those with various risk factors for coronary artery disease and heart attacks (table 2), sedentary people, and those with other chronic disorders often lack physical and certainly cardiovascular fitness.

Overall, 4 percent to 20 percent of all heart attacks (fatal and nonfatal) occur after a bout of moderate to heavy exertion, especially among the least fit individuals. For example, the risk of a heart attack after a bout of strenuous physical activity such as snow shoveling for a fifty-year-old, sedentary, out-of-shape man is more than 10,000 percent greater than for a regularly exercising and well-conditioned man of the same age.

Oxidization of the bad LDL cholesterol in the bloodstream and within the wall of our coronary arteries is the earliest event that damages the lining of the arteries and eventually causes a heart attack. *Short bursts of exercises in unconditioned and infrequent exercisers increase the oxidization of LDL cholesterol.* This is because an unconditioned person produces a large amount of oxidants (or free radicals) during these occasional bouts. However, the body of a regular, fit exerciser produces far fewer oxidants, but generates plenty of antioxidants.

How Much, How Often, and What Kind of Exercise?

Exercises do not have to be rigorous or very long, certainly not in the first several weeks. Even light to moderate exercise begins to pay dividends within a short time—some tangible and visible, others intangible but just as important. Although *the benefits of exercises will increase with intensity and duration,* even briefer and less intensive exercises are still helpful. Certainly exercise regimens must be individualized and intensified slowly. They should take into account such factors as age, weight, coexistent cardiovascular and degenerative joint diseases, the environment (heat, humidity, or chill factor), equipment or facility cost, as well as the availability of various sports clubs, gyms, city/county recreational centers, or even safe neighborhoods and streets.

I often hear people say, "I just don't have the time to exercise." Almost always what they mean is that they don't have a convenient time. Before you say or even think that you have the same problem, let's look at it from a different perspective. There are 1,440 minutes to each 24 hours. You should be able to come up with 40 to 60 of those minutes every day, or certainly four to five times a week, to spend on your health, your weight, and your quality of life. Forty minutes less TV, Internet, chatting, shopping, sleeping, or "vegging out" is what your body has been begging for. This is where you need to draw the line, *today! It's not going to get any easier tomorrow, next week, or next month than it is right now.*

The body resets its energy-burning mechanisms after a certain period of regular exercise, usually within several weeks, so that we begin to burn less energy (calories) for the same amount or type of exercise. This adaptive catch-22 obviously reduces the impact of exercise as a weight-reducing tool. It also explains why some people cannot lose weight even though they continue to exercise on a regular basis. That does not mean it's okay to stop exercising! It simply reemphasizes the importance of a dual approach—both dietary intervention and exercise—to weight management.

Another common reason for the failure of exercise to help people lose weight is that *people sometimes sabotage or negate the benefits of exercise by overeating*. It is counterproductive (and often incorrect) to assume that you burn off the "reward" calories, or to tell yourself, "I lost fat and gained muscle." Remember we gain and lose both fat and lean body mass. Many 300-plus-pound offensive and defensive linemen in American football with massive abdominal obesity (and an extremely high risk for diabetes and premature cardiovascular events) are overcompensating and overeating exercisers.

We do not have a biological bank somewhere in our bodies where we can store the benefits of any good deed: nutritional, lifestyle or any other. It would be very nice indeed if that were the case; we could eat properly or exercise adequately for a month or two, then fall off the wagon while still being able to withdraw the dividends of our short-term good behavior. Unfortunately, the benefits of exercise fade quickly, usually in less than twenty-four hours.

An estimated thirty-four million Americans belong to a health or sports club. Regrettably, membership doesn't mean active membership; people join these clubs (more so in winter months), and then within several weeks they gradually slacken or stop going with any regularity even though they keep paying their monthly dues. Many sports club personnel suggest that all you need is two or three sessions a week. This is often an economic, not a health-based, recommendation. It is designed to avoid overcrowding the premises so other clients won't be turned off or turned away. Some physicians or other health care providers also make a similar mistake, but their reason is primarily misinformation. To derive the benefits listed in table 68 and to increase your energy expenditure, you should exercise at least four or five days a week, and preferably every day.

Each exercise session, from the warm-up to the end of the cooldown, should be about an hour long, for a total of approximately four to five hours a week. Even though the benefits of exercises are both time and intensity dependent, do not jump into your exercise routine without a warm-up, especially if you are past the age of forty. You should always allow several minutes for a slow warm-up and stretching, and for a cooldown. To "save" time, many novice exercisers ignore this advice, ending up with various preventable musculoskeletal injuries.

How Many Calories Do We Burn with Various Exercises?

Although calorie counting is often a waste of time and nearly always inaccurate, I have listed the average calories you *may* burn by various exercises in table 69. Keep in mind that these averages are obtained by testing a small number of young, healthy, and usually fit people. They do not apply to everyone, particularly to people with weight problems or cardiovascular disease, or those who are out of shape. The number of calories you burn during any activity varies greatly from day to day, and depends on how intensely you do it. These numbers also vary from person to person, by gender *(women burn approximately 20 percent to 30 percent fewer calories doing the same exercises than men)*, and by age (younger people burn more).

The number of calories burned during exercise also depends on your weight (body mass index), the amount of muscle you have, even the time of day (you burn more calories in the morning than you do at night), the ambient temperature, the incline of the street or treadmill or the resistance of the bike pedals, and your adeptness at exercise. For example, good swimmers are very efficient with their strokes, and burn far fewer calories than the novice (or poor) swimmer who struggles and thrashes with every muscle just to stay afloat. Poor swimmers may burn two or three times as many calories to swim for the same ten or twenty minutes as the good swimmers, which explains in part why poor swimmers can quickly get exhausted. Similarly, good tennis players don't flail and chase the ball all over the court when a smooth glide of the feet or a flip of the racket accomplishes the same objective. Keep in mind that if you weigh more than 200 pounds (or have a body mass index greater than 30), the calories you burn with any of these activities are about 20 percent to 30 percent lower than the listed numbers. (See table 70 for healthy weight and body mass index).

In practical terms, these numbers can give you a rough estimate of how hard it is to burn surplus calories. In fact, it is a lot harder than you think. For example, a Double Whopper with Cheese Sandwich (Burger King) has 950 calories. You'd have to pedal for approximately one and a half hours on the bike to burn off those calories. Add another forty-five minutes to an hour if you have fries and a Coke! You don't even want to know how many hours of walking you'd have to do to get rid of those calories (if you insist, the answer is more than three hours for the Whopper alone!).

What Kind of Exercise?

The simplest and the correct answer to "What kind of exercises should I do?" is whatever activities or exercises you can do, or are available to you! You can choose among a variety of activities listed in table 69 that you feel comfortable with. Or you can choose two or three, and cross-train on alternating days. Choosing different workouts has the added advantage of exercising different muscle groups, and reduces the likelihood of getting bored with the same routines day in and day out. *What is important is not the type of exercise(s) you choose, but whether you are likely to stay with it.* You also need to factor in all the variables listed above to match the right exercises to any limitations or health issues you might have.

Before you even think of buying exercise equipment or joining a sports club, start by walking about a mile or so every day, do some low-impact exercises (there are numerous versions on video for rent), choose any other light activity that you like, or join any group exercise program that does not require long-term membership. You may find that you enjoy these activities to the point that you might not even need expensive exercise equipment or a sports club.

Of course, if you have some degenerative joint disease of your knees or hips, you shouldn't jog on neighborhood streets or the treadmill; an elliptical exerciser is more suited to your needs. Elliptical exercisers are pedaling machines that do not involve lifting the feet and provide reasonable, weight-bearing workouts, even for people with knee problems. In addition, these machines offer an arms-and-upper-body workout, a feature that makes them even more attractive.

TABLE 69
Energy Expenditure of Common Activities
Calories per Minute*

	Men	Women
Sleeping or lying down	1.5	1
Sitting & watching TV or reading	1.5	1
Standing (salesperson)	2	1.5
Driving a car	2	1.5
House chores/gardening	3	2.5
Biking (easy gears)	3.5	3
Walking (20 min/mi)	3.5	3
Mowing (self-propelled)	4	3.5
Golf (not using the cart)	4	3.5
Softball/baseball/tennis (doubles)	4	3.5
Swimming (good swimmers)	5	4.5
Walking (15 min/mi—flat surface)	5	4.5
Square dancing	6	5
Volleyball	6	5
Skating	6	5
Ping-Pong (table tennis)	6	5
Tennis (singles)	7	6
Exercise bicycle (medium)	7	5
Skiing (without too many stops)	10	8
Swimming (novice swimmers)	10	8
Stair climber (light)	10	8
Biking (low gears)	11	9
Exercise bicycle (hard)	12	10
Treadmill & elliptical exercisers (light)	14	11
Soccer	15	12
Basketball	16	13
Rowing	16	13
Running (10 min/mi)	16	13
Treadmill (10 min/mi)	16	13
Stair climber (hard)	17	14

* Factors listed in the text can change these numbers by ± 30 percent.

Do not go out and buy an exercise bike, a rowing machine, a treadmill, or anything else (or join a sports club with hefty membership dues) in the first month or two. Too many of these impulsive and emotional purchases, no matter how sincere your intentions or commitment, end up gathering dust somewhere in the house or the apartment, usually within a few short weeks. *Wait* until you have gone through your initiation phase (at least a few weeks); then you can decide whether you need to buy exercise equipment or join a club. By then, you should have visited a couple of fitness stores or sports clubs, tried different exercise equipment, and figured out which equipment is most suitable.

It is a major mistake to buy cheap exercise equipment. Don't do it! To enhance your well-being, and to dramatically reduce your risk of a host of chronic disorders and cancers, you need to exercise regularly on a long-term basis. Thus, you should opt for durable exercise equipment that you can use for a long time, not something that may be difficult to use, unstable, boring, noisy, or liable to fall apart in a few months. In general, people are less likely to abandon or give away their treadmills (with useful features and monitors) or elliptical exercisers than other exercise equipment. But here again, your preference is more important than the advice of an outsider, a friend, or a salesperson.

Aerobic Versus Resistance Exercise

Given the choice between aerobic and resistance exercises (or bodybuilding), you should choose both! Each serves different purposes, all of which are synergistic. Resistance exercises increase lean body mass, reduce insulin resistance (the early stage of diabetes), increase your good HDL cholesterol level, and add tone and firmness to your body. Aerobic exercises, on the other hand, improve your cardiovascular fitness, help you with your weight loss efforts, and reduce your risk of diabetes, cancers (of the breast, colon, and prostate), osteoporosis, dementia, and other serious conditions.

For most sedentary people, the cardiovascular benefits of exercise start when they begin regular light exercise to reach and sustain a heart rate of about 40 percent of their maximum capacity. The weight reduction benefit also starts at about the 40 percent capacity level and increases progressively. The maximum heart rate is calculated by subtracting your age from 220.

For people without a significant cardiovascular contraindication, a reasonable guide for moderate-intensity exercises is to raise the heart rate to 60 percent to 80 percent of your age-adjusted maximum heart rate, and maintain it at that level for thirty to forty-five minutes. For example, the maximum heart rate for a forty-five-year-old person is 220 − 45 = 175. The desirable exercise pulse rate for this person then is 105 (60 percent of 175) to 140 (80 percent of 175).

Of course, this guide is not applicable to people with certain cardiovascular diseases, or to sedentary people whose pulses jump to 140 when they climb one flight of stairs. For these individuals, it is safer to start at a slower pace of about 40 percent of their maximum capacity, gradually increasing it over the next several weeks as tolerated.

To be effective, exercise should be sustained for thirty to forty-five minutes, not including the five-to-10-minute warm-up and cooldown time. Window-shopping, taking the pooch out for a walk, getting yourself wet in the pool and stretching out to sunbathe, routine house chores, painting leisurely, walking back and forth, and even going up and down the stairs to do chores at home or at work have too many interruptions to achieve the desired benefits. People sometimes argue that these activities are better than nothing. Well, something barely better than nothing is unlikely to have a significant health benefit. A few reasonable exercises include brisk walking, jogging, biking, lap swimming, aquatic exercises, Jazzercise or "dancercise" classes, and other aerobic exercises, preferably combined with some resistance exercises.

Power Bars, Power Drinks, and Power Powders . . .

An average-size adult stores about one kilogram (2.2 lb) of glucose as glycogen in the liver and muscles (chapter two). This amount of glycogen provides sufficient energy for muscles and other organs for three hours of moderate to intense exercises. With the exception of marathoners or other elite athletes, more than 99.9% of adults in the U.S. or elsewhere do not spend three or more hours a day at this type of exercising. *So why would anyone need a power or energy bar? The answer is unequivocal; no one needs these useless products!*

Power bars (or powders or drinks) with a few exceptions have high concentrations of fat (including saturated or trans-fatty acids), carbohydrates (mostly sugar or corn sweetener), low quality proteins, and an occasional touch of this or that vitamin. The purpose of exercising is the vast benefits listed in table 68, but not to add another 200 to 300 more calories along with a big dose of sugar and harmful fats to your diet. As you can see on page 205, the majority of these products have unacceptably high THI scores (for a snack), making them quite undesirable. Importantly, they have no magical ingredients (regardless of their deceptive advertisements) to make them any better than a glorified and expensive candy bar (some bars cost $2 to $2.50 each). Why would you want to eat a big candy bar when you are trying to lose weight and enhance your health? A healthful and far superior "power" snack (assuming that there is ever any need for it) is 10 to 20 pieces of chocolate raisins or chocolate almonds, or raisins mixed with some nuts such as almonds, hazelnut, pistachios or walnut.

The THI Scores of "Power" Bars

Atkins Advantage*	+13	Kellogg's Krave*	+9
Balance*	+9	Kellogg's Nutri Grain	+3
Carb Solutions*	+5	Kudos (choc. chip)*	+7
Cliff Bar	+4	Met-RX Protein Plus*	+8
Cliff Luna*	+6	Nature Valley (Granola)	+2
Dr. Soy*	+7	Powerbar Harvest*	+6
EAS Advant-Edge*	+8	Powerbar Performance	+3
Ensure (choc. peanut)*	+11	Powerbar Pria*	+6
Gatorade (chocolate)*	+5	Powerbar Protein Plus*	+8
General Mills (Honey Nut)*	+5	Quaker Low Fat Granola	+2
Geni Soy (Ultimate)*	+9	Slim-Fast Choc. Brownie*	+9
Kashi Go Lean*	+13	Zoneperfect*	+8

---

*AVOID

What You Should Do

If someone offered you an easy-to-do, safe, no-cost or very low-cost "treatment" that would reduce your risk of heart attack, stroke, diabetes, and cancers of the breast, colon, and prostate by 30 percent to 50 percent, would you refuse that offer? But there's more: It'll lower your risk of osteoporosis, depression, anxiety disorders, and dementia by more than 50 percent. And it'll help you lose weight, prevent weight regain and muscle wasting, give you firmness and fitness, and improve your immune system and sexual functioning. That marvelous, readily available, life-saving treatment is exercise!

A word of caution: If you are a sedentary person, have any major coronary risk factor listed in table 2, or have a heart or respiratory disease, you must see your physician *before* you start any kind of active or intense workout. You will also require an exercise ECG or an exercise echocardiogram (an ultrasound test of your heart muscle during exercises) to make sure you do not have a significant, albeit silent, cardiovascular disease. Remember, the goal of exercise is to make you healthy (or healthier), without increasing your risk of an exercise-related cardiovascular event. The visit to your health care provider also gives you the opportunity to have a full set of blood tests for the detection of insulin resistance, diabetes, and various coronary risk factors (listed in table 2), and thyroid gland function and blood count.

No matter what kind of exercise you choose, start today, but in small and nonintensive doses. Over the next several weeks, slowly increase both the intensity and the duration of your exercise.

Chapter Eight

The Scientific Principles of Losing Weight Safely

Most people with weight problems are veterans of many weight loss battles with occasional short-term successes and many more retreats to the starting line (about 85 percent of the time) or even greater weight gain. Today nearly two out of three adult Americans, or well over 110 million men and women, and more than 30 million children and adolescents have a weight problem.

For the more than sixty million Americans who have severe weight problems, weight is not just a cosmetic issue. They have a chronic disorder with a visible cosmetic presentation, but it carries a very high risk for various complications, some quite serious.

The majority of these severely obese people and more than one half of those with moderate obesity have an ominous cluster of abnormalities called the *metabolic syndrome*. This is a combination of

It would be ridiculous to turn millions of otherwise healthy people with a slight weight problem into instant patients. But it is negligent to ignore the more severe weight problems with their numerous complications, including diabetes, hypertension, high blood cholesterol, heart attack or heart failure, stroke, liver damage, sexual dysfunctions, degenerative joint disease, social profiling, and stigmatization. More than three hundred thousand Americans die each year of weight-related diseases. This is seven times greater than the number of people who die of breast cancer, and five times higher than the death toll from colon cancer. So ignoring, downplaying, or dismissing weight problems as a cosmetic issue does nothing but perpetuate the problem.

abdominal obesity, abnormal blood cholesterol and triglycerides, hypertension, insulin resistance or diabetes, a sedentary lifestyle, enlargement of the heart and almost always a fatty liver (which may progress to liver failure). In fact, today, nearly 25 percent (one of four) adult Americans has the *metabolic syndrome,* setting the stage for self-perpetuating and simultaneous epidemics of diabetes, cardiovascular diseases, kidney and liver failures, and the addition of millions of medically disabled persons to our already high numbers.

In a recent report, researchers examined the life expectancy of 3,457 participants in the Framingham Heart Study (Massachusetts) who were thirty to forty-nine years of age at enrollment into the study. Life expectancy and the probability of death before seventy years of age were significantly different for obese men and women compared with healthy-weight subjects. In fact, a forty-year-old obese nonsmoker (man or woman) lost an average of seven years of life expectancy because of the weight problem; *smokers lost an average of thirteen and one-half years of life expectancy!*

In a recent American Cancer Society study, nine hundred thousand men and women who were free from cancer at enrollment were followed up for sixteen years. Among the obese members of this study, death rates from cancer were 52 percent higher in men, and 62 percent higher in women. Stomach and prostate cancers in men and cancers of the cervix and ovary in women were most closely associated with severe weight problems.

So why does the public and the health insurance industry still look at weight as a cosmetic issue? Why do we allow unqualified, self-appointed diet gurus to gamble with our lives and trivialize our weight problems with such nonsense as grapefruit, cabbage, or rice diets, this fruit but not that one, this zone or the other, this herb or that supplement, and other gimmicks?

Today, 16 percent (one out of six) children and adolescents in the U.S. are overweight or obese. Obesity among children, especially abdominal obesity, is associated with stiffness and dysfunction of their arteries and abnormal blood cholesterol levels, which predisposes them to premature coronary artery disease, hypertension, and chronic kidney failure. In a report presented at the 2003 annual meeting of the American Heart Association, researchers presented alarming data concerning children and adolescents. Elevated blood pressure was found in 4.4 percent of nine-year-old children, 16.7 percent of thirteen-year-olds, and 19.7 percent of sixteen-year-olds. This trend for hypertension among children was even more alarming in those with moderate to severe weight problems. We now see a large number of children and adolescents with a variety of weight-related diseases that until ten or fifteen years ago were limited to people past the age of forty. Today, for example, more than five hundred thousand youngsters in the U.S. have type II (or maturity onset) diabetes. Fatty liver, a precursor of cirrhosis and liver failure, is also on the rise, raising the fear that as this generation of young people reaches their thirties and forties, we may face an epidemic of liver failures.

The burden of obesity is not just an American or a Western problem. It is also spreading among developing or undeveloped countries, commingled with undernutrition or malnutrition. In China, the obesity rate has tripled among men and doubled among women in the past ten years. A similar trend is spreading across the Indian subcontinent, South America, and Africa. Sugared products, edible vegetable oils and fats, televisions, computers, and E-mail time (instead of outdoor activities) are major contributors to the growing worldwide epidemic. Nearly half of all new cases of diabetes come from China and the Indian subcontinent, whereas ten years ago they were less than 20 percent.

The Origin and Growth of Fat Cells

Where does the surplus fat in your body go? Is there no limit to how much fat we can store? Why do some people gain so much weight while others remain slim? The answers are the size, the number, and most importantly the location of fat cells in our bodies.

Fat cells appear in the human fetus at about the fifteenth week of gestation. For the next eight weeks their numbers increase rapidly and then at a slower pace throughout the remainder of gestation. There is no strong evidence to suggest that children born to overweight or obese parents have more fat cells at birth than other children. From birth until the age of two, fat cells increase in both size and number (assuming the infant has adequate nutrition). The number of fat cells continues to increase slowly in normal-weight youngsters, but much more rapidly in overfed and sedentary children. After the age of fourteen, the number of fat cells remains stable throughout adult life (in people who do not gain a large amount of weight). However, the size of those fat cells may vary by as much as five times in different parts of the body.

On average, a normal-weight person has approximately ten billion fat cells distributed throughout the body. However, the number may range from as low as two billion to well over fifteen billion. Adults who were obese as children or adolescents have a higher number of fat cells, a burden that places them at a great disadvantage. This abundance of fat cells predisposes them to gain weight, and makes losing weight more difficult.

As adults continue to gain weight, their fat cells enlarge to accommodate the extra fat. However, this expansion is not limitless; once the fat cells expand to 170 percent of their original size, they cannot grow any larger. At this point, newer fat cells begin to emerge and take in the surplus fat. *Adults with an increased number of fat cells almost always have a body mass index of well over 30 (they are more than 70 pounds over their healthy weight).* Once those new fat cells appear, they're forever; short of liposuction or removing them by other surgical means (lipectomy), they stay where they are.

Larger and older fat cells are the first to lose any of their fat content when you lose weight; the newer and, therefore, not fully engorged fat cells essentially remain unchanged. On the other hand, as soon as there is any surplus fat, these newer fat cells furiously compete with the original (older) fat cells and ravenously gobble up every last morsel of fat in their path. This mischievous behavior of new fat cells makes successful weight loss and weight maintenance in very heavy people even more difficult, and increases their chance of regaining their lost weight even with minimal dietary or lifestyle infractions.

How Should We Measure Weight?

At present, there is no fully satisfactory way of classifying or defining different types of weight problems. For example, if you are 30 or 40 pounds over your healthy body weight (*let's never say "ideal body weight"*), it makes an enormous difference whether this additional weight is due to an increase in your lean body mass (such as what one might expect in athletes, bodybuilders, and large-framed persons) or is the result of fat accumulation. Also, the *distribution* of fat is even more important than the number of extra pounds. A body fat distribution around the waist and inside the abdomen has a distinctly different relevance to health than that which involves the rest of the body (see below).

Excess body weight is not just due to fat accumulation. When people gain weight, their muscle cells—even the heart muscle cells in those with a severe weight problem—become enlarged (develop hypertrophy). *In fact, as much as 30 percent of the excess weight may be due to an increase in lean body mass* (all tissues, including bones, minus fat).

In addition, up to 10 percent of the weight gain may be due to water retention. Thus, *fat accounts for approximately 60 percent to 70 percent of excess weight*. This is an important point to remember because when you lose weight, you don't just lose fat, you also lose muscle mass and water. The goal of a rational weight reduction program is to maximize fat loss, but keep muscle wasting to a minimum.

1. *Weight on the basis of height.* Although this tool has been popular in the U.S. for several decades, it is a highly inaccurate way of determining or measuring weight problems. Even though tables indicating weight for height are readily available, I won't contribute to our reliance on these arbitrary charts by including one here.

2. *Waist circumference (WC).* The abdominal girth or circumference is perhaps the most useful tool for measuring obesity in a nonpregnant person. The importance of increased abdominal girth (or abdominal obesity) is that *fat cells inside the abdomen and around various organs are distinctly different from fat cells in other parts of our bodies.* One of their major disadvantages is that more than 70 percent of people with moderate to severe abdominal obesity develop *insulin resistance, which may progress to diabetes.*

To measure your waist circumference (WC), stand upright without tucking your tummy in. Use a tape measure around your tummy about 1 inch (2–3 centimeters) below the navel. For men the WC should be less than 40 inches (less than 100 centimeters) and for women less than 36 inches (90 centimeters). A practical way of knowing whether you have abdominal obesity is to stand erect and look down. (Do not tuck your tummy in. It defeats the purpose.) If you can't see your knees, you have abdominal obesity. To compensate for body frame, a 2-inch variation for a large frame, and a negative-2-inch variation for a small frame, are allowed for men and women.

3. *Body mass index (BMI).* The BMI is currently the standard tool for expressing the status of a person's weight, and is used in medical and scientific studies worldwide (though it, too, is imperfect, especially for athletes). To obtain your BMI, divide your body weight in kilograms by the square of your height in meters, or *BMI = W/H x H* (almost all countries except the U.S. use the metric system). To obtain the BMI in pounds and inches, you'd have to use a different formula: First multiply your weight in pounds by 700. Then square your height in inches, and divide the first number by the second (*W x 700/H x H*). Table 70 provides you with an easy tool to determine your own BMI.

The healthy BMI for both men and women ranges from 22 to 25. A BMI of 25 to 30 signifies overweight, and over 30, obesity. These cutoff points roughly correspond to weights of up to 40 pounds, and more than 40 pounds, over healthy body weights, respectively.

Table 70
Body Mass Index (BMI) Based on Weight and Height

BMI	19	20	21	22	23	24	25	26	27	28	29	30	31	32	33	34
Height (Inches)							**Body weight in pounds**									
58	91	96	100	105	110	115	119	124	129	134	138	143	148	153	158	162
59	94	99	104	109	114	119	124	128	133	138	143	148	153	158	163	168
60	97	102	107	112	118	123	128	133	138	143	148	153	158	163	168	174
61	100	106	111	116	122	127	132	137	143	148	153	158	164	169	174	180
62	104	109	115	120	126	131	136	142	147	153	158	164	169	175	180	185
63	107	113	118	124	130	135	141	146	152	157	163	169	175	180	185	191
64	110	116	122	128	134	140	145	151	157	163	169	174	180	186	192	197
65	114	120	126	132	138	144	150	156	162	168	174	180	186	192	198	204
66	118	124	130	136	142	148	155	161	167	173	179	186	192	198	204	210
67	121	127	134	140	146	153	159	166	172	178	185	191	198	204	211	217
68	125	131	138	144	151	158	164	170	177	184	190	197	203	210	216	223
69	128	135	142	149	155	162	169	177	182	189	196	203	209	216	223	230
70	132	139	146	153	160	167	174	181	188	195	202	209	216	222	229	236
71	136	143	150	157	165	172	179	186	193	200	208	215	222	229	236	243
72	140	147	154	162	162	169	177	184	191	206	213	221	228	235	242	250
73	144	151	159	166	174	182	189	197	204	212	219	227	235	242	250	257
74	148	155	163	171	179	186	194	202	210	218	225	233	241	249	256	264
75	152	160	168	176	184	192	200	208	216	224	232	240	248	256	264	272
76	156	164	172	180	189	197	205	213	221	230	238	246	254	263	271	279
77	160	168	177	185	193	202	210	219	227	235	244	252	261	269	278	286
78	164	173	181	190	196	207	216	224	233	242	250	259	268	276	285	293

To calculate any body mass index not listed above; (1) multiply weight (pounds) by 700 (2) multiply height by height (inches). Then divide number 1 by number 2 *(BMI = W x 700/H x H).*

An American Cancer Society study of more than one million adults in the U.S. (457,785 men and 588,369 women) who were followed up for an average of fourteen years showed that among non-smokers, **men with a BMI of 23 to 25 and women with a BMI of 22 to 24 had the lowest risk of dying from all causes.** A higher BMI was associated with a nearly three-times-higher risk of deaths from all causes. Lower BMI levels, such as those below 22, and especially below 20, are actually associated with much higher rates of various diseases including infectious diseases, respiratory problems, osteoporosis, muscle wasting (which also involves the heart muscle), decreased immune function, and, in older persons, various cancers. What is important to your health is *fitness and firmness, not thinness!*

4. *Other weight measurement tools.* Some sports clubs, gyms, fitness centers, and health clinics use other tools or approaches to measure body fat or lean body mass. They include measuring skin folds (more applicable to children than adults), body density (underwater weighing), total body water (from which the percentage of body fat is calculated using an unreliable formula), bioelectrical impedance, use of inert gases, or CAT scans or MRI. None of these methods has any advantage over BMI and WC, but they are expensive and, except in research settings, are often used to make you feel "high-tech," so you can part with your money more generously!

What Happens to the Calories We Eat?

Do you ever wonder where the nutrients and calories go and what happens to them after we've enjoyed our food? Can we expedite or increase their disposal or burning so we won't be left with a bagful of calories after each meal?

Our bodies use dietary energy (calories) to provide needed nutrients to all our tissues, like powering a vast biological factory. There are three separate compartments through which calories are allocated. Calories that escape this triad are mainly converted to fat and stored in fat cells. Consequently, the more calories you dispose of through the triad, the less likely it is that you will gain (or regain) weight.

1. *Food energy expenditure (FEE).* As with all electric or electronic instruments, large or small, every function of every cell in your body needs energy. The digestion (breakdown of food in the stomach and the small intestine) and the absorption of foods (in the small intestine) are no exception. *Proteins burn 20 percent of their calories* during their trip from the mouth to the stomach, the intestine, and finally the bloodstream. In other words, they pay a heavy energy tax, or FEE, of 20 percent of all the calories they contain as we put them in our mouthes. The FEE for carbohydrates is very low at 4 percent, but the FEE of fats is a miserly 2 percent. In other words, *a meal or snack*

containing 100 calories of fat behaves like 98 calories, compared with 96 calories for carbohydrates, but only 80 calories for proteins.

Obviously we rarely eat a single nutrient by itself. With a few exceptions, foods are a mix of various nutrients. Thus the more protein a given meal has, the higher is the FEE, and conversely, the more carbohydrates or fat, the lower is the FEE. On average, the overall FEE for an adult is about 10 percent of the total daily energy intake, but depending on the nutrient mix, it may vary from 5 percent to 15 percent. Your goal should be to raise the FEE from the lower range to the higher range. For example, the difference between a FEE of 15 percent and one of 10 percent in a diet that contains 2,000 calories is an extra energy expenditure of about 100 calories (10 percent of 2,000 equals 200, versus 15 percent of 2,000 equals 300 calories). This is equal to the calories in one and one-half slices of white bread. But the true benefit of a high-protein diet (with a high FEE) is that such meals replace other foods containing fats and carbohydrates that have far more calories.

The FEE is genetically set for everyone with only minor variations. However, certain ingredients of foods such as hot spices; alcohol with meals; and tea and coffee may increase the FEE slightly. In general, short of changing the ingredients of foods, such as increasing the proteins and decreasing fat and carbohydrates, there isn't a great deal you can do to increase your FEE.

2. *Basic energy expenditure (BEE) or basic metabolic rate (BMR).* Even when we're at rest, the muscles, heart, lungs, kidneys, brain, and all other organs still work, albeit at a lower pace. All these basic functions need energy (calories). There is also the matter of repairing, rebuilding, and rejuvenating various organs. When we shower or bathe we wash off millions of cells from our skin, which are replaced. The lining of our digestive tract, from the mouth to the rectum, is continuously being sloughed off and replaced by new cells. All of these repair and renewal processes, too, use energy. In fact, we burn approximately 60 percent to 70 percent of our total daily calories just to keep these essential functions going. We call this energy expenditure the basic metabolic rate, or basic energy expenditure *(BEE)*.

The BEE among different individuals *may vary by as much as 80 percent.* The wide variations in BEE give some credence to those who claim, "I have a slow metabolism." Several studies have shown that among newborns, babies with the lowest BEE gained the most weight subsequently (because they did not burn as many calories as other newborns who had a "faster metabolism"). Everyone knows someone who eats like a horse without ever gaining an ounce! Conversely, there are also people who plead, "I can look at a cookie and gain three pounds!" These and other observations strongly point to a genetic predisposition for faster or slower BEE.

Clearly, a slow metabolism (low BEE) can, over

Nearly all tissues except fat behave like electrical instruments; they need and burn a good deal of energy. Fatty tissues, on the other hand, are like electronic instruments; they use very little energy. Even when they are busy and produce various hormones, they are very frugal and energy efficient. Moreover, they use their own in-house, stored calories (fat) for whatever meager energy needs they have. Thus our lean body mass (all tissues and organs except fatty tissues) accounts for nearly the entire *BEE*. *Bigger people sometimes eat bigger meals in part because they (mistakenly) assume that they require and burn more energy than other people.* This misconception or disconnect often perpetuates the high calorie intake and the energy surplus, especially among men.

time, contribute to weight gain and make weight loss more difficult. However, a low BEE is often aided and abetted by eating more calories than we need or can burn. Studies in identical twins have shown that in spite of their identical genes, different dietary habits and lifestyles create different weights. In other words, we can *override* our genetic predispositions to a host of disorders ranging from cancers to heart disease and obesity. *Most of our genetic predispositions, unlike the color of our eyes or skin, are not inevitable; they can be manipulated, modified, or suppressed.*

Can We Change Our BEE?

The BEE accounts for approximately 60 percent to 70 percent of energy intake, and it offers far more flexibility and opportunity for change than the FEE. *Time of eating* can affect the BEE significantly. For example, our BEE after breakfast and lunch is significantly higher (by about 10–15 percent) than after dinner. You should use this higher metabolic rate during breakfast and lunchtime to your advantage; instead of skipping breakfast or lunch, make them your more important meals, and try to cut down the carbohydrate and fat content of your dinner, in favor of a protein-rich (and hopefully small) meal. Seafood (not deep-fried), skinless chicken or turkey, or a small piece of lean red meat with lots of herbs, spices, and vegetables is each a reasonable choice for dinner. *Capsaicin* in spicy foods containing black, red, or chili peppers, caffeine in tea and coffee, and alcohol (no more than 2 drinks) can also increase the BEE by a few percent each.

Body frame also affects our BEE. Tall thin people have higher BEEs than their shorter and more compact counterparts, which is why many tall people tend to be slender. One reason is that lean tissues burn more calories with exercise as well as at rest. This also explains the higher BEE in men, who have more muscles than women.

The slower metabolic rate in overweight people makes their task of losing weight even harder. However, as they get leaner, their metabolism is reset at a faster pace. Alas! After a period of time, usually within two or three months, the BEE begins to regress toward its original slower pace, but fortunately doesn't quite reach it. At this point we need the help of regular, moderate-intensity exercises to keep our BEE at a faster pace.

Heat and cold can increase the BEE, for different reasons. *In the heat,* blood circulation of the skin is increased to allow perspiration and the evaporation of sweat, through which the heat we generate internally can be dispersed. This requires some extra calories, since every function of the body uses energy. *In the cold,* the body burns more calories to generate enough heat to prevent hypothermia.

Certain disorders such as an underactive thyroid gland or depression can slow down the BEE. Some medications, especially beta-blockers (used for the treatment of high blood pressure and other cardiovascular disorders), also can slow down the BEE. On the other hand, an overactive thyroid gland, an anxiety disorder, restlessness, and stimulants) even caffeine and xanthines in tea and coffee) can increase the BEE by several percentage points.

Fever also increases the BEE by about 7 percent for each degree Fahrenheit (or about 10 percent for each degree Celsius). During long, febrile illnesses people are often sedentary. Theoretically, this inactivity should partially offset the weight-losing impact of poor appetite and reduced food intake when we are sick. However, the increase in BEE due to fever sabotages this energy-saving mechanism, so most people in this setting tend to lose some weight.

Smoking and coffee can individually increase the BEE very slightly. However, smokers who drink several mugs of coffee daily can raise their BEE by about 5 percent. On the other hand, the artificially raised BEE in smokers drops when they quit, and over the ensuing months may contribute to an average weight gain of five to ten pounds. Of course people who quit smoking also experience a surge in their appetites, and many tend to nibble on candies or other snacks as substitutes for their cigarettes, which explains why some people may gain far more than just a few pounds after they quit the habit. Which takes us back to square one: It is eating too many calories—not the lack of cigarettes—that is responsible for most weight gain. Quitting the habit has its own merits, so you shouldn't allow the fear of gaining a few pounds to deter you.

Children and adolescents have a BEE that may be twice as high as that of middle-aged people, and three times faster than that of older people. The much higher metabolism in part explains why children and adolescents can seem to be eating constantly without gaining too much weight.

Menopause is also associated with a reduced BEE (and a lower exercise energy expenditure or EEE—

see page 226). *This downshift in energy-burning is another contributing factor to weight problems, especially abdominal obesity, in postmenopausal women.* Estrogen replacement therapy reverses this process to a great extent (even if at times it may cause slight water retention).

Regular vigorous activity resets the metabolism of the muscles and the liver to a higher level. In other words, the BEE of these tissues does not quickly drop to the pre-exercise level. Instead, it'll take them many hours (up to twelve to eighteen) to go back to their slower basic metabolic pace. This heightened metabolism means that after vigorous exercises, various tissues and organs will use up more fuel, i.e., calories, than if they were not activated.

A sedentary lifestyle artificially lowers the BEE, for example, from 70 percent to about 60 percent. Remember, what your body cannot use will mostly turn into fat. This is even more of a problem in people who eat big, calorie-rich dinners, stretch out on the sofa, and snack on chips and sweets or anything in-between until their bedtime. In this (regrettably too common) scenario, everything that can go wrong does! Here, the total energy intake is increased, and at the same time energy expenditure through all three parts of the triad (FEE, BEE, and EEE) is considerably reduced.

Weight loss through diet alone (without adequate exercise) may cause a 10 percent to 20 percent *drop* in the BEE within a few months. This adaptive catch-22, i.e., a lower BEE after weight loss, makes it much harder and slower to lose additional pounds. It also explains in part why these people tend to regain weight at the drop of a hat! (They burn fewer calories!) To illustrate this, let's take the example of a woman whose weight has dropped to 200 pounds (or to a BMI of about 32) and who is eating 1,600 calories a day. If her BEE has now dropped from 70 percent (or 1,120 calories) to 60 percent (or 960 calories), she will be storing 160 extra calories. In a way, her diet behaves as if it does not contain 1,600 but 1,760 calories! Isn't this an unfair and unfriendly kick in the shins? This is where the value of regular physical activity becomes even more relevant (see below).

3. *Exercise energy expenditure (EEE).* As you exercise, not only your muscles but also practically every organ works at a much faster pace. The brain, heart, liver, kidneys, and digestive tract, even your bones, are in a hectic and busy metabolic mode, all of which requires extra energy (calories). *The longer and the more intense your exercises are, the more calories you burn.* Duration and intensity of exercises have a hand-in-glove relationship. Increase one, the other, or both, and you burn more and more calories.

Since our lean body mass (all tissues except fat) utilizes and burns most of the calories, it is not surprising that people with weight problems have another catch-22 to deal with. For example, if two persons, one lean and the other heavy, walk the same distance shoulder to shoulder, the lean person burns, let's say, 100 calories. The heavy person may burn no more than 60 or 70 calories. You see the problem? Because of the lower BEE and EEE, unless we also reduce our energy input, we might have to exercise almost twice as much to offset the body's energy-conserving attitude.

On average, the EEE for someone who has a sedentary job and is not an exerciser is about 2 percent to 10 percent. Regular, rigorous exercises can increase the EEE to between 20 percent and 30 percent of total daily energy input. Elite or endurance athletes can increase their EEE to more than 100 percent. Obviously, these athletes need a lot more calories to keep up with their energy expenditure; otherwise they wouldn't have been such elite athletes in the first place! People with a weight problem, on the other hand, need to burn as many calories as they can, and as regularly as they can, without defeating the purpose by compensating and eating more calories.

You Are Not the Prisoner of Your Genes!

Almost everyone knows someone who eats like there is no tomorrow without gaining any weight. In fact, many sedentary "skinny" people may eat far more calories than overweight people. So it isn't just the *excessive calorie intake*, but how our bodies can *balance the calorie intake and the calorie disposal*.

Genetic or familial predisposition to weight

disorders is neither a mystery nor a destiny. It is caused by one or more defects in the chain of events that controls the appetite and food intake, on one hand, and by how we burn calories, on the other. The stomach and small intestine, muscles, fat cells, and brain produce numerous hormones that collectively help regulate our energy balance. Regrettably, not all parts of this complex system work smoothly in everyone, a problem that affects millions of people with weight problems. *(In the appendix, I'll try to open the door and walk you through these fascinating interactions.)*

Nearly all biological aberrations that contribute to weight problems are genetically determined. In other words, we are born saddled with genetic "baggage" we did not choose. None of us can ask for a recall, reselect our parents, or pick and choose the genes we want and reject the ones we don't. However, in most cases, we <u>can</u> counteract and modify the impact of these genetic miscues, and minimize their mischief.

People with weight problems may have several genetic aberrations or glitches in their energy-handling system. This can hinder their personal efforts to lose weight, and regrettably cause so much frustration that they give up what is left of their dietary and lifestyle defenses. Very much like those who have severe diabetes, hypertension, high blood cholesterol, or any other chronic disease, these people may also need aggressive medical intervention.

Genetic factors undoubtedly play a major role in predisposing people to develop weight problems, and account for about 70 percent of variations in weight or body mass index. However, genetic or familial influences do not mean inevitability. They can be provoked to express themselves, or suppressed and prevented from causing any disease. Recent studies of Pima Indians in Mexico and Arizona showed that although they share the same genetic background, obesity, diabetes, and cardiovascular diseases are far less common in Mexican Indians than in the more "Westernized" Arizona Indians.

Why are there such glaring differences? The principal reason is that traditional Mexican Indians eat a diet that is low in saturated fats and trans-fatty acids, and high in complex carbohydrates. Even more important, Mexican Indians burn more calories through physical labor and other activities, and drink alcoholic beverages very infrequently. Most Arizona Indians' dietary and lifestyle practices as well as alcohol consumption are 180 degrees different from their Mexican cousins'.

As a result of these lifestyle and dietary factors, and their genetic predisposition, nearly half of middle-aged Arizona Indians have diabetes, the highest rate in the world, and a much greater number have abdominal obesity.

Studies of identical twins have also shown that lifestyle, eating, and exercise habits play major

> *Obesity is a consequence of an imbalance between energy (calorie) intake and energy output (burning of calories).* This simple fact is so essential and obvious that, amazingly, we have a hard time grasping it! *Without an energy (calorie) surplus we cannot gain weight, and without an energy deficit we cannot lose weight!* Fluid retention has no relevance to obesity, even though on occasion it can cause some weight gain.

roles in determining weight. Also, having two overweight parents means a 70 percent chance of growing up overweight (a 40 percent chance if one parent is heavy). Obviously, if identical twins don't weight the same, and not everyone with overweight parents is overweight, there are other factors in weigh besides genetics. For example, children of heavy parents may not only have inherited genetic signals to develop obesity; they may also copy their parents' eating and lifestyle practices.

Cultural and Learned Behaviors

Eating (or lifestyle) behaviors are not imprinted on our genes; they are learned behaviors. Unfortunately, it is often difficult to get rid of, or liberate ourselves from, many entrenched behaviors, even when we can readily see that they are harmful to us. You know all the examples, including eating disorders, smoking, alcohol and drug abuse, sedentary lifestyles, and others. We learn many of our habits as children and adolescents, but as we grow older (and presumably wiser), we often make very little or no effort to change the unhealthy ones.

A recent study showed that given a choice between spicy snacks or sweet ones, more than 50 percent of Mexican children opt for spicy ones. In contrast, only 1 percent of American children do so. Sweet and bitter tastes are innate, meaning that we are born with them; all other tastes are acquired. (In fact the gene for a sweet tooth has been discovered to be on chromosome 4.) Even though Mexican children have the same innate taste for sweets, their food culture essentially overrides their genetic tendencies. On the other hand, very few American parents encourage their toddlers to eat spicy foods. Instead, they bribe, cajole, reward, or appease their children by feeding them all sorts of sweets. This sweet-food culture perpetuates and strengthens children's genetic tendencies, an unhealthy legacy that they carry into their adult life.

Recent studies have shown that weight problems occur at a much faster rate among African-American and Hispanic women than in their white counterparts. In fact obesity is increasing at an alarming rate in the first two groups. Although black and white males have a similar rate of severe weight disorder, obesity occurs at a much faster pace and higher rate among Hispanic males. There is no doubt that a substantial amount of these differences are due to dietary and lifestyle practices. For example, because of a host of socio-economic factors, African-American and Hispanic women eat a large amount of deep-fried fatty foods and energy-dense snacks, while at the same time engaging in fewer regular physical activities.

Food cultures are not always negative. In fact many ethnic foods and eating patterns are quite healthful when they are not tampered with, adulterated, or "Westernized." How can one argue with a *Southern Mediterranean* diet of plenty of fruits and vegetables, as well as nuts, seafoods, free-range poultry, lean red meats from grazed cattle, olive oil, and a glass of wine or two with a meal, but without loads of butter, margarines, shortenings, and cooking fats, or energy-dense, high-fat, high glycemic snacks and desserts?

Traditional *Japanese foods* also carry far fewer calories, saturated fats and trans-fatty acids, and high glycemic carbohydrates. Unfortunately, the waves of Westernized foods and snacks have already changed the diet of this generation of Japanese, resulting in surging epidemics of weight problems and diabetes. In fact, the rate of stroke among Japanese is twice that among Americans, and their rate of heart attacks (although still well below most Western countries) is also increasing rapidly.

Spicy foods are not only tasty but contain a number of health-promoting compounds. For example, black, chili, or red peppers have high concentrations of capsaicin (which is responsible for the hot, spicy taste). Capsaicin in spicy foods increases the burning of calories, and may partly explain the lower rates of obesity among populations who often eat spicy foods. Herbs such as basil, chives, oregano, rosemary, sage, savory, thyme, and watercress have a vast number of antioxidants and aspirin-like compounds that help reduce the risk of cardiovascular diseases, certain cancers, and premature aging. They also add taste, aroma, and personality to foods, enabling you to use less fat for flavor enhancement (and thus fewer calories).

Xanthines and caffeine in tea and coffee reduce the appetite and also increase energy burning. The net result is a lower tendency for weight disorders among those who drink several cups of tea (black or green) or coffee per day.

Southern cooking and its more contemporary variations are often based on deep-frying in cooking fat with high concentrations of trans-fatty acids (see chapter 2). These dietary practices are partly responsible for the high rates of weight problems, hypertension, diabetes, and various cardiovascular disorders in many Southern states in the U.S.

Many *Chinese foods* (at least in the U.S.) are drenched in peanut oil or other fats that literally cover every morsel of meat and vegetables in the dish. Moreover, during stir-frying, various vegetables and meats sponge in a substantial amount of fat (see table 71), making many Chinese dishes very deceptive calorie traps. Similarly, *northern*

TABLE 71
Amount of Oil Absorbed During Chinese Stir-frying
per 3.5 oz./100 g

	Grams
Shredded low-fat pork	4
Fresh soybeans	5
Cubed chicken	7
Green peppers	8
Kidney beans	9
Onions	11
Pea pods	12
Cabbage	13
Cauliflower	13
Spinach	13
Carrots	14
Eggplant	14
Mushrooms	14
Bamboo shoots	15
Broccoli	15

Italian cooking (especially as served in U.S. restaurants) carries a heavy burden of fat, quite different from its *southern Italian* counterparts.

Most *British and other northern European* foods are also atherogenic (contribute to coronary artery disease) and obesogenic. And not surprisingly, the risks of weight disorders, heart attacks, and strokes in these populations are among the highest in the world. Although the diet of a large segment of the population in the *Indian* subcontinent is vegetarian, heart attacks, abdominal obesity, and diabetes are epidemic in India and Pakistan. One reason for this dramatic reversal of fortunes, in spite of relatively low calorie intake and prevalent malnutrition, is their heavy use of vegetable shortening and cooking fats, which contain not only a high concentration of saturated fat, but also trans-fatty acids. The consequence of this shift in their diet is that saturated fats and trans-fatty acids constitute a major portion of their total calories. This devastating trend, which began over forty years ago, has now started to inflict its heavy toll, not only in the indigenous population, but also among those living abroad. In fact, the risk of heart attack among Indians and Pakistanis living in England is even higher than in the English!

A recent study of women who were admitted to four Boston area hospitals for heart attacks is also instructive. The risk of heart attack was two and one-half times greater in those who had had the highest intake of margarine, shortening, and cooking fats than in those with the lowest intake. As noted previously, among the 42,504 U.S. health professionals who were studied for twelve years, the risk of diabetes was 1,100 percent higher in those who were obese (BMI greater than 30) and ate a typical Western diet than in those who were not obese and ate a "prudent" diet similar to the THI diet introduced here. In two large studies, women eating a typical Western diet also had a similarly high risk of developing type II diabetes as men.

Our Environment and Weight Problems

There is no doubt that *socioeconomic* factors have a significant impact on weight, especially among women. For example, the rate of obesity (BMI greater than 30) among lower-income women is twice that of middle-class women, and more than three times greater than in upper-class women. African Americans, Mexican Americans, and especially Native Americans have much higher rates of obesity, especially abdominal obesity, than other groups, and the poorer they are, the higher is their risk. Why? Certainly this is not a genetic trait or predisposition.

There are two major reasons: the availability of fat- and sugar-laden fast foods or other calorie-dense foods and snacks, and a sedentary lifestyle that affects more than 90 percent of the urban poor in the U.S.

In addition, the less affluent are often "forced" to choose the wrong foods. For example, regular ground beef at most supermarkets may have about 28 percent to 32 percent fat, but the extra-lean versions have only 7 percent to 8 percent. Since the cost of the extra-lean version is often as much as 50 percent to 100 percent higher than the regular ground beef, the less affluent shoppers most likely choose the less expensive one for financial reasons.

Undereducation and lower socioeconomic status also contributes to a less proactive attitude toward almost all health-related issues and preventive measures. Unfortunately, this is the segment of our population that can least afford to get sick or develop a chronic, disabling disease. To make matters even worse, they also tend to delay timely interventions to correct various weight-related disorders, often until they experience serious complications. This is even more relevant to the forty million Americans who do not have health insurance.

Psychological Factors and Weight Gain

Let's start by acknowledging that various emotional and psychological factors can and do play a role in weight problems. Unresolved grief, anxieties, depression, isolation, and lack of love, support, hope, and self-worth all can contribute to overeating and a sedentary lifestyle in *some* people. However, *for the majority of people, calorie surplus and weight problems are unrelated to or predate the onset of any psychological disorder.*

Depression and anxiety disorders are common among the general population of the U.S. and other Western nations. Ten to 12 percent of adult Americans have various degrees of clinical depression, and another 10 percent (higher among women) have anxiety disorders. Thus, of the estimated 110 million adult Americans with weight problems, it is quite logical to assume that about 20 percent to 25 percent may have *coexiting* emotional or psychiatric disorders. However, not all those who have an emotional or a psychological disorder have a weight problem, or resort to overeating and fre-

237

quent snacking. Nor do they pick up smoking, drinking, or drug abuse.

Researchers at Georgia State University recently studied the eating behavior and the activity level of a group of men and women who were gaining weight, and compared them with weight-stable, matched control subjects. Participants recorded their activity levels, everything they ate or drank, and the environmental and psychological factors surrounding each eating episode for seven days. The study showed that the weight-gaining group on average ate 1,650 calories more than the weight-stable group during the week. Importantly, the weight gainers did not report different environmental or psychological factors from the stable group. In other words, the weight gain was a physiological response of the body to calorie surplus, but not to their emotional state.

About 10 percent of overweight people are true "emotional" eaters. They do indeed eat when ner-

---

Although alcohol, most illicit drugs, and nicotine are addictive, *there is no evidence that any food is addictive*. As such, eating behaviors including nervous eating can be changed without any withdrawal reaction or negative outcome. The point is that *we should stop trying to explain or rationalize people's weight problem as a compensatory emotional response*. This is a simplistic (even if sympathetic) approach that is patronizing and may reinforce the culprit behaviors.

It is inappropriate and makes no sense to turn everyone with a weight problem into an instant psychiatric patient. But that is precisely what untrained and self-appointed diet gurus preach on various talk shows and infomercials. To be sure, most people who have a weight problem wish, and express the desire, to be lean or less heavy, and are disappointed or even sad that they are not. But we cannot and should not confuse or equate these wants and disappointments with psychological disorders, hide behind them, or label people with them. We gain weight because of an imbalance between energy (calorie) intake and energy output. This imbalance or calorie surplus is caused by our eating behaviors, and may or may not be aided by a host of biological, cultural, psychological, or genetic factors, *but it is not caused by our emotions.*

vous, under pressure, frustrated, angry, rejected, lonely, or depressed. But emotional eating is not the only reason, or even the main reason, for their weight problem. They (as well as the other 90 percent who are not "nervous" eaters) have other eating behaviors or biological disorders that contribute to their calorie surplus (see below). And of course, there are millions of emotional eaters who have no weight problems.

The majority of people (75 percent to 80 percent with weight problems, especially men, do not have significantly higher rates of psychological disorders than the general population. Certainly there is no correlation between the severity of the weight problem and the presence and severity of any associated psychological disorder. In other words, these are separate and independent entities that may coexist in 20 percent to 25 percent of adults with weight problems. Although in some people each of these separate disorders may aggravate the other, there is no primary cause-and-effect relationship. Moreover, many depressed or anxious persons have a poor appetite and cut down their eating, so they may even lose weight or are underweight (see figure 1).

Still, there is a sizable segment of our population that tend to eat, snack, and nibble when they aren't hungry. In an environment of food abundancy and availability, and constant cues from advertisements for foods or snacks, there is a great deal of temptation to reach for food when not otherwise occupied. Acting upon these temptations is not limited to, or the trademark of, people with emotional disorders. Very few people with or without weight problems escape these traps.

Carbohydrate Craving

Many people have told me they crave carbohydrates, especially when they are upset or during their premenstrual phase, or just randomly. Regrettably, almost always these cravings are for "comfort foods" or snacks, which are energy-dense, with a high concentration of sugar and hidden fats. In

Figure 1

**INTERACTION OF MULTIPLE RISK FACTORS
IN WEIGHT DISORDERS***

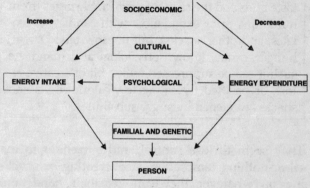

The contribution and the strength of these risk factors vary from person to person, and even for the same person at different times.

other words, people who crave carbohydrates actually crave sweets—not legumes, fruits, potatoes, whole wheat bread, or oatmeal, all of which are rich sources of carbohydrates.

Binge Eating Disorder (BED)

Because of unrealistic, rigid diets and a sense of deprivation or frustration, and often for no particular reason, about 20 percent of people with weight problems engage in binge eating, randomly eating unusually large amounts of energy-dense foods or snacks, often when they are not even hungry.

Contrary to a common misconception, low blood sugar is rarely the reason for sweets cravings; low blood sugar may occur after eating sweets, due to an insulin surge. Sweets craving is the function of taste buds and the recall of pleasurable tastes (from numerous prior experiences with candies, chocolates, and other snacks), but not low blood sugar, hunger, or any known physiological demand. As such it can be suppressed with a bit of creative effort, or pacified by eating low-calorie foods and snacks sweetened by sugar substitutes.

They seem to lose control, and surrender to the all-or-nothing temptation of overeating or snacking on whatever they can get their hands on. Bingers often become distressed and at times grow quite angry about their behavior, responding differently from the usual overeaters, who may merely regret their indulgence. Bingers are also different from bulimics, who often resort to behaviors such as induced vomiting, laxatives, or both, to get rid of the culprit foods they have eaten. Most binge eaters do not engage in purging, even when they feel guilty about their overeating.

A large number of binge eaters have a history of frequent weight cycling and repeated dieting. They jump from one to another "new" diet, hoping "this time it'll be different." Although the majority of bulimics are women, the distribution of BED is the same among men and women. Recent studies suggest that some binge eaters with a severe weight problem may have a compulsive eating disorder that is partially caused by low concentrations of serotonin, a neurotransmitter in the brain, whereas nonbingers with a similar weight problem do not seem to have this particular abnormality. Some drugs that fully or even partially restore the brain's serotonin level are effective in significantly improving compulsive eating disorders, but have no role in the treatment of other weight disorders, which are often unrelated to brain serotonin levels.

Weight Gain and Eating Behavior

There is no doubt that eating patterns and behaviors play an essential role in energy imbalance and calorie surplus. How we respond to our hunger signals, and whether we eat or overeat even when we are not hungry, will have a significant impact on weight gain or weight maintenance. Recent studies have shown that in all age and socioeconomic groups, *dietary disinhibition,* the tendency to overeat large portions indiscriminately even in the absence of hunger, is the most important eating behavior causing weight problems.

If you serve the same meal to ten people, and then ask them to give you an estimate of how many calories they just ate, chances are you will receive ten different answers! That's because people are not food biochemists, and they cannot be expected to know the precise nutritional values of every meal, or how much of which ingredients is present in this or that food. A recent study of a group of dieticians at Louisiana State University showed the difficulty of guessing or estimating the caloric content of any given meal. Although these were dieticians with a good working knowledge of the caloric content of foods, when they were served the same meal, their estimates of its calories varied by more than 100 percent.

People who have weight problems are no different; they tend to underestimate their total food/ calorie intake, and may not remember or even recognize their overeating. This is frequently an honest underestimation, but on occasions, some people just can't or won't admit to overeating.

Although dietary restraint can prevent calorie surplus, overeaters only occasionally practice restraint. They may cut down what they eat for breakfast and lunch, or even skip lunch or breakfast altogether. Regrettably, dinnertime and the rest of the evening are when dietary disinhibition overwhelms the good intentions of dietary restraints practiced during the day. The consequence of this imbalanced eating behavior is almost always an energy surplus and weight gain, or a failure to lose or maintain weight.

What You Should Do

The absolute, inviolable, and inescapable fact is that you will lose weight if you create an energy deficit by taking in fewer calories than you use. Creation of *a negative energy balance, or an energy shortage,* is so essential that without it there is no possibility that anyone can lose any amount of weight! But creating an energy deficit is not as hard as you think!

To succeed and maintain a healthy weight, *you have to take advantage of both arms of your energy equation: decrease energy input and increase energy output.* Although you can manipulate your FEE and BEE by 5 percent to 10 percent, the most direct way to significantly raise your energy expenditure (and minimize your energy surplus) is to alter your EEE. Even moderate but regular exercise (four or more times per week) can increase the EEE from your usual 5 to 10 percent to greater than 20 percent.

Regular, moderate exercise combined with doable dietary changes offers you a no-fail plan to lose your unhealthy weight and stop weight cycling. When you lose weight, you lose fat and water, but you also lose muscle mass (protein) along with it. Regular exercise helps rebuild your muscle mass and prevent flabbiness, or fatigue. But as summarized in table 68, there are thirty-four reasons to exercise!

Losing weight is never a medical emergency despite how the prospect of a wedding, a reunion, and/or the sunbathing season makes you feel. So think and plan ahead. To start reaping the cardiovascular and other health benefits, a 7 percent to 10 percent weight reduction over three to six months is a good start. In other words, if your current weight is 200 pounds, your target weight loss should be 15 to 20 pounds in the next few months. *Do not set an impatient, emotional, or outlandish goal* that can pour ice water on your enthusiasm if you don't achieve it. After the first three to six months, you can reset your goal for another 7 percent to 10 percent for the next several months. This practical, *phased* goal-setting enables you to lose weight without making your whole life revolve around it.

In the U.S., approximately 13 percent of women and 5 percent of men with weight problems are enrolled in various commercial weight loss programs. Most programs are based on faddish, gimmicky, or plain nonsensical dietary regimens that are designed to make profits off of vulnerable people who fall prey to infomercials or Internet advertising, and testimonials of well-paid "personalities." A few commercial programs, such as Weight Watchers, provide a service that is practical for some people. But how effective are they? To find out, researchers from six U.S. academic centers enrolled 211 overweight or obese men and women in the Weight Watchers program. They also assigned 212 to a self-help group who were advised to cut down calories and increase exercise. After two years, those enrolled in the structured Weight Watchers program with regular attendance at meetings and weigh-ins, on average, lost 2.7 kilograms (6 pounds) more weight than the self-help group. Is 6 pounds more weight loss in two years worth the time, effort, and cost? Do it yourself—Eating for Life—offers you a far better alternative.

More than 70 percent of people with moderate to severe weight problems (those who weigh more than 30 to 40 pounds over their healthy weight, or have a body mass index greater than 30) have a host of weight-related disorders. This is especially true in those who have abdominal obesity. If you fall in this category, especially if you are over forty, *see your physician* for a full evaluation and appropriate blood tests to make sure you do not have any of these coexisting disorders.

Try to keep your total THI scores of all foods, snacks, and drinks under +30, and preferably as close to +20 as you can. *It is essential that you follow the five DOs and the five DON'Ts,* so that you can incorporate them into your daily routine. If you keep your breakfast THI score below +5, and lunch below +10, you have another +10 points (or so) for your dinner (and beyond). But if you go beyond +30 here and there, the world will not collapse. Don't get frustrated or go through a new round of self-flagellation. What matters is the long-term trend, not a single meal or a day of dietary indiscretion. Just move on!

Here is a quick and condensed guideline to remind you what you should do.

The Scientific Principles of Losing Weight

Diet:

Avoid: Mayonnaise, margarines, shortening and cooking fats, which means *avoid* cakes, cookies, chocolates, donuts, croissants, pastries, pies, chips and *deep-fried anything* (such as KFC, French fries, wings, etc.). Also *Avoid* butter, creams, and creamy or butter-based sauces such as Alfredo, Béarnaise, or Hollandaise, greasy cuts of meats, sausages, hot dogs, pizzas, and *any food or snack with THI SCORE OF MORE THAN +10.*

Cut down (by at least 50 percent: All sweets including sugar, especially high fructose corn sweeteners (in sodas, canned fruit, syrups, ice creams, most sherbets and other sweet snacks), "sugarized" and frosted cereals, and *all starches* including *white bread, bagels, pasta, rice, and potato.*

Eat: *Four seafood meals a week reduces your risk of a heart attack by 40 percent, and the risk of a sudden death from a heart attack by 70 percent! No medicine in the world could do that!* Eating several seafood meals a week also helps you lose weight, and reduces your risk of developing diabetes, kidney disorders, coronary artery disease, stroke, dementia, hypertension, irregular heart rate, and improves these problems if you already have them. Since the benefits of seafoods are due to their omega-3 fat, "fatty" fish (salmon, tuna, mackerel, etc.) with higher concentration of omega-3 fat are preferable to lean fish (such as flounder, perch, or other white-flesh seafood). However, all seafoods are better than chicken and turkey. [Do not use vegetable oils or fats to cook your seafood. The omega-6 and trans fats in these products defeat the purpose of eating seafood. Instead, use olive or canola oil.]

Also, eat *"tons"* (!) of deeply colored vegetables and fruits!

Use *olive oil, canola oil, or hazelnut oil (instead of peanut, corn, safflower, soybean, or any other oil)*, for all your cooking, baking, or marinating needs.

Lean meats are fine. The culprit is the white fat, not the red meat!

Small amounts of certain nuts such as almonds, hazelnuts, pistachios, and walnuts are reasonable substitutes for sweet snacks. The "operative" word here is *small*. However, you should avoid peanuts, cashews, Brazil and other nuts.

Exercises: Remember: *"He who rests, rots!"* You should exercise at least 4–5 times a week, about 45 to 60 minutes each session, including the warm-up and the cool-down periods. *Do not become a vulnerable weekend athlete!*

A Few Meal Suggestions
(to Make Losing Weight Easier)

The purpose of developing the Total Health Impact Diet was to liberate you from the constraints of having to follow someone's rigid recipes and menus. Instead you have the freedom to use your taste, preferences, mood of the moment, and culinary imagination to choose foods you enjoy. All you have to do is to make sure your total THI scores of all foods and snacks remain under +30 per day. So, instead of a long list of required menus, here are a few practical suggestions.

Breakfast

One slice of toasted nonwhite bread, or half of a pita, or an English muffin, with a thin spread of (no-sugar-added) fruit jam or marmalade, but without butter or margarine. You can replace the jam with a small amount of low-fat cheese spread.

Or a bowl of nonfrosted cereal with 1 percent milk (or Lactaid milk if you are lactose-intolerant), with sliced strawberries, peaches, or nectarines, or even half of a banana.

Or a bowl (a packet) of Cream of Wheat with 1 percent milk but without added butter or margarine.

Or one or two eggs, soft- or hard-boiled, sunny-side up, or prepared as an omelette (use olive oil or canola oil spray). You may still have a slice of toasted bread or an English muffin without butter, margarine, jam, or marmalade.

Or a bowl of fruit cocktail, strawberries or mixed berries, an orange or a grapefruit, or half of a cantaloupe, or any other fruit.

Or a cup of yogurt (plain or with fruit, but *without sugar*) with a slice of toast, or half a muffin.

Of course you can enjoy your cup of tea or coffee without sugar or cream, (but fat-free creamers are fine). A glass of 1 percent fat or skim milk (or Lactaid), or a glass of orange juice (but preferably an orange or an apple or a peach, instead of fruit juice), should further satisfy you so that by ten o'clock in the morning, you are not hunting for food.

Sorry! No donuts, croissants, bagels with cream cheese, sausages, pancakes with syrup, Egg McMuffins and hashed brown potatoes, three-egg cheese omelettes, etc. However, an occasional "infraction" (two or three strips of bacon with Sunday breakfast, for example) will not capsize the world! Enjoy it and move on!

Lunch

Here you have a vast amount of choices limited only by your schedule, location, and imagination. With a bit of creative culinary planning, you should find plenty to eat.

For example, a chicken, turkey, or ham sandwich with mustard, pepper, black or green olives, and lettuce or watercress, with or without pickles, but *definitely with no mayonnaise*. Use only half a pita or a small roll. No 12-inch cheesesteak subs, please! (You are actually better off making your own sandwich and taking it to work, instead of relying on fast-food eateries.)

Or a can of tuna with some Dijon mustard or salsa or chopped chives, parsley, green onions (scallions), celery, or anything else you like. A touch of fat-free mayonnaise is fine, but no regular or "light" mayo. Commercial tuna fish sandwiches invariably have mayo (with plenty of omega-6 fatty acid), which defeats the purpose of eating seafood in the first place, and also throws in a lot of unnecessary calories.

Or a small "sub" sandwich with chicken, turkey, ham, or beef (but no cheeses or processed meats, such as bologna). You can make your sandwich even more zesty with all kinds of tasty relishes, herbs, spices, sliced black or green olives, tomatoes, capers, onions, peppers, or mushrooms (none of which should be fried). Again, no added oil or mayo.

Or a grilled chicken salad with a small amount of olive oil and vinegar, or a low-fat/ low-calorie dressing of your choice.

Or a (lean) roast beef sandwich without butter, margarine, mayo, or fast-food sauces. You can add a side salad (without cheese) to this, but use only low-fat/low-calorie dressing. No French fries, potato chips, fried mushrooms or onion rings, bacon, or processed cheeses.

Or grilled, broiled, baked, or poached seafood (any seafood you like) or chicken, with a small dinner roll. Many restaurants have the bad habit of brushing anything they grill, bake, or broil with a heavy dose of melted cooking fat before or after seasoning, and then pouring some more on it when they transfer it to your plate. Make sure you tell your server that you do not want any fat added to your fish or any other dish you've selected. Béarnaise, hollandaise, tartar, cream, Alfredo, and most other sauces contain unacceptably high *THI* scores and too many calories.

Or a Caesar salad with the sauce on the side (not pretossed) is reasonable, but use less than 1 tablespoon of dressing (otherwise you defeat the purpose).

Or a yogurt, with any fruit or even a couple of ounces of nuts (almonds, hazelnuts, pistachios, or walnuts, but not peanuts, Brazil nuts, or cashews).

Of course you can have water, tea, coffee, or, if you must, a sugar-free soft drink with your lunch, but *SKIP THE MIDDAY COCKTAILS OR WINE!*

Pizzas, steaks, chops, chicken wings, potato skins, and deep-fried dishes are all wrong choices. *Desserts* (except for mixed fruits or berries) are often more energy-dense than the main entrées and have high THI scores, making them totally inappropriate.

Dinner

Dinner meals are frequently easier to choose, especially since you are more likely to be at home. In your own environment you have more control over how you cook, what ingredients you use, and of course the portion size. Here are a few suggestions (among thousands of choices).

Baked, broiled, poached, or sautéed seafoods—from albacore tuna to whitefish, and all the others in between—with a small amount of olive oil, herbs, and spices. You may marinate your fish using a bit of salt and fresh pepper (most chefs prefer black to white pepper, even for fish), a dash of paprika, fresh crushed garlic or shallots (depending on your taste), a touch of Dijon or country mustard, the juice of half a lemon, and ½ to 1 tablespoon of olive oil. You can use something similar for shrimp, but without the oil. (Oil covering the shrimp may prevent it from searing to a golden brown color to let you know it is ready. Don't use oil or you may overcook it to a rubbery texture. The *two most frequent mistakes people make are buying an old piece of fish and overcooking it.* Both of these infractions can stink up your kitchen and discourage you from experiencing the pleasures of eating seafood, both at home and away.

Or season a piece of chicken breast with salt, pepper, a shake of garlic powder (or a small amount of crushed garlic), and a touch of lemon juice. Sauté the chicken for three or four minutes on each side (at high heat, olive oil smokes, so use canola oil instead). In the same sautéing pan, you can brown some diced onions (with or without diced tomato). After you transfer your culinary creation to a plate, sprinkle it with some chopped chives, green onions, or parsley for color and flavor. In less than ten minutes you've made a lovely dinner! Don't forget the salad side dish. If you like, you can have a *small* serving of pasta or rice, or a small dinner roll.

Or buy 7-percent-fat ground beef from your supermarket. Add a bit of salt, pepper, and, if you enjoy Mediterranean-style cooking, herbs such as basil, oregano, or thyme, or a touch of all three. You can now grill your patties or sauté them in a pan using olive oil or canola oil spray. Do not use a big hamburger bun or a large roll. A plate of salad is a great side dish, provided you use low-calorie/fat-free dressings.

Or a small (4-to-6-ounce) lean fillet of beef or London broil, or portion of beef kabobs, or a lean piece of pork or veal. Stay away from, for example, a veal scallopini dinner that is drowned in butter- and cheese-based sauces. A seafood entrée that is covered with creamy, buttery, or cheesy sauces is equally counterproductive.

Or a small plate of pasta with tomato sauce (with a touch of grated parm) without any bread. Add a big plate of salad and you have a filling and satisfying meal.

Or a huge plate of salad with baby spinach, romaine lettuce, broccoli florets, watercress, some sliced mushrooms and red onions, and a bit of goat cheese. You can make your own salad dressing with small equal amounts of lemon juice and balsamic vinegar; some salt, fresh ground pepper, and garlic powder; and a dash of Worcestershire sauce. As you mix these ingredients, slowly add an equal amount of water (or white wine) and extra-virgin olive oil. You can also use any commercial low-fat/

low-calorie dressing. You can have a small dinner roll along with your salad dinner.

Or any sandwich as suggested for lunch, but no deep-fried anything!

Use your imagination and modify any recipes you know of or have enjoyed in the past. As long as the THI scores remain low, you should have no problem. Chances are you will have to dramatically reduce the fat or the carbohydrate content of your old favorites. Remember you are not breaking any law by altering a recipe! Compromise in favor of your health, not somebody's recipe!

You can have water, tea, coffee, sugar-free sodas, or a glass of 1 percent or skim milk (or Lactaid). If you have no personal or philosophical objection, one or two glasses of wine with dinner are fine. For dessert, your best choices are berries or other fruits. However, a serving of low-fat/sugar-free ice cream, chocolate pudding, or frozen yogurt can satisfy your craving for sweets, especially if you have a sweet tooth.

Avoid dietary "celibacy"; please your eyes and taste buds by choosing a wide variety of foods with personality—taste, texture, flavor, color—although not those with high THI scores. This way, instead of getting bored and frustrated, you are more likely to adhere to your diet. The THI scores provide you with the tool with which you can choose a vast number of tasty and nutritious foods. When you "lust" for a "forbidden" food, eat it—but in small portions. The THI Diet is not intended to be punitive or strict and deprivational. Just remember, in addition to losing weight you also want to reduce your risk of chronic diseases and cancers. So try to be faithful to its ten commandments.

Do not make a U-turn!

Appendix

Hormones, Genes, and Our Weight

In the long-running biological play *Our Weight*, there are four major actors, each performing a specific role, but capable of improvising in response to cues from other actors.

1. Stomach and small intestine. The stomach produces a hormone called *ghrelin* (pronounced *gre-lynn*). Blood levels of ghrelin rise shortly before every meal and drop sharply soon after eating. Ghrelin reaches the appetite/satiety center in the brain (hypothalamus) and *stimulates the appetite and food intake*. Soon after eating, the stomach nearly halts the production of ghrelin, so the appetite is no longer stimulated, and satiety sets in.

The small intestine produces another hormone that plays an important role in signaling the body to store dietary fat in fat cells instead of burning it for fuel. The hormone, *gastric inhibitory poly-*

peptide (GIP), is secreted after one eats fat and carbohydrates. Blocking the action of GIP in rodents significantly reduces the storage of fat and weight gain. At present, there are numerous studies under way to assess the role of GIP in humans. It is quite likely that at least some people with a weight problem produce too much GIP.

2. Fat cells. Far from being lazy or out-of-the-loop cells, fat cells produce a torrent of hormones and other bioactive compounds. For example, in response to eating, fat cells produce a hormone (a protein) called *leptin,* from the Greek word *leptos,* meaning thin (another name for leptin is *the obesity protein,* or *OB protein*). Leptin's effect on appetite is the opposite of ghrelin; it *suppresses the appetite*.

Leptin reaches the appetite/satiety center in the hypothalamus via the bloodstream, and enters these cells through special entry gates called *leptin receptors* (figure 2). Without adequate receptors, leptin cannot get inside the brain cells to prompt them into action and send appropriate satiety signals to the rest of the brain and the digestive tract. On the other hand, when leptin enters the hypothalamus through its designated receptors, it signals the nerve cells to release a number of hormones, among them *melanocortins*. Melanocortins serve two important functions: one, they *decrease the appetite* and food (calorie) intake, and two, they *stimulate the muscles to burn more calories* at a faster rate.

No one would be overweight if this scenario

held up every time, and in everyone. Much to the dismay of millions of people, it does not! In people who are overweight and especially in those who are severely obese, one or more components of this cycle may be abnormal and derail this smooth operation.

One of the most common findings in overweight people is that their *leptin receptors are defective* and, therefore, unable to receive and respond to leptin. In fact, most obese people have very high concentrations of leptin in their bloodstream, instead of the expected low levels. This is because their fat cells are working hard to correct the problem, producing a lot of leptin in an effort to signal or kick the hypothalamus to wake up and do its job.

Without adequate leptin inside its neurons (nerve cells), the hypothalamus cannot respond and produce enough melanocortins to break this vicious cycle. So, in people with defective leptin receptors, even when fat cells flood the bloodstream with leptin, there is no response. In other words, these people have become leptin-resistant.

In other people, the leptin itself may be defective and, therefore, hypothalamus receptors can't recognize it to let it in. The end result is the same: There is no surge in melanocortins in response to feeding. Still other people may be unable to produce enough melanocortins, or any they do produce may be dysfunctional.

Fat cells also produce the hormone *resistin,* which increases insulin resistance and may cause diabetes. On the other hand, to keep resistin in check, they also produce *adiponectin* and *CD36*, both of which reduce insulin resistance.

3. Brain. Appetite is the result of coordinated actions of the stomach, intestine, liver, fat cells, and brain. Sensory stimulations such as the sight, smell, taste, or mouth feel of food play major roles in awakening or stimulating the appetite. Sensory stimulations can be real or simply imagined.

Advertisers rely on these stimulations to promote their products. Frequently, we respond to their messages based on our past experiences with these or similar products. Sometimes with the help of advertisers, we subconsciously use a bit of our own imagination to provoke or spike our appetite. If we didn't use our subconscious or our voluntary imaginations, there would be very few new food products, and even fewer advertisements.

The habit of eating at certain times of the day can also arouse our appetite even when we are not truly hungry or need any calories. How well our internal signals, sensory stimulations, and blood sugar, protein, and fat levels interact has a significant impact on our food intake, and our weight. The brain coordinates and directs all these various interactions, which are simplistically called the *set point* (a rather useless and confusing term). Many obese people find it a constant struggle to establish a lasting balance among these various factors, losing the battles far more than winning them.

Satiety, the opposite of hunger, requires a number of interactions beginning with stomach fullness and the composition of the food. As the blood level of ghrelin drops in response to eating, even before the food is digested and absorbed, the hypothalamus produces another hormone, called *cholecystokinin (CCK)*. CCK jump-starts the process of satiety until the other supporting cast (leptin, ghrelin, and melanocortins) can take over. Here, too, in some people the CCK release or the hypothalamus response to it may be defective. The consequence of this defective response to food is that satiety does not occur in a timely manner, allowing overeating or snacking to contribute to calorie surplus and weight gain.

4. Muscles. Recent studies have unraveled how melanocortins turn on the energy spigot. These hormones signal the muscle cells to produce a compound called *uncoupling protein (UP)*. The uncoupling protein encourages the muscle cells to burn more calories and convert them into body heat. *Humans and some laboratory animals with low levels of uncoupling protein in their muscle cells fail to lose weight even with low-calorie diets and moderate to intense exercise.* That's because they simply cannot burn enough calories in their muscles to maintain a reasonable balance between calorie intake and calorie output (burning). They also tend to quickly gain back a good deal of their weight with any dietary infraction or decrease in their activity level. In a way, mutations or abnormalities in UP turn these people into very energy-efficient machines when in fact they need to be more like gas-guzzlers. In contrast, thin people who overeat without gaining weight are lucky, because they may have high levels of UP in their muscles.

Recent studies have shown that *in people with various infections, fever, chronic diseases, or cancers, the muscles produce high levels of Up and release some of it into the bloodstream.* High blood levels of uncoupling protein contribute to poor appetite, decreased food (calorie) intake, and a faster rate of energy burning, all of which are made even worse by pain or an inability to eat for a variety of other reasons. This combination of abnormal miscues can result in significant weight loss and, if continued, eventually emaciation.

Unfortunately, the more players and props there are, the greater is the risk of one or more things going wrong. People with several biological "glitches" tend to gain enormous amounts of weight, usually exceeding 300–400 pounds, and have a terrible time losing any weight, or not regaining whatever amount they lose. Because of these biological aberrations and confusion, the severely obese respond to their abnormal internal cues by overeating, or snacking frequently, even when they are not truly hungry. These unfair biological disadvantages create a vicious cycle that makes weight management even more difficult.

To summarize (see figure 2):

Figure 2

Biological Interactions and Body Weight

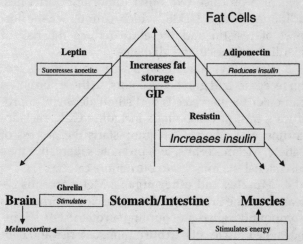

As long as these interactions are smooth and orderly, we can maintain our weight. Any disruption in, or inappropriately high or low production of these compounds can derail weight management. The majority of people with a severe weight problem have one or more abnormalities in these interactions.

1. Stomach and small intestine: In response to hunger the stomach produces a hormone called ghrelin, which stimulates the appetite. After eating, the stomach applies the brakes and brings the ghrelin production to a halt, so we can stop eating. The small intestine secretes another hormone, GIP, which increases the storage of dietary fat in fat cells.

2. Fat cells: In response to feeding, fat cells produce leptin, which suppresses the appetite. They also produce resistin, which causes insulin resistance and diabetes. To keep resistin in check, fat cells also produce two other important hormones, adiponectin and CD36, which counteract the impact of resistin and therefore reduce the risk of insulin resistance and diabetes.

3. Brain (hypothalamus): The brain provides leptin receptors and ghrelin receptors, so these hormones can enter the nerve cells and stimulate them to produce a host of compounds including CCK, melanocortins, and others. CCK jump-starts the process of satiety. Melanocortins, too, promote satiety, but they also signal the muscles to burn more calories.

4. Muscles and other organs: Melanocortins released by the brain signal the muscles to produce a compound called uncoupling protein. UP stimulates the muscle cells to burn more calories and convert them to heat. Also, the muscle and liver cells are targets for the opposing actions of resistin on one side, and adiponectin and CD36 on the other.

Selected References

More than four thousand scientific papers were reviewed for preparation of this book. The following is only a small representative of this large database.

1. Mokdad, A. H. et al. 2001. The continuing epidemic of obesity and diabetes in the United States. *JAMA* 286:1195–1200.
2. McCullough, M. J., et al. 2002. Diet quality and major chronic disease risk in men and women: Moving toward improved dietary guidance. *Am J Clin Nutr* 76:1261–71.
3. De Smet, P. A. 2002. Herbal remedies. *N Eng J Med* 347:2046–56.
4. Jones, D. W., et al. 2002. Risk factors for coronary heart disease in African Americans. *Arch Intern Med* 162: 2565–71.
5. Stampfer, M. J. et al. 2000 Primary prevention

of coronary artery disease in women through diet and lifestyle. *N Eng J Med* 343:16–22.

6. Salmeron, J., et al. 2001. Dietary fat intake and risk of type II diabetes in women. *Am J Clin Nutr* 73:1019–26.

7. Fung, T. T., et al. 2001. Dietary patterns and the risk of coronary artery disease in women. *Arch Intern Med* 161:1857–62.

8. Hu, F. B., and W. C. Willett. 2002. Optimal diets for prevention of coronary artery disease. *JAMA* 288:2569–78.

9. Van Dam, R. M., et al. 2002. Dietary patterns and risk of type II diabetes mellitus in U.S. men. *Ann Intern Med* 136:201–9.

10. Saydah, S. H., D. Byrd-Holt, and M. I. Harris. 2002. Projected impact of implementing the results of the diabetes prevention program in the U.S. population. *Diabetes Care* 25:1940–45.

11. Lakka, H. M., et al. 2002. The metabolic syndrome and total, and cardiovascular disease mortality in middle-aged men. *JAMA* 288:2709–16.

12. Mohanty, P., et al. 2002. Both lipid and protein intakes stimulate increased generation of reactive oxygen species by polymorphonuclear leukocytes and mononuclear cells. *Am J Clin Nutr* 75:767–72.

13. Samaha, F. F., et al. 2003. A low-carbohydrate as compared with a low-fat diet in severe obesity. *N Eng J Med* 348:2078–81.

14. Foster, G. D., et al. 2003. A randomized trial of a low-carbohydrate diet for obesity. *N Eng J Med* 348:2082–90.

15. Bravata, D. M., et al. 2003. Efficacy and safety of low-carbohydrate diets. *JAMA* 289:1837–50.
16. Poppitt, S. D., et al. 2002. Long-term effects of ad libitum low-fat, high-carbohydrate diets on body weight and serum lipids in overweight subjects with metabolic syndrome. *Am J Clin Nutr* 75:11–20.
17. Bazzano, L. A., et al. 2001. Legume consumption and risk of coronary artery disease in U.S. men and women. *Arch Intern Med* 161:2573–78.
18. Fuentes, F., et al. 2001. Mediterranean and low-fat diets improve endothelial function in hypercholesterolemic men. *Ann Intern Med* 134:1115–19.
19. Rodriguez, V. M., et al. 2002. Olive oil feeding up-regulates uncoupling protein genes in rat brown adipose tissue and skeletal muscles. *Am J Clin Nutr* 75:213–20.
20. Joshipura, K. J., et al. 2001. The effect of fruit and vegetable intake on the risk for coronary heart disease. *Ann Intern Med* 134:1106–14.
21. Brigelius-Flohe, R., et al. 2002. The European perspective on vitamin E: Current knowledge and future research. *Am J Clin Nutr* 76:703–16.
22. Van't Veer, P., et al. 2003. Fruits and vegetables in the prevention of cancer and cardiovascular disease. *Public Health Nutr* 3:103–7.
23. Bazzano, L. A., et al. 2002. Fruit and vegetable intake and risk of cardiovascular disease in U.S. adults: The first National Health and Nutrition Examination Survey follow-up study. *Am J Clin Nutr* 76:93–109.
24. Andersson, A., et al. 2002. Fatty acid composi-

tion of skeletal muscles reflects dietary fat composition in humans. *Am J Clin Nutr* 76:1222–29.

25. Harper, C. R., and T. A. Jacobson. 2001. The role of omega-3 fatty acids in the prevention of coronary artery disease. *Arch Intern Med* 161:2185–92.

26. Thies, F., et al. 2003. Association of n-3 polyunsaturated fatty acids with stability of atherosclerotic plaques: A randomized controlled trial. *Lancet* 361:477–85.

27. Albert, C. M., et al. 2002. Blood levels of long-chain n-3 fatty acids and the risk of sudden death. *N Eng J Med* 346:1113–18.

28. Hardman, W. E. 2002. Omega-3 fatty acids to augment cancer therapy. *J Nutr* 132:3508S–12S.

29. Rose, D. P., and J. M. Connolly. 1999. Omega-3 fatty acids as cancer chemoprotective agents. *Pharmacol Therap* 83:217–44.

30. Wallac, H. M., et al. 2001. Plasma leptin and the risk of cardiovascular disease in the West of Scotland coronary prevention study. *Circulation* 104:3052–56.

31. Toborek, M., Y. U. Lee, and R. Garrido. 2002. Unsaturated fatty acids selectively induce an inflammatory environment in human endothelial cells. *Am J Clin Nutr* 75:119–25.

32. Bendixen, H., et al. 2002. Effect of 3 modified fats and a conventional fat on appetite, energy intake, energy expenditure and substrate oxidization in healthy men. *Am J Clin Nutr* 75:47–56.

33. McDevitt, R. M., et al. 2001. De novo lipogenesis during controlled overfeeding with sucrose or

glucose in lean and obese women. *Am J Clin Nutr* 74:737–46.

34. Connor, W. E., 2001. N-3 fatty acids from fish and fish oil: Panacea or nostrum. *Am J Clin Nutr* 74:415–16.

35. Anderson, G. H., N. L. Catherine, and D. M. Woodend. 2002. Inverse association between the effect of carbohydrates on blood glucose and subsequent short-term food intake in young men. *Am J Clin Nutr* 76:1023–30.

36. Chaudhari, N., and S. C. Kinnamon. 2001. Molecular basis of sweet tooth. *Lancet* 538:2101–2.

37. Liu, S., et al. 2002. Relation between a diet with a high glycemic load and plasma concentrations of high sensitivity C-reactive protein in middle-aged women. *Am J Clin Nutr* 75:492–98.

38. Foster-Powel, K., S. H. Holt, and J. C. Brand-Miller. 2002. International Tables of glycemic index and glycemic load values. *Am J Clin Nutr* 76:5–56.

39. Ludwig, D. S. 2002. The glycemic index: Physiological mechanisms relating to obesity, diabetes, and cardiovascular disease. *JAMA* 287:2414–23.

40. Ruitenberg, A., et al. 2002. Alcohol consumption and the risk of dementia: The Rotterdam Study. *Lancet* 259:281–86.

41. Sandhu, M. S., I. R. White, and K. McPherson. 2001. Systematic review of the prospective studies on meat consumption and colorectal cancer risk. *Cancer Epidemiol Biomarkers Prev* 10:439–44.

42. Hughes, R., et al. 2001. Dose dependent effect of

dietary meat on colonic endogenous N-Nitrosation. *Carcinogenesis* 22:199–202.

43. Mirvish, S. S., et al. 2002. Total N-Nitroso compounds and their precursors in hot dogs and in the gastrointestinal tract and feces of rats and mice: Possible etiologic agents for colon cancer. *J Nutr* 132:3526S–29S.

44. Peters, L.I., et al. 2003. Dietary fiber and colorectal adenoma in a colorectal cancer early detection program. *Lancet* 361:1491–95.

45. Brownson, D. M., et al. 2002. Flavonoid effects relevant to cancer. *J Nutr* 132:3482S–89S.

46. Alberts, D. S. 2002. Reducing the risk of colorectal cancer by intervening in the process of carcinogenesis: A status report. *Cancer J* 8:208–21.

47. Nilsen, T. I., and L. J. Vatten. 2001. Prospective study of colorectal cancer risk and physical activity, diabetes, blood glucose and BMI: Exploring the hyperinsulinemia hypothesis. *Br J Cancer* 84:417–22.

48. Giovannucci, E., 2001. Insulin, insulin-like growth factors and colorectal cancers: A review of the evidence. *J Nutr* 131:3109S–20S.

49. Giovannucci, E., M. J. Stampfer, and G. A. Colditz. 1998. Multivitamin use, folate, and colon cancer in women in the Nurses' Health Study. *Ann Intern Med* 29:517–24.

50. Zhang, S., et al. 1999. A prospective study of folate intake and the risk of breast cancer. *JAMA* 291:1632–37.

51. Voorrips, L. E., et al. 2002. Intake of conjugated

linoleic acid, fat, and other fatty acids in relation to postmenopausal breast cancer. The Netherlands Cohort Study on Diet and Cancer. *Am J Clin Nutr* 76:873–82.

52. Chen, W. Y., et al. 2002. Use of postmenopausal hormones, alcohol, and risk for invasive breast cancer. *Ann Intern Med* 137:798–804.

53. Petrek, J. A., et al. 1994. Breast cancer risk and fatty acids in the breast and abdominal adipose tissues. *J Natl Cancer Inst* 86:53–56.

54. Moradi, T., et al. 2002. Physical activity and risk of breast cancer: A prospective cohort among Swedish twins. *Int J Cancer* 100:76–81.

55. Littman, A. J., et al. 2001. Recreational physical activity and endometrial cancer risk. *Am J Epidemiol* 154:924–33.

56. Colbert, L. H., et al. 2002. Physical activity and lung cancer risk in male smokers. *Int J Cancer* 98:770–73.

57. Cottreau, C. M., R. B. Ness, and A. M. Kriska. 2000. Physical activity and reduced risk of ovarian cancer. *Obstet Gynecol* 96:609–14.

58. Bertone, E. R., et al. 2001. Prospective study of recreational physical activity and ovarian cancer. *J Natl Cancer Inst* 93:942–48.

59. Michaud, D. S. et al. 2001. Physical activity, obesity, height and the risk of pancreatic cancer. *JAMA* 286:921–29.

60. Liu, S., et al. 2000. A prospective study of physical activity and the risk of prostate cancer in U.S. physicians. *Int J Epidemiol* 29:29–35.

61. Friedenreich, C. M., and I. A. Thune. 2001. A review of physical activity and prostate cancer risk. *Cancer Causes Control* 12:461–75.

62. Norman, A., et al. 2002. Occupational physical activity and risk of prostate cancer in a nationwide cohort study in Sweden. *Br J Cancer* 86:70–75.

63. Byers, T., et al. 2002. American Cancer Society guidelines on nutrition and physical activities for cancer prevention. *Cancer J Clin* 52:92–119.

64. Yoshizawa, K., et al. 1998. Study of prediagnostic selenium level in toenails and the risk of advanced prostate cancer. *J Natl Cancer Inst* 90:1219–24.

65. Hu, F. B., et al. 2003. Television watching and other sedentary behaviors in relation to risk of obesity and type II diabetes in women. *JAMA* 289:1785–91.

66. Clark, L. C., et al. 1998. Decreased incidence of prostate cancer with selenium supplementation: Results of a double blind cancer prevention trial. *Br J Urol* 81:730–34.

67. Kraus, W. E., et al. 2002. Effects of the amount and intensity of exercise on plasma lipoproteins. *N Eng J Med* 347:1483–92.

68. Shuldiner, A. R., R. Yang, and D. W. Gong. 2001. Resistin, obesity and insulin resistance: the emerging role of the adipocyte as an endocrine organ. *N Eng J Med* 345:1345–46.

69. Wisse, B. E., and M. W. Schwartz. 2001. Role of melanocortins in control of obesity. *Lancet* 358:857–58.

70. Arcaro, G., et al. 2002. Insulin causes endothelial dysfunction in humans: Sites and mechanisms. *Circulation* 105:576–82.

71. Altman, T. J. 2001. CD36, insulin resistance and coronary artery disease. *Lancet*. 357:651–52.

72. Tounian, P., et al. 2001. Presence of increased stiffness of the common carotid artery and endothelial dysfunction in severely obese children: A prospective study. *Lancet* 358:1400–1404.

73. Kenchaiah, S., et al. 2002. Obesity and heart failure. *N Eng J Med* 347:305–13.

74. Janssen, I., P. T. Katzmarzyk, and R. Ross. 2002. Body mass index, waist circumference, and health risk. *Arch Intern Med* 162:2074–79.

75. Calle, E. E., et al. 2003. Overweight, obesity and mortality from cancer in a prospectively studied cohort of U.S. adults. *N Eng J Med* 348:1625–38.

76. Sinha, R., et al. 2002. Prevalence of impaired glucose tolerance among children and adolescents with marked obesity. *N Eng J Med* 346:802–10.

77. Tchernof, A., et al. 2002. Weight loss reduces C-reactive protein levels in obese postmenopausal women. *Circulation* 105:564–69.

78. Hays, N. P., et al. 2002. Eating behavior correlates of adult weight gain and obesity in healthy women aged 55–65 years. *Am J Clin Nutr* 75:476–83.

79. Bloomgarden, Z. T. 2002. New insight in obesity. *Diabetes Care* 25:789–95.

80. Knowler, W. C., et al. 2002. Reduction in the incidence of type II diabetes with lifestyle intervention or metformin. *N Eng J Med* 346:393–404.

81. Freedman, D. S., et al. 2001. Relationship of

childhood obesity to coronary artery disease risk factors in adulthood: The Bogalusa study. *Pediatrics* 108:712–18.

82. Fisher, J. O., and L. L. Birch. 2002. Eating in the absence of hunger and overweight in girls from 5 to 7 years of age. *Am J Clin Nutr* 76:226–31.

83. Pearcey, S. M., and J. M. de Castro. 2002. Food intake and meal patterns of weight-stable and weight-gaining persons. *Am J Clin Nutr* 76:107–12.

84. McTigue, K. M., J. M. Garrett, and B. M. Popkin. 2002. The natural history of the development of obesity in a cohort of young U.S. adults between 1981 and 1998. *Ann Intern Med* 136:857–64.

85. Peeters, A., et al. 2003. Obesity in adulthood and its consequences for life expectancy: A life-table analysis. *Ann Intern Med* 138:24–38.

86. Rolls, B. J., E. L. Morris, and L. S. Roe. 2002. Portion size of food affects energy intake in normal-weight and overweight men and women. *Am J Clin Nutr* 76:1207–13.

87. Nielson, S. J., and B. M. Popkin. 2003. Patterns and trends in food portion sizes, 1977–1998. *JAMA* 289:450–53.

88. Heshka, S., et al. 2003. Weight loss with self-help compared with a structured commercial program. *JAMA* 289:1792–98.

About the Author

Dr. Michael Mogadam is Clinical Associate Professor at George Washington University School of Medicine in Washington, D.C., specializing in nutrition and cholesterol disorders. He is the recipient of several awards for peer-reviewed research that has challenged outdated medical "standards" and introduced novel and successful alternatives. He is the author of *Every Heart Attack Is Preventable*. He lives and practices in Alexandria, Virginia.